Praise for Dee Davis

Midnight Rain

"Psychological suspense is expertly combined with action and romance to form one of rising star Dee Davis's best books to date. *Midnight Rain* is a top-notch romantic suspense."
—*Romantic Times*

Dark of the Night

"A highly entertaining read, both as a mystery and a love story. The story has a surprising climax, embracing all the components that a reader could want."
—*Rendezvous*

Just Breathe

"Rising star Dee Davis returns with a new story of sizzling romance and danger. *Just Breathe* is sure to please Ms. Davis' growing list of admirers."
—*Romantic Times*

After Twilight

"Dee Davis provides her fans with a powerful romantic suspense. *After Twilight* is an entertaining tale that works because the characters seem real and their interactions quite genuine."
—*Affaire de Coeur*

Also by Dee Davis

**AFTER TWILIGHT
JUST BREATHE
MIDNIGHT RAIN
DARK OF THE NIGHT**

DANCING IN THE DARK

DEE DAVIS

IVY BOOKS • NEW YORK

Dancing in the Dark is a work of fiction. Names, places, and incidents either are products of the author's imagination or are used fictitiously.

An Ivy Book
Published by The Random House Publishing Group
Copyright © 2003 by Dee Davis Oberwetter

www.ballantinebooks.com

ISBN 0-8041-1978-3

Manufactured in the United States of America

First Edition: September 2003

10 9 8 7 6 5 4 3 2 1

For my father-in-law, Manro,
who gifted me with a love for Frank Sinatra's music . . .

"When I am close to you, the world is far away,
The words that fill my heart, my lips can't seem to say.
I want you so, more than you'll ever know,
More than you dream I do, I dream of you . . ."

♬ ♪ ♬ ♪ ♬

It was the perfect song. Exactly what he wanted to tell her. Only she wasn't listening. He fought against the rage, its heat threatening to consume him. Patience was a virtue. All he had to do was wait. The time wasn't right. And until it was, he'd simply have to appease the darkness inside him. Feed the hunger in other ways.

He turned to the woman on the bed. Her hands were bloody. A pity, as it was her fingers he craved. She struggled against her bonds, eyes wide with fear. He suppressed a smile. Fear was such a lovely thing. He'd discovered long ago that it held a priapic power over him that could never be explained in normal company. The smell of it excited him, filling him with ecstasy, lifting him higher and higher until there was nothing that could stop him.

Nothing.

He walked to the bed, and stroked the woman's cheek, his body tightening in anticipation. She fought to avoid his touch, but there was nowhere to go, and he smiled, moving her legs apart with one hand, the autographed baseball bat held firmly in the other. It was clear that she loved the thing, a cherished possession that prepossessed all other devotion.

But nothing could be allowed to stand in his way. He'd

prove to her that no one could ever replace him. The bat slid home, and he closed his eyes, forcing a rhythm. First he'd teach her a lesson, and then—he'd watch her die.

Chapter I

Austin, Texas

The shrill sound cut through the night.

It reached deep into Sara Martin's subconscious, jerking her from sleep, vanquishing her dream, dissipating like smoke on the wind. Angrily, she pushed upright, grabbing the phone.

"Hello?"

The line was silent, except for the soft hiss that meant someone was there.

"Hello?" She wasn't certain why she asked again. He never answered. Just waited, listening. As if he knew what he was interrupting—but that was impossible. With a release of breath, she slammed the receiver into the cradle, dismissing the prank. It didn't matter.

Nothing mattered.

Not anymore.

Moonlight, filtering through the curtains, cast intricate shadows across the room, and she watched as they danced across the ceiling. Closing her eyes, she tried to recapture the dream, but as always it was illusive, coming only when it chose, never on demand.

Tears welled, and she pushed them away. Time, it seemed, did not heal wounds. It only left them to fester, the memory of all that was good tantalizing in its obscurity. Here in the dark, reality seemed a cruel joke. A punishment for a crime she'd never committed.

Still fighting tears, she reached for the lamp, and with the flick of a switch banished the shadows back into the night. Reflexively, she turned, her eyes searching the pillow next to hers. Wanting to find an indentation, a scent. Anything.

She traced the contours of the pillow, letting her imagination remember other times. Better times. But they were gone, along with her husband and son. Forever. Squeezing her eyes shut, she rolled over, fighting for control.

It was always worse at night.

Maybe it would be best if she'd just stop dreaming. At least that way the past would stay where it was supposed to be. But even as she had the thought, she knew she didn't mean it. The dreams were all she had left.

The smell was the first thing he noticed, and it wasn't as if he were new to crime scenes. But this one was bad. He could tell just from the sickly sweet stench of decaying flesh. With a sigh, Eric D'Angelo pushed past the crowd of homeless people and ducked under the yellow tape, steeling himself for the task at hand.

No matter how many murder scenes he worked, it was always one too many.

"Wondered if you were going to grace us with your presence." Tony Haskins ambled over as if it were Sunday at the park. His partner's girth and slow gait hid an astute mind and a quick wit.

"I was across town, and there were a few things I had to handle before I could leave."

"Right." Haskins' eyebrows rose, not missing a beat. "Anyone I know?"

"No." The single word brooked no further discussion. "So what have we got here?"

"Dead female. Caucasian. Looks to be somewhere between sixteen and twenty, and based on the clothing, I'd say she was a little bit more than just the kid next door." Tony shifted so that Eric could see the body.

A woman was sprawled beside a Dumpster, refuse scattered around her like a picture frame. Even without Tony's caustic comment, he'd have guessed at her profession. The gold lamé halter combined with the hiphugging skirt could have been considered chic, if it weren't for the fact that they were about two sizes too small. A smear of lipstick marred one cheek, blood staining the other, the two reds at odds with each other, the effect garish.

"She was left like this?" Eric frowned, trying to visualize the situation.

"No." Tony shook his head. "The guy over there found her. Evidently he pulled her out of the Dumpster to get at the stuff underneath, and then couldn't be bothered to call it in."

"Or wasn't able to tell the living from the dead." Eric shot a look at the old geezer. Between the grime and the layers of clothing, it was hard to tell what he really looked like, but the vacant gaze was apparent even from here. He'd seen it a hundred times over the years.

"Well, fortunately for us, he wasn't the only one digging in the garbage." Tony nodded toward a woman sitting on a crate, huddled over a Styrofoam cup of coffee. "She's the one who called. From over there."

Eric looked across the alley to the open door of a club, light slashing across the pavement like a rip in the asphalt. "How long since she called it in?"

"A couple of hours. Took the uniforms a little while to locate her."

"So what else do we know about the vic?" Eric walked over to the body, his seasoned mind already absorbing details.

"Not much. There's no I.D., although they haven't finished searching the Dumpster. There's no sign of struggle and very little blood. Which isn't consistent with her wounds. This woman was stabbed repeatedly, and unless I've missed something, that isn't easy to accomplish without leaving one hell of a mess."

D'Angelo bent down for a closer look. "There's blood all

over the body, but most of it's dried." He frowned, reaching out to carefully touch her cheek. "Rigor's set in. And the smell alone indicates she's been dead more than a few hours."

"Wouldn't be impossible for her to have been in the Dumpster awhile."

"Not impossible." Claire Dennison joined them, her eyes narrowed in thought. Claire was a forensic specialist—a damn good one—and Eric was glad she'd responded to the call. "But not the case here. There's no blood in the Dumpster either. And even without an autopsy, it's fairly clear she bled out."

"So where's the blood?" Eric stood up, his gaze meeting hers.

"Could be anywhere." Claire studied the body with the cool eyes of a professional. "If we're lucky we'll find something to tie her to the killer. If not, maybe a fiber or two will at least give us a location."

Eric nodded, turning his attention to Tony. "Why were we called in?" They were technically off duty, and under normal circumstances, the murder should have fallen to someone else.

"The woman was raped."

"Kind of hard to tell with a hooker, isn't it?"

"Not when someone leaves their bat behind." Tony tipped his head toward a bloody piece of wood protruding beneath the skirt.

"Jesus." Eric forced his gaze away from the body, frowning at his partner.

"It gets worse. The guy took her fingers."

His eyes were automatically drawn to the hand folded against her breast. The lamé hid part of it, but now that he was looking—really looking—he could see that all five fingers had been cut off.

A quick glance at her other hand confirmed that it too had been altered.

"Son of a bitch." He swallowed a mouthful of bile, his gaze locking with Tony's. "He's back."

*   *   *

The soft sound of music filled the air, and Sara let the notes wash over her, the rhythm carrying away some of her tension. Taking a sip from her wineglass, she let the dark, smoky taste of merlot run down the back of her throat. Drinking alone was a dangerous luxury.

But, tonight, she needed it.

She took another sip, and stared at the phone. It would be so simple to pick it up, to call Ryan or Molly. But that would mean confessing her state of mind and, to be honest, she wasn't certain she had the energy. Besides, she was a firm believer in maintaining a stiff upper lip. A throwback to her days in foster care.

Never let 'em see you sweat.

She smiled despite herself. The music and the wine were working, the shadows that haunted her life withdrawing. She looked around the living room, pleased with the soft colors and fashionable antiques. Her home was almost a diametric opposite to the house she and Tom had shared.

Tom had loved the sleek and modern. An architect, he delighted in simplicity. Form and line. Their house had been beautiful. Perched on a cliff, soaring above the treetops, it had been like living in a fantasy of glass and light. After the accident, the house had become a horrifying symbol for all she'd lost.

So she'd sold it, and moved to the center of Austin. As far away from the hills as she could get without leaving the city altogether. The Hyde Park Victorian was a far cry from Tom's designs, but it suited her somehow. And with time she'd actually grown to love it. There was something cathartic in making a place for herself. Almost as if the walls themselves had the power to heal her.

The doorbell rang, breaking her reverie. Frowning, she set the wineglass down, wondering who could possibly be visiting so late. Cautiously approaching the door, she grabbed an umbrella from the stand, and stood on tiptoe to peer through the peephole.

Releasing a breath, she replaced the umbrella and un-locked the door, swinging it open. "Damn it, Ryan, you scared me half to death. It's the middle of the night."

Ryan Greene smiled, his eyes crinkling with the gesture. "Sorry. I was on my way home and saw the light."

Sara moved away from the door, gesturing for him to come in. "It's awfully late to be working. Looming deadline?"

"No." He shrugged sheepishly. "Actually, I was follow-ing up on a story."

Ryan was the editor in chief of *Texas Today*, a weekly magazine with a large regional reader base. But he'd never been able to totally give up the thrill of chasing a lead.

Case in point.

"So what's the story?"

He crossed over to the wine bottle and poured himself a glass. "There's been another murder."

A chill chased down her spine. "The same guy?"

"They're not saying. There's a press conference sched-uled for tomorrow. Until then, we won't know anything for sure. But the M.O. is similar. The main difference seems to be that the body was left in a trash bin."

"Where?"

"Downtown. In an alley behind a bar."

The press had been consumed with the brutal murders of two prostitutes over the last eighteen months. Speculation was that the deaths were the work of the same man. But two cases weren't enough to establish a pattern. Three, on the other hand . . .

"Were you there?"

"Yeah." His eyes darkened, his features harsh. "It wasn't a pretty picture."

"You should have called me. I could have gotten some shots." Although she didn't normally photograph murder scenes, she'd done it several times over the years. Usually when she was nearby or there wasn't anyone else available.

Ryan's gaze met hers, his expression softening. "I wouldn't subject you to that. Considering all that you've been through, I didn't think it was appropriate. Besides, I can pull pictures off the wires." He sat down beside her on the couch. "How was your date?"

"Nothing to write home about. I still can't believe Molly set me up."

"She was just trying to help."

"I know. And I appreciate it. But blind dates have never been my forte, especially now."

"Then maybe it's just as well it didn't work out." He shrugged, taking a sip of wine, studying her over the rim of his glass. "Maybe you need more time."

"That's the first time you've said that. I thought you were a staunch member of the Sara-should-move-on club."

"I am." He frowned, his eyes reflecting concern. "But that doesn't mean I think you should try to accomplish it all in one day, or with the wrong person."

"I know. It's just some days it's harder than others."

"Which explains the merlot at midnight. Look, Sara, I know you miss them. But sooner or later you're going to have to let go of the past."

"I know that. I do. It's just that I can't." She rubbed the gold of her wedding ring, wishing it were a magic lamp. A way to change time. To change fate.

His eyes flashed regret. "I didn't mean to push."

"It's okay. Your heart's in the right place." She stood up, smothering a yawn. The wine had done its job.

"You're tired." Ryan stood up, too, still looking uncertain. "I should go."

She reached up to lay a hand on his cheek. "Thanks for watching out for me."

He covered her hand with his. "That's what friends are for, Sara."

She stepped back, embarrassed suddenly. She wasn't usually given to outbursts of emotion. In fact she prided herself on maintaining control. It's just that sometimes it was so damn hard. "You want me to try and get some photos at the press conference tomorrow?" She walked with him toward the door, firmly steering the conversation back to business.

He shook his head. "I already called Satchel. But I do still need you at the mayor's office. He's not an easy man to photograph, and I'm counting on you to pull the best out of him."

"I'll do what I can."

"That's my girl." He walked out onto the porch. "Try and get some sleep. I'll see you in the morning."

Nodding, she lifted a hand to wave, then shut the door, throwing the dead bolt. Turning around to face the empty room, her eyes were drawn to a picture on the wall. Tom and Charlie smiled out at her from the frame and her heart twisted with longing.

Reaching over she traced first her husband's face, then her son's, her mind conjuring the feel of Charlie's baby-soft skin, the smell of Tom's aftershave. Ryan was right, it was time to move on. Time to make a new life. But truth be told, she simply didn't know how.

Eric D'Angelo stared down at the pictures on his kitchen table. He'd arranged them side by side so that he could examine each victim in context with the others, hoping that one of them at least would have something to tell him.

But so far the ladies were being stubbornly silent. The differences between the three women were as numerous as the similarities. Location had varied, although, until the last one, the body had always been found at the site of the murder. One was a confirmed prostitute, and another had been known to sell her body when she ran out of money for liquor and drugs. The third looked like a member of the same sisterhood, although the fact had not yet been confirmed.

None of the ladies were exactly cream of the crop. But that didn't mean they'd deserved to die. Not like this. Hell, not at all. He picked up the picture of the first victim. Laurel Henry was well over thirty, and she'd obviously lived a hard life. Her cheeks were pockmarked, and a tiny scar ran from the corner of her mouth down her chin.

She had a rap sheet a mile long. Everything from solicitation to petty larceny. Like the other two, she'd been raped repeatedly, then stabbed and left to bleed out.

She was also missing her ears.

His stomach twisted with revulsion. He saw the results of humanity's inhumanity every day, but something like this still had the power to shake him.

He picked up the second picture, studying the lifeless black woman. Candy Mason was the diametric opposite of Laurel, her curly dark hair and chocolate brown skin a tintype negative of the older blonde woman. She had also been stabbed, after an umbrella had been used in ways he didn't even want to contemplate. Like Laurel there'd been angry wounds, and blood everywhere.

But this time the killer had cut out her tongue.

He picked up the last of the photos. The latest victim was nothing like the other two. Younger by maybe ten years, she couldn't be more than eighteen. Her overly mascaraed eyes stared vacantly up at him, her hands crossed almost virginally across her chest.

Another kid on the streets with nothing to lose—except her life. The body appeared to be the least marked up of the three, but that didn't negate the horror.

Even in death, pain seemed to radiate from her. As if her soul were still there, calling to him from the photograph.

Which was, of course, nonsense.

He put down the picture, rubbing the bridge of his nose. It was late, and he wasn't getting anywhere. Tomorrow, after the M.E. was finished with her, they'd know more. Like maybe her name. And why she'd been dumped there.

Maybe her murder wasn't connected to the others. She was younger, softer somehow. And the others had been found at the scene. This girl had obviously been moved. Still, there were commonalities between the three. The use of a knife, the missing body parts, and the impersonal savagery of the rape. But there was one major difference.

The music.

When the first two women had been found, there'd been Sinatra music playing, an endless recording of soft swelling notes, the love song forming a poignant counterpoint to the brutal violence that had ended their lives. He looked down at the picture of the third woman.

There'd been no music—at least not in the alleyway—but then she hadn't actually died there, and D'Angelo had the feeling that when they found the murder site, they'd find the music. It was a marker of sorts, the reason the press had dubbed the perp the Sinatra Killer.

He blew out a breath, and leaned back in his chair, closing his eyes. One thing was definitely for certain; there was twisted logic in every move a guy like that made. Which meant he was still out there somewhere, waiting, watching, and sooner or later, he was going to strike again.

The only real question was when.

Chapter 2

"So, how was the date?" Molly Parker shot Sara a pointed look, blue eyes sparkling. A true redhead, Molly was round and freckled, and one of the kindest people on earth. Friends since college, Sara couldn't imagine her life without Molly.

Just at the moment, however, she was questioning the fact. "It wasn't a date. It was a setup. An ambush actually."

"I think ambush is a bit strong. I gave you a heads up." Molly waved her coffee cup in the air for emphasis, nearly colliding with a passing waitress.

Kerby Lane Cafe was packed. A mishmash of Austinites that included buttoned-down business types, scrubs-clad personnel from the nearby hospital, and the usual collection of bleary-eyed college students. A throwback to Austin's hippie days, Kerby Lane was still staffed by free spirits, making breakfast a truly cultural experience.

"Yeah, about two minutes before he knocked on my door."

"I'll admit my methods may have been a bit guerrilla, but hell, it was the only way we could think of to get you to actually go."

"We?" She choked on the word, automatically reaching for her water glass.

"Bess and Ryan and me." Molly wrinkled her nose. "Well, really Bess. Ryan did say he thought it was a bad idea."

"Now there's an understatement."

"That bad, huh?" Finally a little remorse.

"The only thing good about it was when it ended."

"All right. Fine." Molly held up her hands. "I was just trying to help. You haven't been out with anyone since Phil was in town."

"Molly, I didn't go out with Phil. For God's sake, he was Tom's best friend. If anything, we were consoling each other. There was nothing romantic going on at all."

"I didn't mean to imply . . ."

"I take it the date wasn't a success." Bess Haskins neatly slid into the vacant chair across from Molly. Tall and gorgeous, Bess was the kind of woman you wanted to hate. Except that she was so darn nice, you simply didn't have the option.

"And then some." Molly lifted her eyebrows in defeat.

Bess leaned forward, frowning at Sara. "Judging from the circles under your eyes, I'd say it was an unmitigated disaster."

"It wasn't much fun, but not enough to keep me from sleep. I'm afraid that honor belongs to my mystery caller."

"I thought you were going to get Caller ID?" There was a hint of rebuke in Bess's tone and Sara felt a twinge of guilt.

"I was. I mean, I *am*. I guess the truth is I haven't been all that upset about it."

"Well, maybe you should be." Molly nodded to underscore the thought. "Have you thought about contacting the police?"

"It's just phone calls. What could they possibly do?"

"Maybe nothing," Molly said stubbornly, "but I still think it's worth a try."

"I agree with Molly." Bess toyed with the corner of her menu, eyes narrowed in thought.

Sara raised an eyebrow in surprise. Molly and Bess were seldom on the same side. A massage therapist by day, Molly spent her nights working in the Austin theater. Which meant drama was her middle name. By contrast, understated was the best way to describe Bess, who worked tirelessly behind the scenes as *Texas Today*'s chief financial officer.

So, the truth of the matter was that although they were friends, they were seldom in agreement about anything. Bess's no-nonsense sensibilities often clashing with Molly's free-floating artistic notions, the battleground leaving Sara stranded somewhere in the middle.

Except this time.

Sara braced herself for the siege.

"I think you should talk to Tony. That way it's not exactly official, and there might be something he can do that the officer of the day couldn't."

"I'm not going to talk to your husband, Bess. He's a homicide detective, for God's sake. I can't foist my little problems off on him."

"Of course you can." This from Molly whose expression hovered somewhere between exasperation and concern.

"And tell him what?" Sara knew she was being obstinate but she hated being railroaded, even when intentions were good.

"Everything." Bess shrugged. "At the very least, he'll be

able to suggest things you can do from your end. Look, if nothing else, it will give you a little peace of mind."

Sara shook her head, accepting the inevitable. "All right. You win. I'll talk to Tony."

Not that it was going to do a bit of good, but it would get her friends off her back, and if by some miracle Tony could help, then all the better. The caller didn't really scare her, but his calls were intrusive and Sara cherished her privacy.

"Looks like we nailed cause of death." Rupert Garcia looked up from the dead woman's body, scalpel in hand. "She definitely bled out. Based on what I'm finding here, I'd say she'd been dead a couple days before the old guy found her. I can probably give you a more precise time after I finish the autopsy."

D'Angelo nodded, keeping his focus on the M.E.'s face. Tony, on the other hand, was watching his work with interest. Tony had always been fascinated with the macabre. "Got an I.D.?"

"Nothing yet. Without fingerprints, it makes it a little harder. I'll send off her DNA, although odds are, unless she has a federal record or has spent time in prison, there won't be a match. And of course I can work off dental records, but that's going to take time."

"And time is exactly what we don't have." Eric blew out a breath, trying to contain his frustration. "Anything to link us to a perp?"

Garcia shook his head. "Whoever did this knew how to play the game. There are traces of latex, so he definitely wore gloves, but other than that, there's not a sign of him. No semen, no hairs, nothing personal at all."

"Just like the other ones." Tony watched as Garcia efficiently sliced through the victim's tissue. "Except he moved the body. Which means he's changed his M.O."

"But not his signature." Eric frowned down at the body, automatically depersonalizing it.

"I've never been exactly clear on the difference between the two." Garcia looked up from his calculated carving.

"An M.O. is learned behavior," Eric explained. "It's what the perpetrator does to commit the crime. It often changes as the killer refines his routine. So, by definition, it's dynamic. A signature is what the killer has to do to get off or fulfill himself. And that never changes. It's the reason why he does what he does." He shot a glance at the plastic-clad bat lying on an adjacent table.

Garcia followed his gaze. "The rape and mutilation."

"If I had to call it, yes. All three women were the victims of object rape. Which implies anger as opposed to the need to control, which is more prevalent with contact rape. And when you couple the anger with the overkill," he nodded toward the stab wounds, "I'd say our guy is one unhappy camper."

"But we can't be sure it's the same guy." Tony, as usual, was the voice of reason. "There's the dump site to consider. It's possible we've got ourselves a copycat."

Eric shook his head. "Could be, but my gut's saying no. What about the amputations?"

"Based on the diameter of the wounds, I'd say he's using a surgical knife or scalpel. Which is a change from the last two. The first vic's amputation seemed almost impulsive. Spur of the moment. The wounds were jagged, and there were hesitation marks. The second was more controlled, but the weapon of choice was still a knife. But this last one," he waved at the woman's hands, "is clearly more surgical. Like maybe he's been practicing."

"That fits the pattern. These guys are always trying to perfect their routine. Hell, by definition a serial killer is a successful killer. He's gotten away with it. And every time he repeats the act, he just gets better at it." Eric studied the woman's body. "Did he use the scalpel to kill her?"

"No. Definitely a larger-blade knife. You can see the serration marks." He pointed at a gash on her abdomen, the torn skin almost ruffled-looking.

"What we need is to find the murder site." Tony crossed his arms, his eyes narrowed in thought. "You got anything that could connect her to a location?"

"Yeah, actually, I had better luck there. I found two different fibers. Forensics identified the first as cotton from a sheet. Cheap one, according to the report." He tipped his head toward a file on the table. "And the second was a carpet fiber. Low grade. The kind used in apartment complexes."

"Well, that should narrow it down." Tony grimaced, obviously disappointed.

"There were also traces of disinfectant. Could be someone tried to clean the scene while she was still present. Anyway, the good news is that it's unique. A biodegradable mix made locally by a company called Earth Free."

"Only in Austin." Tony's sarcasm was tempered with a hint of excitement. "How many clients you figure they have?"

"Of the low-rent variety? No more than a hundred or so. It's not easy to be ecological on a budget." Garcia lifted the victim's head with one hand, scalpel in the other. "It's a start. And for the moment, I'm afraid it's all you've got."

"It's enough. We've got a possible link to the first two murders, and a lead on figuring out where she was killed. With an I.D. we might have enough to pull it all together."

"I'll let you know if I find anything else." Garcia made an incision, intent now on the autopsy.

Tony pulled Eric toward the door, his mind obviously already on the next step. "Odds are that if the vic really is a hooker, she's got a sheet."

"And you're thinking if we go through the computer records we might just get a hit."

"It'll be time consuming, but it's a straight sight better than waiting for dental records on a Jane Doe. And we can go at it from the other side by getting a client list for Earth Free."

They walked out into the sunlight, the glare blinding after the subdued lighting of the morgue. D'Angelo reached for his sunglasses. "Want to flip for who gets stuck with the computer?"

Tony smiled, a wicked glint shining in his eyes. "Not necessary. You're not exactly noted for your tolerance of the Birkenstock set. You'd be better off back at the station with the computer. No sense in getting all those ecological left-wingers up in arms."

"Great." Eric put on his shades, and pulled out the keys to his car. Truth was he hated desk work almost as much as he hated liberals.

Sara had been standing outside police headquarters for almost fifteen minutes, trying to convince herself to abandon ship and skip the whole thing. As a kid, she'd learned that the cops weren't always your friend, just as she'd learned that the system didn't always live up to the hype. Reality was sometimes a long harsh ride from propaganda.

But she wasn't a scared kid anymore, and she wasn't here as a part of the system. She was here to get help. And if nothing else, she'd promised her friends she'd do it. Still, walking into the building was proving to be a lot harder than she'd thought it would be. In her life, nothing good had ever come from crossing that threshold.

All the more reason to cross it now.

Besides, it wasn't like she was confessing to murder or something. She simply had a crank caller. Millions of people received calls like that every day. Squaring her shoulders, she walked toward the building.

"Sara? Is that you?"

She pivoted at the sound of her name, her gaze traveling across the plaza searching for a familiar face. Nate. With a smile she changed directions, coming to a stop in front of her friend. "What are you doing here?"

"Looking for you." Tall and angular, Nathan Stone had missed being handsome by a hair. A burgeoning writer, he was paying his dues by working as an assistant at the magazine, filling in wherever he was needed. "Ryan wanted me to find you. Your phone's not on, so I'm playing message boy. The mayor's shoot is off."

She frowned, then nodded, understanding dawning. "The press conference."

"Exactly. Satchel's stuck in Fredericksburg, so Ryan wants you to take pictures. I've been assigned to assist. He thinks maybe there's a tie-in to the story you've been working on." She was doing a photo essay on teen runaways, focusing on prostitutes in particular.

"Works for me. Always glad to have you on my team." Sara glanced down at her watch. "Is the press conference still scheduled for two?"

"Yeah. I just thought if I could catch you early, maybe we could grab some lunch." His smile was playful, but she could see the shyness hiding in his eyes.

"I can't. I have an appointment." She tilted her head toward the building. "I'm meeting Bess's husband. I've been getting some prank phone calls." She shrugged, striving for nonchalance. She liked Nate, had even confided in him a time or two, but she didn't see any value in getting into her personal life in the middle of the busy plaza.

"I didn't think the police would do anything about prank calls." He frowned, narrowing his eyes in thought. "Still, I guess it's worth checking out."

"That's what Bess and Molly thought. I've got to say I agree with you, though. I think it's just a huge waste of time."

"You want me to come?" He looked like he'd rather walk across a parking lot filled with broken glass.

"No. You go have your lunch. I'll be fine. I'll meet you at the press conference."

"You got it." His smile was back to genuine. "Good luck in there." He waved, and turned toward the parking lot, his lanky gait making him look almost adolescent.

She turned back to face the building. She didn't need luck. It was only a conversation after all. And besides, Nate was right. There wasn't a thing anyone could do to help her. Certainly not the police. She'd just have to weather the storm. Sooner or later the caller would lose interest and move on to something more entertaining.

Jane Doe had a name. And a rap sheet. He'd have to wait for confirmation to be certain, but fortunately for him Lydia Wallace looked much the same in death as she had in life. In and out of foster care for most of her young life, the girl hadn't been a stranger to hard times. On her own for the last few years, the sheet showed a series of arrests for solicitation and drug use.

Eric hit the print button and waited for the machine to spit out a hard copy of her file. Hopefully he'd find something that would give them a lead on where she'd been killed, although kids like Lydia weren't exactly known for frequenting the same places.

Still, everyone had a territory. And all they needed to do was establish hers. Then, with a little help from Earth Free, they'd be able to narrow down the possibilities. Police work was like a puzzle, and each piece had to be linked to the others before a complete picture emerged. And it took patience. Lots of patience.

But then, that's what he was good at.

At least professionally.

Personally, he wasn't as good at putting it all together. He'd given marriage his best shot. He and Lauren had tried, but in the end, it simply hadn't worked. The job just took too much out of him, and Lauren had deserved better—had demanded it, actually. He smiled, his thoughts bittersweet. The fact that he'd failed her still rankled, despite the passage of time.

The phone rang, and he reached for the receiver, his thoughts turning back to the case. The past was the past. And best he could tell there was no need to keep reliving it. Lauren had a new life and he had his work. All's well that ends well—or something like that.

"D'Angelo."

"Any luck?" As usual, Tony didn't mince words.

"As a matter of fact I was just running her sheet. Name's Lydia Wallace. Small-timer, but a constant fixture in night court."

"Told you she was a pro."

"Looks that way. Hopefully that'll play in our favor if she was killed on home turf. How are things coming at Earth Free?"

"They offered me herbal tea." Tony's disgust carried solidly across the telephone lines.

"You drink it?" Eric fought to contain his laughter, the picture of Tony with a teacup almost his undoing.

"No." The word spoke for itself. "But I'm stuck here waiting for a printout. There's been a technical glitch and Mac here," Tony's voice faded as he turned away, "is working to fix it."

"Not a problem. It'll take me a while to get through this file. I'll try to establish a perimeter and then we can plug your findings into the mix."

"Actually, the case isn't why I called." Tony now sounded distinctly uncomfortable, and Eric had the sudden urge to hang up the phone. "I, ah, promised Bess I'd have a talk with one of her friends."

"Here?"

"Yeah. She's due any minute."

"And you want me to talk to her." Just what he needed, an afternoon spent baby-sitting one of Bess's friends.

"Well, it seemed the obvious solution. I'm here, you're there." He could almost hear Tony shrug. "It's not that big a deal. She's been getting crank phone calls. Just wants some advice on what to do. Shouldn't take you more than ten minutes, tops."

"Fine." Eric sighed. "I'll do it." As if there'd ever been a choice. "What's her name?"

"Sara Martin. Bess says she's a real looker."

As if on cue, a woman walked into the room. Tiny and

perfectly formed, she moved with the elegance of a dancer, blonde hair shimmering in the artificial light. A small mole accentuated the corner of her mouth, adding a touch of exotic to an otherwise American pie face. Blue eyes, blonde hair. The girl next door with a twist. Exquisite was the word that popped into his mind—along with a vivid image of her naked.

He shook his head. If this was Sara Martin, the visual wasn't the best way to start a conversation. He watched as she walked across the room, her stride and body language indicating a careless confidence.

But Eric wasn't fooled. There was vulnerability, too, carefully sequestered under an artfully constructed facade. He doubted most people would notice. But then he wasn't most people. And the anomaly made her all the more appealing, the combination of sexuality and mystery serving only to pique his interest.

The woman stopped just in front of the desk, her lips curling into a cautious smile. "Are you Tony?"

He shook his head, realizing he was still holding the phone. "His partner. Eric D'Angelo."

She licked her lips nervously, the gesture only making her seem more sensual. He'd obviously lost his fucking mind.

"Eric, you still there?" Tony's voice brought him back to reality in a heartbeat.

"Yeah." He answered, nodding like a moron.

"So is she there?"

"Yeah." He repeated again, his eyes still locked on the woman in front of him. "And Tony—Bess was right."

Chapter 3

"Right about what?" Sara Martin studied the detective curiously. Even seated she could tell that he was tall, a big man who'd no doubt dwarf her when standing. Reflexively she stood a little straighter.

"Punctuality."

"I beg your pardon?" She asked, more than aware that she was staring at him.

His hair was dark, almost blue-black, and just this side of too long, the effect rakish and at odds with the harsh lines of his face. His eyes were a peculiar shade of gray, light and dark all at the same time, his gaze piercing.

There was a small scar on his chin and another at the corner of his left eye, the marks adding character, making him seem more human somehow. Eric D'Angelo wasn't conventionally handsome, but he was definitely compelling, and her fingers itched for her camera. His was a face she'd like to photograph.

"I was just talking to Tony." He stood up, extending his hand. "Bess said you'd be on time."

She had the distinct feeling that wasn't what Bess had said at all, but she wasn't about to push for anything more. His hand engulfed hers, his skin warm and dry, the palm a little calloused. His gaze held hers, his eyes seeming to look deep inside her, and just for a moment she imagined that the air between them crackled with electricity.

Which was, of course, ridiculous.

Pulling her hand away, she licked her bottom lip nervously. "I take it Tony isn't coming."

"No." He shrugged, the corner of his lip quirking upward in the smallest of smiles. "I'm afraid you're stuck with me."

"How about if I just talk to him another time? I'm sure you have more important things to do than talk to me. I feel like I'm intruding on your day." She gestured at the papers piled on his desk.

"Actually you're a welcome break. Have a seat." He gestured to a chair by the desk, and she sank down onto to it, feeling a bit like a lamb in the lion's den. More so even when he perched on the corner of his desk, his proximity almost as intimidating as his physical presence. "So tell me how you know Bess and Tony."

"I know Bess from the magazine. We usually have lunch a couple time a week, and we take the same aerobics class at the gym. I've never actually met Tony." Which sounded lame. And now that she really thought about it was probably bordering on rude. Bess had been a good friend, and although Sara adored her, she'd purposely kept her at arm's length.

"His schedule doesn't make him easily accessible." D'Angelo's smile was meant to be soothing, but seemed to have just the opposite effect on Sara.

"I guess he told you why I'm here?" She'd meant it as a statement, but it came out more of a question, and she fought to pull her rioting emotions under control. He was so close, she could actually smell him, and on some chemical level, her body was reacting to the olfactory onslaught. Pheromones speaking to pheromones.

He leaned back, crossing his arms over his chest, the movement taking him farther away. "He said it was something to do with a crank phone call?"

She couldn't tell from his expression what he was thinking, but she couldn't imagine, considering the kinds of things he probably dealt with daily, that her phone calls were anything to cause particular concern, and she felt compelled to tell him so. "I feel silly, really. Now that I'm here. It's honestly nothing to be alarmed about."

"Why don't you let me be the judge of that?" His eyes narrowed as he studied her, his scrutiny making her want to squirm. She suspected that Eric D'Angelo had elicited more than one confession with an expression like that.

She nodded, trying to order her thoughts. "It started about a year ago. The phone would ring in the middle of the night and when I'd answer it, there was nothing but dead air. In the beginning, I wrote it off as a wrong number. There were only a handful of calls, and those sometimes months apart. But recently they've started coming with more frequency. I've kept a log." She reached into her purse and handed him a small notebook. "The first few dates are estimates. I didn't think to write them down until later."

"I'm impressed. Most people wouldn't have thought to do this at all." He flipped through the pages, stopping to study an entry or two. "Seems to be consistent about the times he calls. Has he ever said anything?"

"No. It's always just silence."

"What do you say?"

"Generally, I ask who's there a couple of times and then hang up. Sometimes, if I pick up the receiver again, he's still there. But not always."

D'Angelo nodded, handing her back the notebook. "Have you considered changing your number?"

She smiled at the question. "I can't. I'm a freelance photographer. My home number is the same as my business number."

"I thought you said you worked at the magazine?" He was frowning again, the lines of his face seeming even harsher.

"I'm not actually a staff member. I contribute a monthly article. A photo essay of sorts. Like *Life* magazine. It gives me the freedom to choose subjects that interest me. They've been kind enough to allow me some office space, and in return I fill in occasionally when they need an extra photographer or someone with my particular skills. It works well." She shrugged. "But, unfortunately, it doesn't pay all the bills."

"Hence the freelancing."

"And the need for a listed phone number." She sighed. "There really isn't anything you can do to help me, is there?"

"Under normal circumstances we can't get involved unless there's an implied threat. And even then, we can't do a whole lot. But there are things you can do. Do you have an answering machine?"

"Of course."

"Well, for starters you can let it pick up any late-night calls." He glanced down at her hand, his frown deepening. "Or, at the very least, let your husband answer."

She twisted her wedding ring nervously. "I'm not married. At least not anymore." She lifted her eyes, not certain she wanted to meet his gaze, yet unable to stop herself. "He died."

Concern washed across his face, his expression softening. "I'm sorry, Sara. I saw the ring and just assumed . . ."

"It's my fault really. I need to take it off." She bit her lip, the gesture almost apologetic. "It's just so hard."

"I can see that it would be." Again his voice was gentle, his eyes kind. "It was six months before I took mine off." He smiled ruefully, glancing down at his ring finger. "And I only got divorced."

"It's been two years," she said simply, as if the words explained everything.

"Two years is a long time."

She searched for censure in his face, but saw nothing other than compassion. "My son was killed, too. In the accident. I guess I'm afraid that if I take the ring off, I'll lose what little of them I have left."

Tears threatened, and she fought for control, mortified that she'd let her emotions hold sway. He was, after all, a

stranger, no matter how compelling, and here she was babbling like an idiot, telling him things she'd hardly admitted
to herself. "I'm sorry. I don't know why I told you all that."

He pulled a Kleenex out of a box on the desk and handed
it to her, the touch of his fingers against hers alarmingly
comfortable. As if they'd touched many times before, in far
more intimate ways. She snatched her hand away, using the
tissue to hide her rioting emotions.

"Everyone has to handle grief in their own way, Sara. I suspect there's no such thing as a right time for dealing with it."

She nodded, wishing that there was a way she could take
all the words back. She didn't normally spill her guts to a
stranger. Maybe it was the atmosphere. Police stations were
supposed to elicit confessions.

But in truth she knew it wasn't that at all. It was the man
himself—*Eric D'Angelo*. There was something about him
that made confiding easy. Almost a compulsion.

She smiled, hoping the gesture gave at least an illusion of
composure.

Whether it did or not, he seemed to be satisfied with what
he saw, his big body relaxing as he shifted on the desk, the
movement subtly increasing the distance between them.
Almost as if he were withdrawing. Sara was surprised to
feel regret.

"What I was going to say," he smiled, purposefully steering them back to the matter at hand, "is that it's good to have a
man record the message. It sounds sexist, I know, but even if
it's only on tape, the presence of a man can act as a deterrent."

"That makes good sense. I should have thought of it
myself."

"Sometimes it's easy to overlook the obvious. Especially
when you're emotionally involved." His smile was comforting, and she had to stifle the urge to ask *him* to make the
recording.

She shook her head, forcing her thoughts back to the
caller. "What else can I do?"

"If you don't already have it, you can try Caller ID. It might not give you an identity, but depending on where the calls are coming from, it should give you a number, and that's a start."

"I did talk to the phone company and they suggested the same. I just haven't gotten around to it. I guess, to be honest, I haven't taken it all that seriously until recently."

"Why the change?"

"A combination of things, really. My friends have all been urging me to do something, which indicates that they're concerned. And, I don't know, there's just something different about the calls now. Nothing concrete, just a feeling I have." She shrugged, words obviously inadequate. "Maybe something to do with what's been in the news lately."

"The murders." He didn't mince words, and she was absurdly grateful for the fact. She'd been right. Eric D'Angelo was the kind of man one could lean on. Trust with anything. But maybe she was mixing the profession with the man.

She nodded, not quite meeting his gaze. "I know it seems silly. But it makes you start thinking about things in a different way."

"I think you're absolutely right to take this seriously. Odds are it's just a prank, but you can't know that for certain, and taking steps to thwart the caller is more than warranted. Besides, in instances like this the more proactive you are, the less likely the caller is to keep coming back."

"So you think maybe if I show him I'm taking action, he'll stop?"

"Something like that. Anyway, it's worth a try. And who knows, if he's stupid enough, Caller ID might just nail him."

"That'd be nice. Even though he never talks, it's still sort of like having a voyeur. Like he's there in my bedroom. You know?"

"I can imagine." D'Angelo was shuffling papers on his desk, and Sara realized she was procrastinating, trying to prolong their conversation. Which probably wasn't a good idea for any number of reasons.

She stood up, holding out her hand again. "Thank you for your time, Detective." The words seemed absurdly inadequate, but she could hardly share her flights of fancy and she'd learned long ago that it was better to err on the side of caution.

"I'm glad I could help." He rose, too, clasping her hand in both of his, the touch strangely exhilarating. "And call me Eric. Any friend of Bess's is a friend of mine." His smile was warm, and just for the moment she allowed herself to believe it was personal. "Call me if anything changes. Or if you actually get a number. I can probably find the owner easier than you."

"Thank you," she said again, suddenly feeling awkward. There was something about him that pulled at her. A connection of sorts that was hard to ignore. Except that of course it was most likely her imagination. Or her libido choosing to make an appearance at a most inopportune moment.

She pulled her hand away, ignoring the hint of laughter in his gray eyes. Surely he couldn't tell what she was thinking? The thought brought on the heat of a blush, and she stepped backward in haste, almost falling over the chair.

He was beside her in an instant, his speed at odds with his size, his hand on her waist, steadying her. "You all right?"

She nodded, unable to find her voice. Their eyes met and held, and she suddenly found breathing difficult.

"Good." He released her and she fought to keep from reaching out to reestablish contact.

She took another step backward, clutching her purse, struggling to radiate some semblance of composure. "I really should be going."

"Maybe I'll see you at Tony's." His smile was slow and sure, his gray eyes glittering silver.

Heated.

Predatory.

Eric D'Angelo was definitely a dangerous commodity.

She hadn't felt anything like this since Tom had died, and quite honestly she wasn't certain she was ready. But even so, she was astute enough to recognize that, despite her misgivings, she wanted to see him again—more than she could possibly have imagined.

Eric stared at papers on his desk, trying to focus on the case, his brain refusing resolutely to cooperate, intent, instead, on concentrating on an image of Sara Martin. He frowned and shook his head, already accepting the fact that it wouldn't do him a bit of good. There was just something about her that made a man's head go a little off-kilter.

And it wasn't just her looks. Although he wouldn't chase her out of his bed. It was more than that. She seemed an enigma of sorts. Vulnerability mixed with strength. Sensuality with intelligence.

He found the combination enticing and puzzling all at the same time. None of which made any sense. He wasn't in the market for a relationship, and Sara Martin was definitely not one-night-stand material.

Not to mention the fact that the woman was obviously still hung up on her husband. If that wasn't a recipe for disaster, he didn't know what was. But despite all that, he couldn't quit thinking about her, his mind obediently trotting out the image of her standing by the desk, her skin soft against his hand, the sweet smell of her perfume seductive in its simplicity.

He blinked his eyes, forcing himself to clear his head. There was work to be done, and he sure as hell didn't need the complication of someone like Sara Martin in his life.

Period.

There was simply no room for anything lasting. He just didn't have it in him to give. Which was an indication right there that his thoughts of Sara were over the top. He'd only just met the woman, and he was already worrying about a long-term relationships. Hell, the reality was he'd probably never see her again.

The thought left him feeling strangely deflated.

"Fascinating file?" Tony seemingly materialized out of nowhere, plopping down at his desk, a know-it-all smile on his face.

"I'm just trying to understand the vic. Maybe narrow down our locations."

"Who you trying to kid?" Tony asked, his smile widening into a grin. "I know you pretty damn well, and unless I miss my guess, you're not thinking about work at all."

"Of course I am." He scowled at Tony, angry at himself for being so transparent.

Tony leaned his chair back against the wall, ignoring the scowl. "I take it things went well with Sara Martin."

"She was a nice enough lady. Intelligent and easy on the eyes. But that's it. I gave her some tips and sent her on her merry way." He shrugged, trying for nonchalant. "She mentioned something about her husband and son dying. You know the story?"

Tony nodded, his expression suddenly grim. "They were killed in a car wreck. I don't know the details. Just that he lost control of the car and both of them were killed. The kid was only four."

"Jesus, I can't imagine." And he couldn't. Despite the fact that he dealt with horrible things day in and day out, it was never personal. At least not like that. "She seems okay, though."

"I think she does all right, but I know Bess is always on her to get out more. Build something new." Tony eyed his partner. "Maybe you're just the ticket."

"Are you kidding? I'm the last thing someone like her needs."

"You sell yourself short, Eric . . ." He trailed off with a shrug.

"I helped her because she's Bess's friend." He emphasized each word as if his friend were deaf. "End of story."

Tony held up his hands in mock defense. "All right already. I get the picture. You don't want to talk about it."

"There isn't anything to talk about." Usually Tony's dogged perseverance was an asset, but just at the moment it was definitely not. He made a point of picking up the Wallace file. "You get anything from Earth Free?"

His partner sobered, realizing that he'd gone far enough. "Yeah. I got a list of local places that use the product. They grouped it geographically. So I figure we concentrate on the places east of I-35 and north of Town Lake. And since the other two women were found in their apartments, I'm guessing we're looking for a residential hotel or apartment building."

"Probably a hotel. An apartment building isn't going to use the same cleaner for each apartment. And this stuff isn't available for residential use, right?"

"Not unless somebody stole the stuff." Tony tossed the list on his desk. "Damn needle in a haystack."

"Maybe not." Eric picked up his notes. "We might be able to narrow the search. Lydia Wallace seems to have frequented an area around Twelfth and Chicon. There's even an old address there. If we cross-check that against your list, we might find something."

"Like where she was killed. You know, maybe we were too quick to assume a change in M.O. Maybe someone else moved her."

"Someone who wouldn't want the attention accompanying a corpse on the carpet? Makes sense. That the list?" Eric nodded at a manila envelope in Tony's hand.

"Yup." He sat down at his desk, pulling out a stack of papers. "So what do you say we narrow it down? It beats the hell out of sitting here watching you moon over Sara Martin."

Just the mention of her name sent his senses reeling, but he had more important things to think about. He reached for a page from the list, firmly pushing all thoughts of Sara Martin out of his head.

It was time to catch a killer.

Chapter 4

"Not much of a place to live." Tony frowned at the peeling paint and fading wallpaper.

"Beats the streets." Maynard Tompkins, the hotel manager, shrugged, stepping back to allow them access to the room.

"I'm not so sure." Eric stepped over warped floorboards, careful not to touch anything. The Tejano Hotel wasn't exactly a five-star establishment. Hell, it probably didn't even rate the moniker *hotel*. It was eleven of twelve on their list of possibles, but perseverance had paid off. Lydia Wallace had called it home.

The room was small. Closet sized, really. A bed and broken-down chest of drawers were the only furniture in the room. The odor of pine cleaner permeated the air. The bed was stripped, and an open drawer gave testament to the fact that the room was empty.

"She ain't been here for a week or so." The older man shifted nervously from foot to foot, eyeing first Tony, then Eric.

"So you emptied the place?"

"She hadn't paid rent in almost a month. What'd you expect me to do?" He edged closer to the door, his eyes darting around the room. "I gotta make a living."

"So much for a caring landlord." Tony exchanged a glance with Eric, and crossed the room to open the closet door. Like the rest of the room, it was empty. "What'd you do with her things?"

"There wasn't nothing here. Honest. I figured she run out during the night." He was biting his lip now, worry creasing his forehead.

"You didn't think to call in a missing person's report?" Eric already knew the answer, but wanted to rattle the guy's cage.

"On someone like that?"

Eric walked over to the bed, searching for something that might yield answers. The guy was a regular bleeding heart. But then maybe *bleeding* was the operative word. He frowned at a brownish stain just at the edge of the bed, leaning over to examine it more closely.

It was small, no bigger than a quarter, with streaks of white where the floor had been scrubbed. Scanning the rest of the floor, he saw similar spots of varying diameter, and recognized them for what they were. Spatter.

Blood spatter. There was a telltale pattern, despite the effort to wash it away.

"Tony, check this out." Eric straightened, nodding at the floor, his gaze locked on the manager.

Tony knelt by the bed, eyeing the stains, then reached up to lift the mattress. The underside was black with dried blood. "Is there something else you want to share with us, Maynard?"

"Like maybe what you found up here?" Eric added.

"I didn't find anything." The man crossed his arms over his chest, his face purposefully blank, but his eyes told a different story as they darted back to the stained mattress. There was fear there. Eric could almost smell it.

"I kind of doubt that. Judging from the blood spatters on the floor, and the stain on this mattress, I'd say you found a lot more than you bargained for."

Maynard backed up, shaking his head. "I didn't do nothing but clean the room. The stains were already there."

"You sure about that? Seems to me it's more likely

you're the one who put them here." Tony's eyes narrowed, his tone harsh.

"No way. I only found her." Maynard stopped, realizing his error, clamping his mouth shut with an audible click, his fear obvious now.

"Found her, how?" Eric moved closer, cutting the manager off from the door.

"Dead." The man's voice broke. "She was all beat up. I ain't never seen nothing like it. And I've seen a hell of a lot."

"So, what, you stashed the body and cleaned up the mess?" Tony's disbelief was palpable.

"No. I called her . . . manager."

"Guy got a name?" Tony pulled out a pad.

"Alturo Ramirez." The man was breathing easier. Maybe there was something to the notion that confession was good for the soul.

"And between the two of you, you tossed the body?"

"Nah. That was Ramirez. I just cleaned up the mess." He shuddered at the memory. "I gotta re-rent the room."

"What time did all this happen?" Tony asked.

"A couple of days. Monday, I think. I knocked, and the door just opened. So I came in and she was there on the bed."

"Dead."

"Oh yeah. Real dead." The man's eyes were locked on the bed now, as if he were seeing her again. "She was cut up bad. And tied to the bed. It was almost like she was sleeping. Except her eyes were open. Wild kinda. Like she was still screaming."

"So why didn't you call the police?"

The man swung around to face Eric. "I didn't need the trouble. And Alturo said nobody was gonna miss her."

"Well, he was wrong."

"So what happens now?" Maynard had deflated, leaving him pale and shaken. "Am I under arrest?"

"What do you think?" Eric eyed the man with disgust.

"But if you help us now, I guarantee it'll play better for you in the long run."

"I told you what I know."

Tony nodded, closing his pad. "Yeah, well, you're going to have to tell us again. Down at the station. And this Alturo person is going to have to corroborate your story. You know where we can find him?"

Maynard nodded. "He lives two blocks down. Above the Roxie."

"How about Lydia's effects? You still say there wasn't anything here?"

"Nah, I got 'em in a box. Downstairs. Figured I'd sell what I could. Make good on what she owed me."

"Guess you figured wrong." Eric reached for his handcuffs, as Tony turned the man around. "Those effects belong to us now. We'll collect them on the way out."

Tony smiled, the gesture not reaching his eyes. "Before they have a chance to disappear."

The three of them walked into the hallway, the manager between them. "One more question, Maynard." Tony's voice was deceptively soft. "Was there music playing? When you found her, I mean?"

"Yeah. Some romantic shit."

Eric looked at Tony, the air suddenly chill despite the suffocating heat of the hallway. "You recognize the singer?"

The little man nodded. "Sinatra. It was Frank Sinatra."

The conference room was packed with press from all across Texas present. Even a few folks from national publications. Serial murders were big news, especially in a society that thrived on voyeurism. The fact that the dead women were all prostitutes only made it better. Insulating the crimes from the mainstream. Providing people with a false sense of security.

There but for the grace of God . . .

Sara shook her head, clearing her thoughts, concentrating instead on the angle of the shot. Ernesto Sanchez wasn't an easy man to photograph. His bald head was perpetually shiny, and he had a way of scrunching his nose that made him border on unattractive, and unfortunately the more nervous he was, the more he scrunched.

Not that it mattered. If they used the mayor's picture at all, it would be a tiny black-and-white buried in the middle of the article. Press conference photos weren't the stock-in-trade of magazines like *Texas Today*. Real-life shots were more the norm. Political statements, as it were. That's why she liked doing pieces for the magazine. It gave her an opportunity to use art to tell a story.

Sanchez turned, the light hitting him just right, and for an instant his emotions were naked for the camera: anxiety laced with fear, and a grim determination that came from experience. She snapped the shot. A moment captured for eternity.

"You get that?" Nate's voice was only just above a whisper.

She nodded, not taking her eye off of the mayor. "He may not have much to say verbally, but it's all there in his face."

"At least we'll have that." Nate's tone was despondent. "So far he hasn't *said* anything that we don't already know."

"You weren't expecting him to, were you?" She cast a sideways glance at Nate. He wore the hopeful expression of a kid, and her heart went out to him. He tried so hard.

"Not really." He shrugged. "But a guy can always hope." His ever present smile was a bit dimmer than usual.

"Your time will come, Nate. You just have to be patient."

The mayor paused for a moment, turning to listen to an aide, the silence demanding their attention. The other man was talking rapidly, his hands moving to underscore his words. Sara felt her skin tingling. Something was happening. Something important.

Nate stepped closer to the podium, his attention focused solely on the mayor. He felt it, too.

Mayor Sanchez turned back to the podium, his expression grim. "Ladies, and gentlemen, I've just been informed that we have an I.D. on the latest victim. It has been confirmed that she was indeed a prostitute." He paused, and Sara could actually hear the pens scribbling on paper. "Sources inform me that she was sixteen years old with no known family."

"You got a name?" someone asked.

The mayor glanced over at the aide, who shrugged in answer. Sanchez turned back to the crowd. "Her name was Lydia Wallace . . ."

Sanchez's voice faded, and Sara's knees buckled, her blood rushing from her head.

"Sara?" Nate's hand clasped her arm, holding her upright. "What's wrong?"

She struggled to find her voice. "Lydia Wallace."

"What about her?" Nate's arm slid around her, the touch comforting somehow.

She looked up at him, his face swimming slowly back into focus. "She's the girl I photographed for the article I've been working on."

"You can sit here looking sullen all you want, Ramirez, but I get to leave when I've got to take a leak. You, on the other hand, are stuck here for the duration." Eric looked pointedly at the two empty Coke cans sitting in front of Alturo Ramirez.

The punk was only a little older than the vic. Cocky and full of false security. He had a rap sheet thick enough to pad a cell, but at the moment he wasn't talking.

"We know you moved the body. And according to some of the other girls, we know you had a fight with Lydia the night she died. So it isn't hard to connect the dots."

The guy frowned, glaring up at him with the kind of insolence only a kid can accomplish. How the hell he'd wound up a pimp was anyone's guess.

"You getting anywhere?" Tony poked a head into the interrogation room, already knowing the answer. He'd been watching the whole thing through the two-way. Hell, the kid probably knew it as well. But the dance had been choreographed and there was no changing the steps.

"Our friend here isn't talking." He walked over to Tony, pitching his voice lower, but not so softly that Alturo couldn't hear. "Not sure he's playing with a full deck anyway."

Ramirez's eyes narrowed even further, but Eric caught a flicker of something in them.

"You tell him we got DNA?" They didn't. But Tony hadn't said they did.

This time they got a reaction. "I didn't do her."

Both detectives swung around, Eric straddling the chair across from Ramirez and Tony sitting on the corner of the table. "Do her, how?"

"*No* way. I didn't do her no way. I fought with her, sure. Even roughed her up some. She was holding out on me. Taking money on the side." His hands cut through the air, underscoring his words. "But I didn't kill her."

"You just helped Maynard move her."

"That old fart? He didn't do anything except come crying to me. I was the one who hauled her ass out of there."

"And put her in a dumpster." Tony's face reflected his disgust.

"Where'd you want me to put her?"

Eric fought the urge to slam the jerk up against the wall. He wasn't worth it. "You could have called the police."

"And wound up here?" The sarcasm wasn't entirely out of place.

Tony smiled. "You're here, anyway. And the way I see it, you're in a world of trouble."

"Look, I moved her." The man's bluster had evaporated. "Maybe I shouldn't have, but I owed Maynard."

It was the beginning of a dialogue and Eric recognized the opportunity. "You tell us what you know, and if it's worth it, then we'll talk to the D.A."

"Not good enough." The hard-eyed stare erased all semblance of youth. "I talk, I want a guarantee."

Tony nodded, slightly.

"All right. You help us, we'll help you."

Their gazes met and held, and finally Ramirez nodded, then looked down at his hands. "Lydia'd only been working for me a couple of months. So I didn't know her all that well. But she was a real piece of work. Mouthing off all the time."

"No respect for authority." Tony put just the right touch of sincerity into his voice, and Eric tried not to smile.

"Exactly." The hands were waving again. Ramirez was on a roll. "Anyway I knew she'd been stiffing me, so I called a meeting."

"What time?"

"Monday night, around ten. We met at the Roxie."

The Roxie was a tit bar close to the hotel. A major hangout for hookers. "And you roughed her up."

"That wasn't my intention. But she took a swing at me. So I hit her. Twice. She promised to pay and I figured we was square."

"When did she leave?"

"I don't know for sure. But the whole conversation only took about fifteen minutes."

"And you didn't see her again until Maynard called you?"

"That's right. He paged me. It was about two in the morning. Said she was dead. And asked me to help him get her out of there."

Eric blew out a breath. "So when you got there, had Tompkins moved her?" He already knew the answer, but he needed to confirm the details.

"No. She was just like he found her. And it was real ugly."

"Describe it." Tony's fist clenched, the only outward sign of his anger.

"She was lying on the bed, her hands tied to the headboard. Her blood was all over the mattress and the floor. She'd been stabbed." Ramirez swallowed convulsively, the memory obviously getting to him. "A lot."

"That it?"

"No." He shook his head, closing his eyes. "Her fingers were missing. We looked for 'em, but couldn't find nothing. And there was a bat. The bastard used a bat—"

"Any idea where it came from?"

Ramirez opened his eyes, and nodded. "It was Lydia's. She was nuts about baseball. Especially the Express. She won the bat at a game. Even got it signed."

"Did you know Laurel Henry or Candy Mason?"

His eyes widened. "The other women? No way. Never even seen 'em. They didn't work the neighborhood."

Tony sat back, crossing his arms over his chest. "How about the night of the murder? You see anyone suspicious hanging around the Tejano?"

"Shit, man, the place is crawling with strangers. That's the whole fucking point. Everyone looks suspicious. No one wants to be seen. You know what I mean?"

Eric nodded. "How about music. You hear music?"

"You talking about that crap that was playing on the boom box?" Ramirez pulled a face. "Some shit about knowing you. The kinda stuff my old man listens to."

"And Lydia?"

"No fucking way. There wasn't a romantic bone in her body. She was heavy into Staind and POD."

Unsure if he was horrified or elated, Eric blew out a long breath. They had confirmation from two sources. Which meant there wasn't any doubt. They were definitely dealing with a serial killer. And he wasn't going to stop with three.

Chapter 5

Sara tried to keep her mind on the traffic, but instead all she could see was the face of Lydia Wallace—too old for her years, but still with the light of hope in her eyes. And now she was dead.

The stoplight in front of Sara loomed red, and she slammed on the brakes, the Accord groaning in protest. The car slid to a stop, but not before skidding to the left, the shimmy in the chassis making her breath catch in her throat, her attention snapping to the present.

Car horns honked behind her, one angry driver gesturing with his hand out the open window. She exhaled slowly, and ascertained that despite her racing heart, everything was okay.

Truth was, she'd never really been comfortable driving, and since the accident it had only gotten worse. She might not have been in the car, but her imagination more than made up for the fact.

And daydreaming wasn't going to help anything.

Lydia Wallace's face flashed through her mind again, and Sara tightened her grip on the wheel. Not exactly a daydream. The light changed and she drove slowly through the intersection, ignoring the traffic streaming by her.

She had to talk to someone, tell them that she'd talked to Lydia, had pictures of her. It might not help anything, but she still had to try. She thought about Eric D'Angelo. She didn't know if he was handling the case, but even if he wasn't, he'd know who she should talk to. Her mind made up, she reached for her cell phone.

It rang before she could dial.

"Hello?"

"Sara? Is that you?" Ryan's voice held a note of excitement. "I just talked to Nate. He told me you took pictures of Lydia Wallace."

She nodded, then remembered he couldn't see her. "Yeah, for the article I'm working on. I was just going to take them to the police."

"No." The word was somewhere between a plea and a command. "If you do that, we lose our edge. Let me print them first. We'll just change the angle of the story."

"I don't know, Ryan. What if there's something there that can help find the killer?"

"Oh, come on, Sara, what are the odds of that? It's hardly likely the man was hanging around waiting for you to photograph him. Besides, what harm can come from holding off a day? We go to print tonight. I can make your photos the lead. Put Lydia on the cover. You can go to the police tomorrow, after the issue hits the stands."

"I don't know." She fought with her conscience. Ryan had been so good to her since Tom's death, she hated to deprive him of what would undoubtedly be a journalistic coup.

"I'll let Nate write the copy," Ryan cajoled.

That cinched it. Even if she hadn't felt an obligation to Ryan, she certainly wasn't about to steal Nate's chance at the limelight. The police would have to wait.

"All right. I'll wait. But only until tomorrow."

"Good girl. Do you have them with you?"

"No. The photos are at home, but the contact sheet is in my office. Nate knows where." She clicked the phone off, praying she'd done the right thing.

"So where the hell are we?" Tony paced around the conference room, his agitation apparent with every step.

"Pretty damned convinced that Ramirez isn't our perp. He and Tompkins are too stupid to be behind the murders."

"I hear that. But they did manage to fuck up the crime scene. Which means we aren't going to find a thing." Tony stopped in front of the window, his hands gripping the sill. "The guy's too damn good for that."

"So we go over the evidence again. And then again, if necessary. There's got to be something somewhere to give us a hint. Someplace he made a mistake. The dimwitted duo may have screwed up the crime scene, but that doesn't mean there isn't anything to find. Claire and her team know what they're doing. We just need to give them a chance to do it. And in the meantime, we go over what we know." Eric walked over to the white board and picked up a marker. "We've got three victims. All more or less in the same profession." He wrote the three women's names across the top of the board.

"Different ages, and race." Tony flipped through the file folders, pulling pictures of each of the victims.

"Yeah." He frowned at the board. "Laurel was the oldest, right?"

"Yup, then Candy and then Lydia. You thinking there's a pattern?"

"Could be. It's hard to tell with three. But it's something." He wrote each woman's age under her name and then wrote the word "age" with a question mark. "What else?"

"Location varies, but, if Ramirez is to be believed, the body is left at the site, and the cause of death has been the same in all three cases."

Eric wrote the location of each murder site under the women's names, along with the word "knife." "And then there's the amputations. First one lost her ears." He wrote the word. "Second her tongue. And Lydia lost her fingers."

"The perp's style is improving, the last amputation cleaner than the first."

Eric made a note of the fact. "But the big question here is why. Why take body parts at all?"

"Maybe a trophy of some sort? These guys like proof of their power."

"Could be. But why body parts? It's not symptomatic of the torture. All three amputations occurred post mortem. And he's not covering anything up. The vics have been readily identifiable, and except for the fingers, he hasn't removed anything that would have deterred discovering I.D. So maybe it's something specific to each woman and the part removed." Eric stared at the board, willing it to yield answers. "Or maybe it's something ritualistic. Something that has meaning only for the killer."

"Which means we have to read his fucking mind?"

"Something like that." Eric slammed his hand against the board, the resulting pain helping him to focus. "We've got to try and think like him. Look at what he's done through his eyes."

"By the light of a full moon?" Tony's tone was teasing, but there was a note of derision present as well.

"No," Eric corrected dryly. "We use our heads. Think like the perp. It's common sense when you think about it."

Tony shrugged. "Can't hurt. Although I've got to say this is one sick son of a bitch we're going to be emulating."

Eric turned to study the board. "So we've got an angry guy with a grudge against women, or maybe more specifically prostitutes."

"Not out of the ordinary. Hookers are low-risk victims. A killer can take them out without raising much of a stink."

Eric frowned, turning to face his partner. "Except that our killer obviously isn't afraid of the limelight. If he was, we'd have seen more of an attempt to cover up his crimes. This guy's practically waving them in our faces."

"Which tells us what?"

"That if he's using hookers as low-risk victims, it's because they're easy to get to. Not because no one cares. Which means that sooner or later it won't be enough to satisfy him. Hell, his pattern's already changing. He's moving toward higher-risk kills."

"I don't follow." Tony frowned at the board. "They're still all hookers."

"Yeah, but they're getting younger, and by definition more innocent. Lydia Walker was just a kid, and a hell of a lot more likely to raise public sympathy than either of the previous victims. Every parent in a hundred-mile radius will be watching their daughters tonight. So he's upped the ante." Eric rubbed the back of his neck, frustration knotting his muscles. "Unfortunately, we're not even sure what game it is we're playing. Which is probably just exactly the way he wants it."

"So we look at what else we've got. The music was present at all three scenes." Tony went back to the file. "All Sinatra, and all played on homemade CDs."

"Well, we know for certain that the music didn't belong to the vic in Lydia's case. And I think we can feel fairly confident that it wasn't in Candy Mason's collection either. Which only leaves Laurel. What about the boom boxes?"

Tony consulted the files. "They were all identical. Probably planted along with the CD. Which still begs the question why?"

"Could be for us. Or it could have to do with the ritual. My guess is both. What about the songs. Any significance there?"

Tony flipped through Laurel's file. "The first one was 'I Think of You.' The second was something about breathing." Tony flipped through Candy's file. "Oh yeah, 'With Every Breath I Take.'"

"And the last one was 'I Dream of You.'" Eric wrote it on the board under Lydia's name.

"How the hell did you remember that?" Tony's eyebrows arched with surprise.

"My mother loves Frank Sinatra. She and my father spent entire evenings listening to albums and dancing around the living room floor. I guess it kinda rubbed off."

"Okay, Mr. Sinatra lover, you see something that might connect these particular songs?"

"No." Eric studied the board. "Not off the top of my head, anyway. But I think it'd be a good idea to get the lyrics. He's playing the music for some reason. Hell, for all I know there's something to the progression of the notes, but not being a musician, I figure it's easier to start with the words."

Tony shrugged, his expression changing to one of resignation. "Fine. I'll get to work on the lyrics."

"It doesn't mean you have to listen to the recording, you know. All you have to do is check out lyric sites online. Not that it would hurt you to listen to a little Frank. Add some romance to your life."

"Hey, buddy, I got all the romance I need. It's just that Bess and I prefer Garth Brooks to Ole Blue Eyes." Tony's eyes crinkled with his smile. "If anyone's lacking in the romance department, it's you."

"I get laid."

"That's not what I'm talking about. You need something more than a one-night stand."

"And I suppose you have just the woman." The minute he said it, he knew he'd walked into a trap.

Tony's smile was slow, almost victorious. "How about Sara Martin?"

All thoughts of the case fled in the wake of images of blue eyes and blonde hair. For a moment, he even thought he could smell her perfume.

He shook his head, trying to clear his mind.

Sara Martin was the last thing he needed. Which had nothing whatsoever to do with the fact that he wanted her.

Bad.

"I can't find anything wrong." Jack Weston ran a hand through his hair, leaving a trail of grease across his forehead.

"You're sure?" Sara felt silly, pushing things. Jack was a great mechanic. And in the last two years he'd been over her car from bumper to bumper more times than she cared to admit.

"Positive." He smiled, the grin making him seem almost rakish. She and Jack went way back. To foster care days. A friendship forged from necessity, but maintained with pleasure. Especially over the last couple of years. "There is nothing wrong with it."

"But I know I felt a shimmy."

"Sara," he reached out for her hands. "Your car is fine."

"I know that—intellectually. But . . ." She pulled her hands away, turning her back to him.

He turned her back to face him. "But you can't let go of the image of their car in that ravine."

She looked up to meet his gaze. "No. I can't."

"And every time you remember, you think something is wrong with your car."

She smiled, knowing the gesture lacked strength. "It's only a small idiosyncrasy."

"An understandable one, but your car is fine." He moved away, the distance between them comfortable. "I talked to Bess Haskins today."

Sara frowned, surprised. "I didn't know the two of you were friends."

"We're not, really. More acquaintances by default. Through you." He picked up a rag and began cleaning off his hands. "Anyway, she wanted to invite me to a barbecue. Want to go together?"

Sara shook her head. "I'm not ready for parties, Jack, but you and Bess get points for effort."

He smiled. "I told her it wouldn't work, but I figured it was worth a try."

"You should still go, though. The Haskinses are good people."

"I might give it a try, but it won't be the same without you."

Sara's smile was genuine this time. "You certainly know how to flatter a girl, but the answer is still no."

Jack held up his hands. "All right. I can take a hint. But if you change your mind . . ."

"I won't."

Although she was tempted. After all, Eric D'Angelo would probably be there. And seeing him again was almost enough to get her to change her mind.

Almost.

Chapter 6

He'd lost his fucking mind.

Eric turned onto Speedway, wondering what in hell he'd been thinking. Obviously, he hadn't. At least not with his head. But that didn't stop him from still wanting to see her. It had been easy enough to find her address. A lot harder to come up with an excuse.

He glanced at the plastic bag on the seat next to him and wondered again what had come over him. Hormones, certainly, but he knew there was more to it than that. He just wasn't certain what.

And so, like a crazed adolescent, he was manufacturing excuses to see her. Which in and of itself was insane. Although it had seemed a good idea in the squad room.

He turned onto her street and started looking for house numbers. The quiet neighborhood was a hodgepodge of eras. Restored Victorians mixed in with cottages from the twenties and bungalows from the forties, along with the occasional ugly apartment building. "Eclectic" at its best.

He slowed as he neared the house, wanting to prolong the moment. Hell, wanting to turn the car around and head for home. But that wasn't his style. And he knew that if he went home, he'd only be back. Besides, there was every possibility that seeing her again would prove him wrong. Maybe there hadn't been a connection.

Maybe he was inventing a fantasy where there was nothing.

The only way to be certain was to see her again. And now seemed as good a time as any.

He pulled up in front of the house. The porch light illuminated the gingerbread trim, giving the place a warm and inviting feel. Just like the woman.

There was a car in the driveway. An old Volkswagen Beetle, the relic at odds with the graceful lines of the house. He wasn't sure how he knew, but he was certain the car didn't belong to Sara. Which meant she wasn't alone.

He hesitated for a moment, not certain he wanted to face her when she had company, suddenly afraid that it might be another man. Then he shook his head at his train of thought. He hadn't even confirmed that there was something to explore, and he was already jealous.

He was acting like a fool. Grabbing the plastic bag, he opened the car door, and before he could change his mind, headed up the sidewalk toward the front door.

The wraparound porch proved to be every bit as inviting as it had looked from the street, wicker furniture and red geraniums making it feel like an extension of the house. Cheerful and welcoming. Despite the November chill, spring lived here, as if time had been peeled away, abandoning the twenty-first century for something cleaner, simpler. Revitalizing.

Laughing at his thoughts, he rang the doorbell and waited for what seemed like an eternity before the painted door swung open.

The woman at the door was not Sara. Embarrassment mixed with disappointment. She did have company.

"I'm sorry," he said, feeling like a complete idiot. "I'm looking for Sara Martin."

The redhead gave him a once-over worthy of someone on the job, and then met his gaze, her eyes slightly narrowed. "And you would be?"

Automatically he reached for his badge. The woman stepped back, the door starting to close. "Detective D'Angelo." He shoved the badge at the remaining crack of open door. "Eric D'Angelo. I talked to Ms. Martin this morning."

And hadn't been able to stop thinking of her since. But that wasn't exactly a great opening remark.

The door swung back open, the redhead's scowl changing to a smile, and she stepped back, gesturing him in. "I'm Molly Parker."

She said it as if that would clear things up for him, but, of course, it didn't. Still there was no sense in letting her know that. "Nice to meet you, Molly, but don't you think you ought to look at the badge before inviting me in?" Using his best cop's voice, he tried to cover his confusion.

The woman gave him another once-over, her examination this time more Mae West than Lennie Briscoe. "I suppose I could do that, but you've got to admit it looks pretty damn official." She shrugged. "Besides, Sara told me all about you."

That seemed like a positive development. At least he had the right house. "Is she home?"

"In the kitchen." She tilted her head in the general direction of a swinging door propped open with a chair. Her smile was mischievous, but her eyes were friendly, and he accepted the odd nature of her banter as part of her charm.

"I, uh, didn't mean to barge in like this . . ." He trailed off, trying not to look toward the kitchen door.

"You're not barging into anything, believe me. In fact, I was just leaving."

He was positive she hadn't been leaving at all, but true to her word, she reached for a sweater hanging from a hook on the hall tree.

"Sara? I'm off, and *you've* got a gentleman caller." With

another impish smile, she dashed out the front door, pulling it shut behind her.

Eric swallowed, and still clutching the plastic sack, walked farther into the room. The house was as welcoming inside as out. An old camelback sofa sat comfortably in front of a leaded glass window, flanked on each side by mahogany tables. An oversize wingback was paired with an ornate gilt-framed mirror, the frame's intricate carving echoing the elegant lines of the chair.

And everywhere there were photographs. On the tables, on the walls. Framed, unframed. Everything from landscapes to portraits. Each artfully arranged so that nothing competed. Fine art at its best.

He picked a simple wooden frame off the table. A boy of about four smiled, gap-toothed, for the camera, his dark hair tousled, his blue eyes the same color as his mother's.

"That's Charlie."

There was a wistful quality to her voice. A hint of sadness that was at once heartbreaking and compelling. He turned to look at her, his breath catching in his throat.

He hadn't been wrong. She was incredible. Even in jeans and a T-shirt, with a dish towel in her hands, she looked alluring. And vulnerable. Or maybe it was the vulnerability that made her so appealing. He couldn't say for sure. Couldn't even think straight. Which should have sent him running for the hills, but it didn't.

"Charlie was your son." The words were inadequate, but he wasn't certain what to say, and he desperately needed to say something.

"He'll always be my son, Detective." There was a gentle rebuke in her words, and she reached to take the photo from him, the touch of her skin against his oddly unsettling.

"I'm sorry, I didn't mean it like that—" He held up a hand in apology, distraught by the fact that he had offended her, distracted by the way she made him feel.

"I know." Her smile was slow but genuine. "It's just that people are always talking about Charlie and Tom in past tense, and while they may be gone on a physical level, I can't accept that some part of them isn't still here," she tapped her heart, "with me."

"I can understand that. My father has been dead for awhile now, but sometimes I'd swear he's still here, talking to me when I need him most." He hadn't meant to say that. Some things were meant to be private. Hell, he hadn't even shared that sort of thing with Lauren.

"So why are you here?" Her gaze met his, blue eyes questioning.

He stepped back, lifting the plastic bag, as if it would create a barrier between them. A barrier he suddenly felt that he needed. There was something about Sara Martin. Something that made him want to throw caution to the wind. Forget good sense, and pull her into his arms.

But that wasn't exactly the polite thing to do, and so instead he held the bag higher. "I brought you a Caller ID box." Once it was said, he had to admit it sounded pretty lame. "I wanted to help. And since there's nothing I can do professionally, I thought maybe this would be a start."

"How thoughtful." Her smile this time lit up her whole face, and just for the moment he felt like the most important person on earth. "I meant to stop and get one myself. But, as usual, I got sidetracked. So this is perfect."

"You'll still have to add the service." He pulled the box out of the bag. "But that can be done with a phone call. Do you want me to install it for you?" There really wasn't anything to it, but he didn't want to leave, and it seemed an obvious ploy.

"That'd be great. Where do you think I should put it? I've got three phones. One in the living room, one in the study, and another upstairs," she gestured with her chin, "in the bedroom."

Just the word *bedroom* sent a slew of less-than-innocent thoughts racing through his head. He blew out a slow breath and forced himself to concentrate. "It should work wherever it is. I guess it just depends on whether you want to see it when the call comes in, or just know that it's doing its job."

She frowned, thinking. "I suppose, since the calls come mainly at night, I'd rather have it in the bedroom. That way I can see if the call is from someone I know and answer it."

"That makes sense. And if you don't recognize the number, you can let the machine get it." He opened the packaging and pulled out the box. "This one will store up to fifty calls and the name and number if it's available."

"Great. How much do I owe you?"

"Consider it a gift. I used my connections." He'd bought it himself, but somehow he couldn't bring himself to tell her that. "Just my way of helping a friend."

"A friend's friend." Their gazes met and held, the air suddenly seeming too thin to breathe. "You're a good guy, Detective D'Angelo."

"Eric." Despite good sense, he took a step closer.

"All right, then. *Eric*." She licked her lips, the gesture provocative.

He reached out to tuck a strand of hair behind her ear, then dropped his hand self-consciously, fighting against the surge of hormones crashing through him. Her perfume surrounded him, filling his senses, making him feel protective and turned-on all at once, the two instincts at war with one another.

Protection won out.

It was too soon.

With a release of breath, he stepped back, purposefully breaking the connection. "Show me where the phone is."

Chapter 7

He was sitting on the edge of her bed, his strong hands connecting the phone line. If Sara listened carefully she could hear his breathing. She swallowed nervously and then licked her lips, her eyes glued to his every move. It was as though things were exaggerated, moving in slow motion—as if she were hyperaware. Every nerve in her body reacting at once.

She shook her head, tightening her hand on the door frame, a futile attempt to ground herself. Eric D'Angelo sent her senses reeling in a way that was frightening and exhilarating all at the same time.

"All done." He stood up, his word at odds with the intensity in his eyes.

She swallowed again, certain that they were communicating on a level that had nothing to do with crank phone calls and Caller ID boxes. "I can't thank you enough."

"Sure you can." His grin was contagious. "You can call the phone company tomorrow and get this thing operational."

"I will. I promise. And in the meantime, I'll let my answering machine take care of my phone calls."

He walked toward the door, and involuntarily she stepped back, something in her, the preservation part, wanting to keep at least a modicum of distance between them.

"All right. Guess I'll let you get back to your evening." He started for the stairs, and all need for distance vanished, replaced by the much more urgent need to keep him with her.

"If it's not too presumptuous . . ." She broke off, feeling stupid, but he turned, waiting, his gray eyes unreadable. "I thought maybe you could record a message for my machine. You said it was better if a man did the recording."

"Sure, it's a good idea. Where's the machine?"

"In the study." She walked past him, their bodies touching briefly, igniting their internal conversation again. There was no denying the connection between them was strong, but that didn't mean it was anything but chemical. "I'll show you."

Study was probably too grand a word for the little room off the living room, but it was her favorite place in the house, a bank of windows on the south wall filling it with tree-dappled sunlight in the mornings and silvery starlight at night.

"It's over here on the desk."

"What a great piece." He lovingly ran his fingers over the carved oak of the rolltop desk, and she shivered as if he'd been touching her. "My grandfather had one like it."

"I never had a grandfather." The words were out before she could stop them, and immediately she wished them back.

He shot her a quizzical look before flipping up the cover of the answering machine.

"I mean of course I must have had one. It's just that I never knew him." She was babbling and feeling more of a fool by the minute. "My mother died when I was still a kid, and I never knew my dad. So grandparents weren't part of the equation."

"I'm sorry. Mine were such an integral part of my life it's hard to imagine someone not having that."

"I did all right, I guess." She shrugged. "You can't miss what you've never had."

His gaze held hers for a moment, his eyes clear, devoid of pity, and she felt a rush of gratitude mixed with embarrassment. She didn't usually blurt out her life story, preferring to leave the memories undisturbed. And she couldn't for the life of her understand why she'd chosen to do so now.

As if sensing her discomfort, Eric held up a hand requesting silence, the action granting a reprieve, bringing them back to the mundane. The recording was to the point. Her number and a request to leave a message, but the timbre of his voice sent her senses reeling anyway.

"All done." His smile was warm, and for the moment, she let herself bask in it. "Once you call Southwestern Bell, you'll be in business. And until then, you've got me."

The thought was enticing, until she realized he meant the recording. "I'll definitely sleep better. Thank you." She took a step toward him, not completely certain of her intent.

He seemed to understand more than she did, because he closed the gap, his breath stirring the hair around her cheeks. She tipped her head back in response, meeting his gaze, her heartbeat ratcheting up a couple of notches as she leaned closer, not certain where this was going but positive she wanted to find out.

"Sara? You in there?" Ryan's voice broke between them with the effectiveness of ice water. She jumped back, hot color flooding her face.

Eric's smile was slow, the gesture not reflected in his eyes. "Saved by the bell?"

"Something like that." She struggled for composure, forcing her breathing to a calmer state.

"Sara?" Ryan walked into the room and stopped, his eyebrows rising in surprise. "God, I'm sorry. I didn't mean to interrupt. I knocked, but figured you were on the phone or something."

"It's all right." It was anything but all right, but Sara wasn't about to tell Ryan that. "Detective D'Angelo and I were almost through." She wasn't certain what made her stress the word *detective*, but Eric's mouth quirked upward in response.

"Eric D'Angelo." He held out a hand. "I'm Tony Haskins' partner."

Ryan took the offered hand, then met Sara's gaze with a pointed look. "I've heard about you from Bess."

Eric nodded, and the two men sized each other up in a way that could only be described as *male*. Sara bit back a smile.

"You all discussing anything I should know about?" The question was pointed, Ryan's gaze probing, his thoughts obvious.

He was afraid she'd told Eric about the pictures. Which of course she hadn't. Although the thought made her feel suddenly guilty. "Eric was kind enough to bring me a Caller ID box."

Ryan relaxed almost immediately, his smile genuine. "Well, it's about time." He shot a conspiratorial look at Eric. "I've been trying to get her to do it for months. I should have known the only way was to show up with the equipment."

"It seemed like a good idea." Eric's words seemed to have secondary meaning, and when his eyes met hers, she felt as if they were bonded in some intrinsic way, the two of them against the world.

Ridiculous thought.

"I brought the article." Ryan waved an envelope through the air, bringing her back to reality with a thud. "I wanted you to see it before I send it to press."

"Kind of late for a deadline, isn't it?" Eric asked.

Ryan shrugged. "The magazine goes to press tonight, and with everything that's been happening, we're rearranging a little. Par for the course in publishing."

Eric nodded, his interest already fading. "I guess I'll go then, and let you get to it."

Sara wanted to stop him, to keep him here with her, but the impulse was irrational at best. "I'll walk you to the door."

Ryan moved to sit on the sofa, his attention on the page proofs in his hand.

Sara and Eric walked into the hallway, stopping at the door. Silence stretched between them, his proximity making breathing difficult. "I'm sorry for the interruption. Ryan has no concept of the word *after hours*. For him work is a never-ending process."

"It's all right. I'm the one who was interrupting."

"Not really. I mean you came to help. That's hardly an imposition."

His smile was crooked. "How do you know I won't demand payment for my services?"

Her breath caught in her throat, her imagination going wild. "How do you know I wouldn't pay it?" They were talking in code again, their bodies moving together of their own accord.

He reached out to push the hair back from her face, the simple touch sensual in its simplicity.

"Sara?" Ryan called impatiently.

"You need to go to home," Sara said.

"I do."

Neither of them moved.

"How about we try this again another time?" Eric asked.

Her mind said no, but her head nodded yes.

"Why don't you come with me to Bess and Tony's barbecue?"

Again she nodded, despite her thoughts to the contrary.

"Until then." His smile was slow, sure. And with infinite grace, he leaned forward, brushing his lips against hers.

The kiss was fleeting and searing all at the same time. Everything and nothing. And as the door swung closed, she realized there were tears in her eyes.

Eric drove mindlessly down MoPac. He ought to go home. Or, better yet, head to the station. But he couldn't seem to do either. So instead he was driving endlessly up and down the highway, trying to figure out what the hell had just happened.

He prided himself on his ability to detach from a situation. It was the only thing that got him through the grim realities of homicide, and for the most part he managed to keep the same kind of control over his personal life.

Until tonight.

What was it about Sara Martin that reduced him to a bumbling school kid? She was pretty, but that alone didn't explain the effect she had on him. There was something deeper going on. Something that he wasn't certain he understood.

And part of him wanted to find out more about it. That was the part that had asked her to the barbecue. But another part of him was certain he'd just jumped off a pier into twenty-five-foot swells—without a life preserver.

The thought was more exhilarating than it should have been.

His cell phone broke through his thoughts, and relief warred with irritation. "D'Angelo."

"Maynard Tompkins is dead." As usual, Tony didn't bother with extraneous dialogue.

"Shit. When?"

"They found him about fifteen minutes ago. He's still warm."

"I thought he had a tail." Eric took the Enfield exit without slowing the car.

"He was holed up in his apartment. Uniforms figured they could take a break."

"Son of a bitch. I'm on my way."

"I'll be here." Tony clicked off the line, and Eric let go with another round of expletives. Tompkins was their primary witness to the crime scene. They'd gotten the basics out of him, but not everything.

Damn it. Why was it always one step forward, two steps back?

Then again, maybe there'd never been a step forward at all.

"Thanks for not telling him anything." Ryan sat back against the sofa cushions, his expression grim. "I know it isn't your style to be duplicitous. And I had no idea you'd have a homicide detective show up at your door."

Sara held up her hand, shaking her head. "It's all right. I promised we'd hold the information until morning and I meant it. Eric will just have to understand."

Ryan reached over to take her hand. "He will. And if he doesn't, then he's not worth the worry."

"Nate did a good job with the article." She forced a smile, purposefully changing the subject, her mind still centered on Eric D'Angelo. What in the world had she been thinking—agreeing to a date with him. "He's a good writer."

"He's got potential, I admit that. Okay for me to run it?"

"Absolutely. And then, tomorrow, I'll go talk to the police."

Ryan stood up, smiling. "Why don't I get out of your hair, and let you get some sleep?" They walked to the door in comfortable silence, then Ryan reached out for her hands. "I promised Bess I'd try to cajole you into going to the barbecue. It would do you a world of good."

Sara laughed. "Not you too. Bess just doesn't take no for an answer. But you can all relax. I'm going to the party."

"You are?" Ryan's smile echoed her own. "That's wonderful. Do you want a ride?"

"Actually, I have a date." At least she hoped she did. Once she admitted holding back her photographs, he might feel differently about the invitation. But she wasn't going to borrow problems; she had more than enough already.

"With who?" Ryan's curiosity was almost palpable.

"Eric D'Angelo." She paused for a moment, afraid suddenly that Ryan would disapprove. "What do you think?"

"I think it's perfect." He squeezed her hands and released them. "It's time for you to start living in the present again, and if D'Angelo can facilitate that happening, then I'm all for it."

She smiled up at him. "You're a good friend."

"I know it." He touched the end of her nose. "Now go get some sleep. Tomorrow we're going to win a Pulitzer."

More likely she was going to be arrested for withholding evidence. But if the arresting officer was Eric D'Angelo, she had to admit the idea actually held a certain appeal.

"What have we got?" Eric stood at the doorway to Tompkins' apartment. A mirror image of the one where Lydia Wallace had been killed, the two scenes couldn't have been more different. Tompkins had taken a single shot to the head. No blood spatters, no sexual overtones. In fact, without a body, the room looked oddly peaceful.

"Shot was a thirty-eight. Clean as a whistle. Someone he trusted enough to turn his back on wanted him dead."

"Any idea who?"

"Could be anyone, but I'd say the best possibilities are our serial killer or Ramirez. Can't imagine he was any too happy that Tompkins turned him in."

"My money is on Ramirez. But I don't think he killed Lydia. Forensics find anything?" The techs had already swept through the room, telltale markers and chalk lines dotting the room.

"Not much on the cursory examination. But there's always hope."

"Yeah, and miracles happen every day. Is Ramirez in custody?"

Tony shook his head. "There's an APB out. My guess is he'll try to hightail it out of town. So we're watching the highways and airport. I doubt he'll get far."

"Until then, what do you say we start canvassing the neighbors? Maybe somebody heard something." He turned his back on the empty room, focusing on the task ahead.

Tony followed. "How'd it go with Sara Martin?"

He frowned over at his partner. "How'd you know about that?"

Tony grinned. "Molly called Bess."

"The world is too damn small, you know that?" He hadn't meant to snap, but he liked to keep his personal life just that—personal.

"Nah. You just move in very small circles. So how'd it go?"

"Fine. I installed Caller ID, recorded a message for her answering machine, and asked her to the barbecue."

"And she agreed to go?" Tony sounded amazed.

"You don't have to act so surprised. It's not like I'm a leper or something. Besides, it isn't a date. It's just your barbecue."

"Right. You're just picking her up, bringing her to the party, and then taking her home again. No way is that a date."

"All right already. So maybe it is a date. But it's only one party, not a marriage proposal, so you and Bess back off, okay?"

"Hey, I'm only interested in your well-being."

"You're only interested in nosing into my private affairs."

Tony pulled a face, pretending to be insulted. "Fine. I can take a hint."

"My ass." Eric grinned, then sobered. "You take the bottom floors, I'll start at the top. We'll meet in the middle, hopefully with a witness. If we're right about Ramirez killing Tompkins, maybe the guy has more to hide than his vocational pursuits."

"Yeah. The question is how it all ties into the other murders."

Eric blew out a long breath. "If it ties in at all."

Ramirez was scum. No question about it. And he certainly had the cojones to off Tompkins. But that didn't make him a serial killer.

Sara tossed and turned, trying to find the blissful escape of sleep, but instead all she could see was Lydia Wallace's face. She'd had so much of life ahead of her. Closing her eyes, Sara sighed. No sense lying in the dark. But before she could reach for the light, the phone started to ring.

Without thinking she reached for it, answering before her machine had the chance to catch the call. "Hello?

The line hissed—empty, mocking.

"Hello?"

She glanced at the Caller ID box, but of course without service, it remained stubbornly blank. Damn it all to hell. She slammed the receiver back into the cradle, anger washing through her.

She was tempted to call Eric, but realized she didn't have his home number. Reaching for the lamp she turned the knob, flooding the room with light, blinking at the brightness. She sat up, her anger evaporating.

There was no point in calling, even if she could find his number. There was nothing to do except talk to the phone company in the morning. Resigned, she climbed out of bed, ready for another sleepless night.

Chapter 8

Eric stood in the conference room looking at the white board. The information on it had grown in complexity since they'd started, pictures of all three vics joining the stats and details. But even with all that, there was nothing to identify the killer, and the fact galled him.

Crossing over to a utility table, he filled a Styrofoam cup with coffee, wishing he'd stopped at Starbucks on the way to work. It had been a late night. Rodriguez had been collared. The stupid prick had been hanging out at the Roxie, seemingly unaware that the whole of the Austin Police Department was out looking for him.

Questioning him hadn't proved any more useful. The bastard was cocky, and no amount of intimidation had convinced him to give up the murder. They didn't have enough on him for a search warrant, which meant no weapon. And that left them hanging in the breeze, although for the moment the punk was still in custody.

"You're in early." Jordan Brady leaned against the table, studying the white board. "Anything new?"

"No. You see anything?" Eric moved to sit beside the

lieutenant. As well as being his boss, Brady was a hell of a cop, and Eric respected his opinions.

"Nothing you probably haven't. The guy is obviously getting better. But that's to be expected. His vics are getting younger. And, given their profession, more innocent."

Eric frowned at the board. "Yeah, I thought the same thing, but we could just as easily be forcing the puzzle in a direction we want it to go. Like Ramirez. I think he whacked Tompkins, but I don't see him as a serial killer."

"He copping to any of it?" Brady's stare was intense. Intimidating. Except that Eric had known him a hell of a long time, and the big black man wasn't even aware of the look. It was part of what made him so good at his job. He scared the shit out of perps without even trying.

"So far he's just blowing hot air. Posturing."

"We don't nail Ramirez for this, we lose him all together. He already cut a deal for moving the body." Brady walked over to the coffee pot and refilled his cup. "He lawyered up?"

"Yeah, that's why I'm in here. Tony's baby-sitting. The attorney's on his way."

"Wagner?"

"Who else? The man has a nose for losers."

"And a track record of getting them off."

"Not going to happen." Claire Dennison walked into the room with a smile. "Got the bastard dead to rights." Crossing to the table, she threw a file down on the desk. "Almost missed it."

Eric sat at the table, opening the file. "So what have you got?"

"At first I thought nothing. The room was so full of fingerprints half of east Austin could have been considered a suspect. And, of course, the weapon wasn't found at the scene. But Tompkins' blood proved to be another story." She leaned over Eric's shoulder, pulling out a picture of the deceased.

"The bloodstain under his head doesn't match the position of the body."

"So he rolled over."

"No chance in hell. This guy was dead before he hit the floor."

"So you're saying someone rolled him over?" This from Brady, who had crossed the room to stand by Claire.

"Exactly. And better still, the asshole left a handprint in the poor guy's blood." Her smile was wicked. "It wasn't apparent to the naked eye, but one of my techs saw it when he was photographing the crime scene."

"And the prints match Ramirez?" Eric frowned, trying to connect the dots.

"They do. We've got three clear and a partial on the other two."

"But couldn't Ramirez argue that he moved the body after Tompkins died? It certainly fits his M.O."

"Not when you add in the ballistics test." She reached over to pull another piece of paper from the file. "There's a unique striation on the bullet we recovered. Traced it to a previous incident, which makes it a gun belonging to one Alturo Ramirez. My guess is you'll find it in his apartment, and I think this more than gives you cause for a warrant."

Brady smiled. "I like the way you work. What do you say we go catch us a murderer?"

He and Claire walked toward the door, still talking, but Eric stopped in front of the white board, the dead women staring out at him. Ramirez wasn't the one. He could feel it in his bones. Which meant that somewhere out there, they still had a murderer on the loose.

A man without a face and an escalating desire to kill.

"So what do you think?" Nate strode into the office, tossing the magazine on Sara's desk.

"I haven't actually seen it, but Ryan brought the article by last night. You did an amazing job." Sara smiled up at him.

Nate shrugged, color flooding his face. "I'm glad you liked it." He ducked his head, clearly uncomfortable. "I wanted it to be special."

"Well, it is. Ryan even said so."

His head shot up. "Really?"

"That's what he said. My guess is he'll be giving you more assignments from now on." She smiled to underscore her words, hoping that she was right. Ryan hadn't exactly said as much, but surely his comments intimated it.

"God, that would be fantastic. Do you think I should go talk to him?"

Sara laughed. Sometimes she forgot how young Nate was. Chronologically he was in his late twenties, but emotionally he was more like a teenager sometimes. "I'd wait for him to come to you. And in the meantime, you need to enjoy the moment."

He ran a hand through his hair, leaving it sticking up every which way. "You're right. I always get ahead of myself. Sorry." His smile was sheepish.

"Don't worry. If it were me, I'd be excited too."

"Oh, God, what am I thinking? It *is* you. I mean, your pictures are the heart of the article, really. Without them it wouldn't be anything but words."

"It was teamwork, Nate."

"Yeah. I guess it was." His expression was joyful, as if the realization was a welcome surprise.

"Well, I hope you're not going to leave the publisher out of this party." Ryan stood in the doorway, his gaze assessing.

"Of course not. We're all part of the process. But right now we're celebrating Nate's first big story." She smiled fondly at the younger man. "And for the moment, I think we should leave it at that."

"Of course. I didn't mean to take away from the moment." Ryan's gaze encompassed them both.

"It's okay." Nate's eyes signaled that it wasn't, but Ryan either didn't notice or was ignoring the fact.

Sara stood up, not wanting to facilitate anything more between them. "Actually, I'm afraid we'll have to save our celebrating for later. Right now, I need to get these pictures over to the police. I've sat on them longer than I'm comfortable with already."

"God, what a conscience." Ryan's smile took the sting out of his remark. "Off you go. And tell D'Angelo I said hi."

"D'Angelo?" Nate frowned.

"Tony's partner." Ryan grinned at Nate, waggling his eyebrows for effect. "Seems he's making the moves on Sara."

"I'm going on a date, Ryan. One date. Nothing more. It's too soon for anything else. I'm not ready." She glared pointedly at both of her friends, ignoring their laughter.

Whether they believed it or not, she was telling them the absolute truth

Sort of.

"So you think this is a ploy?" Tony walked toward the interrogation room with Eric following on his heels.

"Hard to say." Eric shrugged. "I mean he was Lydia's pimp, so there's a chance he knows something. But then again he's also facing the needle, so I'd say there's motive to lie."

"Only one way to find out for sure." Tony pushed the door open and strode into the room. Ramirez was sitting at the head of the table, head in hands. The cocky boy from last night had vanished, Claire Dennison's evidence damning enough to deflate his attitude. Lamont Wagner sat confidently in the chair cattycorner to Ramirez, his smirk indicating he thought their information would buy the kid's way out of a sure date with death.

"So, you ready to tell me what happened to Maynard Tompkins?" Eric straddled a chair, while Tony leaned cross-armed against the wall.

"My client has nothing to say until we're certain a deal is in place. Is the district attorney coming?" Lamont was a slimy bastard, always protecting the guilty, drug runners and pimps his specialty. Eric believed in justice for all, but he drew the line when it involved manipulating the law to protect the guilty.

"I spoke with the district attorney fifteen minutes ago. And provided Ramirez here gives a full confession and that any information he provides pans out, you have his word."

"No death penalty."

"I thought you said you'd get me out of this?" Ramirez's head popped up, a hint of his former bravado resurfacing.

"I said I'd keep you alive. Other than that, they've got a damn good case."

It wasn't often that Lamont admitted a client's guilt, let alone praised the department. Eric swallowed the urge to thank the man. "So we got a deal?"

Wagner's eyes met Ramirez's and the younger man nodded, his gaze returning to his hands.

"Why don't we start with the confession." Tony moved to sit at the other end of the table.

"I did Tompkins." Ramirez's face showed no remorse. Hell, it didn't show anything, except maybe regret for getting caught. "He didn't have any business turning me in to the cops."

"For moving the body?"

"Yeah." The kid fidgeted with a bracelet on his arm. "And then he tells me I can't work the hotel anymore. Like it was my fault the bitch got herself killed."

"So you shot him."

Ramirez shrugged. "Wasn't a big loss. Tompkins was a bottom feeder anyway."

As if Ramirez was the cream of the crop. Eric swallowed his revulsion. "So how's all this relate to Lydia Wallace's murder?"

"It doesn't. Not directly." He shot a look at Wagner, and then continued. "I didn't tell you everything the other day."

"And you want to tell me now."

"Sure," he almost looked Eric in the eyes, but at the last minute looked away again, "if it helps keeps me alive."

"Noble intentions." Tony's sarcasm was lost on the man. "So let's hear what you got."

"Ain't much." He mumbled, but the room was designed so that even a whisper could be clearly heard. "I told you I met up with Lydia that night."

"Yeah, and beat up on her."

Ramirez frowned. "She had it coming."

"Just tell them what you know." Wagner's voice was soothing. And if Eric didn't know better he'd have thought the lawyer actually gave a shit.

"I accused her of stiffing me. She swore she'd been giving me everything, that she hadn't been doing nothing on the side." Ramirez shrugged. "I didn't believe her. So I asked her how come she missed appointments." He looked up at Lamont, who nodded briefly. "She said she'd been meeting with a journalist. Some big story. Told me she even had a meeting that night."

"But you said you met with her at ten."

Ramirez nodded. "That's right. So I'm figuring there must be something pretty special going on if it called for a late-night meeting."

"You think maybe she was jerking your chain?" Tony asked.

"I don't know. She seemed on the up-and-up."

"And you just didn't think it was important enough to mention the first time we talked?"

"Maybe I forgot." The kid smiled, some of his swagger restored.

"Or maybe you wanted a get-out-of-the-death-penalty-free card?"

"Hadn't killed anybody then. I just forgot."

"Nice of your memory to come back." Eric's gaze met Tony's, and then returned to the pimp. "So, this journalist, he have a name?"

"Wasn't a he." Ramirez smiled, his gold tooth glinting in the florescent light. "It was a woman. Name's Sara. Sara Martin."

Chapter 9

It shouldn't have rocked his world, but it did. Damn it. It did. If Ramirez was telling the truth, then Sara just might have been the last person to see Lydia Wallace alive. A little fact that she'd omitted telling him. And that, in and of itself, was enough to throw him off-kilter. But when you added in the fact that she'd also kept her photographs of the girl a secret—well, there wasn't any way to quantify his frustration and confusion.

Eric threw the magazine on the desk, Lydia Wallace's face mocking him from the cover. Brady had brought it to him. Along with a few choice words about the press. One photographer in particular.

He picked up the phone. Best to just get it over with. Sara Martin had a lot of questions to answer. He punched in the magazine's number, listening to the hollow ring of the phone, his mind scrambling for the proper way to handle the situation. He probably should have let Tony deal with it, but he prided himself on facing things head-on.

No matter how difficult.

The receptionist finally answered, only to inform him that Sara was out. *Great*. After hanging up the phone, he picked up the magazine, flipping to the article inside. He'd read it three times, and on the surface it was nothing more than a human interest piece, the tragic plight of a kid without choices and the system that had failed her. But the fact that the girl had ended up the victim of a serial killer changed everything, every word and picture taking on new meaning.

Particularly when coupled with the fact that Sara Martin might have been the last person to see Lydia Wallace alive.

"Eric?" The voice was timid, but he recognized it immediately, looking up to meet Sara's guileless blue eyes. "They, ah, said I should talk to you." Her gaze dropped to the journal in his hands. "I guess you know why I'm here."

"Evidently I don't know anything about you." He tried but couldn't keep the sarcasm out of his voice.

She swallowed nervously, dropping into a chair. "If it matters, I wanted to tell you. Well, not *you* exactly. I didn't know you were in charge of the case. But I wanted to tell the police."

"So why didn't you?" He fought to keep his voice level. This was professional. There was nothing personal going on here. Or if there was, he certainly couldn't allow it to interfere with business.

"Ryan asked me not to."

"And you always do what Ryan tells you?" So much for objectivity.

"No. But he wanted first shot at the article." She waved at the magazine, anger flashing in her eyes. "And I thought it would be okay to wait a day."

"You should have let me be the judge of that."

"I said I didn't know it was you specifically. Besides, I'm a journalist, too, remember? And I made my decision based on that fact. Which is exactly what I should have done. And *now* I'm bringing the pictures to you. I even brought the negatives." She tossed a manila envelope on the desk. "So we're square."

He pushed the envelope aside. "Not quite. There's still the little matter of your meeting with Lydia Wallace the night she was murdered."

Sara's eyebrows rose, her surprise genuine. "I've no idea what you're talking about."

"According to my information, the meeting was scheduled just before she died. Which means except for the killer, you were the last person to see her alive."

"Thank you for that." Her response was dry, her eyes narrowing as she considered what he was telling her.

"For what?"

Her smile didn't reach her eyes. "For not accusing me of murdering the woman."

"Women are rarely serial killers, Sara."

"So that's the only reason you're ruling me out?" She leaned forward, anger darkening her eyes.

"That's ridiculous. It never even occurred to me that you could have killed her."

"But you don't believe that I didn't meet with her?"

"It's not like you didn't give me a reason." He waved a hand at the pictures, wondering how the conversation had degenerated into a verbal battle. Personal feelings overcoming rational thought.

"I never lied to you. I just didn't tell you about the pictures."

"Or your meeting with Lydia Wallace."

"There was no meeting." Her voice had risen, each word carefully enunciated.

Eric came around the desk, aware that others in the squad room were watching them. "Let's go somewhere we can talk privately." He tipped his head at the people behind him, and she nodded, acquiescing, the line of her shoulders reflecting her anger.

He led the way to the conference room, the staccato click of her heels the only sign she was behind him. He closed the door, working to bring his emotions back into check. He was overreacting, and he knew it. And quite honestly he hadn't any idea why.

Well, maybe some idea.

"Oh, sweet Jesus." The words were low. A whispered plea.

Eric swung around to look at her, concern washing away all traces of anger. She was standing with her back to him, her eyes locked on the white board, the dead women's pictures stark against the pale background. Sara swayed slightly, and he moved to support her, one arm circling her shoulders as he guided her to a chair.

"I'm sorry, Sara. I forgot they were in here."

"It's okay, really. I've seen worse." She nervously twisted the band of her wedding ring, her face a clear indication that she hadn't. Or at least not in quite so much detail. "I just wasn't expecting it."

"Here, take this." He handed her a cup of water, grateful to see that her color was returning.

"Thanks." She sipped the water. "I'm usually not this squeamish. I guess maybe this one hit too close to home."

He had a feeling she was talking about more than Lydia Wallace, but he knew better than to push. It was better to let it come in her own time. Right now he needed to know about the meeting.

Sara blew out a breath, putting the cup on the table, evidently reading his mind. "So what in the world makes you think I had a meeting with Lydia Wallace the night she died?"

He sat across from her, purposely sitting so that his body blocked the photographs. "We arrested her pimp on a related charge and he told us."

"That I had a meeting with Lydia?" She was frowning now, obviously trying to digest what he was saying. "But that doesn't make any sense. Does he claim he was there?"

"No. He had his own meeting with Lydia. At a bar called Roxie. He evidently roughed her up pretty good. Something to do with business on the side."

"She wouldn't have had time for that. The man kept her busy."

"And you know this because—"

"Because I talked to her. Listened. She wasn't a risk taker."

He lifted an eyebrow, knowing his skepticism was painted across his face.

"At least not the kind that would put her in danger. She knew what kind of man Ramirez was." Sara reached for the cup again, finishing the water. "There are rules, Detective. Even on the streets."

So they were back to "detective." He wasn't at all happy about the prospect, and the thought surprised him. "You got all this from talking to her?"

"Some of it. Some of it I learned on my own. I wasn't exactly the poster person for happy childhoods. Foster care isn't all that different from the streets."

"I see." He didn't, not really. But it was all he could think of to say.

"Probably not. But that's okay. It was a long time ago." Her smile was weak, but genuine. "So, in the middle of getting beat up, Lydia volunteered that she had a meeting with me?"

Put that way it sounded ludicrous. Eric shrugged, suddenly tired. "That's what he said."

"So maybe it was a ploy. A way to get out of there without making him any angrier."

"It's possible, I suppose. But why pick you?"

It was her turn to shrug. "I was safe. I mean, if she was meeting with me, then she couldn't be putting one over on Ramirez. Maybe it was meant as reassurance of a sort. In situations like that, you'll say whatever it takes."

Eric frowned, considering the idea. "So she just used the first name she thought of."

"She used someone she knew would keep her off the streets for a little while."

"So when was the last time you actually met with her?"

"The day before she died. I needed a couple more shots, so we met at El Azteca and I bought her lunch, then we walked a bit and took some pictures."

"And you didn't see her or talk to her again."

Sara shook her head. "I had what I needed. And she really wasn't all that comfortable talking to me. I think she was having second thoughts."

"About the article?"

"Yeah. Maybe. I'm really not sure. I just know she was edgier than usual. And I got the feeling she was happy to see the last of me."

Eric sat back, trying to put the pieces together. "But if

she wanted you to go away, then why mention a meeting?"

"I don't know. Anything I say will just be speculation. But I promise you, I didn't schedule a meeting with her. I was home in bed."

"I believe you." He did, too, but he wasn't as convinced that the use of her name had been strictly coincidence. "Sara, what time was your phone call?"

"I don't remember exactly. It's in the journal. But it was sometime after midnight. Why?"

"I was wondering if Lydia Wallace could have been the one calling. But according to the M.E., she died around eleven thirty. You're sure the call was after that?"

"Yeah. Ryan came by a little after one and I hadn't been up that long. So that'd mean the call had to be after midnight. Besides, the calls started before I met Lydia."

Eric swallowed his frustration. "It was just a thought."

She reached over to cover his hand, the contact jarring. "You're going to find this guy. I know it."

"Yeah, we'll get him. But I don't know how many more women will die before then." He sat back, trying to keep his focus on the case and not Sara Martin. It was damned hard. Especially when she touched him. "Was Lydia the only prostitute you photographed?"

She glanced over his shoulder at the board. "Yes. She was all I needed. The original concept was to do a photo spread on the invisible population, people most of us cross the street to avoid. The homeless, runaways, drug addicts—"

"And prostitutes." He finished for her.

"Exactly. But I got interested in Lydia. And switched the piece to her instead." Her eyes locked on the dead girl's photograph. "Of course I never imagined it would end like this. Never."

"Did she mention her family? Next of kin?"

"Nothing at all. I got the feeling she was on her own, though, and had been for a long time."

"How about friends? She hang out with any girls in particular?"

"No. Not that I saw. Although she was friendly with people she saw on the streets. And several other girls knew her by name. You think maybe they can help you?"

"It's possible. I'll look at the photographs you brought. Are there interview notes, too?"

Sara shook her head. "My pictures are the only notes."

"But there is an article. Nate somebody."

"Nate Stone. He wrote the copy. But he was only there the last day I shot."

"All right. We'll go with what we've got, although I may have more questions later. And I may want to talk to Mr. Stone."

Sara leaned forward, her hands clasped together on the table. "I'm sure he'll help in any way he can. Everyone wants to find this guy, Detective."

Eric leaned forward, too, covering her hands with his. "Considering you're going out with me tonight, don't you think calling me *detective* is a little formal?"

She bit her lower lip, surprise flickering across her face, but she didn't move her hands. "I thought with all that had happened, maybe you'd rather not—" She broke off, looking decidedly uncomfortable.

"On the contrary." He grinned, squeezing her hands. "I think it's imperative that I keep an eye on you. After all, you never know when you might remember something else you've forgotten to tell me."

"True. And if you weren't around when I remembered, well, I might just forget again." The sparkle in her eye sent hot shards of desire flooding through him.

Truth was someone needed to watch over her, and that being the case, he was more than ready to volunteer for the job.

Sara stuck her key into the lock and opened the front door, her mind still on the conversation with Eric. The idea that Lydia had used her name wasn't all that surprising, but the thought that she'd needed sanctuary, even a fictional one, was heartbreaking. And Sara wished somehow she could have done more.

She hung her coat on the hall tree, and started sorting through her mail. The house was quiet, the only noise the steady ticking of the grandfather clock at the end of the hall. Normally, the silence provided peace. But today, in light of all that had happened, she felt edgy instead. As if she were waiting for the other shoe to drop.

She tossed the mail on the credenza and walked into the living room, bending automatically to pick up a photograph that had fallen to the floor. Tom's face smiled up at her, and despite the fact that it was only a picture, her heart lightened. Tom had always made her feel so safe. So secure. What they'd lacked in passion, they'd more than made up for with their commitment to each other and to Charlie. He'd given her the family she'd never had.

Which made it that much harder to have lost them both. In so many ways it seemed as if she'd died right along with them. But that was a cop-out, an easy way to deal with the pain. She put the frame back in its place on the wall. She *was* alive. And, if anything, the death of Lydia Wallace had crystallized that fact.

Sara turned her back on the room, heading for the staircase, forcing her thoughts to the present. More specifically, her date with Eric D'Angelo. Except for Molly's setup, she hadn't been out with anyone since the accident. Add in ten years of marriage, and she wasn't even sure she remembered how it was supposed to go.

One step at a time, no doubt.

With a smile, she walked into her bedroom, stripping off her clothes, heading for the bathroom. Tossing her shirt on the bed, she noticed the Caller ID box. Squinting, she read the number, smiling. Molly had called.

Southwestern Bell had obviously connected her service. Peace of mind in a little black box.

Naked, she went into the bathroom and turned the taps,

then reached down to close the drain. A hot bath was just what she needed. A little time to pull herself together before Eric arrived.

Eric.

Just the thought of him sent a wave of heat rippling through her. Her nipples puckered, and of their own volition, her hands traced the soft curves of her breasts. The water lapped around her body, caressing in its touch. She closed her eyes, giving into the heat and her imagination . . .

A noise broke the stillness of the bathroom, jerking Sara from sleep, cold water sloshing over the edge of the tub with the movement. Straining into the silence, she waited, her mind working to put a name to what she'd heard. Intellectually, she knew it was probably nothing; possibly she'd even imagined it. But with everything that had happened, she was jumpier than usual.

She stood up and grabbed a towel, wrapping it securely around her. Moving cautiously, she stepped into the bedroom, exchanging towel for robe. The floorboards in the hallway creaked ominously, and she reached for a candlestick, not certain what she was going to do with it, but positive it was better than nothing.

Another creak, this one closer, set her in motion, and she scrambled across the bed, intent on reaching the telephone.

"Sara."

The whisper stopped her short, and she turned, breath lodged in her throat, fingers tightening on the candlestick.

"Jack." She dropped the candleholder, her heart still hammering a frantic rhythm. "What the hell are you doing up here? You scared the life out of me."

"I'm sorry." He held up both hands in apology. "I rang the bell. But you didn't answer, and your car was in the driveway, so I used my key . . ." He trailed off looking miserable, relieved, and sheepish all at the same time. "Considering I scared you to death, not my best move, huh?"

"No. But your heart was in the right place. I assume you had a reason for coming over?" She sat on the bed and picked up the towel, drying her hair with it.

"Yeah." He dropped down into an easy chair by the window. "I came by to bring you the results from the diagnostics I ran on your car."

She dropped the towel, turning around to look at him. "You find anything?"

"No. The tests just confirmed what I already knew. The car is fine, Sara. You're as safe as anyone else is who drives around in a two-ton tin can."

"I know you think I'm being silly, Jack, but I'm just trying to protect myself." She started to tell him about Lydia Wallace, the pictures, and the alleged meeting, but stopped. She wasn't ready to discuss it with anyone. Not even Jack. "And I've been a little distracted of late."

"Eric D'Angelo?"

"God, does Molly ever shut up?"

"Nope." Jack grinned. "Although I'd rather have heard it from you."

She felt a tug of guilt. Jack fancied himself her protector. The big brother she never had. "It's really no big deal. He's just taking me to the party."

"The one you're not going to?" Jack's eyebrows rose with the question. "Must have been a hell of an invitation."

"That's not it at all. I just decided you were right. It is time for me to get on with my life. Eric's invitation just happened to come at the right time."

"Funny, from where I'm sitting, I'd say it's more about the man than the timing."

"Well, I say it's not." Laughing, she lobbed the wet towel at him. "You're just imagining things." But, of course, he wasn't. Jack always saw more than she wanted him to. More than she wanted to see herself.

In truth, it was absolutely, positively, one hundred percent about the man.

"I knew this was love the moment I found you.
So I planned my life; it's built all around you.
Give me this chance, darling, if you only would.
I could make you care. I know I could."

♫ ♪ ♫ ♪ ♫

Things were changing. But not as he'd planned. She was supposed to have chosen him. But she hadn't. *She hadn't.* Anger seared through him, and he fought for control. There was time, still. The game was not lost. He just needed to make her understand. Make her care. And until then, he'd simply have to make do.

Lyrics blended with music, filling him from the inside out, soothing his tortured soul. There was something cleansing in the notes. Something beyond all reality: the past joining with the present, the future beckoning bright.

He stroked her hair. Heavy like silk, golden in the soft light of the lamp. She struggled, trying to turn away, but there was no escape. She was his.

At least for now.

He picked up the knife, enjoying the wide-eyed fear it induced. She wasn't like the others, innocence combining with terror to produce an aphrodisiac beyond anything he'd experienced before.

Punishment had its rewards. And hers would free him, allow him the time he needed to wait. To gain his ultimate reward. And in the meantime, he'd make do with the surrogate. A tribute. Testament to his power. Testament to all that was lost and all that was still to be gained.

He stroked her hair again, this time lifting it high. It was beautiful. The color and texture a perfect match. With a smile, he raised the knife, and began to slice.

Chapter 10

"Hi, guys." Bess Haskins' smile bordered on delight as she eyed Sara and Eric.

Eric's hand tightened on Sara's elbow, and she reveled in the feel of his skin against hers. Silly, really. But sometimes in life it was the little things. And she'd forgotten how nice it felt to be part of a couple. At least for an evening.

Bess stepped back, motioning them inside. "Come on in."

Tony and Bess lived in an older house in Northwest Hills. Bought when property values had plummeted in the late eighties, the house had more than doubled in value. Still, it had a decidedly suburban feel, with live oaks gracefully framing the stone house. The inside was as homey as the outside, Bess's quilts and French country furniture giving it a farmhouse feel.

"I hope we're not too early." Sara said, handing Bess the flowers they'd brought. "We actually drove around the block a couple of times."

Eric laughed, the warm sound echoing through her like a rumble of thunder. "Sara didn't want to be the first to arrive."

"You're not early," Bess assured them. "But you are the first. The phone's been ringing off the wall. Seems everyone has been delayed. Molly's still at rehearsal, Ryan's stuck in traffic. And Tony's at Randall's buying more beer. Which means that I'm delighted to see you."

"So you can put us to work." Eric's smile was wry.

"Got it in one." Bess laughed. "If you'd start the grill that would be wonderful. I've a feeling when people do get here, they're going to be hungry. Sara, you can help me in the kitchen."

With a squeeze, Eric released her elbow and headed for the backyard. Bess propelled Sara into the kitchen. "So tell it all." Bess leaned back against the work island, eyes sparkling.

"There's isn't anything to tell. Eric asked me to the party and I said yes. End of story."

"Hey, this is me you're talking to. Except for our misguided attempt to set you up, you haven't been out with anyone since Tom died, and Eric hasn't brought a girl over here since he and Lauren divorced. So you still going to try and tell me it's nothing?"

Sara ducked her head, hot color flooding her face. "It's just a date."

"I swear, you're more closemouthed than he is." Bess frowned, her smile negating the gesture. "But the fact remains that this has to be something pretty special or neither one of you would be doing it. Which means there's hope."

"Hope for what?" A big man with a teddy bear smile walked into the kitchen, and judging by the adoration in Bess's eyes, Sara figured it was Tony.

"Eric and Sara." Bess returned her gaze to Sara, her smile a little wicked.

"I take it she's matchmaking again?" Tony gave his wife a quick squeeze and then stuck out his hand. "Sara Martin, I presume."

Sara nodded. "One and the same. I'm glad to meet you."

"And I'm glad you're here." Tony's tone turned conspiratorial. "Bess tried everything she could think of to entice you. It was turning into a personal challenge."

"Well, if I'd known it was as easy as introducing her to Eric, I wouldn't have had to go to all the trouble to enlist her friends." They were talking as if she wasn't there, locked into the casual bickering that marked a happily married couple.

"Hey, I'm still here remember?" She held up her hands,

laughing. "And while I appreciate all the concern, I am capable of taking care of myself."

"I can attest to that." Eric walked into the kitchen, just the sound of his voice sending slivers of heat chasing through her. "And if you all want me to get a second date, I suggest you lay off."

Tony shrugged, exchanging an amused look with Bess. "Consider it done. Besides, this won't be much of a barbecue if I don't get the meat on." He picked up a platter and headed for the sliding glass door. "You coming, D'Angelo?"

"In a minute." He looked down to meet Sara's gaze, the concern reflected there almost taking her breath away. "You okay?"

"I'm fine." She reached up to cup his face in her hand. "Honest. So go on, help Tony."

He covered her hand with his, and for a moment the world shrank until it was just the two of them.

Then Bess cleared her throat. "This is supposed to be a party, remember?" Her voice was full of laughter.

"There're all kinds of parties, Bess." Eric's smile now was just plain wicked, and despite herself, Sara shivered, anticipation pooling hot and heavy in her gut. It had been a long time since she'd felt like this.

"Go." She shooed him out of the room, and then turned to meet Bess's grin.

"Nothing going on. Right." Bess walked to the refrigerator and opened the door, pulling a bottle of wine from the refrigerator. "Methinks the woman is full of shit."

"*Bess*," Sara protested, but not with much vigor. It was sort of hard to argue in light of what had just happened.

"Well, you can't deny that *he's* interested." Bess filled a glass and handed it to Sara.

"Honestly, I'm not sure what's happening. I mean, I just met him, and—"

"*Kaboom.*" Bess smiled. "Sometimes it just happens like that. And when it does, believe me you have to grab on for everything you're worth."

"Grab on to what?" Nate walked into the kitchen, still wearing in his sport coat and tie.

"Life," Bess said, and Sara let out a sigh of relief. It wasn't that she didn't want Nate to know. It was just that discussing it seemed sort of crass, somehow. What was between her and Eric, if anything, was private, and until they decided what they were doing, she didn't really want to share it. Not even with her friends.

"Amen to that." Nate loosened his tie. "Hope you don't mind my just walking in. The door was open."

"Not at all." Bess pulled a bag of produce out of the hydrator. "Glad you're here. But don't you think you're a little overdressed for a cookout?"

"I came straight from work. Traffic was hell. I sat on MoPac for at least forty minutes. Anyway," his grin was contagious, "that's what you get for having a party on a weekday."

"It was supposed to be Tony's day off." Bess rolled her eyes. "Like that ever happens."

"I saw Molly pulling up as I came in. Looks like she brought one of her actor friends. Hope he's better than the last one."

"You mean the one with the nasty habit of breaking into soliloquy?" Bess washed the lettuce and then started chopping.

"Exactly." Nate's laugh echoed through the room. "So am I the only one here without a date?" He shot a significant look at Sara, then ducked his head shyly.

"No. Sara's friend Jack is coming on his own. Right?" Bess asked.

"Unless he meets someone on the way over here." Sara smiled at Nate, who had relaxed a little. "What about Ryan? Is he bringing someone?"

"Yeah," Bess said, adding dressing to the bowl. "Flavor of the month. A reporter from the *Statesman*. I didn't recognize the name."

"I'd like a flavor of the month," Nate sighed as the doorbell rang. "I'll get it."

"Thanks," Bess called, carrying the salad over to the buffet, her mind centered on the party again.

Sara sipped her wine, for the moment content. Good friends, good food, and Eric D'Angelo. Who could ask for anything more?

"So Bess said you're Sara's mechanic?" Eric studied the younger man, sizing him up. He was handsome in a rugged kind of way, with the sort of blond good looks that got a woman's attention, but there was something cagey about him as well. As if he kept himself buried deep inside, only showing the world what it wanted to see.

"Among other things. Sara and I go way back." Jack took a sip of beer, his eyes straying across the pool to where Sara stood talking to Ryan Greene and his date.

She looked up and flashed them both a smile. And just for a moment, Eric felt the tug of jealousy. "So how'd you meet?"

Jack studied the label on his bottle. "We were in the same foster home for a while. When we were kids."

"After her mother died."

Jack looked up, nodding, his gaze serious. "She had a pretty tough time of it. I tried to take care of her best I could, but once we were separated, it wasn't as easy."

Eric remembered Sara's comment about Lydia Wallace. Something to do with foster homes not being that far removed from the streets. Coupled with Jack's protective stance, it was fairly easy to deduce that there was more to the story. But it was Sara's story to tell. He could wait. "But you stayed friends."

Jack smiled. "That we did. I even walked her down the aisle."

"You knew Tom?"

"And Charlie. They made one hell of a happy family."

His hand shook ever so slightly, but Eric was more obser-
vant than most. "It almost killed her to lose them. At first she
wouldn't believe that they were gone. And then, when she
began to accept that, she wouldn't accept that it had been an
accident."

Eric frowned. "Did someone check the car?"

"It was ruled an accident, so the police only gave it a
cursory examination. I checked it more thoroughly." Again
there was a tiny pause. "But there was nothing to find.
Bottom line, Tom lost control of the car. It was raining, and
they were on twenty-two twenty-two." He shrugged, the
sentence damning in and of itself.

2222 was a curving highway that cut through the north of
Austin, the hills forcing the road to twist and turn as it followed along the cliffs above the river. There'd been work
done to widen it, but there were still places where it was a
death trap. Especially when it was slick.

"Jesus." It was inadequate and a blasphemy to boot, but
Eric couldn't think of anything better to say.

"And then some." Jack smiled, the gesture not quite
reaching his eyes. "But she's better now. Her being here
with you is a sure sign of that."

"Sign of what?" Sara sat down next to Eric, looking first
at Jack and then back at him.

"I was just commenting on how happy you're looking."
Jack's smile moved to his eyes, his feelings for Sara clearly
reflected there. "And I was telling D'Angelo that if he hurt
you, I'd personally see that he regretted it." There was teasing in his tone, but Eric recognized the seriousness of the
promise, and he found himself liking Jack Weston. Loyalty
was a trait he admired.

"I want to know when discussing my life became a national pastime?" Sara shot a pointed look at both of them.
"Surely I'm owed a modicum of privacy?"

"Of course you are." Jack was quick to assure. "But I've
been checking out your boyfriends since we were kids.
Surely you don't expect me to stop now?"

Sara opened her mouth, then closed it again, clearly recognizing the futility of arguing.

"Sara says you're heading up the Sinatra killer investigation." Jack's eyes reflected only mild curiosity.

"Tony and I are lead detectives."

"Anything new?" Again the question was almost a throwaway.

"Nothing for public consumption." Nothing at all, actually. But he hated to admit it. "We're working on a couple of angles. But I can't say if they'll pan out."

"I saw your pictures in the magazine," Jack said, turning to Sara. "When was the last time you saw her?"

"The day before she died." Sara was looking uncomfortable again. "She was just a kid, Jack." He reached out to take her hand, and Eric suddenly felt like an outsider. "Like us."

"Except that we didn't work the streets."

Again Eric had the feeling that there was something more here. Something more personal than just sharing a foster home. But it was hard to say for certain, and this certainly wasn't the time to ask.

"Did Sara's pictures capture anything that might give this guy up?" Jack's question was earnest, his attention still on Sara.

"We don't know yet." Eric resisted the urge to pull the guy's hands off Sara. Not exactly the way to impress her. "These days, with computers, we can manipulate a lot. If there's something there, we'll find it."

"Enough," Sara said, pulling her hands away from Jack. "This is supposed to be a party, remember?"

Eric smiled, pulling her to her feet. "No more shoptalk. I promise. What do you say we refill that drink of yours?"

"Sounds perfect." She tipped her head back to look at him. "Thanks." Her eyes reflected more than just gratitude, and relief washed through him. Whatever her bond with Jack, it obviously wasn't romantic. And for that he was grateful.

Absurdly grateful.

*   *   *

"So how's it going?" Molly snagged her arm and pulled her over to a quiet corner. The party was winding down; only the diehards remained.

"Pretty good. Except that people keep asking me that question." Sara smiled at her friend. "Besides, I could ask you the same thing." She tipped her head in the direction of Molly's date, a tall, angular man in pressed chinos and a sweater. "Not your usual style."

"I know." Molly grinned. "He handles the accounting for the theater. He may not be much to look at, but the chemistry is amazing. So I figured, why not ask him out?"

"I've always wished I had your moxie."

Molly studied her friend, her eyes serious. "You have more strength than you give yourself credit for, Sara. And when you really want something, you don't let it go. Speaking of which," her grin was back, "I think your detective is looking for you."

Sara followed Molly's gaze to where Eric was standing, surrounded by a group of chatting party-goers, Nate and Bess among them. With a slight tilt of his head, he motioned her toward the cabana on the opposite side of the pool.

She nodded, and grabbed a wine bottle from the table, tucking it, along with some plastic cups, under her arm.

"You go, girl," Molly whispered, shoving her playfully in the cabana's direction. Sara hurried, determined to make it before anyone could waylay her.

After the brightly lit patio, the cabana was dark, and Sara made her way cautiously, not certain where the light switch was. The building was small, no more than two rooms, this one apparently for storage. Two small windows were sealed shut, the light they allowed only enough to add definition to the shadows. The air smelled musty, almost sweet, the stale essence of summer encapsulated forever.

Not exactly the best place for a rendezvous.

After failing to locate the light switch, Sara decided to

make her way across the room to the barely discernable door opposite. Hopefully, the second room would be more hospitable. She inched her way forward, trying to avoid hitting anything that might be protruding out of the dark.

"Eric?" The word came out on a whisper and hung in the air, taunting her with the lack of reply. She called again, this time louder. "Eric? Is that you?"

Something scurried across her foot and Sara shuddered with revulsion. With a muffled yelp, she jumped back, wine and cups crashing to the floor, her only thought retreat.

Dark, damp places reminded her too much of the last year with her mother. More specifically, the hovel they'd called home. A box more than a room, it had been infested with all kinds of vermin. Human and otherwise.

Light flooded the room, the effect blinding, and she spun again, this time colliding with something solid, something human.

"Sara, it's okay. It's just me. I came in from the other way." Eric's voice was a panacea for her fear, and she felt it ebb away as his arms tightened around her.

"I'm sorry. There was a rat. And then the light, and then you . . ." She stopped, chagrined to have overreacted so completely. Pressing her face against his chest, she let the smell of freshly ironed cotton and soap fill her senses, soothing in their simplicity.

Light speared through the room. "Everything okay?" Nate stood in the open doorway, his face etched with concern.

She pressed closer to Eric, feeling even more ridiculous.

"It's okay. Sara heard a rat, and it startled her. We'll be out in a minute." His tone brooked no argument, and Nate retreated with a nod.

She tipped back her head, chewing on her lower lip, her gaze meeting his. "I feel so stupid. It's just that I'm really scared of rats."

He traced the line of her cheek with one finger. "I suspect you scared him more than he could have possibly scared you."

"I don't know. They're a pretty vicious lot." She shivered again, remembering.

"Sounds like you're talking from experience." He frowned down at her, seeing too much.

"It was a long time ago." She shrugged, pulling away.

"Sometimes childhood fears aren't so easily conquered." His silvery eyes were shimmering with something she couldn't put a name to, but it made her tremble, heat washing through her from the inside out. "Want to tell me about it?"

"Not much to tell really. I told you my mom died. She had congenital heart disease. Which meant she was sick for a really long time, and it was hard for her to hold a job. Especially in the end. And that meant we couldn't afford the best of apartments. Our last place had only one room. And at night you could hear the rats scurrying around." She shuddered at the memory. "I still hate them."

He stepped closer, his eyes glinting silver in the light. "I'm sorry it took me so long to get here. I got stuck talking to Ryan and his friend. A very yuppie discussion about the price of property on Lake Travis." It was his turn to sound chagrined. "I see you brought wine." He tilted his head toward the shattered glass, and despite herself, she smiled.

"I had planned a better use for it."

"I suspect as a rat deterrent, it works pretty well. And just at the moment," he bent his head, his lips inches from hers, "I don't think we'll be needing it."

Chapter 11

Eric's mouth brushed against her cheek, the warmth of his lips against her skin making her tremble. It had been so long.

Maybe forever.

His kiss was like fire, filling her with a heat she'd forgotten was possible. Her mouth opened of its own accord, giving as much as it got, reveling in the feel of his tongue, hot against hers. There was an urgency she couldn't define, a sensual onslaught unlike anything she'd ever experienced.

Eric D'Angelo was a take-no-prisoners kind of guy, and she knew without question that if she let him in, there would be no going back.

Not that she wanted to.

She pressed herself closer, letting the smell of him surround her. Almost a tangible thing, it caressed her senses, leaving her reeling. His hand found her breast through the soft cotton of her shirt, his fingers kneading, massaging, leaving her quivering for more. It was almost as if she'd been waiting for him. Holding some part of herself in reserve.

The thought both elated her and frightened her.

As if sensing her dilemma, he retreated, his kiss more gentle, his hand circling, soothing, but the fires inside her had been too long denied, and she deepened the kiss, pushing against his hand.

And with a groan, he obliged her, his hands needy, his lips possessing.

Then his beeper went off.

Followed by a pounding at the door.

Reluctantly he pulled away, and she fought for breath, not sure if she felt relieved or deprived. Both, most likely.

"Eric?" Tony called. "You in there?"

Eric mumbled an assent and held his pager up to the light. "There's been another murder."

Sara's blood ran cold, passion replaced with horror. "So soon?"

"It might not be the same M.O. We won't know till we get there."

The door swung wide, and Tony stood impatiently in the entrance. "We've got to go."

"I know." Eric reached over to kiss her again, this time tenderly. "Can you get home okay?"

"Not a problem." She forced a smile, her emotions still in a tangle. "I'm sure Molly or Jack can give me a ride."

"Molly would be preferable." His smile was warm, but there was a hint of possessiveness.

"I'll be fine." She nodded for emphasis, a signal that he could go.

He turned and started to walk from the cabana, and before she could stop herself she called after him. "Eric?" He swung around to look at her, his mind obviously already on the case at hand. "When you finish, if you need to talk . . ." She trailed off, feeling all of about thirteen.

His smile was slow, his focus returning to her. "I'll look for a light. If it's out, I'll know you've gone to bed."

She nodded again, seemingly incapable of anything but gestures. "I'll be waiting."

It seemed so basic, waiting for someone to come home. So connected. And some part of her, some long forgotten part, rejoiced at the knowledge that there just might be someone out there worth waiting for.

Electronic flashes popped as the forensic team photographed the body, the bright light only serving to make a gruesome sight more horrific. The victim was tied to a chair in her kitchen.

The woman had been stabbed repeatedly, her body twisted awkwardly as if she had been trying to escape the blade. Blood covered the body and what remained of her scalp. Whatever hair she'd had had been removed. And from the looks of it, in something less than a surgical manner.

"We got an I.D.?" Eric turned his attention to a uniform standing off to one side. Although he was valiantly trying not to show his reaction, his face gave him away.

"She's a social worker." The officer pulled out a notepad, swallowing convulsively, an obvious effort to keep his stomach contents firmly in place. "Allison Moore. Twenty-six, according to her driver's license. We talked to the next-door neighbor, and got a little bit more information. She's lived here about three years, alone. She kept to herself, but was friendly in a guarded kind of way."

"Any sign of someone in the house?"

"Nothing. Place was neater than a pin. Only thing I found was this." He held up the body of a doll—Barbie from the looks of it. The head was missing.

"Where was it?"

"In the hall. Couldn't find the head. But there are more dolls in the bedroom. Neighbor said she collected them."

"Put that one in an evidence bag. We'll have the lab examine it. Any sign of forced entry?"

"Nope. Place was locked up tighter than a drum. No security system, but there were double locks on the doors."

"So she knew the killer." Eric narrowed his eyes, trying to assimilate the facts.

"Yes, sir. Or at least thought she could trust him enough to let him inside."

"Neighbors call it in?" If so, maybe they'd seen more than they were admitting to.

The kid shook his head. "No. But we're running a check to see where the call originated."

"How about a weapon?" He already knew the answer, but he still had to ask the question.

"Not so far, but the forensic people are looking. You want me to canvass the rest of the neighborhood? Maybe there's someone out there who saw something." What he wanted was to get out of the room.

And, frankly, Eric didn't blame him. "Yeah, take someone with you."

Steeling himself, he turned back to Allison Moore. Claire Dennison was examining the body, her movements calculated not to disturb anything that might be evidence.

Eric walked over to crouch at her side. The body was slumped forward, bound hands the only thing keeping it in place. The eyes, though fixed and dilated, still reflected terror. Allison Moore's last minutes on earth had not been pretty ones.

There were still strands of hair on the floor, silent testament to what had occurred here. He'd read about scalping, of course. Seen it alluded to in countless Westerns, but he'd never actually witnessed the results firsthand. The reality was beyond anything he could possibly have imagined. There truly weren't words.

"Unfuckingbelievable." Or maybe there were. Tony ambled over to the body, his pace at odds with the grim expression on his face. "This bastard should be strung up by his balls."

"Not a bad idea."

Tony held up a compact disk, gloved fingers only touching the edges. "Found it near the back door, along with a boom box."

"Frank Sinatra?"

"Yeah. Homemade, just like the others. Tech says it's a song called 'I Could Make You Care.'"

Eric stood up, suddenly feeling tired. "Wishful thinking from the looks of it."

"Yeah, but no question it's our guy."

"So why her?" He gestured toward the body. "She's obviously not a prostitute." A new thought worked its way front and center. He looked over at Claire. "Any sign she was raped?"

"Nothing conclusive. Her panties are missing." Claire lifted the woman's skirt to underscore the fact. "But there's no visible bruising, and I haven't seen anything to indicate fluid. Although the last is consistent with what we've found at the other scenes."

"You find anything around the body that could have been used as a phallus?"

"Nothing protruding. And nothing on the floor. But, hell, Eric, this is a kitchen." She waved toward a counter covered with appliances and cooking utensils. "We'll know more after we get an autopsy."

Eric nodded, blowing out a slow breath, turning back to Tony. "How come the music wasn't playing when we got here?"

"One of the uniforms turned it off. Not exactly a fan of the classics." Tony grinned as they walked into the living room.

"So the guy's moved uptown."

"Or our girl had a connection with prostitutes."

Eric frowned. "Moonlighting from her day job?"

"Right. Allie does Austin." Tony's laugh held no amusement. "Jesus, Eric. Think. The woman was a social worker. Social workers help the downtrodden. Maybe Allison here was working with one of our girls."

"So, what, she was killed because she knew the wrong people?"

"I don't know." Tony's frustration carried with every word. "I just figure there's got to be logic here. These guys always have a pattern. No matter how obscure it seems, it's there."

"Yeah, I know." Eric ran a hand through his hair. "I didn't mean to snap at you. It's just that I feel like he's taunting us."

"Maybe he is." Claire walked into the room, holding a plastic bag containing a knife. "My tech found this in the dishwasher. It's still hot."

"He washed the dishes?" Tony's remark was off the cuff, his tone flippant, but it was only a second before the significance registered. "Oh, Christ, you're saying he washed the murder weapon."

"Looks like a definite possibility. The blade width matches the length of the stab wounds, and at least a cursory examination shows serration that could match the pattern of injury. We'll know for certain after we run some tests."

"Arrogant bastard." Eric's fought the urge to hit something. The man was playing them like a well-strung guitar. "What the hell does he think he's doing?"

"Yanking our chain, if I had to call it." Tony shrugged. "But you got to give the sick son of a bitch points for creativity."

"Give me five minutes alone in a room with him . . ."

"I'll be right there with you." Tony's smile was tight. "But we've got to find him first."

"Right." Eric rubbed the bridge of his nose. "So we've got a change in M.O., but he's still overkilling and amputating."

"I don't know if *that*," Tony nodded toward the kitchen, "is considered an amputation."

"Maybe not per se, but whatever's driving this bastard to cut them up is still in play."

"Escalating, if I had to call it," Claire said.

"Meaning what?" Eric frowned.

"The victim was alive when he scalped her." Claire's eyebrows drew together to form a grim line. "That's why there's so much blood. The others were dead when he cut them."

"Which means it was either an afterthought—"

"Or a conscious effort to spare them pain." Eric finished Tony's thought.

"I vote for the first one," Tony said. "He wasn't concerned with anyone's pain."

"I'll buy that. But I don't think the amputations were an afterthought." Claire crossed her arms, her gaze encompass-

ing them both. "If anything, it's part of the reason he's doing this. And if that's the case, then the violence is definitely
increasing."

"Something's pissing him off." Tony dropped the CD
into an evidence bag.

"Maybe. But there's no way I can know that for sure. My
job's with the scene. I extract what it's got to tell me and
pass it on to you. I can tell you *what*. But you've got to figure out *why*."

"Which means we've got our work cut out for us." Tony
exchanged a glance with Eric. "We can canvass her office in
the morning. Someone there might be able to connect her to
one of the other victims. Which would go a long way toward giving us a link between the murders."

"One thing's for certain," Claire said, peeling off her
gloves. "This is going to scare the hell out of the city.
There's no safety zone when the vic is white-collar. Unless
you find your connection fast, every woman in Austin is going to feel like a target."

"When will Garcia do the autopsy?"

Claire's smile was tired. "As soon as they get the body
back to the lab. Mayor's in on this one, and he wants answers fast."

"He's not the only one." Tony nodded toward the reporters camped out at the door. "Word spread pretty damn
fast."

"It'll be impossible to contain this one, boys." Claire
shrugged. "It's too soon after the other one. This guy is on a
roll, and he's not likely to let up anytime soon."

"Thanks for the ride." Sara leaned down to look in the
window of Nate's old Crown Victoria.

"Not a problem. Guess that's one of the disadvantages of
dating a cop." He smiled up at her, his hands still on the
steering wheel.

"I guess. Considering it was only our first date, I'm not
much of an expert."

"You going to see him again?" His tone was light, but there was a hint of something resembling worry in his eyes.

"I honestly don't know. You got a problem with it?"

"No." He held up his hands. "Of course not. I just worry that getting involved with a detective comes with its own set of problems. Long-term relationships don't seem to be congruent with the job."

"What about Tony and Bess?"

"Okay," Nate shrugged, "so they're the exception. But Eric already has a strike against him. He's divorced."

"So are a huge percentage of adult Americans. Come on, Nate. Life is about taking chances. Besides, you're jumping the gun a little. I've only been out with him once. And I didn't even get to complete that."

"There you go." He tapped the steering wheel for emphasis. "Exactly what I was talking about. That's going to happen a lot."

"Where's all this coming from?" She leaned down for a better view of his eyes.

He shifted uncomfortably on the seat. "Nothing about Eric D'Angelo, if that's what you mean. I just don't want to see you get hurt."

She reached over to cover his hand with hers. "Stop worrying. I'm not committing to the man for life. I'm just testing the waters. Okay?"

"Okay." He smiled sheepishly. "You want me to walk you to the door?"

"Nah. I've got my keys right here. Besides, you know you're dying to follow up on whatever it was that called Eric and Tony away."

"So I'm predictable." He grinned, then reached down to turn the key in the ignition. "I'll talk to you later."

"Tomorrow. And, Nate," she leaned in to kiss his cheek, "thanks for caring."

Beet red, he put the car in reverse and backed out the driveway. She stood watching until he was out of sight, his words still ringing in her ears. She'd lied, of course, when she'd said she could take care of herself.

At least where Eric D'Angelo was concerned. She'd never met anyone like him, his strength of character at once comforting and daunting. She was fairly certain, if she'd let him, he'd turn her soul inside out. He was the kind of man who demanded all or nothing.

And just at the moment *all* might be more than she had to give.

Chapter 12

The photographs were haunting, and not because they were particularly well-done or because the subject had led a tragic life, but because Lydia Wallace was dead. All hope extinguished in an instant.

Her choices in life might have been limited, but she still had a life, and someone had taken that life away. Sara picked up a picture, remembering the vibrance and laughter captured there. For one isolated moment, Lydia Wallace could have been any other teenager. Endless possibilities stretching out in front of her.

Sara tossed the photo on the table with the others, leaning back in the chair, her mind turning to Eric. Her stomach tightened at just the thought of him, and she pushed away from the table, crossing to the wine bottle on the bar. After pouring a glass, she walked to the sofa, sinking down on the cushions, closing her eyes.

Frank Sinatra crooned from the stereo. Probably macabre,

considering the circumstances, but Tom had loved his music, and by playing it, somehow she always felt closer to him. But sitting here now, listening to a song about dancing in the dark, it wasn't Tom she saw in her mind's eye. It was Eric.

Longing tangled with logic and guilt, emotions twisting together to leave her confused and conflicted. She had loved Tom so very much, and the idea that some other man could occupy his place was an abomination.

Yet, Eric made her heart sing in ways she'd never even imagined. It was almost as if there were two of her: one living firmly in the past, holding on to Charlie and Tom, clinging to what had been. The other wanting only to move forward, to live life again. To find happiness—and perhaps even love.

She gripped the stem of her glass, the feel of the cool crystal grounding her in the present. The past was behind her, the future only a dream. It was today that mattered. The decisions she made now affecting everything.

She sipped her wine, the liquid warming her from the inside out. Intellectually she knew that being with Eric wasn't a betrayal of Tom. But her heart wasn't as certain.

The music crescendoed, and she let it surround her, the notes comfortable like old tennis shoes or a favorite blanket.

The phone rang, the shrill sound startling her out of her thoughts. She reached for the receiver, then stopped, remembering Eric's admonition to let the machine get it. With a sigh, she walked into the study, listening as the machine clicked on, red light turning green in the process.

"Sara? You there? It's Molly. Pick up."

She reached for the phone. "I'm here. I just wanted to see who it was."

"Well, I'm glad I rated an answer." There was laughter in her voice. "I just thought I'd check on you."

"I'm fine. Just sitting here unwinding."

"Worrying is more like it." Molly's voice was kind. "You hear anything from Eric?"

"Not yet. He said he'd come by if it wasn't too late, but I'm having second thoughts about it."

"Why? He seems like a great guy." She could hear a note of frustration in her friend's voice.

"That's the problem, I think. He's too appealing." Which sort of summed things up nicely. "When I agreed to go out with him, I wanted to test the waters, not jump into the deep end."

"Well, I think he's worth the risk."

"Then maybe you should go out with him."

"You mean it?" Enthusiasm colored Molly's voice, making her sound almost breathless.

"No." Sara was surprised at the fervor of her response. "Of course not."

"Gotcha." The enthusiasm turned to laughter. "I knew you liked him."

"I never said I didn't. I'm just questioning the wisdom of following through on it."

"If you're already in the deep end, then I suspect you don't have a choice."

Which, of course, was exactly what she was afraid of. Sara hung the phone up with a smile. Molly might be a bit overbearing in her opinions, but her heart was in the right place. Except that she was wrong about choices.

Eric had said he'd stop if there was a light. So, with a flip of a switch, Sara turned it off, and headed for bed.

"Just got the autopsy report." Lieutenant Brady walked into the conference room, throwing the white envelope onto the table.

Eric picked it up, and pulled out the thin sheets. "Not much here."

"There's enough. Keep reading."

He skimmed the first page, then turned to the second. "This guy's a real sicko."

"What's it say?" Tony peered over his shoulder, trying to read the tiny print.

"Garcia found the missing Barbie head."

"Oh, shit, tell me it isn't what I'm thinking." Tony took a

step backward, as if by doing so he could distance himself from the brutal reality.

"The head was inside the victim. Traces of vaginal fluid on the doll's body confirms that it was used to rape her." He lowered the pages, his gaze meeting the lieutenant's. "Tell me they found something to identify this guy."

Brady shook his head. "Claire's people have a positive I.D. on the knife. It matches the victim's wounds. But other than that it didn't tell us a lot. The serration is different from what we found on the other wounds, and the knife was clean as a whistle, not even a trace of the guy. Bastard's probably at home right now having a good laugh."

"Allison Moore have any kin?"

"Yeah," Brady's lips tightened, "a mother and sister. They live in Abilene. They'll be here in the morning. I don't have to tell you the press is going to have a field day with this. How about the journalist's pictures? Anything come of that?"

"Preliminary report turned up nothing. But I sent them over to the computer lab. If anyone can work a miracle, they can. We should know something tomorrow."

"Early would be good. In the meantime, go through the evidence again. Maybe with the additional victim something will shake out that wasn't apparent before." Brady turned and strode through the door, leaving silence behind him.

Eric was the first to break it. "Shall we start at the top?"

"Works for me." Tony pulled a photograph from a file and tacked it up on the white board. Allison Moore. The newest addition to the Sinatra club. "They're all so damn different."

"So that rules out look-alikes." Eric narrowed his eyes, studying the wall. "We've got three Caucasian, and one African-American. And four different body parts. Ears, fingers, tongue, and hair."

"Interesting combination. Maybe he's building a woman."

"Seems like there are easier ways." Eric blew out a long, frustrated breath. "Hell, Tony, truth is, it could be a million different things."

"All right, then let's look at the rape instruments." Tony pulled another sheet from the file. "We know that at least two of them were special to the victims. The bat and the doll. Which leaves us a wine bottle and an umbrella." Tony consulted the report. "Wine was Turning Leaf. Nothing special. I suppose you could make the argument that since Laurel Henry was an alcoholic, a wine bottle would have been a prized possession."

"Or a syringe." Eric stared up at the white board, willing it to yield answers. "Anything to indicate Candy Mason had a thing for umbrellas?"

"Not in the file, but that doesn't mean it isn't so. Maybe we can reinterview her friends, establish something about the umbrella." Tony pulled out a photo of the murder scene and studied it. "Come to think of it, it doesn't look like a regular umbrella. It's all pink and frilly."

"So maybe it's a parasol." Eric frowned down at the picture. "You know, the kind women use for shade. Where's Candy originally from?"

"Says here Alabama."

"Southern makes some sense. Maybe it did have sentimental value. Either way, I think you're right. We should talk to her buddies again. The more information we can pull together, the closer we'll come to understanding how this bastard's mind works. What makes him tick. Once we have that, all of this," Eric waved in the direction of the white board, "is going to make a hell of a lot more sense."

"Well, one thing we know for certain." Tony stood up, pacing alongside the table. "He's getting better at what he's doing. Claire says the amputations are more professional, and although there was more blood at the last site, it was primarily because he took her hair while she was alive."

"Which points to an escalation in violence."

"Yeah, but without a motive. He could be getting angry, or he could just be building tolerance."

Eric nodded. "Needing to inflict more torture to get off. But that wouldn't explain the increased frequency of events.

The first two murders were months apart. Three and four were practically back to back."

Tony pulled out a chair and straddled it. "I looked into the lyrics of the songs. Composers, too. Lyrics and music are all over the board. No commonality as far as authorship is concerned. All the songs are love songs, but then that pretty much defines Sinatra. There is a vague pattern of sorts. The first lyrics are almost wistful, same with the second. Giddy love sort of thing. But the last two seem to have more of an implied threat."

Eric raised his eyebrows in question. "You think Sinatra's threatening?"

"No. But I think the lyrics could be interpreted that way. It isn't as apparent when you listen to the songs, but it's different when you read them—especially for me, because I don't know them and so I don't hear the music in my head. The catch-phrase from Lydia's song is 'more than you dream I do, I dream of you.' Sort of an unrequited love thing. But also a hint that the singer is thinking of her—"

"Obsessing on her," Eric finished.

"Exactly. And the next one's worse." Tony reached for a piece of paper. "I had Claire's folks transcribe a copy. There's a line about 'building a life around you.' Again with the obsession. And it ends with 'I could make you care. I know I could.' It might be a stretch, but I think you could argue that we've gone from passive attraction to active obsession."

"Which would explain the escalating violence. But it also raises another important question." Eric's gaze locked on the white board, and the bloodied victims. "Who the hell is the object of his obsession?"

Sara tossed restlessly in her bed. Tonight even her dreams weren't cooperating. Instead of comforting images from the past, all she could think about was Eric D'Angelo—the way his mouth felt on hers, the way his hands burned her skin, the steely gray of his eyes.

With a sigh, she flopped onto her back, opening her eyes, waiting for them to adjust to the dark. There was no moon tonight, and even with the curtains open the room was shadowed more than usual, the dark almost a living, breathing thing. But it was friendly. An extension of the house, wrapping her in the cool velvet night.

She wondered if Eric was still working. Or if he'd come by to find her house silent and dark. She'd taken the coward's way out and she knew it. But some part of her wasn't ready for what he was offering. Or what she thought he was offering.

The whole thing was too much to contemplate in the middle of the night, but her brain evidently hadn't gotten the memo, and steadfastly refused to drop the topic, despite the pleas of her heart. In the space of forty-eight hours everything had changed, her carefully orchestrated life turned topsy-turvy in the whirlwind of her emotions. Eric D'Angelo made her feel things she'd never felt before.

And all of that added together made her want to throw caution to the wind—let the chips fall as they might. In short, ignore every screaming atom of common sense she possessed.

Not exactly her usual mode of operation.

She rolled onto her side, adjusting her pillow, the cool feel of cotton comforting. Closing her eyes, she concentrated on sleep, pulling to mind every pastoral scene she could think of.

Nothing.

Except that Eric D'Angelo kept popping up in English fields and tropical islands. So much for the power of meditation.

When the phone rang it was almost a relief. Escape from her mutinous imagination. She reached for it reflexively, the receiver already to her ear before she realized she was supposed to let the machine answer.

"Hello?"

There was silence, then she thought perhaps the faintest hint of music, the sound so soft it was impossible to recognize the melody. She counted to three, and then quietly replaced the receiver.

Her caller had changed his style.

Annoyed at herself more than him, she switched on the light and looked over at the Caller ID box. The words 'unknown caller' flashed green, the rhythm mocking her.

"So much for modern conveniences." She glared at the box, then remembered to hit the scroll button. A number replaced the original message.

"Gotcha." With a grim smile, she copied the number on a pad by the table. It was tempting to call Eric right that minute, but since the whole idea had been to avoid seeing him tonight, she fought the urge. Tomorrow would be soon enough.

She lay back in the bed and was reaching for the lamp, when her ears caught the faint sound of music. Rolling onto her side, she checked the phone to make certain she'd hung it up. She had.

Which meant the music was either in her imagination or in her house.

She waited, straining to hear something. Anything. And then faintly, as if on a crescendo, the music wafted up the stairs again. Swallowing nervously, she swung out of bed, and padded to the top of the stairs.

The dark at the bottom didn't seem as friendly as the light in her bedroom. The music was louder, obviously coming from her living room, but still too soft to discern a tune. Heart thudding, she walked down the stairs, hitting the switch at the bottom, flooding the living room with light.

The stereo light glowed green, the music loud enough now to identify.

Frank Sinatra.

She'd obviously left the CD player on. The song she'd thought she heard on the telephone had actually been playing down here. What had seemed ominous was suddenly ridiculous, and she sank onto the sofa, her fear morphing into giddy relief.

The doorbell probably should have scared her, but since hysteria was working hand in hand with relief, it only seemed to heighten her sense of the absurd. Holding back laughter, she peered through the peephole and saw Eric on the other side.

Delight warred with caution, her sensible self reminding her firmly of the risks of opening the door. But then she couldn't just leave him standing there. After all, he was a friend if nothing else.

So with a smile worthy of Scarlett O'Hara, she opened the door.

And immediately sobered. He looked so tired. As if something had sucked the soul right out if him. Her petty worries disappeared in an instant, and all she wanted to do was find a way to restore his vibrancy.

"Come in. You look awful." She moved aside so that he could pass her, but he held his ground, his face grim.

"I'm not good company. I shouldn't have come."

"Of course you should have." She lowered her voice, trying for soothing. "Was it really bad?"

"As bad as it gets, I guess." He moved into the foyer, his feet seeming to have a will of their own. She linked her arm through his, and drew him into the living room. Frank was still singing.

"Sit here." She helped him onto the sofa. "How about a drink? I think I have all the basics."

"Scotch would be great." He sat like an automaton, his face still set in what seemed to be a permanent grimace.

She walked to the bar and poured a jigger of Glenlivet, then added extra just for good measure. "Ice?"

"A cube." The words were almost a whisper, as if even talking was more effort than he could afford.

She carried the drink over to the sofa, crystal and ice adding musical accompaniment to the movement. "Here." She handed him the glass. "Drink this. It'll make you feel better." She stressed the last, not knowing for certain that the words held truth.

He sipped the scotch, savoring the taste, swallowing only after letting it linger on his tongue. Then, tipping back his head, he closed his eyes, and she resisted the urge to put her arms around him.

"I'm assuming it was the same guy." It wasn't a question; his face more than told the story.

He nodded, taking another drink from his glass. "We're up to four. Only this one was worse than the others. If that's possible."

She reached over to cover his knee with her hand, the gesture inadequate but all that she had to offer. "I'm sorry."

"Sorry he did it?" His eyes were still closed, but somehow it only increased his intensity.

"I suppose that goes without saying. But what I meant was that I'm sorry you're having to go through it all. I can't imagine what it must be like to see something like that."

"I'm supposed to be immune." The words actually held a note of bitterness.

"That's ridiculous. You've managed to steel yourself, perhaps. Insulate yourself in the most basic of ways. But there's no way to be immune. And nobody would expect that of you."

"Maybe I expect it." He opened his eyes to look at her, the pain and exhaustion reflected there almost taking her breath away.

"Here's what I think." She leaned forward, her gaze colliding with his. "You spend too much time taking care of other people and not enough time taking care of yourself. What you need to do right now is rest."

"You're right." He sat up. "I should go home."

"That's not what I meant. You don't need to be alone. Stay with me. Let me take care of you for a while."

He looked at her for a moment as if she were speaking a foreign language, and then nodded, the faintest wisp of a smile curling his lips. "Just what did you have in mind?"

"Nothing insalubrious, I promise. Just a shoulder to lean on."

"Figuratively or literally?" His silvery gaze held hers, the current running between them promising things she wasn't certain she wanted.

"Literally, if that's what you need." She patted her shoulder. She wasn't sure why she'd offered. Certainly it was contrary to her instinct to keep a distance between them. But he needed her. And it had been a long time since she'd felt needed.

He studied her for a moment, and then evidently satisfied with what he saw, settled against her shoulder with a sigh, his feet stretched out on the sofa. "Some first date, huh? I'm a regular Prince Charming." The words were low, underscored by the soft rhythm of his breathing, and she smiled, smoothing back his hair.

"I don't know, sometimes fairy tales aren't all they're cracked up to be." She waited for an answer, but was rewarded with silence.

It seemed that Prince Charming had fallen asleep.

Chapter 13

Eric woke with the horrible sensation of not knowing where he was. His eyes shot open, the dark shadows playing against the ceiling doing nothing to relieve his anxiety. A soft sound to his left clarified things in an instant.

Sara.

He was on the sofa with Sara. They had shifted in sleep so that they were lying together, legs intertwined. It would have been a wonderful moment, except that he'd fallen

asleep in the middle of a conversation. At least he thought
he had.

He was a little fuzzy on the details. He remembered having a drink. One Scotch. Certainly not enough to incapaci-
tate him. They'd talked about the murder. And he'd meant
to go home, but she'd offered her shoulder, and somehow it
was just what he'd needed. He couldn't remember the last
time someone had offered to take care of him.

And now he was here with her, in the middle of the
night, sleeping on a sofa. It was provocative and comforting
all at the same time. A heady combination. There was something about Sara Martin. Something that reached out to him,
soothed the angry parts of his soul.

Or maybe he just wanted to jump her bones.

Hell of a dichotomy.

With a sigh, he rolled onto his back, careful not to disturb her, trying to sort through his riotous thoughts.

"You're awake." Her voice was soft like a whisper of
wind, and it sent a shiver down his spine.

"Yeah." The word hung in the air, taking on a life of its
own.

"I'm glad you got some rest." She paused for a moment,
clearly embarrassed. "I didn't mean to sleep here. I guess I
just drifted off."

He turned to face her. "I can think of worse things than
waking up with you."

"We didn't . . . I mean, if that's what you're thinking."
Even in the dark he could tell her face was red.

He reached out to trace the line of her jaw. "Believe me,
if we had, it's not something I would forget. In fact, I'd bet a
month's salary that it would be the memory of a lifetime."

She sat up, clutching a pillow in her lap. "I, ah, just
thought you needed the rest."

He sat up, too, reaching over to cover her hand, stilling
her nervous fingers. "I did. And for what it's worth, I feel
better now."

"Ghosts vanquished?"

"I don't know that they're gone, but at least for the moment they're subdued. And, believe me, that's something." He smiled, feeling oddly at home despite the situation. "What about you? Looks like I've managed to steal most of the night from you."

"It's not a problem." Her smile was wistful. "I don't sleep all that much anyway."

His eyes narrowed as he studied her face, noticing for the first time the shadows there. "Because of your husband?"

"In part." She stared down at the pillow in her hands. "Charlie, too. It's just that sometimes it doesn't seem real." She lifted her head to meet his gaze. "Especially at night."

"When you dream."

She nodded, her eyes narrowing in surprise. "You sound like you've been there?"

"Not to the same extent. But I remember how my mother was after my father died." He tightened his fingers around hers, oddly relieved when she didn't pull away. "She had dreams, too. Sometimes comforting, sometimes downright scary. But either way, very real. And for a while, I think, she wanted the night to go on forever."

"It's the only way to stay connected." The words came out on a whisper, and Eric knew Sara wasn't just talking about his mother.

"But it passed, Sara. Not the memory of my father, certainly. She'll have that forever. But the need to live in the past is gone. She's got a new life, now. A new man."

"And the dreams?" Her eyes reflected apprehension and hope, the two emotions at odds with one another.

"They're gone."

"Maybe that's what I'm afraid of." She looked so vulnerable, so lost. "It's already getting harder to remember their faces. I close my eyes and I can't even hear the sound of their voices. I'm losing them, Eric. And it makes me feel so disloyal. As if I never loved them at all."

"Sara, that's not ever going to be true. No matter what else you do in your life, you'll always love them, always remember them. Maybe not in the tangible way you do now, but they'll live in your heart forever."

"I want to believe that. To let go. But I'm so afraid of losing them all over again."

"I can't prove it's true. I can't even tell you I understand your pain. But I *can* tell you I care. And if you'll let me, I want to help."

"You don't even know me." She ducked her head, but didn't pull her hand away.

He reached out to place a finger under her chin, lifting her face, forcing her to meet his gaze. "I like what I do know."

She leaned forward slightly, her breath warm against his face. The first touch was gentle, an exploration, each of them learning the feel of the other, then, as if of its own volition, the kiss deepened. She opened to him, surrendering, her need enveloping him, lighting fires deep inside. He ran his hands down her back, settling on the smooth curve of her hips, fingers splayed, massaging.

Her heat radiated through her clothes, the intensity shooting through him like skyrockets run amuck. She pressed against him, trailing kisses along the line of his jaw, the swell of his neck, her tongue tracing the curve of his Adam's apple.

He shivered, and with a groan, framed her head with his hands, pulling her lips back to his. There was passion in their touching now, the frantic need of new lovers to memorize everything about their partners. He recognized the sensation, but not its intensity.

Never had he wanted a woman this way. Not so completely. Her hand found the opening to his shirt, sliding inside, her palm smooth against his chest, her heat branding him. Her fingers were tentative, fluttering like a captured bird. And he covered her hand with his, his heart beating wildly beneath their fingers.

Their gazes met and held, and he saw a world of hope reflected in her eyes, hope for a future he wasn't certain he could give. And almost as if she'd read his mind, she pulled away, her eyes turning uncertain, determination replacing vulnerability.

"I'm don't think I'm ready for this." Her voice quivered, and she looked so uncertain, so insecure, he had to fight not to pull her back into his arms.

"I understand." He pushed a strand of hair behind her ear, and felt her shiver at his touch.

"Do you?" Blue eyes searched his, her lips curling in a faint smile. "Then you're one up on me."

"It was my fault really. I just read the signals wrong." He was apologizing, and he wasn't really certain why. Frowning, he released her.

"No. You read it right." She held out a hand, beseeching. "I do want to be with you. It's just that I haven't done this in a long time."

"And you're thinking about Tom." The idea rankled, but there was no avoiding it.

Her eyes widened. "Tom has something to do with it, certainly, but it's more than that. It's about me. I just don't make love with someone on a whim."

"And you're not ready to be with me."

"Oh, believe me, I'm more than ready." Her smile was crooked, endearing, and he felt his heart flutter in response. "It's just that I want it to be right. To be special. You know?" She sat there, chewing on her bottom lip, eyes begging him to understand. And he knew in that moment that he'd do anything for her.

Anything.

He reached out to cover her lips with his finger. "No worries. We'll wait until it's right. Okay?" She nodded her agreement, and he dropped his hand, standing up. "What do you say you walk me to the door?"

"Probably not a bad idea. Between you and the caller, I haven't had a lot of sleep."

Eric frowned, alarm flashing through him. "You didn't tell me there'd been more calls."

"I sort of got sidetracked," she said, her expression

sheepish. "He's called twice more. Once before I got the service turned on. And then again tonight."

"The same M.O.?"

"You sound like a cop."

"I am a cop." It was his turn to smile. "So tell me what happened."

"It was exactly the same. The phone rings. I pick it up. Dead air." She frowned for a moment, remembering something.

"Something was different?" he prodded.

"No. It's just that I thought I heard music in the background this time, but when I hung up, I could still hear it. So I went downstairs, and realized it was just the stereo. Stupid, huh?" Her laugh held no humor.

"No. You're just jumpy. Are you certain the music was the same?"

"I'm fairly sure. I mean, I'd been listening to a CD earlier, and when I came downstairs, I realized it was still on."

"How about the message. Did you record it?"

She shook her head. "I was asleep, and when the phone rang I just answered automatically. But I did get a number off the Caller ID. Hang on, and I'll get it." She stood up, then ran up the stairs, and Eric fought the urge to follow her, his professional instinct for once in alignment with his personal need. At all costs, no matter what else happened between them, he wanted her safe. And he intended to do everything in his power to see that it was so.

"Here." She was back, intruding into his thoughts in person just as she did when she was gone. "There wasn't a name or anything. Just a number."

He took the piece of paper, his fingers brushing against hers, the resulting heat rekindling his desire. "This should be enough. I'll get back to you as soon as I know something. In the meantime, let your machine answer the phone. Okay?"

She nodded, and they stood there, still touching, neither of them wanting to be the one to say good-bye.

"All right, then." He reached up to touch her face, letting his fingers memorize the feel of her lips. "I'll talk to you tomorrow."

She nodded again, clearly unable to say anything. And so he let himself out, turning at the driveway to look back. She still stood in the doorway, illuminated against the night, a beacon of hope, hope that maybe there was a life out there for him after all.

Only time would tell.

He tightened his fist around the paper with the phone number on it. But first he was going to nail this bastard to the ground.

Sara leaned against the closed door, trying to sort through all that had had happened. Everything was different, her whole world tilted on its axis, Eric D'Angelo the source of her confusion—and exhilaration.

Strong one minute, vulnerable the next, he was a marvelous contradiction of character. Wonderfully human—completely man. She dipped her head in embarrassment, even though she was alone. She'd forgotten the heady insecurity that came with interest in the opposite sex. It was evidently not a state that changed with age, because she felt very much like a teenager with a crush.

An incredibly hormonal crush.

She'd meant what she'd said about not letting things move too fast. In fact, even with Tom, it had been more him than her. At least in the beginning. She'd just never been able to convince herself to open up enough to let someone in. Tom had been particularly persistent, and it had paid off for both of them. He'd been the first man she'd ever really trusted.

Except maybe Jack. But that was a totally different thing.

Eric wasn't like any man she'd ever met. It was as if he were a planet, pulling her into his orbit, the attraction so strong it was impossible to keep any kind of distance. Which scared her as much as it excited her. There was simply so much at stake.

She'd promised to love Tom forever, and, more important, she'd promised to honor him. And even though they'd been parted by death, she wanted to live up to those promises. But with the passage of time, it was harder to be alone. Memories couldn't keep her warm at night or share the intimacies of life.

In the span of a few days, she'd begun to realize all that she'd been missing. And she'd wanted to do something about it. Tonight. With Eric. And amazingly enough, in the heat of the moment, he'd seemed to want her, too.

At least she thought so.

She shook her head, her thoughts back where she'd started. The past calling to her, the future compelling, the two seeming mutually exclusive. Fighting tears, she realized how tired she was. There would be no answers tonight. And as the saying went, tomorrow would be another day.

The question was what she wanted to do with it.

Flipping off the hall light, she walked into the living room, automatically reaching out to straighten the picture of Tom and Charlie, the frame listing to the left. She obviously needed to check the nail.

But not now. It was almost daybreak, and except for the time on the sofa, she hadn't had much sleep. And, truth be told, sleeping with Eric had been anything but restful.

She smiled at the memory of their legs tangled together, their hearts beating almost in tandem. It was an intoxicating feeling. One she'd almost forgotten. But now that her senses had been reawakened, she knew that they wouldn't easily be quieted.

And despite her guilt, she knew in her heart that she didn't want them silenced. It was time to face the future head-on, and if she had anything to say about it, she fully intended for Eric D'Angelo to have a part in it.

Quite possibly, a starring role.

Chapter 14

"You're in early." Tony stood in the doorway, Starbucks cup in hand.

"Never went home, actually." Eric looked up from the printout in his hand, squinting at the overhead light.

"That would explain the rumpled look." His partner sat down at his desk, extending the cup. "I think you need this more than I do."

Eric took it and sipped the scalding brew, the acidic taste doing wonders for his aching head. "Sara had another call last night. So I thought I'd run the number and see if I got a hit."

"What'd you find."

"Not a damn thing. The call was placed from a pay phone in northwest Austin. The caller used a prepaid card, so there's no way to trace him."

"Where was the phone booth?"

"Highland Lanes."

"So maybe somebody there saw something."

"I already checked it out. The phone's just outside the entrance, but no one remembers seeing anything. Which isn't surprising, I guess, when you consider it's a bowling alley."

"Look, you know as well as I do that as long as the guy stays the strong and silent type, there's not much chance it will escalate beyond phone calls."

"I know. I just don't like the idea of some creep out there stalking Sara even if it's only across the phone wires."

"We'll keep an eye out. If things change, we can always stake out the bowling alley. But as far as you know, this could have been a one-time locale."

"Yeah." He took another sip of the coffee. "It's just that I promised her I'd take care of it."

"Tall order."

"Maybe. You got anything new on the Sinatra killer?" Eric nodded toward a manila envelope in Tony's hand.

"A little something. Got the lab report back on the CD players." He pulled out a sheet of paper and passed it over to Eric. "They were clean. No fingerprints at all. Which pretty much rules out ownership by the victims."

"Which was a sure bet anyway, considering their financial circumstances." He studied the report, still sipping the coffee. "What about the CDs?"

"They were generic. There's a serial number, but no way to trace it beyond a lot number. Basically we could figure out whether it was from Best Buy or Fry's, but that's as far as it goes. They were burned by an amateur. No label. And no fingerprints. The only signature at all was electronic."

"Meaning what?"

"Well, if I understood correctly, there's a volume label on a CD like on a hard drive, and the default is the date information is burned. There's a date and time on each CD. They each correspond with the respective killing within twenty-four hours or so, which tells us the killings are premeditated in that he's burning the CD prior to the kill. He knows he's going to do it, and then selects the perfect song."

"And leaves it playing." Eric frowned. "Why not take it with him?"

"Because he wants us to find it. Just like the knife. These bastards love to flout authority. I think the choice of song is part of the ritual, but leaving it playing is about getting his rocks off at our expense. All it costs him is a CD and a boom box."

"Well, he obviously has money. According to the guy

at the lab, the player our perp favors retails around $80 a pop. Not to mention the computer equipment required to burn a CD."

"Pretty standard these days, I'd think."

"It is. But the system still costs about a grand. And you have to know how to do it. I'm thinking at least minimal geekiness is required."

Eric smiled despite himself. "So our guy loves to flout authority, has disposable income, and knows his way around a computer. Wonderful. That fits half the population of Austin."

Sara stared at the proof sheet, trying to force the pictures into focus.

It wasn't working. Instead of photos of the mayor, all she could see was Lydia Wallace, her mind's eye insisting on revisiting the photographs she'd taken of the girl.

Laying the proof sheet on the table, she blew out a breath, rubbing the small of her back. "You look tired." Ryan stood in the doorway of the photography lab, his concern reflected in his eyes. "Long night?"

"Something like that. At the moment I can't seem to get Lydia Wallace off my mind."

"That's understandable, considering the circumstances."

"She was just so young, Ryan. So full of life."

"She was a prostitute, Sara. Not exactly the profession of winners."

She looked up at him in surprise. "Are you saying you think she deserved what happened to her?"

"Of course not." He came over to sit beside the desk. "I just don't want you to gloss over the situation. She put herself at risk just by being out there. And I don't believe for a minute that there's anything you could have done that would have changed what happened."

"I know you're right. It's just that I can't help but wonder what would have happened if I'd reached out more, tried to help. I mean, all I did was take pictures."

"If you'd tried to reach out, she'd have rebuffed you.

Sara, you know what it's like to be on your own at so young an age. You don't trust anyone. Especially not an adult."

"I just wish I'd tried." Sara sighed.

"You did. More than you realize. Just being there counts for something. And I saw the photos, remember? You couldn't have taken pictures like that if you didn't care."

She forced a smile. "Thanks for that."

"You talk to D'Angelo?" She nodded, and Ryan leaned forward, his eyes alight with curiosity. "He tell you anything about last night's killing?"

"Nothing specific. Just that it was grizzly." Actually he hadn't even said that much, but she'd seen it reflected in his face. "I read about it this morning, of course. But other than that, I don't know anymore than you do. Probably less, in fact. Did you go to the site?"

Ryan shook his head. "I considered it, but decided to send Nate instead. He seems to have taken a personal interest in the story."

"Because of Lydia Wallace?" They'd come full circle.

"Yeah. I guess so. Anyway, figured I'd let him run with it awhile. He did a good job with the copy for your article."

"He's a good writer. And he really wants to succeed. I'm glad you're giving him a chance."

"More than you realize, actually." Ryan smiled cryptically, not offering any more. "Unfortunately, he didn't get anything except the party line. Victim's name and a few details about the murder. The police are keeping a lot of it under wraps to keep the public from panicking." He casually crossed one leg over the other, his stance at odds with the grim nature of the conversation. "Of course the mere fact that the woman wasn't a prostitute will set off a frenzy of fear. Every woman in the city will be looking over her shoulder now."

"Not a bad idea." Nate walked into the lab, carrying a huge bouquet of flowers. "Because it doesn't look like the police are any closer to catching the killer." He set the vase on Sara's desk with a smile. "Special delivery."

"From you?" Sara looked first at the roses, then back at Nate.

He blushed. "No. There was a delivery man at the front desk. I just happened to be coming this way."

"See if there's a card," Ryan said, his interest apparent.

She felt carefully amidst the roses, finally locating a small white envelope. She opened it and slid out the card. Frowning, she read it out loud. "All I can do is think of you."

"That's all? There's no signature?" Ryan reached for the card, rereading it. "I suppose it's a nice sentiment."

"I'll bet it's from your detective." Nate's smile was conspiratorial. "He seemed quite smitten at the party yesterday."

"Smitten?" Ryan could hardly contain his laughter. "Detective D'Angelo doesn't seem the smitten type."

Nate glared at Ryan. "Well, he's interested. Anyone can see that."

"Okay, guys, could you maybe lay off talking about my love life? I mean, it is *my* life."

They turned to look at her as if just realizing she was in the room. "Sorry," they said, almost in unison.

Sara pointedly ignored them, turning her attention to the roses. She reached out to caress the velvety softness of one red petal, her eyes falling to the card again. *All I can do is think of you.* It was a lovely sentiment. And one she totally reciprocated.

But then, Eric D'Angelo was a hard man to forget.

"Can you zoom in on that corner?" Eric stared at the computer screen over the tech's shoulder.

"Sure." The tech typed several commands and centered a white circle over the part of the photograph Eric had indicated. One click later, and the area in question had been enlarged, the result grainy but still clear.

"There's nothing here. Just a mob of people." Tony squinted at the screen. "We can enlarge until hell freezes over, but odds are against us finding anything. Hell don't even know what we're looking for."

"Can you enlarge it any more?"

"A little maybe. But much more and you're going to lose clarity." The man resized the picture so that it was larger, the graininess increasing, but the images still discernable.

"So what are you seeing?" Tony asked, moving closer to the screen.

"I'm not sure. Does anyone here look familiar to you?"

"Nope, but then it's hard to tell for certain."

Eric studied the screen, trying to pinpoint what it was he was seeing. Pulling in a breath, he focused on the upper corner, a lamppost. "Wait a minute. There. Can you focus in on that?" He pointed to a figure standing behind the streetlight.

The tech typed in some commands, and the lamppost grew larger, the man standing behind it suddenly clear.

"Jack Weston." Eric's voice echoed his surprise. "What the hell's he doing on a street corner in East Austin?"

"The same corner as our murdered girl." Tony reached across the tech's shoulder to point at the image of Lydia Wallace. "Hell of a coincidence."

"Yeah," Eric said. "Except that I don't believe in coincidences."

"Nate, I can't believe you picked this restaurant." Molly waved a hand at the dining room behind her. "It's a little macabre under the circumstances, don't you think?"

"What do you mean?" Nate looked up, his mouth full of spaghetti, his gaze questioning. "Frank and Angie's has great pasta."

"I think she's referring to the theme." Sara shot a pointed look at the pictures of Frank Sinatra adorning the walls. "It hits a little too close to home, don't you think?"

Nate glanced at the wall in front of him, then did a dou-
b̶l̶e̶ ̶t̶ake, realization crashing in. "Geez, I didn't think about
̶ ̶ ̶ ̶ ̶I'm not sure I ever really even noticed it before."
̶ ̶ ̶ ̶ ̶you think the Frank in Frank and Angie's
̶ ̶ ̶ ̶ ̶d her ice tea, eyes flashing with laughter.

"I never thought about it one way or another." He was turning red again. "I figured Frank was the owner or something."

Sara reached over to pat his hand. "That's totally under-
standable. I wouldn't know it myself except I asked once.
Angie is the owner's mom. And she had a thing about
Frank Sinatra. So there you go—Frank and Angie's."

"I didn't mean anything by it, honestly."

Molly laughed again. "Of course you didn't. It's just that
I thought, under the circumstances, this place was a little too
on point. You know?"

"I can see where you'd think that." His grin was weak,
his discomfort fading.

"So why don't you tell us how the new assignment's going?" It wasn't, strictly speaking, a change of subject, but at
least it had a more positive focus.

"I don't have a lot yet. But I've scheduled an interview
with Allison Moore's family. I thought if I presented things
from their point of view, it would go a long way toward hu-
manizing the piece. It seems that with murder, especially
this kind, the victims often get lost in the shuffle."

Sara nodded her approval. "I think it's perfect. How'd
you manage the interview?"

"I'm not sure, really. I expected to be turned down. In
fact, I think she planned to turn me down. But then, when
she heard that I was the one who'd written the article about
Lydia Wallace, she changed her mind."

"Sounds like a coup to me." Molly raised her glass in
salute.

"Thanks." Nate ducked his head, swallowing another
mouthful of spaghetti. "But I've still got to turn it into
something marketable. You think maybe I could get you to
take some photographs?"

"No problem. Just tell me when." Sara frowned, another
thought pushing its way front and center. "Has Eric talked
to you?"

"We talked a little at the party, but I haven't heard anything more."

"I suspect he's been a little busy." Molly leaned back in her chair with a sigh. "It seems like every time we turn around there's been another murder."

Sara took a sip of ice tea, eyeing her friends over the rim of the glass. "It does seem as if things are escalating."

"In a sick kind of way. The killer's a real piece of work. I'm betting he can't even get it up." Despite her words, there was anger in Molly's voice.

"Maybe he has a reason," Nate offered tentatively.

"Like what? Voices in his head telling him what to do?" Molly glared at Nate. "You think there's an excuse out there that would validate what he did?"

"No," Nate said, staring down at his bowl, avoiding her gaze. "I just meant that despite the horror of the results, there's usually an explanation of some kind."

"I'm sorry, Nate." Molly's smile was genuine. "I didn't mean to lash out at you."

"It's okay." He sighed, his tone indicating that it really wasn't.

Sara started to say something to try to smooth things over between them, but before she could get the words out, her phone rang. Signaling to Molly and Nate, she grabbed the phone, and headed for the restaurant's entrance.

"Hello?"

"Hello yourself." Eric's voice washed through her, warming her in places she hadn't even realized she was cold. "Am I interrupting anything?"

"Nothing important. I'm at Frank and Angie's having lunch with Nate and Molly."

"Seems an off choice of venue." There was a hint of laughter in his voice.

"Believe me, we've more than covered that ground. It was Nate's idea."

"Well, I won't keep you. I just called to let you know I tracked down the number."

Sara couldn't help the intake of breath, her heart rate accelerating as she waited to hear what he'd found.

"The call was placed from a pay phone at a bowling alley. Highland Lanes. Can you think of any connection you or someone you know might have with the place?"

"I don't even bowl." Disappointment mixed with relief.

"It's probably random, but think about it and let me know if you think of anyone you know who might frequent the place."

"Is there anything else I can do?" It was frustrating to feel like her hands were tied. "It's like this guy is running my life. Or at least my nights."

"Unfortunately there isn't anything to do at this point except wait for another call. If it's from the same place, then we can try a stakeout. If not—"

"Then we're back to square one," she finished for him on a sigh.

"Not necessarily." There was a pause, and when he spoke again it was with conviction. "We'll find him, Sara. It just takes time."

"All right." She forced a smile. "I'll keep a good thought."

"That's my girl." The words weren't meant as an endearment, but nevertheless she was absurdly pleased with the way they sounded. "You have plans for dinner?"

"No. You got something in mind?"

"You." This time there was no mistaking the intimacy of the word.

She swallowed, suddenly nervous. "I think that can be arranged."

"Good. I'll pick you up at seven." There was a definite smile in his voice. "And I'll be thinking about you until then."

His words reminded her of the flowers. "I almost forgot. Thank you for the roses. They're beautiful."

"I'd love to take credit, but I didn't send roses, Sara. What made you think they were from me?"

Disappointment threatened to silence her. She sucked in a breath, forcing her emotions into control. "I just assumed . . ." she paused, striving for nonchalance. "There was a note, but no signature."

"What did it say?" His tone was suddenly coplike.

" 'All I can do is think of you.' I think that's it."

"Nothing else?"

"No. That's it."

"Did you check with the florist?" Eric sounded angry now.

"Of course not. I thought they were from *you*."

"I'm sorry, Sara, I didn't mean to grill you. It's just that I don't like the idea of you getting anonymous flowers."

She wondered if he was talking professionally or personally. Hopefully a little of both. "I'm sure there's an explanation. Someone I've photographed or something." Which, of course, made absolutely no sense at all, but she didn't like to think about the alternative.

"Look, whoever it is, we'll get to the bottom of it." He blew out a breath. "I'd come by sooner, but I've got my hands full with this murder investigation. Will you be all right until seven?"

"Of course. I'll be fine."

"Okay." He didn't sound like he believed her, but in truth there wasn't anything he could do about it. "I'll see you tonight, then."

He hung up, and she stood staring stupidly at her cell phone, Frank Sinatra crooning in the background. Her eyes widened, and she strained to hear the lyrics. Frank's voice soared, the notes underscoring the words, *"All I can do is think of you."*

She shivered, a horrible thought pushing its way into her head. But the idea was preposterous. There was no connection between her and the Sinatra killer. She was jumping to conclusions. The words on her flowers were not from a song. Anyone could have said them.

The big question, of course, was who?

Chapter 15

"Got a minute?" Eric and Tony stood beside a '65 Chevy, talking to Jack Weston's feet.

The mechanic rolled out from under the car, frowning up at them. "Can't it wait until I finish?"

Eric shook his head. "I'm afraid we need to talk now."

Jack stood up, wiping his hands on the back of his coveralls. "How can I help you?"

Tony shot a look at the busy garage. "Why don't we talk in your office?"

"All right." Jack nodded to another mechanic, who took his place on the dolly. "This way."

They walked in silence, and Eric took the opportunity to study the younger man. Here in the garage he seemed rougher around the edges than he'd appeared at the party. Maybe it was just a product of the environment, or maybe there was more to Jack Weston than appearances. Either way, he intended to find out what Weston knew.

They walked into a small cubicle, with a window looking into the garage. Jack wound the blinds shut, then indicated two chairs sitting in front of a beat-up old desk. "So tell me what this is all about." He sat behind the desk, his eyebrows raised in question.

"You tell us." Tony dropped the photograph on the desk.

Jack picked it up, studied it for a moment, then put it down again. "I was standing on a corner. Is that against the law?"

"Normally not. But this particular corner just happened to

be where Sara was photographing Lydia Wallace. I'm guessing your being there is a little bit more than coincidence."

Jack blew out a long breath. "I was following Sara."

It was Eric's turn to frown. "I don't understand."

"It's really simple. I worry about her. So I watch out for her."

"Without her knowing?" This from Tony.

"Yeah, if necessary. I don't see much point in alarming her. Besides, if she knew, she'd be madder than hell. Probably send me away. So sometimes I watch over her from behind the scenes." He shrugged. "Whatever it takes."

"And the reason you've appointed yourself Sara's guardian?"

"I care about her. Look, D'Angelo, I told you yesterday that Sara and I go way back. I've been looking out for her since we were kids. It's a habit I've carried right into adulthood. Especially with Tom gone."

"You're telling us the only reason you were on Chicon that day was to check up on Sara?" Tony wrote something in his notebook, the repetition a ploy to keep Jack talking.

"To watch over her, yeah. In case you haven't noticed, it's not the safest environment."

"And she had no idea you were there?" Eric studied the other man, trying to judge his honesty.

"None at all. Unless she saw me in the photograph."

"Did you know Lydia Wallace?" Tony asked, the question a not-so-subtle shift of subject.

"The dead girl? No. I saw her, of course, with Sara, but I never met her. You guys thinking I had something to do with her death?"

"We're just checking all the angles, Jack. Looking for a connection."

"Well, you won't find it with me, or Sara, either, for that matter."

"You mentioned protecting Sara at the party, too. Something to do with foster care. Can you tell us a little more about that?"

Jack fixed his narrow-eyed gaze on Eric. "You asking professionally or personally?"

"A little of both, I guess." Truth was, he didn't know for sure.

"I don't see how it could possibly impact your investigation, but there's no big secret about it. Our so-called foster father was a little too free with his hands." Jack's voice was bitter. "We tried to get social services to remove her, but they wouldn't listen. Told us it was all in her imagination."

"But it wasn't."

Jack shook his head, lost in the past. "The bastard cornered her in her room one night. She screamed for help; I came running."

"Sara was molested?" Eric fought against emotion, trying to maintain professional perspective, but it was hard.

"No. I hit him over the head with a poker before he could hurt her. We thought he was dead, and so we ran."

"You could have claimed self-defense."

"You obviously have never been in the foster-care system. No one listens to the kids, believe me. Anyway, we didn't want to take a chance. So we hid out until social services caught up with us."

"What happened?"

"We found out the pervert wasn't dead. And, of course, in an effort to keep his awful secret, he hadn't told anyone anything other than that we'd run off. So they relocated us. Separately." The last was said with anger.

"But you stayed in touch."

"Hell, yeah. Sara was the only family I ever had. I wasn't about to let the system take her away from me. Anyway, we persevered and here we are. Successful, and for the most part emotionally healthy." His smile was crooked, almost charming.

"And you still watch out for her."

"Damn straight. Always will."

"She's lucky to have a friend like you," Eric said, the faint pull of jealousy coloring his perception of the man.

"No, D'Angelo, you've got it wrong. I'm the lucky one."

"I think you should tell Eric." Molly was sitting on the edge of Sara's desk. Sara had waited until they were alone to share her fears.

"I called the station. He wasn't there. So I figured I'll tell him about it tonight. It's probably nothing. I mean the words in the note were pretty generic after all. Just because I heard them in a Sinatra song, doesn't mean they're from the Sinatra killer."

"I know. But you can't take a chance." Molly frowned, her eyes narrowing as she glared at Sara.

"All right already. I told you I'll tell him." Sara raised a hand in defense.

"I'm sorry." Molly's expression changed to apologetic. "I just want you to take care of yourself. Besides, even if the note isn't a lyric, the whole thing is still really weird." She shot a look at the roses. "I mean, someone had to have sent them to you."

"I called the florist, and they couldn't help. Whoever bought them paid cash, so there's no record. And the woman who was working the counter doesn't remember anything. Evidently they've been really busy with the holidays so close; centerpieces and door decorations."

"Anything special about the roses?"

"You mean something that might identify the sender? No. They're just stock roses. Not a special order or anything. Whoever sent them obviously wanted to stay anonymous."

"So are you going to keep them?"

Sara shook her head. "To tell you the truth they kind of give me the creeps. Do you think it'd be awful if I threw them away?"

"No way. Frankly, I would have already done it. Why don't I take them on my way out?"

"That'd be great. I haven't been able to bring myself to

touch them. I know it's stupid, but I feel like they're tainted or something."

"I wouldn't go that far, but I do think you'll feel better when they're gone."

"Out of sight, out of mind." She reached over to hug her friend. "Thanks for not thinking I'm a total loon."

"Hey, I already thought that." Molly returned the hug, then grabbed the vase, already heading for the door. "Call me when you get home from dinner with Detective Dashing. I want to hear every single detail."

"Some things are not meant to be shared, Molly." Sara laughed.

"With your best friend?" Molly pretended to be offended as she peered over the top of the roses, their crimson color clashing with her fiery hair. "Tell me it isn't so."

"Okay. I'll call. I promise." Sara held out her hands in supplication. "Now go. You're going to be late for rehearsal."

"I'm on my way. Right after I dump these flowers." Molly turned and left, her laughter echoing down the hallway, one red rose petal wafting silently to the floor.

"Your government dollars at work." Tony grimaced at the cubicle-filled room, the decor sadly lacking.

"Hey, beats the hell out of our offices. At least they have cubicles." They came to a stop in front of what had been Allison Moore's office space. A black balloon marked the spot, a fellow employee's idea of a tribute.

It hadn't been a particularly productive day. First Jack Weston and then a series of pointless interviews with the second victim's so-called friends. No one had an explanation as to why she had a parasol, but several remembered her carrying it with her everywhere. So at least they had a reason to believe it fit the pattern.

"Can I help you?" A frazzled-looking man with a bobbing Adam's apple popped out of the cubicle across from Allison's. Tony flashed his badge, and, if possible, the man looked more frazzled. "You're here about Allison."

"Just a few questions." Eric purposefully pitched his voice lower, soothing. "Were you a friend of the deceased?"

"We worked together."

"You're a case worker, too?" Tony asked, notebook in hand.

"No. I'm a supervisor. Allison reported to me."

"Harold Cummings?" Tony consulted his notes. The man nodded. "Great. Mind if we talk for a bit?"

"Anything to help. Why don't you come in and sit down." He moved to the side, gesturing with his hand toward the cubicle. Situated in a corner, it was larger than the others and had a window. Perks of the job.

Eric took a seat across from the desk, while Tony perched on the windowsill. Cummings sat down, twisting his hands nervously. "So what can I tell you?"

"Can you think of anyone Ms. Moore had a beef with? Someone who would want her dead?"

"Providing protective services for children isn't an easy proposition, Detective. Case workers constantly run into volatile people. Especially in abuse situations. And Allison often dealt with the more difficult cases. She had a knack for drawing out even the most troubled child."

"Would she have had cause to work with runaways?"

"Possibly. Although it's not the norm. Usually indigents are handled by other organizations. Triad, for one." The man swiveled his chair to face the credenza behind him, pulled out a drawer, and then, finally, a file. "This is her case record for the last six months." He turned back to face them, handing the folder to Eric.

Eric thumbed through the pages, disappointed to find no mention of Lydia Wallace. "Everything she was working on is here?"

Cummings frowned. "I assign the cases, so the list should be inclusive."

"Any chance she was taking cases on her own time?" Tony's question brought a frown to the other man's face.

"It happens. Not often, and not with my approval, certainly. But sometimes our people come across situations that warrant attention, attention my department either can't or won't take on. Last year we investigated just under three hundred thousand child abuse and neglect cases, Detectives. And that's just the tip of the iceberg. The truth is we simply don't have the money or the manpower to handle it all." He shrugged, his expression grim. "So when a child falls through the cracks, sometimes a social worker will work the case off the record."

"Which means there isn't any way to know for certain if she was working with Lydia." Tony's comment was meant for Eric, but Cummings perked up.

"You think that there's a connection between Allison and the other dead girl?"

"We don't know anything for certain, Mr. Cummings. We're just trying to gather all the information we can. Is there anyone else here who was close to Ms. Moore?"

"Amy Whittaker was her friend. At least I think so. Her cubicle's in the next aisle." He stood up pointing across the partition behind Eric. "Maybe she'll know more about what she was doing outside the office."

They shook hands, and then walked back into the maze of cubicles.

"Well, that was a wash." Tony flipped his notebook shut, and slipped it into his pocket.

"Maybe not. At least there's still a possibility of a connection." They turned the corner and began to scan the cubicles for Amy Whittaker's name. It was the last cubicle in the row.

"Ms. Whittaker?" Eric poked his head through the door, a petite brunette squinting up at him through oversized glasses.

"I'm Amy Whittaker. How can I help you?" She stood up, tilting her head, studying them quizzically.

"Detective D'Angelo." Eric stuck out his hand. "And this is my partner, Tony Haskins." She shook his hand, then released it, settling back into her chair. "Mr. Cummings said you and Allison Moore were close."

"I don't think Allison was close to anyone, Detective. But, yes, we were friends."

"Can you think of anyone who might have wanted to hurt her?" Tony sat on the edge of her desk.

"With this job the list can be quite long." She frowned up at them. "But I thought the papers said it was the Sinatra killer."

"That doesn't change the fact that your friend knew the killer."

Amy's eyes widened. "How could you possibly know that?"

"There was no forced entry," Eric said. "She had to have let him in. Did she have a boyfriend? Someone new she'd been seeing, maybe?"

"Not as far as I knew." The woman looked down at her hands nervously. "I wish I could be of more help."

"How about the other victims? Any chance she knew them?"

"I can't think of any reason Allison would have been dealing with prostitutes, Detective. We work with children here."

"Lydia Wallace wasn't much more than a child, Ms. Whittaker." Tony picked up a pencil, twirling it absently. "She was sixteen."

Amy's head shot up. "What was her name?"

"Lydia," Tony repeated. "Lydia Wallace."

"Oh, my God." Amy's face turned ashen, and she swallowed nervously. "About a week ago, Allison and I were having coffee and she was asking about the runaway hotline. I used to volunteer there. She wanted to know how it worked, that kind of thing. She said she'd received a call about a girl living on the streets. Allison thought maybe she was a runaway. But here's the important thing," Amy said, "I'm almost positive the girl's name was Lydia."

Chapter 16

"I feel like this bastard has us running in circles." Tony took a swig of beer and leaned back in his chair.

"I know it doesn't feel like it, but the pieces are beginning to fit. We've got a pattern emerging. We've just got to put it together in a way that identifies a perp." Eric reached for his long neck, propping his feet up on the table. Dry Creek Saloon was a tiny hole-in-the-wall at the top of Mount Bonnell Road. A favorite place for the two of them to talk about cases.

It wasn't a bar so much as a grocery counter with a couple of tables under a Schlitz beer lamp. The choice of beverage was beer, whatever was in the refrigerator comprising the choice of brand. Outside, there was a small rooftop patio with a couple more tables.

It wasn't fancy, but it was comfortable, and private. Exactly what they needed.

"So what do we know now that we didn't know this morning?" Tony frowned, looking out across the trees at the lake.

"Jack Weston was following Sara, which at least indirectly connects him to Lydia Wallace. Although at least for the moment I'm inclined to think the link's circumstantial. If Amy Whittaker is to be believed, it looks like we can connect Allison Moore to Lydia, as well."

"Except that it's unlikely the kid called her directly. So that means there's a middleman somewhere, which could be our guy, or it could be someone totally unrelated. The only connection we have between the other victims is profession. But Allison Moore wasn't a prostitute. So maybe she posed a threat to the killer somehow."

"Like what, she was on to him?" Tony shook his head, dismissing the thought even as he voiced it. "That could explain the change in profession, but not the fact that he still followed the ritual. If he killed her to keep her quiet, as opposed to choosing her as part of the fantasy, it wouldn't have the same significance. But the signature was exactly the same, right down to the object rape."

"With something she treasured." Eric closed his eyes, realizing his head was pounding. "But even that pattern's iffy. We know for a fact that Lydia Wallace collected baseball paraphernalia. And we know that Allison had the Barbie collection. But the link between Candy and her parasol is a lot weaker, and it's almost nonexistent for Laurel. So maybe that part of the ritual is developing?"

"It's possible." Tony shrugged. "Maybe the first time out he raped with what was at hand, and that somehow evolved into using objects the women cherished. You've got to admit there's a certain degree of irony in the action. Most of the time these things are about control, proving he's got the upper hand. If this is really about punishment, what better way than to degrade someone with something that has personal value?"

"All right. So let's think like a serial killer. Our guy feels like some part of his life is slipping. His anger builds, and instead of tackling the problem head-on, he deals with it indirectly by torturing and then killing. Only he's not killing the primary source of his anger. He's using surrogates, which is why we're seeing the same thing over and over."

Tony leaned forward, putting his bottle on the table. "And if it's a surrogate, I'm betting the primary source is a woman. Someone from the past, maybe. Someone he couldn't control."

"Or maybe the first one *was* the real thing."

"Laurel Henry? Possibly. Her murder certainly seems less organized than the later killings. But according to Claire, there was already forensic method. Cruder than the later amputations maybe, but still not the work of a beginner."

"Generally, with a serial killer, fantasy precedes acting out, which means that there's been considerable thought put into the act before it ever occurs. Still, the first instance is usually pretty crude, a way to test the waters. And you're right, Laurel Henry's murder wasn't crude. The guy was prepared, and most of the ritual seems to already have been in place." Eric dropped his feet to the floor. "Which means he could have practiced somewhere else. Let's check N.C.I.C. again. Maybe we missed something. These guys usually don't wander very far, but I'd rather err on the side of caution."

"All right. And in the meantime, I'll check with some of the old-timers, see if any of them remember anything in the past that sounds like it might be our guy."

Eric nodded, glancing at his watch. "Hell, I hadn't realized it was getting so late. I'm due at Sara's at seven."

"Another date?" Tony's grin was just this side of a smirk.

"Seemed like I ought to at least try and make up for last night."

"You tell her about the bowling alley?" Tony stood up, glass clanking as he picked up his empty beer bottles.

"Yeah, she's not a bowler."

"So no leads."

"Nothing. And you know as well as I do that the odds of tracking down someone who used a pay phone are basically astronomical. I told her we'd see where the next call came from, then go from there."

"Why don't we go one better and pull her phone records?" They walked down the rickety stairs into the bar, handing over the bottles, then continued on into the parking lot. "Didn't you say she kept a log?"

Eric nodded. "I've got a copy at the office."

"So I'll call the phone company in the morning. In the meantime, I'll have a look at the log."

Eric looked pointedly at his watch. "In case you missed the memo, it's now officially after hours."

Tony shrugged. "Bess is going out with Molly tonight, so I'm on my own. Might as well work."

"I'll come with you."

"No dice, buddy," Tony said, his tone goading. "You're meeting Sara, remember? And I, for one, am not going to be responsible for you screwing up your second date."

"No worries." Eric smiled. "Believe me, I'm more than capable of doing that all by myself."

"I'm meeting Molly for dinner after her rehearsal." Bess walked into the photo lab, dropping down into the chair by Sara's desk. "Want to come?"

"Can't." Using her mouse, Sara zeroed in on a section of a photograph, cropping it with the precision only a computer could provide.

"All work and no play makes Sara a very dull girl." Bess's tone was teasing, but her eyes remained serious.

"Hey." Sara held her hands up in defense. "I'm just finishing up here. Then I have a dinner date."

"With Eric?" Bess didn't even bother to hide her delight.

"Yes. With Eric. Happy?"

"Ecstatic. For both of you, actually. He's a good guy."

"So what happened to his first marriage?" Sara tried for nonchalance but didn't quite make it.

"Typical story. Eric and Lauren dated from high school right into college. Couldn't wait to get married. So junior year, they did. And for the next five years or so they had a pretty good thing going. But then they just sort of grew apart. Even in college Eric knew he wanted to be a police officer. Probably before that, too. And I think Lauren thought it was a romantic notion. Someone to protect her, that kind of thing. But the reality is a heck of a lot different. And Lauren wasn't cut out for the life."

"The life?"

"Yeah." Bess nodded, her expression resigned. "It's hard to have a husband who's never there. The truth is part of him belongs to the job, and in many respects that's always going to come first. Particularly in homicide. You never know when he's going to get called away. Vacations are nonexistent, and I can't think of a major holiday we've managed to make it all the way through."

"Like being married to a doctor."

"Sort of. Only when you're married to a doctor, you don't worry about your husband coming home in a body bag." Bess shuddered, delicately, then smiled. "Anyway, Lauren wanted more than Eric could give. And she wasn't shy about asking. Don't get me wrong. She's a good person, just not the right woman for Eric."

"But he thought so."

"Yes, he did. And I think he blames himself for their breakup. Eric's the kind of guy who doesn't make commitments lightly. When he got married, he thought it was forever. I don't think it even occurred to him that something could go wrong. So when it did, it hit him hard, and he took full responsibility, even offered to quit the force."

"But he belongs there. It suits him somehow."

Bess shrugged. "He wanted to save his marriage more. But by then Lauren had already made up her mind. I never knew for sure, but I think maybe she'd already met her second husband. Either way, she was determined to get a divorce. So Eric gave it to her, along with their house and most of their possessions."

"Was he bitter?" She couldn't imagine anyone letting Eric go, but it was easy to see how much it would hurt him if they did.

"Maybe a little at first. But whatever he felt, he kept it pretty contained. I never saw him angry or anything. Just certain it had all been his fault. Even after he and Lauren made peace, he still was convinced that he simply wasn't cut out for a relationship. He believed he was married to the job."

"And now?"

Bess smiled. "Now there's you. He hasn't dated anyone

seriously since the divorce. So the fact that he brought you to the barbecue says a lot."

"You can't know that for sure."

"Sara, I've known Eric for a lot of years now, and I'm telling you this is serious stuff. He doesn't date lightly. And certainly not publicly. I know you've only just met, but the fact remains that you matter to him. So treat him gently, okay?"

"I will. But I think the sentiment needs to go both ways. I'm not exactly an old hat at this dating thing."

"Hey, you two. Go home." Ryan poked his head around the corner, his grin lightening the mood immediately.

"I was on my way out." Bess stood up, shooting a significant look Sara's way. "I just stopped to wish her luck on her date tonight."

Ryan raised his eyebrows. "Another one? Aren't you turning into the social animal?"

"I hardly think a quiet dinner qualifies as painting the town red."

"I guess it's all a matter of degree," Bess said, heading for the door. "I've got to get going or I'll be late."

"I'm assuming you're going out with Eric D'Angelo again." Ryan's face was inscrutable, but Sara had the distinct feeling there was disapproval there.

Best to face it head-on. "You don't like him?"

"I don't know him." Ryan shrugged. "Just promise me you'll go slowly. Okay? I'm sure D'Angelo has the noblest of intentions, but that doesn't mean he's the right guy for you. To repeat a cliché, there are a lot of fish in the sea. So there's no hurry to find a keeper."

"God, I've reduced you to fishing analogies." She opened her arms for a hug, and he pulled her close, his smell familiar, comforting. "Stop worrying. I'll be fine."

He pushed back to look into her eyes. "You're sure?"

"Yeah."

His smile was slow, but genuine. "Then that's good enough for me."

Chapter 17

Gray clouds hugged the craggy cliffs, hiding vegetation beneath a cottony canopy, thin fingers of mist stretching across the highway. The combination of rain and dusk made visibility difficult, which was only complicated by the fact that Eric's thoughts were as foggy as the air outside.

Everything was tangled together in what seemed to be an inextricable knot. The Sinatra killer, the dead women, his career. All of it somehow interdependent on each other, the newest link in the chain being Lydia Wallace's apparent relationship with Allison Moore. He needed to corroborate Amy's statement, and to figure out whether Lydia had come to Allison on her own or had had help.

The truth was it seemed that every turn brought new information, but instead of clarifying matters, they only made everything more murky. He wondered suddenly how many deaths it would take until the bastard made a mistake.

Despite all the technological advantages of police work today, there were more unsolved homicides than ever. Partially because the face of murder was changing. The triad of motives—jealousy, greed, and revenge—had morphed into a nebulous concoction of twisted minds and indefinable motivation.

It was a world of predators, strangers cultivating and hunting their victims. And he was a part of that world, out there day after day, up close and personal with man's inhumanity to man. It was a fight to the death, good against evil, and sometimes he was pretty damn certain they were losing the fight.

Not exactly what he'd signed on for.

He tightened his hands on the wheel, trying to clear his head. Self-pity wasn't his style. He was a problem solver, pure and simple. He found the what, and then worked backward through the whys until he got to who.

Which meant that most of the time, the bad guys bit the dust.

Most of the time.

The car in front of him slowed abruptly, tires squealing, red taillights cutting through the gloom, reflecting off the slick pavement. He swerved, slamming on his brakes, surprised when his foot met no resistance. Pumping rapidly, he waited for the brakes to catch, but nothing happened.

The Mustang slid sideways, hydroplaning on the wet road. He jerked the wheel to the right, steering into the skid, his foot still pumping the brakes. He was aware of cars honking around him, and the screech of braking vehicles, then it seemed that everything went into slow motion.

He fought for control of the car, but it careened across two lanes of oncoming traffic, the impact of a glancing blow jerking him hard against the seat belt. Next thing he knew the car was airborne, the ground below him rocky and brush covered.

Bracing himself the best he could, he gritted his teeth, preparing for impact.

It came quickly, surprisingly quiet, draped in black velvet that seemed to swallow him whole.

He was late.

Sara looked at her watch for at least the hundredth time, trying to contain her frustration. Part of her was certain she was being stood up, and the other, saner part knew that he'd probably just been called away on a case. Still, surely nothing was so pressing he couldn't find time to call.

She felt like a bitch, but she knew it was just fear talking.

Fear that he'd changed his mind. Fear that somehow she'd just imagined the chemistry between them. It had been a long time since she'd been out there. Maybe she'd mistaken lust for something more. Maybe he was only interested in a good time.

Even as she had the thought, she knew she was selling him short. If he was only interested in a physical relationship, he'd have taken advantage of her last night. But he'd respected her wishes, agreeing to hold back until the time was right.

An honorable man.

Which meant that he'd been delayed, and she'd just have to sit tight. Bess had made it more than clear that Eric's life wasn't his own, and if Sara wanted a part of that life, then she had to be prepared to live within the parameters of his world.

No time like the present.

She started to turn on the television, but hesitated. There was enough stress in her life without adding the world's problems. Even the comedies dealt with issues these days. She could veg with some *Nick at Nite*, but the thought of unwinding with a glass of wine and some music was far more enticing.

Not to mention a nice mood-setter for when Eric did arrive.

Selecting a Nancy Griffith album, she opened the case, and placed the CD in the player. In moments, the house was filled with the mellow sounds of guitar, Griffith's soft alto swelling with each note of "Across the Great Divide."

Crossing to the bar, she poured a glass of wine, and turned back to survey her kingdom, as it were. The rain beat a counterpoint to the music, rattling against the tin roof. The lamplight fell golden against the cushions of the sofa, brightening the colors with its cheerful glow.

She loved her home. It was the first thing she'd ever created for herself. A sanctuary in the middle of the confusion and sorrow that marked her life. And she was proud of it. Of herself. Other women might have capitulated to the pain, but she hadn't. Molly was right. She was strong, a survivor. She'd just been tested more than most.

Putting her glass on the table, she picked up the discarded CD from last night, returning it to its case, her thoughts suddenly on Frank Sinatra and the song she'd heard at lunch. Grabbing her glass, she sat cross-legged on the floor in front of the two racks that held her CDs.

One half of the first one was filled with Sinatra albums. Tom's legacy. Pulling out first one and then another, she searched lyric sheets and titles, trying to find one with the phrase from the card. The Nancy Griffith CD had finished, along with most of Mary Chapin Carpenter, by the time she found it.

A song called "I Think of You." She hadn't been mistaken. The card's message was literally the fourth line verbatim. A chill ran down her spine, and suddenly the room didn't seem so warm and comforting.

As if to underscore her unease, the phone rang, the shrill sound discordant against the syncopated rhythm of "I Feel Lucky." Standing, her muscles sore, she realized suddenly how late it was. And Eric hadn't come.

Surely, then, this was him. Torn between annoyance and concern she picked up the phone, disappointed to hear Bess's voice on the other end.

"Sara? Are you there?" Her friend sounded strangely somber, and the chill was back.

"I'm here." She sucked in a breath, bracing herself. "What is it?"

"Sara, it's Eric." There was a pause. It seemed like hours and seconds all at once, time suddenly having no meaning, and in that instant, she was back in her old dining room, dinner on the table, Charlie and Tom late. Only they'd never come home.

Never.

"Sara, honey, are you still there?" Bess's voice sounded far away, but she forced herself to concentrate, to keep the receiver to her ear.

"What happened?" She pushed the words out, her breath coming in gasps.

"There was an accident." Again the pause. As if Bess were consulting with someone. Her friend sighed, and Sara clutched the phone as if it were a lifeline. "His car went off the road . . ."

Blue and black shadows danced before her eyes, her chest tightening until she thought it might explode. She struggled to focus, to stay standing, and then, just when she was certain she couldn't hold on anymore, Ryan was there, taking the phone, helping her to sit down.

"Bess? It's Ryan." He lowered his voice, his concerned gaze never leaving her. "I told you to wait until I got here."

They talked some more, but she couldn't focus, couldn't follow the words. All she could think about was Eric. "Is he . . ." She trailed off, unable to finish the question.

"We don't know. Bess got a call from Tony, and she called me. Tony didn't have any specifics. Just that it was bad."

She nodded, trying to stand. Ryan was by her side in an instant, his strong arms helping her to move, to stay upright.

"It's going to be okay, Sara. You've just got to hang in there. Whatever's happened, we'll face it together."

She nodded, her brain churning so fast she thought it might spin right out of her head.

It couldn't be happening again.

Oh, please, dear God, not again.

The waiting room at St. David's was crowded. People in various stages of agony. Pain hanging heavy, almost a physical presence. Ryan ushered Sara to the nearest chair, but she didn't want to sit. She needed to do something. To know something.

"Wait here," Ryan said, pushing her firmly down on the chair. "I'll see what I can find out."

She half rose, opening her mouth to argue, but thought better of it, and sank back onto the chair, twisting her ring. She didn't have the energy for a fight. She watched Ryan weave through the throng to the admissions desk, and then scanned the room for Bess or Tony. Surely they were here somewhere.

"Sara?" Molly's voice sang through the waiting room, and Sara burst into tears when Molly and Jack materialized at her side. "Are you all right?"

She shook her head mutely, trying to force words to the surface without success.

"Bess called us," Jack said, sliding an arm around her shoulders. "Have you heard anything?"

"Ryan's checking." The words were low, almost a whisper, but at least she'd gotten a sentence out. She wiped angrily at her tears, reaching deep inside for control. "Did Bess tell you what happened?"

Jack shook his head. "Just that the car went off an embankment on twenty-two twenty-two."

Sara shuddered feeling suddenly like she was trapped in an episode of *The Twilight Zone*—the one where the same events kept happening over and over.

"He'll be all right." Molly reached out to squeeze her hand. "You've just got to have faith."

Sara nodded, then held her breath, watching as Ryan made his way back to the chairs.

"He's fine, Sara. Bruised and a little beat up, but fine."

She released the breath on a whoosh, tightening her hand around Molly's. "Can I see him?"

Ryan nodded. "He's been asking for you. Tony and Bess are with him now."

Shooting Jack and Molly a faint but triumphant smile, she made her way over to where the nurse stood waiting. Following behind the scrubs-clad woman, she sent a silent prayer heavenward.

Eric was sitting up on the side of the bed, minus his shirt, a bandage on his head, and another around his ribs. His shoulder was beginning to purple, but other than that, he looked whole and healthy.

And wonderful.

Tony was standing at the end of the bed, reading a report of some kind. Bess was helping Eric take a sip of water. Standing there watching them, Sara suddenly felt like an outsider. They'd all known each other forever, and, she supposed, formed a family of sorts. One she didn't belong to.

She was taking a step backward, thinking of retreat, when Eric looked up and saw her, his gaze meeting hers, the message there more powerful than any words. Silently, he held out his hand, and she crossed the room to take it, the feel of his skin against hers exquisite.

"You're all right." The words came out a whisper, her eyes still locked on his. "I thought, oh, God, I thought . . ."

He stood up, pulling her to him, holding her close, the beating of his heart the most marvelous sound in the world. "I'm okay. Just a little banged up. Believe me, it'll take more than a car wreck to take me out."

Reluctantly she pulled away, not wanting to hurt him, but still firmly holding on to his hands. "What did the doctor say?"

"That I was lucky. And that I should expect to be sore for a couple of days."

She looked to Tony and Bess, trying to ascertain if he was telling her everything.

Tony shrugged. "His ribs are pretty bruised, but nothing's broken, and his head took a beating, but it's too damn hard to have sustained any serious damage. Except for a mild concussion, he's good to go."

"They want to keep him overnight, just for observation," Bess added.

"Like hell." Eric straightened, grimacing in pain. "I'm fine. And I'm definitely not staying here."

Sara moved so that she could slip an arm around him, offering support. He leaned into her slightly, but held his ground. "You need to do what the doctors say."

"I need to get some rest, and I'm not going to get it here."

"Well, you can't go to that hellhole you call an apartment. I bet it hasn't been cleaned in a month." Bess's tone was firm. "Besides, someone's got to watch over you."

"I'll do it." The words were out before she had a chance to talk herself out of it. "You can stay with me."

Tony opened his mouth to say something, but before he

could say anything, Bess elbowed him silent. "I think that's
a great idea." Bess's enthusiasm was overdrawn, her motives almost transparent.

"I don't need an excuse to see Sara, Bess." Eric smiled.
"But I'll take it just the same." His hand tightened on hers,
and her synapses went into overdrive, neurons firing with
the power of small cannons, the resulting electricity shooting through her like lightning.

"Tony, why don't you come with me, and we'll see what
we can do about getting Eric released." With a hand firmly
under his elbow, Bess guided Tony from the room, winking
at Sara as she passed.

"Not exactly subtle, our Bess." Eric laughed, reaching
for a shirt hanging across the back of a chair.

"Let me help you with that." She took the shirt, and held it
as he slid his arms into the sleeves. "Are you in a lot of pain?"

"It hurts when I breathe, but not too much. The doctor
gave me a shot."

She buttoned the shirt, straightening the collar when she
finished, the exercise feeling oddly intimate. As if they'd
stood like this a thousand times before. She stepped back,
but he stopped her with a hand, forcing her to look at him.

"I'm glad you're here. All I could think of when I woke
up was seeing you."

Her breath caught in her throat and tears filled her eyes.
She reached up to trace the line of the bandage over his eye.
"I'm just glad you're okay."

He covered her hand with his. "What do you say we get
out of here and go home?"

It was just a sentence. It wasn't even his home, but somehow the words held more meaning, as though they were
predicting the future. A future she was at once desperate for
and frightened of.

As if reading her mind, he pulled her close again, the silence broken only by their breathing. And just for the moment, she allowed herself to believe that everything would
turn out all right.

* * *

"Are you sure you're feeling okay?" Sara chewed the side of her lip, earnestly studying his face, no doubt looking for signs of imminent collapse. She'd been fussing over him for the last hour, arranging and rearranging his pillows as if their proper positioning had the singular power to heal him. If she hadn't looked so worried, he'd have laughed. Instead, he reached for her hand, pulling her down to sit on the bed beside him.

"I'm a little sore, but other than that, I'm fine."

She scrunched up her nose, eyes narrowing as if she didn't believe him. "The doctor said you had a concussion."

"It's only a mild one, so stop worrying. Everything's going to be okay."

She nodded once, as if convincing herself, her hand tightening on his. "So do you want to tell me what happened?"

It was his turn to frown. "I'm not certain, actually. I was heading to your house and a car in front of me slammed on its brakes, and when I followed suit, my foot hit the floor. I guess I shouldn't have put off that tune-up." His effort to make light of the situation sailed right over her head.

"It might not have mattered." She shook her head, still holding on to his hand. "Tom was obsessive about that sort of thing. He had the Mercedes checked and rechecked constantly. Most *people* aren't as well taken care of as that car was."

"I think most men feel that way about their automobiles."

"I suppose so, but with Tom it wasn't just one. He was also rebuilding a 1961 Jaguar with Ryan. The two of them worked on it every spare minute." She looked out the window, her thoughts obviously in the past. "Anyway," she said, turning back to him, "the car was in pristine condition. I even had Jack check it over after the accident."

"He told me. And that the consensus was that the accident was driver error. Which on a rainy night is always a possibility."

"I know, but I didn't want to believe it. I needed for it to have been something else's fault. Something that didn't have to do with Tom." She met his gaze, begging him to understand.

"You didn't want to blame him for Charlie's death."

She nodded. "It sounds awful, I know. But I needed for him to be innocent. For him—and for me. So I asked Jack to look at the car. The police didn't find anything. But Jack worked on the car regularly, so I thought maybe he'd find something they missed." She sighed, staring down at her hands. "Whatever happened that night, it wasn't about the car."

"I'm sorry."

"Because the car wasn't at fault?" She lifted her head to look at him. "It wouldn't have mattered if it was. I thought it would, but I was wrong. Either way, they were still dead."

"And today you thought it was happening again. With me?" The last was a question, one he suddenly needed to hear an answer to.

"Yes." Her smile was muted. "But it didn't. And that's what we're going to concentrate on. You're here to heal, not listen to my sad tales." She started to stand, but he kept her hand, holding her there at his side.

"Stay with me for a while." He shot her what he hoped was a charming grin, and felt her relax.

"Only if you promise to rest."

He closed his eyes obediently, then opened them again. "You haven't mentioned the roses. Did you find out who sent them?"

She shook her head. "No. But I do think maybe there's something odd about the card."

"Odd how?" His stomach tightened, the telltale uneasiness signaling something significant.

"I think the line on the card was from a song." Her gaze collided with his. "A Sinatra song. It's called 'I Think of You.'"

Chapter 18

"Jesus Christ," he whispered, the tone more alarming than if he'd yelled. "Why the hell didn't you tell me sooner?"

"You've been a bit busy, in case you forgot." Sara tried but couldn't keep the indignant note from her voice. She'd explained it all to him. Starting with lunch right through to Molly disposing of the flowers. And now he was yelling at her.

"I'm sorry." He was immediately contrite, and she felt guilty for being angry at him.

"The truth is it could be a coincidence. I mean, everyone has Sinatra on the brain."

"But you don't know who sent you the flowers, and when you combine that with the phone calls, I'd say the odds of coincidence are reduced dramatically."

"So what? You think the Sinatra killer sent me flowers?" The idea made her stomach churn.

"I'm not jumping to any conclusions, but I think we need to look into this. Do you still have the card?"

She shook her head. "It was with the flowers when Molly took them."

He nodded and reached for her phone. "What's her number?"

"You're calling Molly now?" She didn't know why it surprised her. Maybe because at the hospital he'd seemed so vulnerable. But whatever he'd been, he was all detective now. And she knew there was no sense in arguing. She gave him the number, watching as he dialed.

They sat in silence as the phone rang—waiting. But Molly either wasn't answering or wasn't home. So he left a message and replaced the receiver in the cradle. "We'll follow up in the morning. And I'll check out the florist as well."

"But no one remembers the order."

His grin was weak, but still rakish. "It's amazing what people remember when the police are the ones asking the questions. Besides, I don't want to leave any stone unturned."

"Well, if someone has to talk to the florist, it'll have to be Tony, because you'll be right here—resting." She crossed her arms, trying for a Nurse Ratched frown.

"We'll see. I can't afford to sit here while that madman is out there. Especially if there's a connection to you."

"It'll keep a day or so, I promise. Besides, it's not like there aren't other police detectives in Austin capable of taking up the slack until you're a hundred percent."

"Maybe." He sounded like a disgruntled schoolboy, and despite the gravity of the situation, she found herself holding back laughter.

"Tomorrow, Detective D'Angelo, is another day. And if you want to have any part in it, I suggest you close those sexy gray eyes and get some sleep."

"Sexy? I like the sound of that." He reached for her hand again, this time bringing it to his lips for a kiss. "In fact, I especially like it coming from you. Why don't you forgo the Nightingale routine and come to bed with me instead?"

His words were intended to fluster her, and they hit their mark with a vengeance, her breath lodging in her throat right beside her heart. "I don't think that's on the recovery plan," she said with exaggerated concern, "but I can certainly call the doctor. In the meantime, though, why don't you try to get some sleep? I'll check on you in a couple of hours."

"You promise?" He still held her hand, but his capitulation was imminent, his eyelids already fluttering with fatigue.

"Cross my heart."

He nodded, already sliding into sleep, and she envied him his complacency. She supposed it came with the job. In order to survive the horrors he faced day in and day out, he needed to be able to let it go, if even just for a couple of hours.

Unfortunately, it meant that she was now alone with her thoughts. All of them confusing, some of them frightening. If the words on the card were chosen because they were lyrics, then it was possible the Sinatra killer had sent the flowers. And if that were true, then she had reason to be afraid.

People he became entranced with—died.

After she left the room Eric waited five minutes, then picked up the telephone, dialing Tony's number. His partner picked up on the second ring.

"Haskins."

"It's me." Eric didn't waste time on pleasantries. "We need to talk."

"I thought you were supposed to be resting." There was a note of patient exasperation in Tony's voice. "I'd have thought with Sara there, you'd have better things to do than think about work."

"Sara's the reason I'm calling. Turns out the guy who sent her flowers used a lyric from a Sinatra song on the card. 'I Think of You.' "

"Same as Laurel Henry." Tony's tone was all business now.

"Exactly. It could be coincidence, but I don't want to take a chance. I want it checked out. Molly threw out the flowers, but there's a chance we can recover the card, maybe find something in the handwriting or better yet a print. I tried her house, but she's not answering. Hopefully, we can catch her in the morning. In the meantime, why don't you send a squad car over to check out the Dumpsters at the magazine. It's possible the card is there."

"Anything else?"

"Yeah, run background on Jack Weston, and put a rush

on Sara's phone records. And it wouldn't be a bad idea to order a drive-by every hour or so. I want someone watching out for Sara 24/7."

"All right, I'll make it happen. By the way, I got the preliminaries on the wreck. The brakes definitely failed. No hydraulics. They're running diagnostics now. If it wasn't an accident, we'll find out."

"Good. And as long as you've got the tech's attention, I want you to pull the accident report on Tom Martin. I want to know what happened that night. You've got to admit there's a certain symmetry. Anything else I need to know about?"

"Nothing new on the Sinatra killer, if that's what you're asking. Brady talked to Katie Brighton. Strictly off the record."

Katie was FBI and an old friend. "She have any thoughts?"

"Nothing we haven't already covered. But she suggested Brady talk to a friend of hers. Another Fed. A profiler. I figure at this point anything goes. Hell, I'd settle for a clairvoyant if she was dead-on."

"I'll take whatever we can get." Eric sighed, his head throbbing.

"So we hold out for a break. And in the meantime, you watch your back."

"It's not my back that needs watching." He lay back against the pillows, Sara's blue eyes flashing through his mind. "And that's what scares the hell out of me."

Sara sat on the sofa, wishing she could sleep, knowing it was impossible. The photo albums called to her as if they had human voices. Charlie, Tom . . . the past. Her life. She tried to push the memories aside, to concentrate on the future, but her past and future were tied together in a way she could never have imagined. Life intrinsically bound in time, nothing escaping without being part of the other.

Silly.

But real, and, as she opened the album, heartachingly tangible.

Sighing, she stared down at the photos. Charlie on his fourth birthday. Chucky Cheese—Madison Avenue's idea of parental hell—the wonder of a preschooler's existence. The memory brought a strange combination of joy and tears.

He'd been so little, so much of his life ahead.

And he'd been everything to her. Her life wrapped up in peanut-butter smiles.

Oh, dear God, she ached.

And there was nothing to take the pain away.

Nothing.

"You must have been an incredible mother."

The words washed over her, and she forced herself to concentrate on the here and now, valuable minutes ticking away, charged against her life account as if they didn't matter at all. She tilted her head, her mind angry at the intrusion, her heart rejoicing that he was there.

There were no words, and she struggled to find something—anything—that captured the essence of what she was feeling. "He was my baby."

"Your heart." Eric's words were simple, and she knew they were honest. God's truth.

"And it died with him." She'd never said that out loud, never admitted her fears, but somehow, with Eric, she needed to tell the truth. Needed him to know where she stood.

"It didn't die, Sara."

She clutched the scrapbook to her chest. "How can you possibly know that?"

"Because the heart is amazingly resilient. It has an infinite capacity to love." He reached out to touch her cheek, his dark eyes seeing far more than she wanted them to. "No one can ever replace them, but that doesn't mean there isn't room for someone new."

She swallowed, fighting against the emotions battling inside her. It was easy to be confused. There were so many questions. So much guilt and worry. She wanted to let go, if only for a minute. To let herself feel something good again.

To lose herself in the gray of Eric D'Angelo's eyes.

"You're supposed to be resting." She needed to change the subject, to steer away from the things that scared her.

"I don't think my head got the memo." He shrugged, the gesture emphasizing the strength of his body—his sheer size, her living room dwarfed by his mere presence.

She held the photo album as if it were a shield—in some intrinsic way, a barrier to the future, protection from life. The thought scared her even as it comforted. Like an ostrich, she'd managed to bury her head in the sand, hiding from all the things that threatened to hurt her. Possibly missing life in the process.

"I couldn't sleep." There was a world of meaning in his words, but she wasn't going there. She couldn't—wouldn't.

"The doctor prescribed a sleeping pill."

"I've no need for a sleeping pill, believe me." His silvery gaze met hers, the truth behind his words hitting home with an impact well beyond the physical.

"So what is it you want?" She regretted the question as soon as the words were out, her body already anticipating the answer.

"You." The word was simple, soul rending. And more frightening than she could have anticipated. Frightening because it was what she wanted more than anything.

Anything.

"I'm not sure I know how to do that anymore."

His smile filled her with hope. "I think it's like riding a bike. You just have to let go and remember." He studied her for a moment, the intensity in his gaze leaving her breathless. "You have to find it in your heart to trust someone, Sara."

"And you think it should be you?" The question left her breathless.

"I do." There was something compelling about the simplicity of his words.

"All right then." She held out her hand, her heart hammering in her throat, a testament to the risk she was taking.

A moment passed, and then another, and she almost

pulled back, fear threatening to overcome her resolve. But then he was there, his hand encompassing hers, his body effectively blocking her fear.

There was nothing between them now. Not her past, not his present. Nothing except the beat of their hearts and the intake of their breath. And, suddenly, she was no longer afraid. It was as if this was meant to be from the very beginning.

Destiny at its most unpredictable.

She'd have laughed, except the moment was deadly serious, the weight of her future hanging in balance.

He tightened his hold, pulling her closer.

"You can't do this." Her words were an excuse. A coward's way out. "You're hurt."

"Don't use my injury as an out, Sara." As usual he read her mind, and she cringed at the thought of it.

"I didn't mean—" She broke off, determined to at least keep her words honest. "Well, maybe I did, but you *are* hurt."

His smile was slow and sure. "I'm well enough for this."

She shivered, forcing herself to meet his gaze. "How is it you can read my mind?"

"Your eyes." He leaned closer, his breath teasing her cheekbones. "I never knew you could read a soul in someone's eyes." He reached out to tuck the hair behind her ear. "You're an incredible woman, Sara Martin."

"No, I'm not . . ." She started, but before she could finish, he was kissing her, and not the tentative touch of a suitor, but the passionate possession of a lover, the kiss of a man who knew what he wanted and would not settle for less.

The feel of his skin moving against hers was exquisite— sensual beyond belief. For the moment, there was nothing but him. His lips, his hands, the hard masculinity of his body. She needed him like she needed sustenance. Basic, like air or water. The very essence of her being.

His hands caressed her, finding the curve of her buttocks and the swell of her breast. The one touch calming, the other exciting in ways she'd completely forgotten. She surrendered to him then, reveling in the heat that resonated between them. The magic of the moment.

His mouth left hers to trail kisses along the line of her jaw, the shell of her ear. His tongue sending shivers of bliss dancing from nerve to nerve, whipping her passion to a fever pitch. They moved locked together, their steps choreographed by a connection both physical and spiritual. Each movement bringing them closer. Hearts beating together, clothing becoming an unwelcome barrier.

Taking her hand, he pulled her up the stairs, the touch of their hands binding in its simplicity. He stopped in the door of her bedroom, his eyes raking over her, his need etched on his face.

"You're sure." Even now his thoughts were for her, and tears sprang to her eyes.

Wordlessly, she reached up, untying the ribbons of her gown, the soft white cotton sliding against her skin to pool around her feet.

The night air was cool, and for a moment she was afraid. But then he was there, his heat consuming her, his mouth and hands worshipping. His kisses gentle, almost reverent.

Fumbling with buttons and zippers, she worked to free him from his clothes, desire spiraling through her with a power she'd never experienced before. It was as if she stood on a precipice, some intrinsic force urging her onward with the promise that she could fly.

Somewhere in the rational part of her mind, she knew this was an illusion, that the magic would vanish with the light of day, but she didn't care.

There was only the night and the man—this man.

Finally, skin to skin, they lay down on the bed, the cool cotton of the sheets a sensual backdrop for all that was to come. He ran his hands down the length of her body, caressing her, learning her. She closed her eyes, and let sensation carry her away.

His mouth was warm, and his touch delicious. He started

with her toes and worked his way to her calves, kissing the tender skin behind each knee. Anticipation built inch by inch, until she wanted to cry out. But she stayed silent, forcing herself to wait, knowing that it would be more than worth it.

His hands moved between her legs, his mouth following the curve of her inner thigh, his hot breath teasing her with its nearness. She arched her back, wanting more, and just when she thought she couldn't stand it, his tongue found her, laving her—loving her.

She cried out then, the joy almost more than she could bear. Clasping the back of his head, she urged him on, her need building with each stroke of his tongue, the fire inside her ratcheting higher and higher, until finally she jumped, leaving the precipice behind, flying higher and higher, reaching for the moon—knowing that it was reflected in the silver of Eric D'Angelo's eyes.

Eric felt her body shudder, and knew she had found release, and sliding up to cradle her against him, he was surprised at the contentment that rocked through him. It was as if he'd come home, found a place of safety he hadn't even known he'd been seeking.

His body ached for her, but still he held her. Wanting to prolong the bliss, the peace. It wasn't often he felt this way, and he knew it was a moment to be savored—cherished.

Her breathing was still erratic, her heart pounding against his, but she moved, pushing the hair back from her face, her gaze meeting his, eyes full of trust. It humbled him. And excited him.

With a groan, he pulled her into his arms, his kiss demanding, absorbing her with each taste, each touch. She met him halfway, her tongue dueling with his, taking as much as she gave. He shivered as her fingers caressed the hard planes of his chest, whispering butterflylike across his bandage to land firmly against his abdomen, her palm tracing circles of fire on his skin.

She tasted his neck, then slid down to take a nipple into

her mouth. Sucking and nipping, she savored him, the warmth connecting directly to his groin. Tightening almost to the level of pain, he throbbed for her, his penis impatiently pressing against the soft skin of her thigh.

"I need you." The words came from some place deep inside him, and were almost guttural in pitch and fervor. He'd never felt like this. As if part of him were missing. As if possessing her was the only way to feel whole.

She smiled up at him, and slid farther down, taking him into her mouth, the moist suction almost his undoing. Circling him with her tongue, she moved her hand as well, the rhythms combining to create pleasure so intense he thought he might explode.

Up and down, squeezing, stroking, he fought his body for control. When he came, he wanted to be buried deep inside her.

Connected.

He moved slightly, the shift enough to separate them. Then, still fighting to hang on to his control, he pulled her up, the friction of their bodies moving together a pleasurable pain. Unable to wait any longer, he flipped over, pulling her beneath him, his body covering hers. Bracing himself on his elbows, he looked down at her—eyes glazed with passion, mouth swollen from his kisses, breasts alabaster against the night.

With a crooked smile, she opened for him, the invitation more than just physical, and with a reverence of spirit, he slid home, her wet heat embracing him. They stayed that way for a moment, eye to eye, linked together as man and woman, the age-old dance suddenly taking on new meaning because he was with Sara.

Then she pushed against him, driving him deeper, her hands pulling him closer, urging him onward. Together they began to move, finding their own private rhythm—in and out, in and out, until there was nothing but the two of them, and the incredible sensation of the dance.

Bodies locked together, dancing faster and faster, until

the world exploded into shards of crystalline light, his body and mind oblivious of everything except the power of his orgasm and the feel of her breath against his skin.

A branch moved against the window, the scratching sound breaking the peaceful silence of the night. Sara rolled onto her back, immediately missing the warmth of the man sleeping next to her. As if reading her thoughts, he shifted in sleep, reaching for her, moonlight caressing his face. It seemed as if she'd been sleeping with him forever, their bodies fitting together like two halves of a whole.

Tom had always needed his space. And, because of it, they'd slept on separate sides of their king-size bed. Even after sex, they'd separated for sleep. It had been comfortable, routine. But now, with Eric's hand thrown possessively across her stomach, she mourned the intimacy she'd lost.

Or maybe it was meant to be different.

That might explain why she wasn't feeling guilty. She was, after all, lying in bed with a man who wasn't Tom. A man she didn't even really know.

Except that she did.

That was the truly amazing thing—she *did* know him. And despite the situation, despite her past, all she felt at the moment was content.

Warm, satisfied, and happy.

And to be honest, she couldn't remember the last time she'd felt this good. Surely that couldn't be a bad thing? Tom would have wanted her to be happy. She knew that. It was just that she hadn't been able to imagine herself with anyone else. Until now.

She blew out a breath, uncertainty replacing euphoria. She'd loved Tom. And he'd loved her. But Tom was dead.

"He'd want you to be happy." Eric was awake, and as usual, reading her mind.

She rolled over to face him, her heart swelling with emotion. "I know that. Honestly I do. It's just that—"

"You feel like you're betraying him. Look, maybe you're

just not ready for this after all." He pulled away, the distance more painful than she'd have expected.

"I don't know if I'll ever be ready. At least not the way you mean. But I'm here, now. And today I realized all over again that life can change in an instant. When Tom and Charlie died, a part of me shut down, and then you came along and for the first time since their deaths I felt stirrings of life. Then Bess called, and I thought it was happening all over again." She reached out, tracing the line of his jaw with her finger. "I thought I'd lost you, too."

"But you didn't." He covered her hand with his, his eyes full of emotions she was afraid to put a name to.

"No. But I could have. And that's when I realized that we only go around once, and I don't want to miss my turn because I'm afraid. I know I said I wanted to go slowly. But I've changed my mind. We're here—now. Together. And that's what matters. The rest of it we can sort through as we go." She swallowed nervously, trying to read his thoughts, praying that she hadn't misread him, that he'd felt the connection between them that she had.

His smile was quick, his teeth white against the stubble of his beard. "I can't tell you where we're going. Hell, I'm not even certain how we got here. But I do know something good when I see it. And together, we're good, Sara. More than good, actually—we're fantastic. So unless you change your mind, I'd say we're in this for the duration."

> *"I've got my eyes on you,*
> *so best beware where you roam.*
> *I've got my eyes on you,*
> *so don't stray too far from home.*
> *Incidentally, I've set my spies on you,*
> *I'm checking all you do, from a to z.*
> *So, darling, just be wise. Keep your eyes on me . . ."*

♫ ♪ ♫ ♪ ♫

The music swelled, then faded, only to start again, the warning clear enough. Fighting against his anger, he struggled for control, letting the music wash away his turmoil. She still hadn't come to him, and the fact annoyed him. Hadn't she seen the sacrifices he'd made? The things he'd done just for her? It was almost more than he could handle. *Almost.*

He turned to the woman on the chair, her blood staining the wall behind her. It had been tempting to cut out her heart. Fitting, since she obviously didn't have one. But it wasn't part of the plan, and he prided himself on his organization. Instead, he'd taken her eyes. At least they were the right color. And he liked the idea of an eye for an eye.

Disgust swirled through him, distorting the exhilaration of the kill. Maybe it was that he knew her. Or maybe it was that she'd been so unresponsive. Cunt. He kicked her for good measure, certain that she was beyond feeling.

The music crescendoed again, and he fought for composure, wondering how long it would take the bastard detective to discover his latest handiwork. If things had gone as planned, the man wouldn't be coming at all. But life was about setbacks. And good things came to those who waited. At least, that's what his mother'd always said. But then what the hell did she know?

Chapter 19

"What have we got?" Eric walked into the conference room, moving more slowly than usual but more comfortably than he'd have expected, considering the circumstances.

"You look well rested." Tony looked up from the file he was studying with a know-it-all grin. "I thought you were supposed to be at Sara's taking it easy."

"And leave you to have all the fun?"

Tony's grin faded as he extended a report. "You're not going to like this."

Eric scanned the piece of paper, then handed it back to Tony. "It says the brakes failed. That I already knew."

"You're missing the fine print." He tapped the paper. "It says here that the brakes failed because the bleeder valves were open."

Eric frowned at his partner. "You want to put that in English?"

Tony shook his head disparagingly, his expression tolerant. "Sometimes you really scare me, Eric. You know that?"

"Just because you think tinkering with cars is synonymous with testosterone doesn't make every guy a car jockey." He shrugged. "I know how to drive, and I know *mechanic* is under *m* in the Yellow Pages. What else do I need?"

"Just at the moment, a lesson in bleeder valves." Tony walked over to the white board and picked up a marker. "Okay, a brake system is really pretty simple. There's a master cylinder." He drew a box on the board. "It's attached to the brake pedal and the brake lines, which run to each wheel." He added lines connecting the wheels to the drawing. "The brake lines are actually connected to calipers that surround the rotor above each wheel." He drew a C-shaped figure around the rotor. "When the brake pedal is pressed, the calipers close and the brake pads push against the rotor, which ultimately slows the car."

"Lovely drawing, Tony, but what's the point?"

Tony blew out an exaggerated sigh. "Each caliper has bleeder valves, located right about here." He made some dark marks on the board and tapped them. "The hydraulic fluid that runs through the brake lines sometimes gets air or other contaminants in it, which makes the brakes feel spongy. The valves are there so that a mechanic can bleed the system and remove the air. Once the problem is resolved, the valves are shut again, and the drained fluid is replaced."

"But mine weren't closed," Eric studied the diagram, and then looked back at the report, "so every time I pressed on the brakes, fluid was draining away."

"And since we know you haven't taken your car for a checkup since Clinton was president, I think we can safely assume that the valves weren't left open by a mechanic. And since they can't open themselves, that means it was intentional, which means that someone wanted you to hit the road in a very literal way."

"Someone who knew cars." A nasty idea presented itself front and center. He looked up to meet Tony's gaze. "Someone like Jack Weston."

"It occurred to me, too. But unfortunately the techs haven't found any evidence aside from the valves. No fingerprints, no trace fibers, nothing. Still, it might be worth asking some questions."

"Anything in his background?"

"I'm still waiting on the file. According to the computer he's got a rap sheet, but I wanted to see the hard copy."

"So we wait. You get the report on Tom Martin's accident?"

"Yeah. The car was totaled and the report lists driver error as the cause. I looked at the photos, but you can't tell a damn thing."

"So it could have been the bleeder valves."

"Yeah, but there's nothing conclusive here to even say it was the brakes. Hell, the guy could have fallen asleep; he could have swerved for a deer. There's just no way to establish cause with what we've got. I even talked to the uniform who took the call. Problem is it was two years ago, and he doesn't remember anything other than what's already here in the report."

"Great." Eric ran a hand through his hair, frustration washing through him. "So all we can be certain of is that someone wants me out of the picture."

"Yeah. But what picture? It's not like you don't have enemies."

"No more than you."

"Yeah, but I'm not the one whose car is totalled."

Eric tipped back his head, rubbing his eyes. "What about the roses? Any luck with Molly?"

Tony frowned. "Still haven't been able to run her to ground. I had a uniform check the Dumpsters at the magazine. He didn't find anything. No card. No roses. Just a few petals. Which, according to the building's cleaning crew, could have come from the floor around Sara's desk."

"So we've hit an impasse."

"Not entirely. I got Sara's phone records." Tony walked back to the table, and picked up a printout. "I had them pull the calls on dates that correspond to Sara's caller. Since she noted the time on most of them, I've been able to pinpoint the calls. And there's an interesting correlation." Tony handed him the report. "Tracking against her log, it looks like Sara received a call within a couple of hours of each Sinatra murder."

Eric frowned down at the sheet, as if by staring at it, he could negate the yellow markings. "Are there other calls as well?"

"Yeah. But they all group around the murders, coming

within a day or so of each killing and then disappearing until the process starts over again."

"Nothing before a murder, though. Everything is after the fact." He looked up at Tony. "What about these numbers?" He pointed to the column that listed the caller's phone.

"Cell phones for the most part. The kind with prepaid minutes. If you pay for them with cash, they're virtually untraceable."

"Wonderful. Disposable phones."

"Yeah, it's a great world we live in." Tony straddled a chair. "There's a couple of pay phone calls, though. The one you traced to the bowling alley and one from a booth on East 12th. Interesting locations." He blew out a breath, his expression darkening. "The bowling alley is two blocks from Allison Moore's house. And the booth on East 12th is within a block of the hotel where Lydia Wallace was killed."

Eric felt the hairs on the back of his neck rise. "And the timing?"

"Dead-on."

"I wasn't expecting to see you this morning." Ryan stopped in the doorway of the magazine's coffee room.

"I'm going with Nate to interview Allison Moore's family. He wanted some pictures." Sara shot him a smile, then turned back to stir cream into her coffee.

"How's Eric?"

Now there was the million-dollar question. Despite all that had happened between them, he'd been gone this morning when she woke up, the indentation on his pillow the only sign that he'd been there at all. That, and a carafe of hot coffee on the kitchen counter.

A chivalrous notion, but she'd have rather had the man. Just the thought of him made her heart beat faster, her body tightening in anticipation, heat pooling between her legs.

None of which she wanted to share with Ryan.

"He's at work. At least I think so. He was gone when I woke up."

"Well, between the murders and his accident, he's got a lot on his mind." He poured a cup of coffee and sat down at the table opposite her. "And considering his profession, he's uniquely qualified to get answers."

"Yeah." She sighed, sipping her coffee. "I just wished he would have stayed in bed another day." *With me.* She didn't voice the rest of the thought, but based on Ryan's expression, she might as well have. Fortunately, he didn't comment.

"Any news on what caused the accident?" he asked, his expression turning thoughtful.

"Just that it had to do with the brakes. Something about hydraulics. The car was in surprisingly good shape, so hopefully they'll be able to find something concrete."

"Well, I'm just glad it wasn't any worse than it was."

"Me, too." She smiled up at him. "I don't know what I would have done if it had happened again."

"You'd have gotten through it, just like you did before. And we'd have all been here to help you." He reached over to squeeze her hand. "But it's a moot point. Eric is fine."

"Right." She stood up, squaring her shoulders. "And right now, I've got a job to do."

"You may be doing it on your own. I haven't seen Nate all morning. We were supposed to go over some ad copy at eight, but he didn't show."

"That's not like him. Maybe he got caught in traffic or something. Or maybe he went straight to the Doubletree." She turned her wrist so that she could see her watch. "We're due there in about twenty minutes."

"Maybe he just forgot the meeting. He was pretty upset last night. He'd heard about Eric, and wanted to go by and see you, but it was late and I suggested he wait."

"More reason for him to have gone without me. Did you try his cell phone?"

"No answer. But I'll bet you're right. He's probably on his way to the hotel."

"Then I guess I'd best get going." She rinsed her cup and put it on the drain board before heading for the door.

"Sara," Ryan called. "You're sure you're okay?"

"I'm fine. More than fine, actually." She smiled at Ryan, her thoughts turning back to Eric. "I'm great."

"Hey." Nate rushed into the room, tie askew, hair going every which way. "I'm sorry I'm late. I overslept."

Sara reached out to pull a rose petal off of his jacket. "In a bed of roses?"

Nate laughed. "No. That came from your desk. Remnants of yesterday's flowers. I was looking for you. Guess this little guy decided to come along for the ride." He grabbed the petal and tossed it into the trash. "Sorry about the ad copy, Ryan. Can we do it this afternoon?"

"No need. I handled it without you." Ryan's tone was just this side of condemning and Nate's face fell, a flash of anger in his eyes.

Sara placed a hand on Ryan's arm. "He said he was sorry."

"I know. I didn't mean to snap." Ryan smiled at Nate, the gesture going a long way toward easing the tension that had suddenly filled the room. "We've all been a bit stressed of late."

"It's okay." Nate shrugged. "I should have been here."

"No harm done." Ryan patted his shoulder. "I'll look forward to seeing your story on Allison Moore."

"Which we won't have at all if we don't get going," Sara said, keeping her voice light. If she hadn't known better, she'd have thought there was real animosity between Ryan and Nate, a veiled anger she'd never noticed before. But Ryan was right. They were stressed, and stress made everything look different.

It also made people connect in ways they normally wouldn't. Which meant that the bond she felt with Eric could potentially be nothing more than illusion. The thought was disheartening.

In a matter of days, he'd come to mean so much to her, and the thought that it might not last was simply more than she could bear. She shot a prayer heavenward, hoping that if God were listening, he'd hear her plea.

She needed Eric D'Angelo in her life—more than she could possibly have imagined.

"Jack hasn't exactly been a good boy." Eric and Tony walked down the hall toward the interrogation room where Jack Weston waited. As he walked, Eric read Jack's sheet. "Juvenile priors for loitering, petty theft, and two counts of aggravated assault."

"Anything current?" Tony asked.

Eric scanned the sheet. "An arrest for a bar brawl and another assault charge. This one a hooker."

Tony frowned. "Guy's obviously got a temper. But that doesn't necessarily make him a murderer."

"Yeah, but the pieces can be made to fit. He's a mechanic, so he sure as hell could have doctored my car. And we know he's got a thing for Sara." The last pulled at him more than he cared to admit.

"Which gives him motive. You're moving in on his territory and he decides to do something about it." Tony shrugged. "And I suppose from that you could make a case that he felt the same way about Tom. But none of it means anything unless we find something tangible to back it up." He stopped just outside the door, his expression grim. "Linking him to the Sinatra killer is going to be even harder. All we have is a series of phone calls with a pattern to suggest they *might* connect Sara to the murders. And except for Sara, we don't have anything that even hints at linking Jack to the killer."

"Except that he was conveniently on site when Sara was photographing Lydia Wallace, which means he was at least aware she existed."

"Still not enough to make a case."

"No. But maybe we can get Jack to help us." Eric's smile

held no humor. "We've established that he has a temper. So maybe we can leverage that into a confession."

Tony's smile didn't reach his eyes. "No time like the present."

Eric pushed open the door, his gaze colliding with Jack Weston's. There was anger there, and caution, but nothing that looked remotely unsettled. If the man had demons, they were tightly leashed.

"So you want to tell me what this is all about?" Jack gripped the edge of the table, as if the physical action was all that was holding him together. "I don't appreciate being hauled down here in the middle of a workday."

Tony crossed the room to sit at the table opposite Jack. Eric walked over to the barred window, leaning back against the sill. "We've come across some evidence that may link Sara's caller to the Sinatra killer."

Jack stood up, still gripping the edge of the table, his knuckles white. "So who the hell's watching out for Sara while we're having this little soirée?"

"We've got that covered, Jack, so please sit back down." Eric came over to perch on the end of the table. Jack complied, but from the look on his face, he wasn't thrilled with the idea.

Tony sat back in his chair, elbows on the arms, fingers steepled. "According to your rap sheet, you have quite a history with assault."

"I've been in trouble a few times. I told you about my background." His expression was wary, the obvious veteran of similar encounters.

"You told us that you spent your time protecting Sara from the big bad wolf. Which makes you a regular Boy Scout." Eric shrugged, deliberately keeping his posture relaxed. "But that's a far cry from what's here in your file."

Jack shrugged. "Ancient history, and I fail to see the relevance."

Tony made a play of reading the file. "Aggravated assault against a social worker seems relevant, no matter how long ago it was."

"The social worker was the bitch who wouldn't believe Sara." Jack met Tony's gaze without flinching. "I did what I did to protect her."

"Right." Eric paused, watching Jack, trying to see behind the facade. "And I suppose Sara is also the reason why you were arrested for assaulting a prostitute last year."

"Hell, no. Sara had nothing to do with that." Anger flared for a moment in his eyes. "I was drinking at a bar on the eastside, and a pro hit on me."

"So you beat her up." Tony prodded.

"No. Her pimp had that honor. Someone found her and called the police. If she'd ratted him out, she'd have been dead, so she fingered me instead. If you'd read the entire sheet you'd know the charges were dropped."

"For lack of evidence. You and your mother get along?"

Jack looked up startled. "My mother? What the hell does that have to do with anything?"

"Just curious." Tony's smile was humorless. "Men who have issues with women often have troubled relationships with their mothers."

"And you think my *issues* manifested themselves in the brutal murders of four women? Jesus, Detective, do I look like a freak?"

"From where I'm sitting you just look like a suspect." Tony closed the folder and leaned forward.

"Well, I didn't even know my mother. She died when I was born. So you'll have to bark up some other tree. I didn't kill anyone." There was genuine revulsion in his voice. "And I'd never do anything that could hurt Sara. If you can't see that, then you haven't been paying attention."

"But you don't like the fact that she's starting a relationship with Detective D'Angelo."

Jack shot a look at Eric, then stared down at his hands. "I don't like it. I admit it. But not because I have anything to hide or because I want Sara for some personal reasons. I don't like it because he's a cop."

"You hate cops?"

"No. I just hate the system. And I don't like the idea of Sara being jammed up in it again."

"I won't let anything happen to her." The words were out before Eric could stop them. Clearly unprofessional— evidenced by Tony's look of surprise. He glanced over at the two-way mirror, hoping like hell that Brady wasn't on the other side.

"You probably really believe that. But look at what happened yesterday. You scared her to death. I haven't seen her look like that since she lost Tom. And you know as well as I do that the odds are it'll just keep happening over and over until one day you don't come back. And where the hell does that leave Sara?"

Their gazes met and held, Jack's daring him to deny the truth.

"So you decided to fast-forward things a bit and take matters into your own hands?" Tony's question cut through the undercurrent, bringing them firmly back to the issue at hand.

"Now you're accusing me of doing something to your car?" Jack's gaze was still locked on Eric.

"I think it's within the realm of possibility," Eric said. "You're a mechanic. A damn good one to hear Sara tell it. And it certainly took someone in the know to sabotage my car."

"You have proof that the accident was deliberate?" Jack's surprise sounded genuine, at odds with his attitude. He was staring down at his hands again, his fingers still curled around the edge of the table.

"Yeah. Someone managed to open my car's bleeder valves, which as you well know made the *accident* a foregone conclusion."

"What did you say?" Jack's head jerked up, his face going white.

"I said that thanks to you my brakes failed."

Jack held up a hand, shaking his head. "No. Not that. I mean specifically what did you say."

Eric frowned, not certain what was happening.

Tony however, appeared to be with the program, whatever the hell it was. "He said that someone opened the bleeder valves."

"Holy shit." Jack buried his face in his hands, his expression bordering on horrified. "Holy fucking shit."

Chapter 20

"You're sure it was the bleeder valves?" Jack's color was a little better, but not much. His chin was resting on his hand, the casual pose at odds with the lines of tension radiating from his shoulders.

Tony tossed the report on the table. "See for yourself."

Jack reached for it, holding it between two fingers as if it might bite him. He skimmed the document, then looked up, his face reflecting his anguish. "I thought it was my fault."

"Thought what was your fault?" Tony's calm voice was a sharp contrast to Jack's discomfort. Designed to disarm, for once Eric thought it wasn't needed. Weston wanted to talk.

"Tom's accident. The car." He spoke in short bursts, as if he couldn't quite get enough air. "I thought I'd killed them."

"But now you don't?" Eric moved to sit in an adjacent chair, his attention now centered on Jack.

"No. Not if it happened to you, too." He motioned to the report.

"You want to tell us what the hell you're talking about?" Tony asked, his eyes narrowed in concentration.

"Sure. But there isn't much to tell." Jack was back to

staring at his hands. "In fact I told you part of it at the party." He shot a look at Eric. "After the accident, Sara didn't trust the police report. So she asked me to look at the car."

"But you told me you didn't find anything."

"I lied." Jack sighed. "There wasn't a lot of the car left, but the left front wheel casing was intact, along with the brake rotor and caliper." He paused, his gaze encompassing Tony and Eric. "The bleeder valve was open. And the only way that could have happened is if someone left it open."

"Intentionally." The word was sharp, Tony's expression harsh, as he considered the possibility.

"Or accidentally," Jack rushed to say, if possible, looking even more miserable. "I worked on the car a few days before the accident. Tom was kind of anal about his car. He didn't like the way the brakes felt. So I bled the system."

"And left a valve open."

"That's what I thought. But I didn't work on your car, Detective."

"It would have been easy enough for you to have access to it. It's not like you need special tools or anything." Tony eyes narrowed as he studied Weston. Judging him.

"I didn't do anything to your car." Jack met Eric's gaze straight on, unflinching.

"But you lied to Sara about Tom's car."

Jack dropped his gaze, his shoulders hunched inward. "It wouldn't have served any purpose. Tom was already dead."

"And you didn't want her to hate you." Tony's observation was dead-on.

The other man's head jerked up. "Would you? I love Sara. I've loved her for almost as long as I can remember. I'd do anything for her. The only constants she'd ever had in her life were Tom, Charlie, and me. If I'd told her that it was my fault she'd never have been able to forgive me, which would have left her with no one."

"Pretty arrogant, don't you think?" Tony asked.

Eric clenched a fist and said nothing.

"Maybe." He shrugged. "But I wasn't going to take the chance. You didn't see her. She was hanging on by a thread. The last thing she needed was to find out I was responsible for Tom and Charlie's accident."

"Of course there's also the fact that you could have been held criminally responsible for what happened. And with your record . . ." Tony purposefully let his words trail off.

"So I did want to protect myself. I'm not pretending to be a saint. But I also wanted to protect Sara."

"Enough to have sabotaged Detective D'Angelo's car?"

"*No.* I didn't do anything to his car. How many times do I have to say it? I wouldn't put Sara through that again. No matter what I think of you." Again he turned his attention to Eric, anger mixing with remorse. "The point here is that in light of what happened to your car, I don't believe I left Tom's valves open at all."

"You're suggesting there's a connection between Eric's car and Tom's." Tony's eyes narrowed as he considered the possibility.

"Yes. Bleeder valves are a simple way to accomplish sabotage, but they're not common knowledge, and you certainly have to know your way around a car to be able to pull it off. Especially without leaving any evidence. It could be coincidence, of course, but given the connection to Sara, and the rarity of the method used, it doesn't seem that big a leap. Someone wanted Tom and Charlie dead, and that same person wanted Detective D'Angelo dead as well."

Eric looked across the table at Tony, who shrugged slightly, his expression guarded. "Did you document what you found on Tom's car?"

Jack shook his head. "I just wanted it to go away. Wanted Sara to get on with her life."

"And with Tom out of the way, you were all set up."

"No." His voice was soft now, his face full of pain.

"But you said you loved her," Eric prompted, trying to keep his personal feelings at bay.

"Not like that." Jack frowned. "Sara is like my sister. I told you, she's the only family I've ever had. And I swear on my life, I'd never do anything to harm her." His eyes locked on Eric's. "Never."

And at least for the moment, Eric was inclined to believe him. Which left two murders, an attempted murder, and no one holding the bag. And, even worse, was the uneasy conviction that the accidents were only a prelude to something big.

Something tied to Sara.

And, quite possibly, to the Sinatra killer.

The Doubletree smelled like chocolate-chip cookies. Even in the private office management had provided for the interview, the smell permeated the air.

Amanda Moore was sitting across from Nate, her emotions securely in check, or perhaps it just hadn't hit her yet. Sara knew firsthand that the heart was capable of rejecting even the most valid of truths if the reality was too painful to bear.

Allison's sister, Paige, was more open with her feelings, wearing her anger for everyone to see. "I just don't understand how something like this could have happened."

"The police say there was no forced entry." Nate's voice was purposefully gentle. "That means she knew her killer. Or at least trusted him enough to let him into the house. Surely you can think of someone that might have had that kind of access."

Paige frowned. "She didn't have a boyfriend, if that's what you're getting at. And as far as I know the only other guys in her life were at work. And any friendship she had there wouldn't have included an invitation home."

"Well, someone got past her reserve." Nate's words were cold, but the sympathetic note in his voice negated the harshness.

"I know, and that's why it doesn't make sense." Mrs. Moore tilted back her head, obviously exhausted. "Allison

DANCING IN THE DARK

had so many locks on her door it made her security system superfluous. She simply wasn't the trusting type."

"How about workmen? Would she have let them in?"

"At that time of night?" Paige said, her frustration evident. "It doesn't seem likely."

"Well, the fact remains there had to have been someone."

"The only thing I can think of is the reporter. But that doesn't make any more sense than the rest of it."

"What reporter?" Nate leaned forward, frowning.

Paige chewed the side of her lip, her eyes narrowed in thought. "The last time I talked to Allie she was all excited about some interview she was going to do. A story on social workers. The reporter told her she was going to the focal point. She couldn't decide what to wear."

Mrs. Moore began to cry, the tears slipping down her face unheeded. Sara centered the lens, framed the shot: mother and daughter immortalized in their pain. Suddenly feeling like a voyeur, Sara lowered the camera.

"It's okay." Mrs. Moore said, brushing her tears aside. "I want you to take the picture." She squared her shoulders, forcing a wan smile. "If my photograph can make the world understand what this monster has done, then it's worth the price."

Sara nodded, wishing there were words to erase the hollow agony reflected in the woman's eyes. But there weren't. There simply weren't. Raising the camera again, she took the shot.

"We just want to avail ourselves of every option," Mrs. Moore said, her emotions once more under control.

"There could be something in the reporter angle. I can check up on that for you. If there was an interview, there should be a record of it somewhere. Austin isn't that big. And if we find the guy, maybe he'll have information that can help."

Hope crested then waned in Mrs. Moore's eyes as she digested the information. "But if he could help, wouldn't he have already come forward?"

"Possibly. Or he's not putting two and two together. Either way, it's worth following up on. Did you tell the police?"

Paige nodded. "I don't think it made much of an impression."

"Probably more than you realize. Sometimes it's the insignificant things that matter the most." Nate reached out for her hand and gave it a squeeze. "They're going to find the man who did this."

Surprise was replaced with gratitude and Paige offered him a timid smile.

Sara adjusted the lens and took the shot, the soft click of the camera seeming loud in the quiet room. Paige pulled her hand back, her expression closing off again.

"Do you have what you need, Mr. Stone?" Mrs. Moore slid a comforting arm around her surviving daughter. "I think we've had about as much as we can take for one day. And there are arrangements to be made."

Nate, who was still watching Paige, fumbled with his notes as Amanda Moore's question brought him back to reality. "I think so. You've been more than gracious. I realize how difficult this is, and I appreciate your taking the time to talk to me."

Mrs. Moore stood up, extending her hand, her smile for Sara as well as Nate. "I'm just glad that Allison's death won't go unmarked. You have my number in Abilene?"

Nate nodded, taking her hand. "I really do appreciate this."

"You just do for Allison what you did for Lydia Wallace and I won't have wasted my time."

Nate swallowed, obviously overcome with emotion. "I appreciate your confidence. I'll give it my best."

"Well, that was interesting." Tony strode into the squad room, his eyes narrowed in frustration. "You think he was telling the truth?"

"Jack? Hard to say for certain." Eric struggled against a rising sense of dread. "But he was pretty damn convincing in there."

"Unfortunately, I tend to agree." Tony sat on the edge of his desk.

"Well, we've got more than we had yesterday. We know that someone deliberately tampered with my brakes, and we know that it's possible that the same thing happened to Tom Martin and his son."

"And we know there's at least a tentative connection between Sara's caller and the time and location for the killings."

Eric nodded, his gut twisting into a knot. "So all we have to do is find a way to connect the dots."

"That's what we do, D'Angelo." Jordan Brady walked into the room, his expression inscrutable. "We find answers where there aren't any."

"Aw, hell, I knew I should have read the damn manual," Tony's eyes crinkled in a smile, then almost as quickly narrowed again. "You talk to the profiler?"

Brady nodded. "Just got off the phone with her. Name's Madison Harper. According to Katie Brighton, she's really good. Been with the bureau a long time, most of it with the Investigative Support Unit. She faxed her report. Figured you guys would want to see it."

"Anything helpful?"

"Yeah, in a weird hocus-pocus kind of way. Read it for yourself." He tossed the fax on the desk. Eric picked it up, Tony moving to peer over his shoulder.

There were a couple of introductory paragraphs restating the facts of the crime, then a list of attributes. It was the list that interested him most.

Average looking white male between the ages of 25 and 35, probably closer to the end of the range, no obvious impairments; no long-term relationships with women; problems with dominant female in his life; orderly; persuasive but also insecure; high IQ; highly manipulative; probably holds a day job; no remorse; drives a dark car; externalizes through killings; repeat offender, possibly in another locale.

"And we're supposed to believe she just pulled that out of thin air?" Tony asked.

"It's pretty damn eerie, but honest to God, once she finished explaining it, she'd turned me into a believer." They walked into the conference room, settling down at the table, Brady consulting his notes. "Why don't we start at the top? I think we can all agree that he's male. The age range is based on the fact that the amputations and planning are well executed, indicating that the guy's fantasy is well formed. That gives us an older killer. But when you factor in the overkill, and the violent nature of it, you're back to someone younger. Older killers tend to be more methodical, which is why she gave us a range."

"I admit that makes sense," Tony said, "but how the hell does she know he's good looking?"

"Actually the report says average looking. Whoever this guy is, he's not outwardly alarming. You know as well as I do that hookers have good radar. And this guy obviously didn't set it off. And in Allison's case, we have an overly cautious woman who just let the guy in. That also fits in with the idea of him being persuasive." Brady tipped his head toward the list in Tony's hand. "The fact that the guy can't keep a girl ties into the fact that he has a problem with a female somewhere in his life."

"That one is pretty self-evident. I mean, we know that in the majority of cases where a serial killer targets seemingly unrelated females, he has an issue with a woman," Eric said. "Usually a wife, mother, or girlfriend. And considering the severity of the object rape here, I'd say our guy is royally pissed about whatever it is and intent on inflicting his own brand of punishment."

"Now there's a blinding glimpse of the obvious." Tony mumbled, still looking at the list. "I'm assuming *orderly* is postulated on the fact that the kills are so well executed. And that there's little evidence at the scenes."

Brady nodded. "That and the fact that he's obviously planning the killings ahead of time." He consulted his notes again. "The high IQ is a given. These guys always skew that way."

"And the day job is based on the fact that except for Allison, the killings all happened late at night." Eric narrowed his eyes, scrutinizing the list.

"His remorselessness is based on the fact that he leaves his vics in plain sight, still bound and not covered in anyway," Brady continued. "And the dark car is evidently a common correlation with highly organized people. And we've already established that given the kill pattern and developed ritual, our guy is seriously methodical. The last two are also obvious, given the others. He's killing face-to-face, externalizing his attacks, and his ritual is too developed for Laurel to have been a first-time kill."

Brady put the paper down and blew out a breath. "So we've got a guy in his mid-twenties, easy on the eyes, who has a hell of grudge against someone."

"You just described half the males in Austin." Tony shrugged. "And we looked for priors, twice, but nothing matched our guy. She say anything else?"

"She thinks that so far the killings are ways for him to externalize his frustration, to sublimate it away from the real target. But the escalating violence is a sign that it's not working as well as it did originally. And, ultimately, she thinks he'll stop using surrogates."

Eric's skin tingled, his heart twisting inside, his mind conjuring images of Sara. He tried to assure himself that the connection wasn't solid, that it was spurious at best, but he couldn't quell the sick feeling in his stomach.

"She's going to continue to study the files, and see what else she can put together." Brady was still talking, unaware of the turn of Eric's thoughts. He forced himself to concentrate on the lieutenant's words. "She also suggested that we let the press know we've contacted the FBI and that their profile of the perp fits closely with the evidence."

"But it doesn't," Tony offered.

"But the press doesn't know that. And, more important,

the killer doesn't know it. These guys like to believe they're winning, so sometimes tightening the noose can flush them out into the open."

"And get someone else killed." Eric wasn't a fan of manipulating offenders. With serial killers there was a tendency for it to backfire.

"Madison also offered to give us access to their database. We can take another look at priors. But the clock is ticking. You know as well as I do that the more distance we have from this thing, the more likely the trail goes cold. Start with the database and see if anything new pops up."

"We're already on it." Eric stood up, rubbing his side, his ribs aching.

Brady nodded, then turned on his heel and walked from the room.

"You didn't tell him about Sara." Tony's frank gaze met his.

"I figured it could wait. It's not like we have anything concrete to tell him." Eric shrugged, reaching for his beeper as it went off. "And besides, for the moment at least, we've got it covered." He read the text as it scrolled across the pager's screen, his blood running cold.

They'd found another woman.

And this time it wasn't a stranger.

Sara stopped at the light, her car idling to the beat of the radio, Toni Price's "Call of My Heart" helping her to lighten her mood. It was hard to see the good side of anything after the interview with the Moores. Life's abrupt turns seemed to blindside the best of people at the worst of times.

But then maybe that's what it was all about. Dodging and turning. Trying to make the best of whatever life gave you. She'd always been somewhat of an optimist, and even with all that had happened, she still couldn't quell the hope that there was a silver lining out there somewhere.

She laughed at herself, and turned up the music, wondering when she'd become a philosopher. Traffic surged forward as the light changed, and her thoughts turned to Eric. It had all seemed so right in the dark of the night. But here she was in the harsh Texas sunlight wondering what exactly had happened between them.

He'd said they were in it for the duration, but then she'd woken up alone. Intellectually, she knew he'd probably needed to get to work, but in her heart there was a glimmer of doubt, the niggling worry that she'd misread the signs, asked for more than he could give.

The truth was she needed to talk to him, to hear his voice, to know that last night had meant as much to him as it had to her.

As if on cue her cell phone rang, and her heart did a little flutter step. She turned off the radio and clicked on the phone. "Hello."

Music filled the car, at first confusing her, then sending shards of ice stabbing through her. The song was an old one, but she recognized it immediately. It had been a favorite of Tom's, the lyrics taking on new meaning as they rang out from the phone.

"I'm checking all you do, from a to z. So, darling, just be wise, keep your eyes on me . . ."

She pulled into a parking lot, afraid that she wouldn't be able to drive, and with shaking fingers fumbled to disconnect the call. But before she could find the button, a tinny voice replaced the music, the automaton quality doing nothing to lessen the impact of the words.

Molly was dead.

Chapter 21

Sara fought for breath, finally locating the phone's disconnect button. Her heart felt as if it was cracking through her chest. She hit the brakes, shifted to park, and beat on the steering wheel, anger combining with terror, the phone still clutched in her hand. The caller was gone, the phone disconnected, but it didn't matter. His voice rang through her ears, over and over again.

Molly is dead, Molly is dead, Molly is—*dead*. The word reverberated in her head, taunting her. Frightening her. She wanted to scream, to throw something. To drive her car through the Jiffy Mart. But none of that would help Molly.

She needed to find her friend. To prove the caller wrong.

She ground the key in the ignition, and it was several seconds before she realized the car was already running. Slamming it into gear, she drove out of the parking lot, heading for Molly's house, already dialing Eric's number at the precinct, praying that he was there.

The number rang for what seemed an eternity and was finally picked up by the switchboard. From there she was transferred to another detective. With a minimum of words she explained herself, trying to convey the urgency of the situation. He urged her to come into the station, but she refused, disconnecting the phone as she swerved onto Molly's street.

There were police cars everywhere, several with lights still flashing, an ambulance blocking the front drive. Her stomach tightened until she was certain it was going to implode, nausea clawing at her throat, the bile bitter. The caller had been telling the truth.

Molly *was* dead.

Sobbing now, she pulled the car to the curb and killed the engine, already opening the door. With a single motion she was out of the car and running across the lawn, imagining the worst. Pushing past an officer, she stopped in the entry hall, her stomach almost giving up the battle.

There was blood splattered across the wall by the window, the pattern lacy and grotesque. The room was a wreck, as if Molly had fought her attacker, her blood staining the carpet and sofa as well as the wall. Dead roses were strewn everywhere, their fading color garish against the white room, a macabre punctuation of the horror that had happened here.

Sara swallowed a scream, her hand crammed into her mouth as if to manually keep it from emerging. A tech was lifting a body onto a stretcher, the telltale red hair a stake right through her heart.

She started to move, but before she could take a step, strong hands closed around her. She fought at first, blind to reality, seeing nothing but Molly's bloody body, hearing nothing but the taunting voice, but finally the tenor of the voice sank in, the sound an anchor amid madness.

Eric.

Eric was here. In the house. He'd know what to do. She swung around into his arms, burying her face in his chest, wanting nothing more than to wake up from the nightmare.

"She's alive, Sara. Molly's alive."

At first the words made no sense, and then they hit home with a clarity that brought relief. "He said she was dead." The words came out on a whisper. "The bastard said she was dead."

Eric's voice was gentle, his hand stroking her hair. "Who said it, Sara?"

"I don't know. He called me." Sara struggled for breath.

"He told me she was dead." She pushed away from him, swiveling around to look at the stretcher, to reassure herself that Eric was right.

A tech was holding an IV, and another was checking for vitals, their pace frenetic as they worked to stabilize Molly for transport. Sara slipped from Eric's grasp, moving forward, intent on reaching her friend.

But she slid to a stop a few feet away, her horrified gaze locked on Molly, her knees buckling, the world spinning into a nauseous blur of crimson and white. She felt Eric's hands, heard his voice, but couldn't understand the words.

All she could see was Molly's face, two bloody gashes where she'd once had eyes.

Eric knelt beside Sara, grateful to see that some of her color had returned. She sat on Molly's front porch in a rattan rocker, clutching his hand as if it were a lifeline. She hadn't said anything since he'd ushered her out here, away from the gruesome sight of Molly's butchered eyes.

Rage boiled inside him, tempered with helplessness. He wanted to make it right somehow. To pull Sara into his arms and promise that her friend would be okay. But he knew it was an empty promise. Molly's condition was critical. She'd lost a lot of blood. It was anyone's guess if she'd survive.

Sara whimpered, almost as if she shared his thoughts, and the idea cut at his heart, the pain almost physical. In an instant, with a phone call, the game had changed. It had become personal. And Eric wasn't going to rest until the bastard was behind bars.

"The ambulance just left." Tony strode onto the porch, his expression mirroring Eric's anger. "She's hanging in there. But just barely."

Sara's head shot up, her eyes locking on Tony. "Where are they taking her?"

"St. David's."

"I need to go. I need to be with her." Sara struggled to stand, faltered, then used Eric to lever herself up.

He rose, too, sliding an arm around her. "You're not in any condition to drive. Officer Jenkins can take you." He nodded to a uniform standing discreetly by the shrubbery. "He'll watch out for you."

She lifted her head, confusion awash in her eyes. "Aren't you coming?"

Regretful, he shook his head. "Right now I'm needed here. I'll come as soon as I can, though."

She nodded, started toward Jenkins, then stopped, lifting her gaze to meet his. "I want you to find him, Eric." Her eyes cleared, and hardened. "And when you do, I want you to make him pay."

He nodded, then bent his head to brush a kiss across her forehead. "We'll get through this, Sara. All of us. *Together*." He stressed the last word, and she nodded again, then turned to go.

He watched her walk away, his heart twisting inside him, the pain in her voice etched inside it. Pulling in a deep breath, he forced his mind back to business, calling on all his years of experience to do it. "Any idea what Molly's chances are?"

"They're not saying," Tony said as they walked back into the house. "But I wouldn't think they're good. She's not conscious and she's lost a hell of a lot of blood. The tech said it probably happened this morning. He can't be certain, of course, until they run more tests. But at least it's a starting point."

"And a change in pattern. Night to day. Question is whether there's a specific reason or if it's just happenstance." Eric's gaze swept the room. "There's a randomness here that's different from the other scenes. It's almost as if this one wasn't planned. Molly wasn't tied up. And, at least from the look of things, I'd say she fought like hell."

"Still, there are similarities. He took a trophy. And it looks like he at least tried to rape her." Tony waved his hand toward a theatrical award that lay in pieces on the floor, the tip bent and bloody. "And there was music."

"Except that the boom box was turned off."

"Maybe there was a technical malfunction." Tony shrugged.

"No way." Eric shook his head. "Everything this guy does has meaning. *Everything*. The techs find anything?"

"They're still working. So far they've found some fibers, but that's about it. No fingerprints. And no weapon."

"Wouldn't want it to be easy." Eric rubbed the bridge of his nose, a headache threatening, the perfect companion to his aching ribs.

"This is a new touch." Tony bent and picked up a rose petal. "They found more of them in Molly's trash. Forensics is going to compare them to the petals found at Sara's office. There was no sign of the card."

"If the flowers are the same, then maybe it explains the escalation of violence."

"How do you figure?" Tony let the petal fall, and they both watched as it wafted to the floor.

"According to Sara, it was Molly who suggested throwing out the flowers. And it was Molly who actually took them away."

"So, what, you think the killer was pissed because Molly threw out the flowers?" Tony frowned, his mind already considering the possibility.

"No, I think it's Sara he's angry with. She's the one who rejected the flowers. Molly's just another surrogate. Considering she helped Sara dispose of the roses, an apropos one, but still a substitute for the real thing."

"All that assuming that the killer and Sara's stalker are the same."

"I think the fact that he called to tell her about Molly makes it pretty damn certain. If the roses are a match, I'd say we're dead-on." The sick feeling was back in the pit of his stomach.

"Nice to see you back in action, D'Angelo." Claire Dennison walked through the doorway, stepping carefully around the trophy. "I should have known a little car wreck wouldn't keep you from a scene. Vic's alive?"

"Yeah. Barely." Eric struggled to push his personal feelings aside. This was still a case, and he fully intended to work it. Now more than ever, he wanted to find the bastard.

"Sounds like she was lucky." Claire knelt by the marker where Molly had lain, scrutinizing the bloodstain.

"Depends on how you look at it, I guess." Tony shrugged. "She's lost her sight for certain, and there's no telling what else the bastard took from her."

"She obviously has a strong will to survive. That'll carry her a long way. This where they found her?"

Eric nodded.

"It's not where she was hurt." Claire lifted a strand of what looked to be carpet thread and dropped it into an envelope.

"How can you tell?" Tony asked, his curiosity getting the better of him.

"Blood pattern." She stood up, her eyes scanning the room. "See over there? It's almost a spray." She pointed at a wall near a ladder-back chair. "I'm betting the perp did his worst over there."

Tony walked over to the chair, leaning over to examine it. "You're right. There's blood on the caning."

"Along with everything else in the room," Eric said, walking over to have a look at the chair himself. "Anything unique in the pattern here?"

"Possibly." Claire joined them, her gaze thoughtful. "See the spatter behind the chair? According to the EMT folks, the perp cut her eyes out, right?"

Tony and Eric nodded almost in unison.

"Right. Well, this stain," she pointed at the wall, "is consistent with that. Along with the pattern here." She lowered her hand to point at the seat. The edges of the seat were spattered, but the center was unmarked, as if something had covered it.

Molly.

"I need to verify it all, of course. See how the evidence lines up. But I'd say your girl was here. And most likely left to bleed out."

"But she moved."

"Exactly."

"So what?" Tony sputtered. "The guy had an attack of conscience? That doesn't seem likely."

"No." Eric said, shaking his head, his eyes meeting Claire's. "She crawled."

"As amazing as it sounds, it looks like that's exactly what she did. Could be she was heading for the phone." Claire nodded at the cordless on the coffee table. "You know who called it in?"

"Dispatch got it from 911," Tony said. "We've got people checking the recording now."

"Well, there was blood on the phone and it was found beside her, so it seems probable that it was her. Either way, her movement probably saved her life. The position of her body acted as a tourniquet of sorts, slowed the blood flow." She scanned the room again, her professional gaze missing nothing. "Whatever the hell's going on here, I'd say things are definitely heating up."

Sara sat in the surgical waiting room, her back pressed into a corner. Even with Officer Jenkins at the door, she didn't feel safe. The vague threat of a serial killer had morphed into something far more immediate. Hitting so close to home, she almost felt like he was here somewhere, watching her.

She'd tracked down Molly's mother. Diana Parker was in London on business, and wouldn't be able to arrive in Austin until late tomorrow. Never particularly close to her daughter, Diana had nevertheless been concerned about Molly, and consulted with doctors to make decisions until she arrived. Until then, Sara was to hold down the fort.

Sara, however, wasn't so certain she wanted the responsibility. But Molly was her closest friend, and she'd do what had to be done. But it would be nice to have reinforcements. Bess and Ryan were on the way, but in the meantime, except for Jenkins, she was alone.

Automatically, she glanced over at the doorway. Jenkins

wasn't much more than a kid, with a fresh-scrubbed face that was at odds with the gun in his holster. Still, he represented safety. And she knew that it came from Eric. If he couldn't be with her, he'd at least sent someone in his stead.

It wasn't exactly the same. But the gesture meant a lot. And in light of the phone call, there could be no doubt that it was necessary.

Molly was in surgery, and probably would be for hours to come. She'd suffered massive internal injury in addition to the loss of her eyes. Sara fought against a gag, the image of Molly's ravaged face clear in her mind.

The doctors hadn't been very forthcoming, only saying that Molly's odds weren't good. But Sara had hope. Her friend was alive, and that had to count for something.

She tipped back her head, rubbing her temples, her thoughts turning to Eric. He'd been worried about her. And angry. She'd seen it in the hard steel of his eyes, the possessive glint confirming his feelings for her in a way that words never could.

She wanted to reassure him, to tell him that she was fine. But it would be a lie. She wasn't fine at all. Her friend was in there fighting for her life, and some sicko was out there laughing at them all.

She wrapped her arms around her waist, wishing for Eric, needing to feel his arms around her, to know that as long as he held her, nothing more could happen, that she was safe.

As if in answer to her plea, Jenkins stepped back, and someone stepped through the doorway. And in less than a heartbeat, she was across the room, stopping short when she realized it was Jack, not Eric.

"Thank God you're all right." He reached for her hands, his eyes telegraphing his relief.

"I'm fine." She wasn't, of course, but it was the easiest response. "How'd you know I was here?"

"Ryan, actually. He called to tell me about Molly."

She nodded. "She's in surgery."

"I know. I talked to the nurse. It doesn't sound good."

"Molly's a fighter." She'd said those words so many times. Now if only they were true.

"Listen, Sara," Jack lowered his eyes, his gaze not quite meeting hers, "there's something I need to talk to you about."

"Can't it wait?" She couldn't see how anything he had to say could be more important than Molly.

"No. It's important, and I need you to hear it from me."

"All right." She wasn't certain she could handle anything more, but she loved Jack, and because of that she was willing to listen. "Tell me."

"I was at the police station earlier today. Your friend D'Angelo believes his car's malfunction was intentional."

"You're saying someone deliberately tried to kill Eric?" The breath whooshed out of her throat, her heart constricting as she considered the implications.

Jack nodded, his expression somber. "Apparently he thought I might be responsible. That's why I was at the station. He had some questions, and quite honestly, there was some pretty damning evidence. I can see why he'd have suspected me."

"But he doesn't anymore." It was a statement, not a question.

Jack shook his head. "Come sit over here." He shot a telling look at Officer Jenkins and pulled her over to the far corner of the room, lowering his voice to a whisper.

She sat down, meeting his troubled gaze. "I don't understand any of this, Jack. Why would Eric believe you tried to kill him?"

"Because someone tampered with his car. And since I'm a mechanic, it seemed a reasonable assumption. Especially when you add in the fact that I was already under suspicion. One of the pictures you took of Lydia Wallace had me in it, too."

Sara frowned, forcing her thoughts away from Eric. "What?"

Jack stared down at his hands, his expression inscrutable.

"I was there that day. I was worried about you going down there on your own."

"So you followed me?" Her head was spinning, the information coming too fast to process properly. "Why didn't you just tell me?"

"Because I knew you'd be mad."

"I might have been. But it would have kept you from looking suspicious to the police. Anyway, you said that Eric doesn't suspect you anymore. So that's the end of it, right?"

He shook his head, still not meeting her gaze. "There's more. It's just that I don't know how to start."

She reached for his hand. "Just say it."

He looked up at her then, his eyes dark with worry. "I lied to you, Sara. I had good reasons, or at least I thought I did. But now, under the circumstances, you need to know the truth."

Confusion washed through her, coupled with alarm, the little voice in her head screaming a warning. "What circumstances?"

Jack blew out a long breath, regret mixed with anguish coloring his expression. "I told you that Eric's car had been tampered with."

"Is there something more?" She gripped his hand, holding on for dear life. "Did something else happen to Eric?" The last came out low, almost a hiss, her throat tightening with fear.

"Nothing happened, Sara. He's fine. This is about Tom and Charlie."

She sat back, struggling for breath, confusion replacing fear. "I don't understand."

"When you asked me to look at Tom's car, I told you I didn't find anything. But the truth is I did find something."

She hadn't thought she had any emotion left, not after all she'd just been through, but she was wrong. Jack's words were like a sucker punch. Blood pounded in her ears.

"Is everything okay over there?" She'd forgotten about Officer Jenkins. Forgotten about everything but Jack's announcement.

She struggled for control, then forced a nod. "We're fine. Just talking about Molly." The lie was unnecessary, but she couldn't bring herself to put the other into words. She returned her attention to Jack, her mind still spinning. "What did you find?"

"The front bleeder valve was open. I thought I'd done it, that the accident was my fault." He shook his head, tears glistening in his eyes. "I couldn't stand the idea of your knowing, so I lied."

She nodded, as if it made sense. But of course it didn't. It couldn't. Jack had killed Tom and Charlie? The idea seemed preposterous. As if she'd fallen down the rabbit hole—everything turned inside out.

"So why are you telling me now?" She pulled her hand away, not wanting him to touch her, wanting more than anything to put distance between them, to take away some of the pain slicing through her.

"Because I think you could be in danger. Look, the bleeder valves on Eric's car were tampered with, too. The same as Tom's. And while I certainly could have been responsible for Tom's accident, I've never been near Eric's car. According to Haskins, nobody has. Don't you see, Sara? Until I saw the evidence, I would have sworn Tom's car was in top shape. I'm a good mechanic and I'm careful."

"Everyone makes mistakes, Jack." She wasn't sure if she was talking about the accident or the lie. Both, probably. And she wasn't sure how she felt about either. There was simply too much to deal with.

"Yes, but I didn't make a mistake. That's the point. Someone deliberately tampered with both cars." He reached for her, but she pulled back, ignoring the resulting pain that flashed in his eyes. "I was wrong not to tell you, Sara, and I'm sorry. But what's important right now is that you understand that if I'm right, and Tom's accident is related to Eric's, then someone out there wants to hurt you."

Suddenly everything seemed clear, the emotions making way for the harsh light of reality. "Tom and Charlie were murdered." The words came out on a breath of air, as if by whispering, she could keep them from being true.

Jack nodded, his gaze locking with hers. "I'm sorry, Sara."

She chewed on her upper lip, trying to keep from crying. Tears wouldn't do anyone any good. Not Molly. Not her husband or her son. Not Eric. She needed to be strong. To face all of it head-on.

Starting with Jack.

She swallowed, realizing she felt numb, her thoughts cascading through her with the velocity of a pinball, the information coming faster than she could possibly process. "I don't know what to say."

"Don't say anything. Just take care of yourself. And remember I did what I did in part because I didn't want you hurt any more than you already were."

"Jack, I think you should leave," Eric said, striding into the room, his silvery eyes flat and cold.

Jack opened his mouth to argue, but Eric's expression brooked no disagreement. Jack nodded, then shifted so that his gaze met Sara's. "I'd never do anything purposefully to hurt you. You've got to believe that."

Sara shook her head, ignoring the plea in his eyes. "Please. Just go." He stood for a moment, devastation etched across his face, then turned to walk from the room.

She tried to get up but her knees refused the order, buckling instead. There was simply too much happening. And everything was coming so fast. In two strides, Eric was beside her, his strong arms closing around her, his strength her undoing.

The tears came with the force of a hurricane. And she let them come, crying for Molly, for Jack, for Tom, for Charlie, for all that she'd lost. And Eric held her. His hands stroked her hair, her back, comforting with just a touch—his body shielding her, keeping her safe from harm.

At least for the moment.

Chapter 22

"I'm sorry," Sara said, her words muffled against his chest. "I don't usually lose it like this. It's just that so much has happened."

"It's okay." He stroked the soft silk of her hair, wishing there was something he could do or say to make it easier for her, something that would simply make it all go away. But of course there wasn't. "Considering everything that's happened, I'd say you're doing remarkably well."

She pulled away from him, brushing ineffectually at her tears, her somber gaze colliding with his. "Is what Jack said true? Were Charlie and Tom's deaths intentional?"

"I don't know for certain. There isn't any evidence. Jack destroyed what he found. But I believe the bleeder valves were tampered with. There's no reason for Jack to have admitted he found them if it weren't true."

"You don't suspect him anymore."

"Not at the moment. But until we figure this out, everyone stays on the list."

"And you? Is it true that someone tried to kill you?"

He thought about lying, but knew he couldn't. She deserved the truth. "It looks that way. Someone definitely tampered with the valves on my car."

"So it's my fault?" Her eyes were still awash with tears.

"Of course not. We can't even say for certain that the two incidents' commonalities are anything other than circumstantial. Jack shouldn't have told you. Not here. Not like this."

She nodded, walking over to the window, watching the traffic below. "But he did. And now I can't get it out of my mind."

He came to stand behind her, his hands on her shoulders. "If there's a connection, we'll find it. And in the meantime, I'll be here to watch over you."

She turned to face him, her gaze locking with his. "And who's going to watch out for you?"

He smoothed her hair. "I'll be fine."

She reached up to touch his face, the simple gesture more telling than any words, then, with a sigh, she turned back to the window. "Did you find anything at Molly's house?"

"Some fibers. A pattern of events. Not much else. There were loads of fingerprints, but nothing, at least on the surface, that looks like a direct link to the killer. We'll know more after they've examined the evidence more closely."

"So the truth is you really don't have any idea who's behind all of this."

He wanted to tell her they had something. That they were going to nail the man. But they didn't. "We have bits and pieces, but nothing conclusive. This guy is playing a game, and it's up to me to try and figure out the rules. Hopefully, then, I'll be able to identify a suspect."

"But he's calling me." The words were low, almost inaudible, as if saying them out loud was more than she could handle.

"I know. And if there was a way I could get to him, stop him, believe me I would . . ."

"You're doing the best you can." She turned to face him. "I know that. It's just that suddenly it's gotten a lot more personal."

He led her over to a chair, straddling the seat next to

hers. "Maybe more than you know. Tony found a pattern in your previous calls. A relation to the Sinatra killer. The calls start just after a murder, cluster there, then taper off until there's another one."

She frowned, saying nothing, fear cresting in her eyes.

"And in addition, there's the fact that the two calls we could trace came from phone booths within a couple of blocks of the respective murder sites."

"Why didn't you tell me?"

"I wasn't sure there was a correlation, but now with the latest call, I don't think there's any doubt."

"So why is he calling *me*?"

"I don't know. I wish to hell I did." He blew out a breath, feelings of inadequacy threatening to overwhelm him. But he knew from long experience that emotion was a detective's greatest enemy. It clouded judgment and colored the facts. With a grimace, he ruthlessly pushed his feelings aside. The important thing now was to concentrate on protecting Sara. Until the killer was found, nothing else mattered. "Look, I know you told me about the call at Molly's. But I want to hear about it again. All the details. You think you're up to it?"

She nodded. "There really isn't much to tell. I was driving home from the interview with Amanda Moore and her daughter."

"The call came in on your cell phone?" He frowned, his senses on alert.

"Yes."

"Do you have it with you?"

"Yeah." She frowned. "But I don't see."

"The number should be registered on the phone."

"Oh, God." She fumbled with her bag, extracting the phone and handing it to him. "I never even thought . . ."

"It's all right. You were thinking about Molly." He hit a couple of buttons and then studied the tiny LCD screen.

"Is it there?"

"There's a number, yes." He held it out for her to see. "Do you recognize it."

She stared at the number, eyes narrowed in concentration and then shook her head regretfully. "I don't recognize it."

"It's okay." He reached over to touch her hand. "I'd have been surprised if it was familiar. I'll have it traced when I get back to the department. So where were you exactly when the phone rang?"

She frowned, concentrating on remembering. "Lamar and Guadalupe. Where the two roads come together. I'd stopped at a light. When the phone rang, I answered. But all I heard was the music."

"Sinatra."

"Yes. A song called 'I've Got My Eyes on You.' I recognized it because Tom used to play it a lot."

"We found the same song at Molly's."

"Oh, God." She wrapped her arms around her waist, sucking in an audible breath. "So you think he was there? At her house?"

"It's possible, but I don't think so. The timing isn't right."

"Either way it was like the guy was there in the car with me. And before I could disconnect, he talked to me."

He reached over for her hand. "Anything you recognized in the voice?"

She shook her head. "It was tinny. Like he was using something to disguise it. And he only said the one thing."

"That Molly was dead."

"Yes. Only she wasn't." Her eyes met his, her gaze questioning. "How come he didn't know she was still alive?"

"We think he left her to bleed out. He probably thought she was dead, or damn close to it. But he underestimated Molly. She managed to crawl to the phone. Maybe even used it. We're trying to confirm it now."

"Wasn't there a recording? Can't they tell if it's Molly?"

"Yeah, but the recording isn't clear. And it's hard to identify the voice."

"So someone could have been disguising their voice?"

"Or Molly could have been having difficulty speaking.

There was blood on the phone, so the odds are on Molly, but there's no way to know for sure until she wakes up."

"And if she doesn't?" Sara eyes brimmed with tears again.

"She will." He tightened his grip on her hand. "I'm just sorry I couldn't be here earlier."

"It's okay. You needed to be there—at Molly's. And Officer Jenkins has been great."

"He's been assigned to watch over you. That way when I can't be with you, I won't have to worry that you're on your own."

"I'd rather it was you." Again the words came out on a whisper, this time tentative, as if she wasn't certain of their reception.

In an instant he was on his feet, pulling her into his arms. "I want it to be me, too."

"But you were gone this morning." Her eyes searched his, the hurt reflected there shooting through him like an arrow.

"I left a note—and coffee." It seemed pathetic now that he'd said it.

She frowned, nervously twisting her wedding band. The gesture more telling than words. "There wasn't a note."

"I left it by the coffee pot," he said.

"It doesn't matter." Except that it did. A lot. It was there on her face.

"Of course it does. I should have woken you. It's just that you looked so peaceful. And," he sighed, running a hand through his hair, "I'm not very good at the whole relationship thing."

"I understand." She nodded, staring at the floor in obvious discomfort.

"No." He lifted her chin, his gaze meeting hers. "You don't understand. It's not that I wanted to avoid talking to you. It's that I was afraid that you wouldn't feel the same way that I did about what happened last night. It's so easy to make promises in the night. But by light of day, I thought you might have regrets. And I guess I just didn't want to face that."

They stood for a moment, their gazes locked, and Eric was afraid to breathe. He wasn't good at expressing his feelings, and he hated to take the risk, but Sara was important, and he wanted to get it right.

Her smile was slow, but genuine, and his heart threatened to break out of his chest. She lifted a hand, her fingers tracing the line of his jaw. "No regrets, Eric. None at all."

He bent to kiss her, the touch of her lips against his sending spirals of heat coursing through him. There was passion in the touch, but something else as well, a feeling of serenity, of peace. And that was something Eric hadn't felt in a hell of a long time.

And he'd be damned before he'd let someone take it away from him.

"Still no luck on clarifying the voice." Tony walked into the conference room, waving a folder. "But at least we can be certain it came from Molly's house."

Eric looked up from the report he'd been reading, the table was littered with them. Every scrap of information they had on the case contained within these four walls. Forensics, rap sheets, notes, everything. And he'd read them all at least fifteen times, all without anything new. "My bet's on Molly."

Tony nodded. "Or the killer, which doesn't make a lick of sense."

"Like any of it does?" His question was rhetorical and Tony underscored the fact by ignoring it. "What about Sara's call?"

"The number's registered to a throwaway." Tony perched on the side of the table. "No way to find the owner, but the fact that he called with news of Molly goes a long way to solidifying a link between Sara and the killer. Anything else come out of your talk with her?"

"Nothing." And everything. But the personal part was going to stay just that. "The salient point seems to be that the guy talked. And since this is the first time, assuming he's the one who made the other calls, the big question is why now?

He's been content to hold his tongue this long, so what's changed?"

"His level of anger, maybe," Tony mused. "Forensics confirmed that the flowers we found at Molly's were the same variety as the ones Sara received. And since we know Molly threw Sara's flowers away, there could be a connection. Sara spurns flowers. Molly throws them away. Killer feels rejected, partially blames Molly, and takes his anger out on the messenger in a very literal way."

"Yeah, that's what scares the hell out of me. If the victims here really were surrogates, and if Sara is the real deal, rejection is a surefire way to get him to up the ante. If he can't have her, no one can." Eric sighed. "But unfortunately, even with what we've got, motive is still just supposition. We can't read his mind, no matter how many profilers we talk to."

"So we chip away at the facts." Tony shrugged. "You talked about the change in pattern based on time of kill, but there's more to it than that. The pattern for Sara's caller shifted as well. Up until now, all of her calls have come at night. This one, conveniently, came during the day, following right on the heals of the attempted murder—on her cell phone."

"From an untraceable phone." Eric sat up, his beleaguered brain trying to assimilate the new information.

"No one said the man was stupid." Tony shrugged. "Just for the hell of it, I took the liberty of checking her home phone. No calls there that can't be identified. Which means that the caller not only knew her cell number, he knew she wasn't going to be home. And that means he's close enough to keep tabs on her."

"Jenkins hasn't reported anything unusual. Although considering we're not sure what we're looking for, it's not out of the question for him to have missed something." Eric stood up, rubbing the small of his back. "Hell, I feel like he's jerking me around by the balls."

"What about the trophies?" Tony turned to scrutinize the list on the board. "We've got ears, a tongue, fingers, hair, and now eyes. What color were Molly's eyes?"

"Blue, I think." He pulled a sheet of paper from the pile. "Yeah. Blue. Why?"

Tony blew out a breath, still squinting at the board. "Sara has blue eyes, right?"

Chills chased across his skin as the train of Tony's thoughts crystallized. "And blonde hair."

"Same as Allison Moore."

"Jesus, he's choosing his vics because they remind him of Sara?" The idea that Sara could be the center of the killer's fantasy was almost more than Eric could contemplate, revulsion threatening to compromise his professional integrity. Forcibly he held his emotions at bay, focusing on the case. "So how do explain the fact that Candy Mason was African-American?"

Tony frowned. "It was her tongue. Maybe she sounded like Sara?"

"Sick bastard." Eric clenched his fists, wanting to find the son of a bitch and castrate him.

"Eric," Tony's voice was cautious, "Brady thinks you're too close to this to do your job."

"I'm fine."

"You're not." Tony shook his head to underscore the point. "But I told Brady that you wouldn't let it compromise the case."

"And now you're having doubts?" He tried but couldn't keep the sarcasm from his voice.

"No. I just thought you ought to know how things stand." Tony stood up, looking distinctly uncomfortable. "You're the best cop I've ever known, Eric. And I'm proud to stand beside you. But this is a tough one. And it's become personal. No one would blame you if you stepped aside."

"I'm not going anywhere until we nail this bastard to the floor." He spit out each word as if it were a bullet. "So you're either with me or against me."

Tony's smile was slow in coming, but it reached all the way to his eyes. "Then it's you and me all the way, partner." He leaned over to pick up a file. "What do you say we try and catch a killer."

Chapter 23

With all the wires and machinery, Sara felt like she was on the set of some sci-fi adventure. Instead, she was at her best friend's bedside.

Intensive care was a small unit with a semicircle of rooms and a nurses' station in the middle. Molly's room was much the same as the others, except that a policewoman stood guard in the doorway, another at the entrance to the ward.

Molly looked almost peaceful, if one could ignore the myriad tubes protruding from her every orifice. A steady beeping signified that she was still clinging to life. Tenacious to the very last. For once Sara was grateful for Molly's stubbornness.

Bandages covered much of her body, the one across her eyes seeming garish against the backdrop of her fiery hair. Her breathing was unassisted, but she hadn't woken since she'd been found. And although there was brain activity, the doctors were being guarded as far as prognosis.

She'd come a long way, but there was still more to come. Another surgery probably. Reconstruction of what was left of her eye sockets. And that wasn't even taking into consideration the psychological hurdles that she would have to overcome.

But she was alive. And Sara knew that Molly wouldn't give up without a fight. The man who'd done this to her had severely underestimated his opponent. And with a little luck, and a lot of prayer, Molly'd find her way back. And Sara would be there. Waiting.

"Ms. Martin?" A nurse bustled into the room, an IV bag in hand. "I'm afraid it's time." Molly was only allowed five-minute visits every half hour. And then only from one person.

Sara stood up, leaned over, and kissed Molly's cheek, careful not to touch the bandages, reaching out at the same time to squeeze her hand. "It's going to be okay, Molly. I promise. You just hold on. Okay?" Tears filled her eyes, and she stepped back, unable to force herself to leave the room.

But when the nurse cleared her throat, the noise meant as a polite reminder, she turned her back and walked away, certain that if hate could take physical form, the man behind all of this wouldn't stand a chance.

She walked out of the ICU with a nod at the police-woman, and made her way to the waiting room. Ryan was standing looking out the window, and Bess was going through the motions of reading a magazine, although con-sidering the rapidity with which she turned the pages, Sara suspected there wasn't much actual reading going on.

"How is she?" Ryan asked, crossing to sit beside Bess.

"Breathing." Sara sat across from them. "I think at the moment that's as much as we're going to get."

"Considering what that monster did to her, I'd say it's miracle enough." Bess's anger mirrored Sara's, and judging from Ryan's thunderous expression, his as well.

"So what did the doctor say?" Ryan asked.

Before she had gone in to sit with Molly, the surgeon had updated Sara on her friend's progress. "He didn't say much, really. The surgery went as well as expected. It stopped the internal bleeding, but she's still dealing with injuries and blood loss, not to mention shock. At this point I think it's a waiting game."

"Molly's tough," Ryan said. "She'll pull through."

"I don't know." Nate walked into the waiting room, coffee cups balanced between his hands. "She lost a lot of blood. And there's no telling how much it's affected her brain. She may come out of it, but you all have to face the very real possibility that she might never be the same."

"Well, that kind of attitude isn't going to help very much." Bess took a cup from him, her tone full of rebuke.

"Sorry." He handed another cup to Ryan. "I just thought it needed to be said. There's something to facing reality, you know. Lying to ourselves isn't going to change the outcome."

"No. But a positive attitude can help." Ryan sipped his coffee.

"Hey." Nate held up his hands in defense. "I didn't mean to set everyone off. I just don't want us clinging to false hope, that's all."

"Sometimes that's all there is." Bess's voice was soft, almost a whisper.

"Look, you guys, we don't need to be picking at each other." Sara's gaze encompassed them all. "Right now we need to stick together. Support Molly."

"Of course." Nate smiled.

"So tell me about the phone call." Ryan reached over to take her hand, his eyes concerned.

She suddenly wished she hadn't mentioned the call. It had seemed natural to tell Ryan. But now what had been private was suddenly public. It wasn't that she minded her friends knowing, it was just that she wanted to compartmentalize it, keep it locked away somewhere inside, where it couldn't scare her. Talking about it made it real. She sighed, pulling away from Ryan, leaning back in her chair. "He called to tell me that Molly was dead."

"Oh, God, that must have been horrible." Bess's eyes widened as the idea sank home.

"It was nothing compared to what Molly went through."

"So your caller is tied to the Sinatra killer?" Nate looked puzzled.

"It looks that way." Sara crossed her arms over her chest,

as if in doing so she was protecting herself. "It really doesn't make a lot of sense, but Eric and Tony are working on it."

"God, the whole thing is so creepy." Bess stood up and began restlessly pacing in front of the window. "It's like the whole world has gone topsy-turvy."

"I think the roses were the worst thing," Nate said. "Do you think they were the same ones you threw out?"

Sara nodded, shivering.

"Well, it was a sick gesture, no matter what." Nate leaned back in his chair, a myriad of emotions flashing in his eyes.

"Nate." Ryan's voice was sharp, a warning. "Let it go. Can't you see you're upsetting Sara?"

"I'm fine, Ryan. And Nate's right. It is sick. Sick that someone could do this to women and even sicker that he wants to talk about it." She blew out a shuddery breath.

Ryan leaned over to take her hands again, his eyes searching hers. "Why don't you let me take you home. I could cook or something."

She shook her head. "Thanks. But Eric's coming back as soon as he finishes at the station."

"That could be hours," Nate said, ever the pessimist.

"It doesn't matter. I'll wait." There was a world of meaning in her words.

Ryan released her hands and sat back, his expression inscrutable. "All right. Then we wait."

"Tony thinks it's someone we know," Bess said, coming to sit beside Sara.

"One of us?" Nate's brows disappeared into his hairline.

"Not *us*—us. But still, someone around us. Maybe someone at work. They even thought it might be Jack."

"But they don't now?" Ryan had his reporter's voice on.

"No." Bess shook her head. "At least I don't think so. I talked to him an hour or so ago. He came to see Molly."

"Why didn't he stay?" Nate frowned.

"Because of Sara." Bess's eyes met hers, her gaze knowing.

"He told you?" Sara fought against a surge of anger.

Bess nodded.

"Told you what?" Ryan asked impatiently.

Sara sighed, struggling for words. "Apparently, when he checked out Tom's car after the accident, he found something. Something that made him believe he was responsible for the accident."

"And he didn't tell you?" Nate looked confused.

"No. He didn't." Nate opened his mouth, but Sara cut him off with a shake of her head. "It doesn't matter why. What's important is that they found the same thing wrong with Eric's car."

"Which means they think both accidents may have, in fact, been the result of sabotage." Ryan, as usual, got it in one.

Sara nodded, and Bess slipped an arm around her. "I really haven't had time to process it. Jack just told me a couple of hours ago."

"Well, he shouldn't have kept it from you." Nate's eyes glittered with anger.

"He thought it was his fault," Bess said.

"Well, it could have been, right?" Ryan's expression was thoughtful, contemplative. "I mean, he is a mechanic."

"He could have done it, but he didn't." Despite what Jack had told her, Sara couldn't stop herself from defending him. "And he's certainly never worked on Eric's car."

"Doesn't mean he didn't do it, Sara."

"Tony seems to think that he's telling the truth." Bess joined Sara in Jack's defense.

"Well, I think you should stay clear of him until they find out who is behind all of this," Nate said.

"I think you should all refrain from discussing what should have stayed a private matter."

"Tony." Bess's voice came out on a squeak.

Tony walked over to his wife, the look in his eyes a combination of rebuke and exasperation. "This is why I don't usually discuss my cases with you."

Bess pulled a face, her nervousness uncharacteristic. "I didn't say anything that Sara didn't already know."

"And how about Ryan and Nate?" Tony tilted his head toward the two men, his expression softening into something akin to loving tolerance.

"Well, I suppose that wasn't the greatest idea. But we're all friends."

"And reporters." Ryan added. "Tony's right. We need to draw some boundaries."

"Boundaries for what?" Eric walked into the waiting room, and the walls seemed to move closer together, breathing suddenly more difficult.

Sara offered a tentative smile. "We were discussing Jack."

"Bess was telling all." Tony shot his wife another look, one big arm draped around her shoulders.

Eric shrugged. "I don't think there's any big secret. Truth is, we thought Jack might be a suspect, but at least for the moment, he's off the hook. But I would ask that you keep the possible tie to Tom and Charlie quiet a bit longer. I want to have some time to investigate it." He reached for Sara's hand, his touch an anchor in all the madness. "Right now we're not certain how it all ties together, or even if it ties together, and I don't want it any more complicated than necessary."

"You're trying to protect Sara." Ryan narrowed his eyes, studying the other man.

"Among other things." Eric's fingers tightened on hers.

Sara wondered suddenly how they'd gotten to this place. Molly in I.C.U. Her friends gathered to sit vigil. Jack revealing secrets that might have been best left buried. And Sara herself the possible center of the maelstrom.

Somewhere out there, a man was killing innocent women. And, somehow, she was a part of it, part of his vicious fantasy, a puppet in a game that had no rules. It was like playing chess with the Red Queen, logic existing only in illogic, everything the mirror image of what it really was.

Only in *Alice Through the Looking Glass* nobody died.

Chapter 24

Visiting hours were long over, but Sara couldn't bring herself to go home. The ever-faithful Officer Jenkins was sitting across the room, but even his eyelids were drooping. Everyone else had gone. Tony and Eric had been called away, Ryan had a meeting, and despite their protests, she'd sent Nate and Bess home.

So she was alone. Which, quite frankly, was the last thing she wanted. But at least in the hospital, she was surrounded by people. Her cell phone was off, which meant Eric couldn't call. But it also meant *he* couldn't call. And just at the moment, the latter was more important. Sara leaned back in the chair, closing her eyes. There was simply too much to think about, and her overloaded brain was rebelling.

"What do you say we get out of here?" Sara's eyes fluttered open, her mouth opening in protest, but Eric put his finger over her lips, silencing her. "It's late. And between the doctors and the guards, Molly is being well taken care of."

"I know. It's just that I couldn't face the thought of going home."

"Especially alone."

She nodded, feeling like a coward. Eric faced horrific things every day, and here she was hiding from a phone and an empty house.

"Look, Sara." He sat down beside her, reaching for her hands. "No one thinks any less of you for being scared. In fact, considering the circumstances, there'd be something wrong if you weren't afraid."

"I just feel so helpless. And I hate it. I can't get his voice out of my head. It's like he's out there, yanking us all around like marionettes."

"That's because part of it's about power. Proving that he's in control."

"Well, I'm convinced."

"Unfortunately that's not enough. This is about something only the killer can truly understand, some perversion of reality that twists around in his head until it's all he can see."

"So how do you figure it out?"

"I don't. At least not completely. What I do, what all cops do, is to try and look at something from back to front. Particularly in homicide, we start with a scene. A victim. And by studying both we can put together a picture of a crime, what happened. That's usually the easy part. Even with the most meticulous killers, there's usually at least a body. From there it's all about why."

"And you can tell that from the evidence?"

"Sometimes. Sometimes it's just a hunch. Experience counts for something, and there are certain patterns that become pretty evident if you do this long enough. Or sometimes one piece of evidence will lead to another until suddenly the why is clear. Once you have the what and why, then the next step is who. Usually along the way you've developed a list suspects."

"Like Jack."

"Yeah." He shrugged. "It's a process of elimination. But every time you eliminate someone, or gain another piece of evidence, or a clue, you tighten the parameters and get a little closer."

"But what if that's not enough?" She wasn't sure why she was goading him. Maybe because she wanted reassurance, or maybe because she wasn't sure a monster like the Sinatra killer could really be caught.

"It isn't always. That's the hard part of the job. There's

never a guarantee we'll win the day. But I sleep at night because most of the time we do. And every time I win one, the world's a better place. Sounds egotistical, I guess."

"No. It sounds noble. Not that many people are willing to take on that kind of battle, and even if they were willing to do so for some personal crusade, they wouldn't do it full-time, for lousy wages, and a lot of bad coffee."

He laughed, and the sound warmed her heart. This was a man she could easily lose herself in. Had already lost herself to some extent. And here they were spending valuable time discussing the very person who wanted to take it all away.

Damned if she'd let that happen.

"You offered to get me out of here." She smiled up at him. "Do you actually have a plan?"

"As a matter of fact, I do." He stood up, offering her his hand. "What do you say, just for a little while, we try and put all of this behind us?"

"You think that's possible?"

"I know a good place to try."

"Where are we going?" Sara pulled her coat close, shivering in the brisk air. A particularly persistent cold front had pushed its way south, and for the moment, at least, it actually felt like November.

"Hang on. You'll see." Eric's fingers tightened on her elbow as he guided her forward past a convenience store and a veterinary clinic.

"See what? Austin at its eclectic best?" The tail end of the university drag, this section of Guadalupe fell somewhere between the student rental market and the Victorian renaissance of her Hyde Park neighborhood. Property here was worth a fortune, but on the surface, you'd never know it, apartment buildings crammed together with houses.

But as they rounded the corner, Sara stopped, her breath lodging in her throat, surprise blending with amazement.

"Welcome to 37th Street." Eric's voice was low, almost a whisper. Or maybe she simply wasn't capable of hearing anymore, the visual onslaught of the street interfering with normal sensory perception.

There were lights everywhere. Hanging from houses, draped across lawns, woven amidst streetlights and telephone wires. Like floating garlands in blue, green, red, and the most amazing shade of purple. A whirlwind of light and color that erupted into the night, leaving the viewer breathless with delight.

It was a wild combination. Picasso, Monet, and velvet Elvis. Abstraction taking form and shape to create an indefinable but amazing whole, the pervading feeling one of joy. Complete and absolute joy.

"But it's not Christmas." The words, when they came, were senseless. There was no way to express what she was really feeling. But as Eric's arm slid around her shoulders, she knew he understood. That's why he'd brought her here.

"Season isn't exactly the driving force on 37th Street."

"It's amazing." They walked slowly up the street, Sara with her head tipped back, her gaze feasting on the blinking, twirling lights.

"There'll be more eventually. All the houses."

"I can't even imagine." Some apartments, along with the first few houses on the block, were dark, sort of a peaceful prelude to the explosion of light to come. They passed a house festooned with white lights, twinkling balls decorating the eaves, reminding Sara of beehives.

Across the street, a waterfall of blue and green fell from roofline to grass, ending in a glittering pool of silvery light, complete with illuminated tropical fish.

"Some people think it's a little much." Eric grinned down at her, pointing to a light-encrusted motorcycle. "But I like it."

"It's incredible." A hedge draped in blinking green was covered with fuchsia "flowers," the effect garish and fantastical all at the same time. They stopped and Eric pulled her close, the combination of flashing lights and crisp cold air more of an aphrodisiac than she could have imagined.

His lips closed on hers, his heated breath caressing her face, and she abandoned herself to the feeling. Lights, heat, cold, and joy combusting. The kiss at once possessing and exploring. Giving and taking. Everything a kiss should be.

He opened his coat, pulling her inside, the beat of his heart a tantalizing tempo. She opened her mouth, reveling in the moment, the man. She stroked his back, then his shoulders, ultimately twining her fingers through the crisp darkness of his hair.

She traced the line of his teeth with her tongue, inhaling him, sucking his essence deep inside, holding it there for a rainy day. There was magic afoot in the swirling lights and the heat of the man. And she wanted nothing more than to have him take her. Here. Now.

A car honked, the occupants yelling their approval, and she pulled back, grinning like a fool, feeling an odd combination of embarrassment and elation. Elation won as she drank in the glory of the night. "I can't believe more people don't know about this."

Eric laughed. "Everyone knows about it, Sara. They've even had coverage in the national press."

"So I'm totally clueless?" She twirled in a circle, trying to take it all in. "How long have they been doing it?"

"Around fifteen years, I think. It started with one guy." He pointed at a house up ahead covered with pulsing spirals of light, a huge oak tree in the front yard literally dripping with color. "Jamie's the mastermind behind it all, but the idea was infectious and the neighbors were soon hanging their own lights. The tradition grew from there. These days, they're having block parties to paint lights."

"That's why the colors are so amazing." She slid back into his embrace, relishing the contact. "How do you know so much about this?"

"I have friends on the street." He pointed to a white frame house with a garden motif, corn and carrot lights bright against the branches of a crape myrtle. Chili pepper lights and miniature palm trees filled another corner, brightly colored parrots in the trees overhead. There was even a small corral of cows—in Santa hats—twinkling on the lawn. "This is where I come when I need a little spiritual revitalization. Sometimes it's easy to forget the world is essentially a good place." He shrugged, stepping over a bed of light-filled pumpkins. "This reminds me."

Part of Sara's ebullience evaporated, reality hovering just at the edge of sight. Eric lived with the worst of humanity every day, constantly dealing with the kinds of things that most people never saw at all, except maybe for six seconds on the ten o'clock news. And yet he hadn't lost the ability to find joy in Christmas lights.

It was comforting and humbling. She pressed close, their frozen breath mingling in the air, the world around them a blinking kaleidoscope of brilliant light. And just for the moment she could pretend that all was right with the world.

After the magic of 37th Street, searching Sara's house for intruders was a less than enchanting return to reality. But a necessary one. Eric flipped on the kitchen lights, searching the shadows.

Sara'd been quiet on the ride home. Not completely withdrawn, but certainly preoccupied. Under the spell of the lights, anything had seemed possible. And just for a few minutes their problems had disappeared.

But, of course, nothing had truly changed, and now they were back where they'd started, a hunter out there, quite possibly with Sara in his sights, her friend clinging to life by a fingernail. And despite his intensifying feelings for Sara, or maybe because of them, he knew the most important thing right now was for him to put emotion aside and concentrate on doing his job.

"Everything's secure," he called, purposefully keeping his voice light. Coming round the corner, he stepped into the foyer where Sara was waiting.

"You're certain." Her gaze darted around the hallway as if she expected something to jump out at her.

"Positive. The house is empty, and Jenkins is right outside. He'll keep you safe."

"You aren't going to stay?" Her attention jerked back to him, fear and longing flashing in her eyes.

"I didn't want to assume." The words were inadequate, but he couldn't think of anything else to say.

"I think maybe we're past that point." Her smile was genuine, and it warmed him through. "Besides, I feel safer with you here. Can we maybe just talk for a bit? I could make coffee."

"Sure." He wasn't certain he was up to small talk. Truth was all he wanted to do was pull her into his arms and make them both forget the problems that surrounded them. But instead, he'd play the game. For Sara.

And that, in and of itself, said a whole lot about the state of his emotions. He wasn't in the habit of catering to someone else's needs. But with Sara, it seemed instinctive. Second nature.

He followed her into the kitchen, automatically reaching for the carafe, filling it with water as Sara opened the coffee, their movements almost choreographed, as if they'd made a thousand pots of coffee together.

Their hands touched, and the spark that shot between them was almost a tangible thing, Sara jerking back, her eyes widening. At least he wasn't alone.

"You think he's out there?" Sara had turned to look out the kitchen window, the dark night obscuring any view.

He moved to stand behind her, not touching her, but close enough to feel the rise and fall of her breathing. "Not in your backyard, if that's what you mean. He's too smart for that."

"That's what scares me." The words were whispered, and he felt her shiver.

"It's not as bad as all that. Tony and I are working overtime to put the pieces together. Forensics is studying and restudying the evidence; every detective on the force is following leads. We've even asked the FBI for help."

"But you said it yourself—he's smart. And whatever is happening here, he's the one calling the shots."

She sounded so hopeless he wanted to lie, but he fought the urge, knowing there was strength in truth. "For the time being maybe. But sooner or later this guy is going to slip up. Maybe he already has. You've just got to hang tough until something breaks."

"Waiting. Wondering." She swung around to face him, tears filling her eyes. "This monster may have killed my husband, my son. He maimed my friend. Put her in a coma. And he almost killed you. And now it looks like it's connected to me. *Me*." She pounded a hand against her chest. "He's hurting the people I love, Eric. And I can't do anything to stop him. Nothing. Not a goddamned thing." She was crying now, her pain raw, unfettered.

He pulled her close, intending to comfort her, but instead she tipped back her head, her lips meeting his, her kiss hot and wanton, desire laid bare. There was an urgency, a need to connect, to become one. Her need combining with his. Combustible.

He'd never known anyone who could make him feel this way. Complete and hungry all at the same time. It was as if madness had set in, wiping away all common sense, leaving nothing but a surge of something primal, something so basic it defied words.

Man and woman. Nothing more . . . nothing less.

He'd have laughed, except that he couldn't breathe. Her tongue probed his, demanding, taking, sucking some part of him deep inside her. He pulled away, sliding his mouth across the smooth skin of her cheek, tasting the salt of her tears.

There was an intensity that had been missing before, the sense that time was important, that every minute they had together had to mean something, count in some intrinsic way. He knew it was probably a product of her fear—their fear. But he couldn't stop it any more than he could stop a speeding train. The gates had been opened and there was no holding back.

She fumbled with the buttons of his shirt, her hands shaking with need. Finally, in frustration, she pulled at the cotton, each button straining in protest, then giving with a satisfying *pop*.

They laughed as he shed the now-tattered shirt, the sound embodying joy. The joy of belonging. Of needing. Of finding magic amidst horror. They belonged together. And at least for the moment, neither of them was fighting the fact.

Her hands were soft against the bruised planes of his chest and back, kneading, stroking, building the heat inside him with every touch, every caress, circling, smoothing, her kisses tracing lines of fire along the curve of his neck and shoulders.

With a passion he hadn't known he possessed, he pulled her lips back to his, some primal need pushing him to brand her, mark her as his own, the soft murmur from her throat, telling him that she was surrendering. And, at the same time, conquering, a mutual drive sending them both on a spiral of pure desire. Need crescendoing into heat so powerful it threatened to unman him.

He slid her sweater over her shoulders, his hands unerringly finding the soft flesh of her breasts, his fingers rubbing the hard buttons of her nipples, feeling them respond to his touch, tightening with each stroke, each rasp of his skin against hers.

She moaned, the low sound sending spikes of raw passion shooting through him, his body tightening to the bursting point, his need ratcheting up to a level he wasn't sure he could survive.

Somehow, they found the sofa, the soft cushions absorbing the thrust of their bodies as they pushed together, grinding in their need for release. For joining.

She laughed again, and he swallowed the sound, drinking her in like some exotic elixir, wanting more with each sip. She reached for his buckle, and before he had time to think about it, had it open and off, the fly of his jeans open as well, her magic fingers already sliding the zipper down, setting him free.

The air hit him, cold and unforgiving, but before he could complete a shiver, her mouth closed around him, her heat sending shards of pure pleasure dancing through him. She moved against him, up and down, deeper—deeper still, until he was shaking with desire. Wanting her more than he'd ever wanted anything in his life.

Filled with urgency, he pushed her upward, his mouth connecting with hers, tasting himself on her lips, the sensation binding in its elemental essence. Her skirt had twisted about her hips, a thin barrier of satin the only thing keeping him from finding his way home.

With the twist of a hand, he heard the satisfying sound of material splitting, and felt the silk of her body against his. Raising on an elbow, his eyes met hers, the promise there taking his breath away.

This was as it was meant to be. Perfection in joining. And with a single thrust, his eyes locked on hers, he slid home, her heat pulsing around him. For a moment, time stood still, and there was nothing but Sara—surrounding him, caressing him, loving him.

Then, with a motion that followed music beyond hearing, they began to move. Body to body, joined together for all time. Deeper and deeper he drove, until they were one, no beginning, no end, just a spiral of pleasure, a promise that nothing could break. An inextricable flash of ecstasy that bound them together forever.

At least that's what he prayed.

Chapter 25

Sara had never felt like this.

Never.

It was as if every neuron in her body had fired at once, expending all of her energy, leaving her like a boneless cat, content against the warmth of Eric's body, which was insane and wonderful all at the same time.

She rolled over to face him, the action taking him deeper inside her. There was something to be said for joining. Soul to soul, a connection that nothing could break. She tried to remember if she'd felt like this with Tom, but had trouble remembering.

Which frightened her and soothed her all at once, the past making way for the present in a way that could only be good.

"We're going to get through this." Eric's voice was rough with emotion, the aftermath of their lovemaking obviously affecting him as much as it had her.

She nodded, not sure she really believed his words but cherishing the emotion behind them. "I always seem to find a way to survive."

"You haven't had an easy time of it, have you? First your mother dying, then the pervert in the foster home."

She pulled away from him, immediately missing the contact, but unwilling to move back. The specter of her past wavered between them, creating a gulf bigger than the simple act of physical separation. "How did you know about that?"

"Jack told me."

She eyed him warily. "He talks too much."

"He cares about you."

Bitterness swelled through her. "That's why he lied to me about Tom."

"He was afraid of losing you."

"But he wouldn't have. At least I don't think so."

Eric reached out and pulled her close again. Part of her wanted to withdraw, knowing that loving brought the potential for great pain, but another part of her relished the contact, his touch making her feel whole again.

Eric was silent for a moment, and then reached down to trace the line of her shoulder, his touch sending heat spiraling through her. "So tell me about it."

"What part exactly?"

"All of it, I guess. Except for Tom and Charlie dying, I really don't know much about your past."

She shrugged, shifting so that she could see him. "Sometimes it feels like someone else's life. After Mother died, I officially became a ward of the state. But at eight I wasn't exactly prime adoption material, and it didn't help that all I wanted was my mother back. At first, every time they placed me somewhere, I'd run away, certain that if I went home, I'd find that the whole thing had been a nightmare, that my mom was still alive."

"But she wasn't." His voice was gentle, touching her somewhere deep inside.

"No." She was surprised to feel the prick of tears. "So I stopped running away, and at first it wasn't so bad. My foster parents were really nice. I even began to call them Mom and Dad. But no one explained to me that foster care wasn't forever. And when the family got transferred out of state, I was left behind.

"It was like losing my mother all over again. And I made up my mind that I wasn't going to care again. Ever. Only then, when I was ten, I met Jack." She smiled at the memory. "He was so gruff and so caring. He listened to me. And despite my misgivings, we formed a family of sorts. Just the two of us."

"And he was there for you when you were attacked."
There was anger in Eric's voice, and he tightened his hold on
her, as if in doing so he could protect her from the memories.

"It wasn't as bad as he makes it sound. The man never
touched me. Just threatened. But Jack lost his temper, and
hit him. And we thought he was dead."

"So you ran again."

She nodded, lost in remembering. "It was a frightening
time. But in a way it was good for me. It made me realize all
that I'd had. Even at its worst, my life was never as hopeless
as the people we met living on the streets. And Jack took
good care of me. We had a room on the south side of Dallas.
Not the Ritz, but it was safe. And it was only for a few
weeks. Social Services tracked us down."

"And separated you."

"Yeah. But it was different after that. I wasn't so afraid of
being alone. Jack gave me that. The strength to believe in myself. Eventually I went on to college, which is where I met
Molly and ultimately Tom. I'd never met anyone like him.

"He was funny. I remember that the most. He could
make me laugh even when there wasn't anything to laugh
about. He was one of those people who saw the good in
everything, no matter the situation. And together we built a
family. A real one. The first I'd had since my mother died."

"And then it got ripped away. Just like before."

She nodded, unable to continue, tears filling her eyes.

He stroked them away. "Sometimes all you can do is go
on, Sara. Build again. Brick by brick by brick. There are no
guarantees in life. None at all. Everything can come tumbling down without the slightest provocation. But I think the
risk is worth it. When you find the right person." He
searched her eyes, seeing something there she wasn't even
certain she could see herself, but the idea gave her hope.

"And are you the right person, Eric?" The question was
whispered, as much to herself as to him.

"I hope so, Sara. Because, God help me, I'm falling in
love with you, and I'd hate to be doing it alone." To under-

score his words, he kissed her, the kind of kiss that went soul deep, cleansing and invigorating all at the same time.

Love was a scary thing. And yet most people fought all their lives to find it. And with almost no effort she'd found it twice. Which meant that she'd be a fool to throw it away.

She rolled against him, deepening the kiss, committing to him with the gesture. He groaned his acceptance, his hands framing her face, his wonderful gray eyes looking into her heart. He was at once masterful and submissive. The quintessential lover. Everything she'd dreamed of. Everything she wanted him to be.

He drove into her, his hardening body a lance piercing her flesh and her spirit, the latter surprising her with its depth. She felt as if they belonged together. Two hearts joined as one. Romantic notion, maybe, but she could feel the empirical evidence in her soul.

His mouth found her breast, his tongue circling, sucking, pulling emotion from her as surely as if he were siphoning her very being. She arched upward, giving in to his ministrations, wishing the moment could go on and on, that she could freeze time forever.

With a smile and a groan, he flipped them, so that she was on top, riding him, a position of power. There was a liberation there. Something she'd never experienced. And with trepidation and then with vigor, she rode him. Up and down, sliding in and out, pushing deeper and deeper, driven by the feel of her body and the increasing cadence of his groans.

Looking down at him, she saw nothing but desire, and acceptance, her need mirrored in his eyes, the strong man she knew him to be surrendering the moment to her. And she held it in her heart like a talisman. Strength giving in to gentle persuasion, her heart wanting only to repay the love.

Up and down she drove, bracing herself against his strength, until the passion carried her away, lifting her to some higher plane, magic mixing with reality, her body shaking in response. Swell upon swell of pleasure threatened to break her apart—like waves crashing against a shore.

She felt his arms tighten, his voice washing over her like a calming sea. "It's okay. Hold on to me."

And she did, riding the night with him. Holding on to today as if it were a lifeline, the crest of emotion taking her away, lifting her high, the stars beckoning, reaching out as they touched the sky.

And for the moment anything seemed possible. Dreams coming true.

The discordant sound of the phone interrupted paradise. Eric leaned across her to pick up the receiver, listened, then met her gaze, the look in his eyes erasing all traces of fantasy.

"Molly's coding."

The florescent lights of the hospital provided perpetual daytime. Even in the early hours of the morning, there was activity. Sara sat with Eric, waiting for Molly's doctor. For the moment at least Molly was stable, her heart once more pumping life through her veins.

But despite all medical effort, she hadn't regained consciousness, and Sara wasn't certain if that was a blessing or a curse. Her friend was unaware of the trauma her body was enduring, but she was also unaware of the world around her. And that wasn't a life Sara would wish on anyone. Particularly Molly.

A gray-haired man with steel-rimmed glasses, wearing scrubs walked into the waiting room. Molly's doctor. Instinctively Sara reached for Eric's hand, comforted by just the simple touch of his fingers.

They stood up as the doctor walked over, Sara's heart beating a rapid tympani against her ribs. "How is she?"

"She's resting comfortably, at least as comfortably as possible considering all that she's been through."

"Any idea what caused the arrest?" Eric tightened his hand on hers, his eyes narrowing with concern.

"Not specifically. Frankly, considering the degree of her injuries, I'm surprised it hasn't happened more often. We changed her meds, which ought to lower the risk of recurrence. But I can't promise anything."

"What about brain activity?" Eric had switched to detective mode. All business. And Sara was grateful for it. Any emotion at all now and she knew she'd fly apart.

The doctor shook his head. "She's still responding, but without cognitive evidence, we can't gauge the degree of damage. At this point the only thing I can tell you for certain is that she's alive. The quality of that life unfortunately is not something I can measure."

"But she *will* wake up." Sara reached out to touch the doctor, as if with contact she could better communicate.

His eyes were somber behind his glasses. "It's possible, certainly. But the longer she remains in the coma, the less likely it is she'll come back."

"So, what, she stays like this indefinitely?" Sara's voice rose with each word, the idea repugnant.

"He's just giving you worst case, Sara." Eric squeezed her hand, the action helping to calm her fear.

"I'm sorry. I just can't imagine Molly living like this."

"When her mother arrives, we'll have to talk about her options. But right now we're concentrating on letting her body heal."

"And so we wait." It was a statement, not a question, and the doctor nodded in response. "Molly is going to pull through. You'll see. It's simply not in her to let that monster win."

"When can Sara see her?" Again Eric's words held reason rather than emotion.

"The nurses are with her now. We still need a couple of tests. As soon as they're finished, it should be all right for Ms. Martin to go in." The doctor smiled, the gesture meant to be reassuring.

Eric nodded his thanks, and they stood, still holding hands, as the man walked away. Then Sara sank down onto a chair, tears welling. "It's all my fault."

"No, it's not." Eric sat beside her, lifting her chin so that she was forced to look at him. "Whatever is happening here, whether you're a catalyst or not, the fault lies with the bastard who tried to kill her. You can't hold yourself responsible for a sociopath's actions."

"Even if those actions are the result of something I said or did?"

"Sara, it doesn't work like that. You're no more responsible for what happened than the other victims. And letting yourself go there isn't going to help anyone."

"On an intellectual level you make all kinds of sense, but just take a look at Molly lying in there," she waved an arm in the direction of the ICU, "and then tell it to my heart."

"I can't, Sara. You're the only one who can do that." His steely-eyed gaze locked on hers, his thumb moving in circles on her cheek, the motion sending tendrils of heat curling through her. "But I can tell you that sitting here blaming yourself isn't going to help Molly."

"You're right." She sucked in a breath, then released it, pasting on a smile. "And the most important thing right now is to find the killer."

"Which is where I come in," he said, standing up, his demeanor shifting with the action, the detective back in full force. "I'll check in when I can. In the meantime, Jenkins is here to watch out for you. Don't go anywhere without him."

"Yes, sir." She was tempted to salute, her grin for real this time.

"I'm not kidding, Sara. Don't go anywhere alone."

She nodded, sobering. "I won't. I promise. Most likely I'll be right here."

"Okay." He sighed, then pulled her close, his kiss hard and possessive. Then, without looking back, he strode from the room, the light seeming to follow him, leaving nothing but shadows in its wake.

"I'm not finding a damn thing." Eric slammed a hand down on the table, a file falling to the floor.

"We're good, partner, but even we can't manufacture evidence out of thin air." Tony bent down to retrieve the scattered papers. "We've been over and over these files. And what we know is all we've got."

"I can't accept that."

"Can't or won't? Either way it's a futile exercise." Tony straddled a chair, studying the white board. "What we need is a miracle."

"Or maybe just some solid police work." Brady stood in the doorway, holding a printout. "Looks like your hunch about Sara Martin's coworkers might be paying off."

"What did you find?" Eric was on his feet in an instant, already reaching for the papers in the lieutenant's hands.

"This just came from the FBI. They ran Sara's list of friends and got a hit. An unsolved from Wichita Falls. And you're not going to believe who the primary suspect was."

Eric scanned the report, frowning as his brain absorbed the information. "Son of a bitch."

"So what does it say?" Tony's impatience was reflected in his voice.

"The primary suspect was Nate Stone." Eric handed the printout to his partner. "Three women were killed. All of them prostitutes. Police never made the case."

"So what made Stone look good?" Tony asked, trying to read and listen at the same time.

"His background." Brady answered, perching on a corner of the table. "Seems he let an adolescent crush get out of control. Followed some girl everywhere. Sent her flowers and gifts. Called her at all hours. Her father finally got a restraining order. Stone responded by breaking into the girl's house, said he was just trying to talk to her. No charges were filed, but it was enough to make the authorities suspicious when the women turned up dead."

"Once obsessive, always obsessive?" Eric wasn't sure why he wasn't more elated. Maybe because Nate was Sara's friend.

"Something like that. Unfortunately, there wasn't enough evidence to pin it on him, so he walked."

"To Austin." Tony put down the file. "Anyone else think this is too easy?"

"Everyone has a past, Haskins." Brady shrugged. "Even a serial killer. The profiler said he'd probably done it before."

"Anything about Sinatra?" Tony asked.

Eric skimmed the report. "Nothing about music, period."

"So the guy could have evolved into it. Or maybe the Sinatra connection is something to do with Sara Martin," Brady said, shooting a meaningful look at Eric.

"Her husband had a collection of CDs." Eric rubbed the back of his head, his ribs starting to ache again.

"Nate would have known that," Tony mused, his eyes narrowed in concentration. "And he fits the profiler's top ten. Age is right. And he's not ugly. To hear Bess tell it, the guy has never had a date. So at least some of the character description fits."

Eric frowned. "Yeah, but I wouldn't have described him as persuasive."

"He's shy, but not to the point of being socially inept. He got an interview with Allison's family. As far as I know, it was the only one they granted. And our dominant woman could be the girl who rejected him."

"It does add up." Eric paced in front of the white board, trying to order his thoughts. "But he's bound to know, these records are out there."

"So maybe that's part of the head trip: Power over authority," Tony said. "We know it's him, but we can't prove it. That'd be a hell of a turn-on. I mean, all we have are priors. There's nothing to tie him to the murders here."

"Gentlemen, you can sit here all day speculating, or you can take your questions to the man of the hour. Me, I'm thinking it's always better to hear it from the horse's mouth." Brady stood up, signaling an end to the discussion.

"So we'll run him to ground." Tony stood up too, and

Eric followed suit. "Who knows, maybe we can get him to choke and confess everything."

"Yeah, right. And then we can drive a Zamboni straight through hell."

"I need to talk." Jack stood by the door of the waiting room, shifting from one foot to the other.

Sara was alone except for Jenkins, her guardian angel. "I don't know what's left to say."

Jack took a step into the room, and Jenkins moved forward, but Sara shook her head. Jack might have lied to her, but that didn't mean he'd hurt her. No matter what lay between them, he wasn't a threat.

"Thanks." Jack sat down in the chair across from her, his hands clasped nervously in front of him.

"There's nothing to thank me for." She searched his face, looking for something to explain what he'd done, some character flaw she'd missed. But all she saw was Jack.

"I didn't sleep much last night."

Guilt flooded through her when she thought of the way she'd spent the night, but it faded as quickly as it had come. She hadn't betrayed him. It had been the other way around. "I don't know what you want me to say."

"I want you to say there's still hope for us, that we can still be a family."

"Jack, you kept my husband and son's murders a secret from me."

"I didn't know it was murder."

"But you knew something was wrong. You even thought you were responsible. And instead of telling me and letting the truth come out, you chose to protect yourself."

"And you."

"That's not good enough, Jack. We're talking about Tom and Charlie. They were part of your family, too. Don't you think you owed it to them to tell the truth?"

"Of course. Jesus, Sara, if I could turn back time and handle it differently I would. But I can't. I screwed up. I let my fear of losing you get in the way of common sense. I thought if I told you what I'd found, you'd never forgive me."

"And this is better?" She tipped back her head, suddenly tired. "God, Jack, after everything we've been through together, I wouldn't have thought it possible. I trusted you."

"I know." He stared down at his shoes, unable to look her in the eyes. "And I let you down."

"With disastrous results. Don't you understand if we'd known what had happened, maybe we could have stopped this thing before it escalated out of control, before those women were killed, before Molly was attacked."

His head jerked up, anger flashing. "You blame me for that."

"I'm not blaming you. I'm stating the truth. It might not have been your fault that Tom and Charlie died. But if they *were* murdered, then the killer got away with it in part because you didn't tell the truth. And that means you share responsibility for the other things he's done." Tears pricked the corners of her eyes, and she fought them. She'd shed enough tears for a lifetime.

"I didn't mean for anyone to get hurt. You know that."

"I do know that. But it doesn't change anything, does it?"

"So that's it, then? Our friendship is over?"

"I can't answer that." She struggled for words. "You lied to me about my husband's death. That's not a small thing. No matter what your reasons were."

"I know. And I also know that this probably isn't the best time to try and deal with this." He paused, swallowing, he eyes on his hands. "It's just that I want to find a way to make it all right."

"I'm not sure you can ever do that, but at the same time I can't imagine not having you be a part of my life. So what do you say we just take it day by day?"

He nodded. "I can wait, Sara. I swear it. As long as it takes. I'll wait."

"*Sara.*" Bess ran into the room, her voice sharp with excitement. "It's Molly. The nurse says she's awake."

Chapter 26

"He's not here." Eric stepped into the cubicle Nate called an office. There wasn't much to designate the space as personal. A calendar from Ireland, and a coffee mug that read *Nerds Do It With Detail*. Other than that it could have been any cubicle anywhere.

"Maybe he's in the building?" Tony's bulk filled the doorway, his gaze accessing.

"It's possible." Eric pulled out a drawer. Nate's files were routine. Articles the man was working on. Expense accounts. Nothing out of the ordinary.

"You were expecting him to have a file labeled *Sara*?"

"I don't know what I expected. I just want to stop the bastard. Keep him from harming her. Is that so much to ask?"

"No. Not if Nate's our man. But right now we don't have anything but priors. And you know as well as I do that doesn't mean a thing. We need something to connect him to the present. Until then, his past doesn't mean shit."

"So I'm trying to find something to connect him." Eric opened another drawer, knowing he was treading a thin line.

"Without a warrant?" Tony crossed over to the desk, closing the drawer. "Anything you find would be thrown out almost before it could be submitted. No matter what's at stake, Eric, we've got to do this by the book."

Eric ran a hand through his hair, trying to shake a building sense of dread. Maybe Tony was right. Maybe this was too personal.

"Can I ask what you're doing?" Ryan Greene stood in the doorway, his frown an indication of his displeasure.

"We're looking for Nate."

"Officially?" Displeasure faded, replaced with confusion. "Is he in some kind of trouble?"

"Right now we just have some questions for him." Eric ruthlessly pushed his fears aside, opting instead for the tools he relied on every day. Observation and logic were a detective's primary allies, and this situation was no different from any other.

"About the murders?" Ryan's tone bordered on incredulous.

"Among other things. Nate has quite a past."

"The girl in high school? For Christ's sake, Tony, the worst you could say of that incident was that Nate used bad judgment."

"You knew about it?" Eric felt a surge of anger. "Why the hell didn't you tell someone?"

"Because it didn't occur to me that it might be relevant."

"I think being accused of three murders shows a little more than bad judgment." He clenched a hand, trying to control his temper. If Ryan had knowingly put Sara in harm's way . . .

"You've lost me now." Ryan shook his head.

"A couple of years ago in Wichita Falls three prostitutes were killed. A series of murders that were never solved." Tony leaned back against the edge of the desk.

"And you're saying they suspected Nate?"

"Yes." Eric crossed his arms, studying the other man. "They questioned him on at least three different occasions, but never could find the evidence to charge him."

"Which could mean he didn't do it." Ryan's denial was weak, as if the reality of the situation had just hit him.

"That's always a possibility." Tony's statement was rote, the politically correct thing to say.

"You interviewed him earlier, right?" Ryan tilted his head in thought. "How come you're only just now finding out about his past?"

It was the question of the hour actually, but Eric didn't see the point in sharing it with Ryan. "It wasn't really an interview. I just talked to him at the party because he'd met Lydia Wallace. He wasn't a suspect at the time, so there wasn't any reason to investigate further."

"Look," Tony inserted impatiently, "we can sit around here all day discussing what ifs, but until we talk to Nate we aren't going to know anything. Is he here somewhere?"

Ryan shook his head. "I haven't seen him all day. I just assumed he was working on a story. Or with Sara and Bess at the hospital. Oh, God." He stood up, clearly agitated, his horrified gaze meeting Eric's. "He could be with Sara right now."

"Sara's fine," Eric said. "She's got an officer assigned to watch over her. And Molly has guards as well."

"You think he'd try to finish what he started?" Ryan flinched at the thought.

"I think it's best to be on the safe side."

"Does Sara know?"

Tony shook his head. "We thought we should wait. No need to upset her unnecessarily. At least not until we know something for sure."

"Jesus." Ryan sat down again, his expression bordering on shell-shocked. "I hired him. Assigned him to Sara's stories. Hell, I might as well have set her up. I should have investigated more. Followed up on Nate's story." Ryan sighed in frustration. "There's a yes/no box on our application. You know, the standard one about being arrested. Nate checked it. I asked and he explained. I thought it was just a juvenile mistake. Hell, we've all let our hormones carry us away, especially as teenagers. He said the charges were dropped. I believed him."

"They were dropped." Eric wasn't certain why he wanted to reassure the man, maybe because he was Sara's friend, or maybe because he looked so devastated.

"But that doesn't change the fact that I hired him."

"This isn't about blame." Tony straightened, his face

grim. "It's about eliminating possibilities. And right now the important thing is to find Nate, figure out if he's our man."

"It just seems inconceivable. Nate is so . . . so timid. I can't imagine him having the courage to ask a woman on a date, let alone rape her."

"It was more than rape, Ryan. It was a calculated play at power, a way to control the situation, to come out on top. The person who did this probably feels out of control most of the time, and the killings are a way to remedy the situation. Truth be told, Nate fits the profile to a tee."

Ryan released a slow breath. "So what can I do?"

"Nothing for the moment. Just call us if he shows up." Eric handed Ryan a card with his cell phone number. "Don't say anything. Try to behave as normally as possible. And if you can, keep him here."

"All right." Ryan stood, for the moment looking a little lost. "For what it's worth, I'm sorry. You have to know I'd never do anything to put Sara in danger. Never."

"You couldn't have known," Eric said. Hell, he'd missed it, too. Talked to the guy on more than one occasion and never suspected a thing. He thought about the profiler saying the killer liked to manipulate things.

Well, it looked like Nate Stone had managed to manipulate them all.

Sara sat by Molly's bedside waiting for a miracle. According to the nurse, Molly had turned her head and tried to say something. Unfortunately, the effort had not been repeated. And now they were saying it had only been a reflex.

Evidently even people in vegetative comas were capable of what appeared to be human response when, in fact, it was simply a muscular reaction to outside stimulus. Logical conclusion, but this wasn't a logical situation and Molly wasn't a vegetable. Which meant that she could wake up.

Sara squeezed her friend's hand, praying with all her

might that God would find a way to send Molly back. It would be a long fight, but Molly would be more than up to the battle. Sara was certain of it. They just needed a little help.

If Molly died, then *he* won. If she lived, then they won. At least a little. It wouldn't bring back Tom or Charlie. But it was something to hold on to. A way to believe that good could triumph.

She leaned her head against the cool sheets, letting the steady beep of the machines wash over her, soothe her.

"It's time to go." The nurse's voice was full of regret. "I hate to ask to you to leave, but Molly needs to rest. And we need to check her vitals."

Sara nodded, rising slowly, feeling suddenly old and tired. "I'll be outside."

"You need to get some rest, too." The woman meant well, probably was right even, but Sara didn't want to leave.

"What if she wakes up and needs me?"

"Then you'll come running. But there's no sense in putting yourself in the bed next to her."

Sara shivered, the woman's words having more meaning than she knew. "I'll be fine. You just take care of Molly."

The nurse shrugged, already turning her attention to Molly, working to replace one of her IV bags. Sara walked out of the room, nodding at the policewoman on guard, and returned to the waiting room.

Bess was standing by the window, the line of her shoulders reflecting her stress. Jenkins sat in a corner, his shy smile a comfort even if he was a stranger.

"She's resting."

Bess spun around, her eyes hopeful. "Did she come to again?"

Sara shook her head. "It was a false alarm. The nurse thinks maybe now that it was just a reflex of some kind."

"I don't believe it." Bess crossed her arms in defiance. "They said she tried to talk. That's hardly a reflex."

"I don't know what to think." Sara shrugged, fighting

against her fatigue. "I want to believe that she's in there fighting. But then I think of all she's been through and—oh, Bess, I just don't know."

Bess crossed to her side, sliding her arm around Sara, sharing her strength. "You're almost asleep on your feet. You need to get some rest. You won't be doing Molly any good if you collapse."

"That's what the nurse said." Sara's smile was wry. "I just feel like I need to be here."

"I understand that. I feel the same way. But this has been harder on you than anyone."

"Except Molly." The words were bitter, the taste vile against her tongue.

"Sara, you can't hold the world up all by yourself. You need to let us help too. So why don't you go home and at the very least take a shower. And I'll hold the fort down until you get back."

Sara started to say no, to explain why she needed to stay, but then thought better of it. Bess was right. She wasn't any good to anyone this way. And the thought of a shower was wonderful. "All right. I'll go. But I'm coming right back."

Bess nodded. "I'll watch over Molly until then. And Jenkins there can watch over you. It'll be okay, Sara. I promise."

Sara sighed, and gave her friend a hug, then turned to go, Jenkins following right behind her, his presence a constant reminder that everything was not going to be okay—at least not as long as there was a killer on the loose.

Eric felt as if the world were missing something crucial, or at least the hospital waiting room was. Bess was sitting in the corner, reading a book, but there was no sign of Sara. Disappointment flooded his gut. "Where's Sara?"

Bess's head shot up, her smile welcoming. "She went home to take a shower. Jenkins is with her. Well, not literally of course."

They both laughed, but like laughing in church, the sound seemed out of place. Abnormal. Hell, who was he kidding? Everything was topsy-turvy. "I got a call that Molly was awake."

Bess shook her head. "False alarm. At least that's what they're saying. Evidently it was just reflex."

"They're sure."

"About as sure as they can be of anything, I guess." Bess put her book down. "The doctor is in with her now. Maybe it would help if you to talk to him."

Eric nodded, already turning to head for ICU. With a nod at the officer on duty, he flashed his badge and headed for Molly's cubicle. The sterile conformity of the ward always left him feeling oddly disturbed, as if in coming here a patient had to surrender their humanity, the need for medical intervention superseding anything personal.

Yet, somehow Molly had managed to evade that, her hair bright against bandages and linens, startlingly unique even in the face of ICU's starched uniformity. There was hope in the thought, and despite himself and the situation, he smiled.

The doctor nodded to a nurse, wrote something on Molly's chart, and then walked over to meet him, offering Eric his hand. "I wish I had better news."

"I take it you're concurring that Molly didn't actually wake up."

"I can't say for certain either way. It's possible that she did wake up. There was a change in her EEG about the same time. But it's also possible that she was reacting instinctively to stimulus within the room. She's responsive to pain. Maybe the nurse jostled her or her pain meds were waning." He shrugged. "I know it's not what you wanted to hear."

"I just want her to get better."

"The surgery seems to have successfully stopped the internal bleeding. Her blood pressure has leveled out, and the sutures in her eye sockets are holding. All of which are excellent indicators that she's starting to heal."

"And the coma?"

"There's no way to tell. She could wake up tomorrow or not at all. Besides the eyes, there's some swelling and a couple of contusions. I suspect she took at least one blow to the head. That, combined with the shock of losing her eyes . . ." The doctor shrugged again, his face impassive.

"But there's brain activity, right?"

"The EEG shows some low-level activity, yes."

"And the spike?" Eric asked, trying to keep his emotions at bay.

"It's a good sign. Especially if she did regain consciousness. I'm afraid the truth of the matter is that other than monitoring her, there's nothing to do but wait."

"Can I see her?" He wasn't sure what it was he hoped to accomplish, but he figured it couldn't hurt. And with Sara gone, maybe Molly would like the company.

"Sure." The doctor smiled, his attention already moving on to the next case, the next patient. Like cops, doctors had to keep their emotions compartmentalized, keep everything at arm's length.

It was the only way to survive, but sometimes he wondered about the cost. Sighing, he pushed the thought aside and walked into Molly's room. There were machines everywhere, all of them making noise, the resulting cacophony comforting and irritating all at once.

He sat down beside Molly's bed, feeling a little awkward. It wasn't as if they really knew each other, but they shared a bond because of their feelings for Sara.

Eric reached for her hand. Molly's skin almost translucent. He could feel the flutter of a pulse. Independent confirmation of life. Frustrated, he leaned back in his chair, wondering if Tony was having any luck tracking down Nate. They'd split up when the call about Molly came in, Eric opting to go to the hospital leaving Tony to the hunt.

Inertia wasn't his strong suit, but he'd hoped that Molly would have something to tell him. And if he were honest, he'd have to admit that he'd wanted to see Sara.

Make certain that she was okay. That the magic of the

night hadn't been one-sided. He'd told her he loved her. Put it right out there front and center. And she'd hadn't responded. At least not with words. The specter of her husband still stood between them, an obstacle he wasn't convinced he could overcome.

Molly's fingers moved beneath his, pulling his attention sharply back into focus. He waited, staring down at her hand, willing it to move again, wondering if perhaps he'd simply imagined it.

Her index finger twitched, was still, and then, with obvious purpose, curled around his. "Molly? Can you hear me?" He leaned forward, his heat pounding. "Molly? It's Eric."

She turned her head, squeezing his hand in recognition, then swallowed struggling to speak.

Eric shook his head, not wanting her to push herself. "Hang on, Molly. I'll get a nurse."

Her hand tightened on his, pulling him closer with surprising force. "Nate." She said, the word faint but clear. "*Nate . . .*"

> *"And then the time will come
> when all the waiting's done.
> The time when you return
> and find me here and run . . ."*
>
> ♫ ♪ ♫ ♪ ♫

It was his favorite song. The one she'd loved the best. And the words were more than appropriate, bringing everything to a fitting finale.

Not that this was the way he'd wanted it. No, he'd had a different ending in mind, but nothing had changed. She'd cuckolded him again, tossing him aside with no thought to the consequences. Spreading her legs at the first opportunity. She was no better than a whore.

And for that, she'd have to pay.

He'd given her all the chances in the world, but she'd chosen someone else—again. And that simply wouldn't do. He'd prove to her once and for all that he was the man for her, the one to make her scream in ecstasy. There'd be no substitute this time. He'd find his release skin to skin.

He sharpened the knife, the whet stone making a lovely whizzing noise as the blade scraped back and forth, back and forth. He closed his eyes, imagining that it was her he was stroking, his body ripping into hers, their blood mixing together, binding them for all time.

The prick of the knife brought him back to reality and he sucked the cut on his thumb, letting the music fill him, the words tantalizing in their promise. Tonight it would be different. She'd finally belong to him. *Forever.*

He'd taste her sweetness, lose himself deep inside her. And then he'd hold her there, tight and hot around him, as he slowly cut her throat and watched her die.

Chapter 27

Sara lay back against the upholstery of the squad car, eyes closed, hovering on the brink of sleep. Officer Jenkins was a wonderful chauffeur, and if it weren't for the situation, she'd probably have enjoyed the ride.

But at the moment there was too much at stake to enjoy anything so frivolous. She opened her eyes, staring out the window. It was a gray slate kind of day, cold and wet, the clouds so low they almost grazed the rooftops. They quilted the trees, draping over bare branches, ice-glazed and ugly, the perfect backdrop for the insanity surrounding them.

The phone rang, and for a moment she didn't even comprehend that it was hers. And then, when she did, the last thing she wanted to do was answer it. But there was no bravery in that, and so, with a sigh, she clicked the "on" button, secure that Jenkins was just in front of her, watching her proverbial back.

"Hello?"

"Hey, gorgeous, how you holding up?" At the sound of Eric's voice, her whole body relaxed, and it wasn't until that moment that she realized just how keyed up she'd actually been.

"I'm doing okay. Any news?"

"Yeah." There was regret in his voice, regret and concern.

"Oh, God." Her heart started to pound. "Is Molly . . ."

"No." He was quick to reassure her, and she leaned back against the seat, shaking her head at Jenkins' concerned gaze in the rearview mirror. "Just the opposite in fact. She actually woke up."

"But the nurse said it was a reflex."

"It wasn't. I was there. She squeezed my hand. She recognized my voice."

"So she's going to be okay?"

"They're still not committing. She slipped back almost as quickly as she came out. But I did get the doctor to admit that it's a positive sign. We know she's in there, cognitively in there."

"But all she did was turn her head."

"She did more than that, Sara. She said something. A name."

"The killer?" Cold chills chased down her spine and she shivered, tightening her hand on the phone, a lifeline to Eric.

"We think so. It tracks with some other information we came across."

"So who is it?" She hadn't meant to sound so harsh, but it was getting hard to breathe.

"We believe it's Nate, Sara."

There was silence as she digested the information, her mind running the gamut from disbelief to amazement. "*Nate*? Surely there's a mistake."

"There was no mistaking what Molly said. And to top it off, Nate's got a past history involving this sort of thing."

"What does *he* say?" She simply couldn't accept it.

"We haven't found him yet. Tony's working on it. Hopefully he'll be in custody soon. Did he come to the hospital today?"

She shook her head, then remembered she was on the phone. "No. I haven't seen him since yesterday." Visions of the interview with Amanda Moore presented themselves front and center, Nate so caring, so concerned. "I just can't believe it."

"It's not confirmed yet, but the facts are beginning to stack up against him."

"Should I come back to the hospital?" She wasn't sure

what she wanted to do, but heading for Eric seemed the wisest choice.

"No. You're fine as long as you're with Jenkins. And I won't be here anyway."

Leave it to him to read her mind. "Where will you be?"

"I'm on my way to talk to Claire Dennison. She paged me, said it was important."

"Okay," she said, forcing herself to sound positive. "I'm going to head on home and grab a quick shower, then I'll head back to the hospital." She started to say something about Nate, something to encourage Eric on his quest, but she knew that wasn't what she really wanted to say. "Eric?"

"I'm here."

"I . . . ah . . ." Why the heck couldn't she just spit it out? The emotion was there, solid and sure; all she needed now were the words. "I just wanted . . ." She twisted her wedding ring, perversely willing it to give her courage, "I just wanted to tell you how much I love you." The words came out in a rush, but once said, she felt as if a huge burden had been lifted, as if someone had opened a window deep in her soul, her heart feeling suddenly light. "And when I see you," she smiled into the phone, "I promise I'll show you just how much."

"I'll hold you to it." There was a raw note of passion in his voice, her insides tightening in response. "In the meantime, sweetheart, don't go anywhere without Jenkins."

Which brought them back to Nate.

Her stomach clenched again, but this time from revulsion, a shudder making its way from her shoulder blades downward. There was no way to truly contemplate the magnitude of Eric's pronouncement—a friend becoming an enemy in the space of a word.

There was a stench to the forensic lab, a sickly sweet combination of death, chemicals, and cleaning fluid that no amount of air freshener could possibly cover. Eric supposed that if one worked there long enough, the smell probably went away. But the fact didn't do a thing to improve the olfactory onslaught he was dealing with at the moment.

"So what's the word?" He stopped just at the edge of a lab table, not in the mood to watch Claire play with her toys.

She looked up from a blood-spattered piece of material; chemicals had turned the stains a luminous blue. "Got something I think you're going to want to see." She stripped off her gloves, already heading toward the door. "I'm guessing it's important."

"All right." He gestured toward the door, then followed her down the hall into her office.

Claire picked up an envelope, sliding out a sheet of paper. "We found a fingerprint at Molly Parker's." She handed him a photographic copy. "It was on the boom box. I ran it through the system and got a hit. Guy named Nathan Stone. He's got quite a record."

The skin on Eric's neck prickled as he stared down at the fingerprint. "Yeah, I know. Tony's out looking for him right now. We've got a few questions for him, and this should sure as hell add fuel to the fire. Any other prints?"

Claire shook her head. "No, not at Molly's. But we did find something else of interest. The fibers I picked up at the scene were hemp."

"Rope?" Eric frowned, trying to process the new information.

Claire nodded. "The same kind we found at two of the other murder scenes."

"So we were wrong. Molly was tied up."

"I'm waiting for a call from the hospital to confirm it. I couldn't check her at the scene, obviously. Saving her life was the priority. But it seems probable that she was restrained. Anyway, the point is it couldn't have been very strong if she was able to free herself. She wouldn't have had a lot of strength."

"Determination has accomplished amazing things, Claire; you know that as well as I do." Another thought surfaced.

"When I asked about fingerprints you said there weren't any more at Molly's. Did you find a print somewhere else?"

Claire nodded, her expression at odds with the gesture, almost reticent. "I'm not sure it's really worth saying anything. But we did find a partial. On one of the calipers on your car."

"And that's *not* something to tell me?"

"Well, it's a bad print. We're working on trying to make it clearer. Hopefully then we can get enough to make a match."

"So you can't say if it's Nate's?"

"I can't say if it's Jack the Ripper's." Claire shrugged. "But we're working on it. And I promise you'll be the first to know if we find something."

Eric's cell phone rang, and he clicked it on. "D'Angelo."

"Hey, partner." Judging from Tony's voice the news wasn't good. "Just thought you'd want to know I've hit a dead end. Best I can tell, Nate Stone has simply dropped out of sight."

The bathroom was warm, the steam from her shower coupling with the vanity lights to dispel some of the gloom of the afternoon. She'd told Eric she loved him. It had been a scary step, but in the aftermath all Sara felt was peace. That, and a giddy sort of joy that made her feel a lot like a teenager again.

She combed through her wet hair, sobering as her eyes dropped to her wedding ring on the counter. Why was it that she constantly felt like she was in two places—called by the past, tempted by the future, tormented in the present? Or maybe that was overstating things.

There were so many people who never had the chances she'd had, even with all the things that had happened to her. And she'd had Jack to watch out for her, then Tom. Now Eric. Maybe that was part of the problem. Maybe she didn't need anyone to look out for her. Maybe she was perfectly capable of standing on her own two feet.

She reached for the ring, then drew back her hand. Or

maybe she simply needed to accept that fact herself. Maybe she'd spent too much time leaning on others, letting other people carry the load.

Maybe, and that was operative word, it was time to believe in herself.

She chewed her lip, staring at the ring. It represented Tom's love. But it was also a tie to the past. And what she wanted more than anything was to let it go, to move on, and hopefully, in doing so, to accept her life for what it was. The good and the bad. All of it. To hold Tom and Charlie close in her heart forever, and, at the same time, to allow room for others—for Eric.

Metaphorically, it seemed so simple. With a shaking hand, she reached for the ring, gold cold to the touch, and with tears filling her eyes, she opened her jewelry box and let it go, watching as it tumbled to a stop, bright against blue velvet.

And despite the ache in her heart, she knew that her tears were cleansing as she sealed the past away in her heart— opening the door on tomorrow.

Eric strode into the squad room, worry blossoming inside him. "Has anyone heard from Jenkins?"

Tony looked up from the file he was reading, his feet propped nonchalantly on his desk. "He made his last scheduled call. Talked to him myself. He was on the front porch. Sara was taking a shower. From the flustered nature of his speech, I'd say he was fighting a hard-on."

The comment brought laughter from the others in the squad room.

"I'm serious." The tone in Eric's voice sobered everyone, including Tony, who sat up, eyes narrowed in concern.

"Is there a problem?"

"I don't know. I just tried to reach Sara at home, and no one was there, not even the answering machine picked up. And then, when I tried to get Jenkins on the radio, there was nothing."

"That doesn't necessarily mean something's wrong, Eric."

Tony's expression contradicted his statement despite his attempt to be comforting.

"Okay, then let's just say I have a really bad feeling." Eric paced in front of the desk, trying to assure himself that he was overreacting, that everything was all right. How many times had he assured an overanxious parent or spouse about that very thing?

And in most cases, he'd been telling the truth. Everything resolved without incident. Funny how different it was when he was the one worried. How different it was when it was Sara whose life was at stake.

He shook his head, trying to clear his thoughts, to center on reality instead of his fear.

"When was the last time you talked to her?" Tony asked.

"I don't know for certain. No more than forty-five minutes. She said she was going home. And then she was heading back to the hospital. I'm supposed to meet her there when we finish up here."

"Well, I wouldn't plan on that anytime soon." Tony's words were caustic. "There's still nothing on Nate."

"All the more reason to worry about Jenkins."

"Don't know if this will help," another detective inserted, "but Jenkins is notorious for turning off his radio. The static drives him crazy. I rode with him for a week last summer, and he had the thing off almost the entire time."

"He should be written up." Eric's words were harsher than necessary, and he knew it.

The guy only shrugged. "He's good, Eric. Just because he isn't always plugged in, doesn't mean he isn't paying attention. I'm sure everything is fine."

Eric met Tony's questioning gaze. "I can't be sure until I talk to her."

It was Tony's turn to shrug. "Then I suggest we take a ride."

*   *   *

It was dark in the house: a product of the steel-gray day and early twilight, the gloom penetrating as if it were an invader. Sara shivered, and shrugged into a shirt, buttoning it and tucking it into her jeans, the flannel some comfort against the suddenly pervading cold.

It was silly, really, to be afraid of her own house. But suddenly without the ring, without Eric, without anything except Officer Jenkins, she was frightened. Taking a deep breath, she made her way down the stairs, concentrating on the idea of getting back to the hospital. To friends and employees and a myriad of other people.

No Nate.

No killer.

The idea that they could be one and the same was still not settling well. She'd thought about it a lot since she'd been home, but the concept didn't seem any more rational than it had when Eric had first mentioned it.

Then suddenly, as if in an effort to be difficult, her mind presented the memory of Nate talking about the rose petals at Molly's. Her blood ran cold.

No one was supposed to have known about them. She only knew because she'd been at the scene. But Eric had sworn her to silence.

She reran the conversation in her mind. Nate had described the scene as if he'd been there. She fought against tears. Eric was right. Nate was the enemy.

She rubbed her finger, missing the comforting touch of the ring, yet liberated by its absence. She could deal with this. Just like she'd dealt with everything else that had happened in her life. She squared her shoulders, hitting the bottom of the staircase with an even stride.

"Jenkins? You down here?" she called. "Kyle?" The second request was more tentative. The first time she'd used his given name.

Nothing.

Moving more slowly now, she edged into the living

room, her eyes searching for his familiar form. But the room was empty. Heart starting to rev up, she fought to keep calm, knowing that nine times out of ten there was a reasonable explanation.

Something that they'd both laugh about later.

But not now.

Fighting to stay in control, she inched her way across the room, stopping in the door to the study, calling Jenkins' name again. Odds were he'd stepped out onto the front porch. Surely he had to check the perimeter occasionally. That made sense in an *Alias* kind of way. She should have paid more attention.

But she hadn't. And so here she was, standing in her living room, wondering where the heck Jenkins was, and what exactly she was supposed to do about it.

Call Eric.

The voice in her head was loud and insistent, and she was grateful for the guidance. Walking into the study, she reached for the phone, and picked up the receiver. Nothing.

She clicked it off and on again, with the same result.

Dead air.

Forcing her breath to come in even bursts, she moved from the study to the living room and the extension there. A land line.

With a shaking hand, she picked up the receiver.

Again nothing.

Clicking the disconnect button she tried again, with no result. The phone lines were dead. A tree limb scratched against the window, sending her running into the hallway, cursing her own timidity. It was just the storm. With all the trees, the neighborhood lost cable and phones at the slightest provocation.

She was jumping at shadows. She needed to find Jenkins. And her cell phone. She walked back into the hallway, trying to remember where she'd left it. Maybe the kitchen. Calling Jenkins' name again, her back to the wall, she inched her way into the hall, wishing suddenly that she had a fraction of the *Alias* woman's moxie.

Not to mention experience with martial arts.

She was losing it. But better over a television show than in real life. At the moment hers certainly rivaled anything a writer could come up with.

A sound behind her had her spinning on heel, facing the door, heart beating a syncopated rhythm against her chest. Someone was pounding on the door.

She froze, her mind screaming to call out for Jenkins. Her heart screaming to run.

But it was a moot point, as neither her feet nor her voice was paying any attention, both of them unable to respond.

The part of her mind that was still working rationally recognized the sound—Nate. Nate was at the door. Pounding. Screaming at her. Demanding entrance. She could hear his voice, and with effort she focused on the words, trying to hear them above the cadence of her heart.

"Sara? Sara? Are you there?"

She opened her mouth to answer and then shut it again. Backing up, freezing in a flash of lightning, praying that he couldn't see in through the frosted glass panels of the door.

Not daring to breath she continued to inch her way backward, praying that the cell phone was on the kitchen counter where she remembered leaving it.

"Sara? Open the door. *Sara*."

She fought the urge to answer, to yell for him to go away, her mind trotting out the image of Molly in bandages, her imagination filling in the blanks.

The pounding increased, and Sara continued to inch backward, her mind screaming *run*, her body obviously not getting the memo.

"I know you're in there." Nate's voice was frantic now, and Sara's heart was beating so loudly she was afraid he would be able to hear it.

Glass sprayed across the floor as the door's window shattered. Sara stifled a scream, then swallowed, her heartbeat echoing in her ears as silence reigned.

She waited—one heartbeat, two—then turned to run,

the kitchen offering her cell phone, a connection to Eric, sanctuary.

Lightning flashed again, and she shot a look behind her, relieved to find the hallway still empty, the gaping holes in the door shining eerily in the half-light.

Rounding the corner, she reached for the light switch, horrified to realize that the phones weren't the only thing affected by the storm. Flipping the switch once more for confirmation, she concentrated on the flash of lightning, using the momentary illumination to get her bearings.

The kitchen counter was just ahead, the black silhouette of her cell phone beckoning. Safety in sight.

A noise behind her made her spin around, arms raised defensively.

Someone caught her, holding her close, and she fought against him, a scream rasping in her throat. Then common sense prevailed, his smell driving home, the sound of his voice coaxing her to be calm.

"Sara. Sara, it's me."

"Ryan." She breathed his name with relief, knowing that everything was all right, that Nate couldn't possibly hurt her now.

Chapter 28

"It's okay, Sara. You're safe." Ryan's voice was soothing, but she wasn't certain she wanted to let him go.

"Nate?" The name came out on a whisper.

"He's been taken care of. Jenkins is with him now."

She nodded, working to calm her shattered nerves. "Then it's over."

"Yeah." He released her, keeping an arm around her, reaching for a Starbucks cup on the counter. "Everything is going to be just fine."

"I should call Eric."

"You're still shaking. Sit here, and drink my coffee. You look like you need it a hell of a lot more than I do." He smiled, offering the cup. "I'll call Eric."

The idea of hot coffee was suddenly irresistible. She took the cup, sinking onto a kitchen chair, sipping the bitter brew with a sigh. "How did you know to come?"

"Eric called and said your phones were out. He wanted me to check on you."

Even in his absence Eric had been watching over her. Sara allowed herself a tiny smile, watching as Ryan dialed the number on his cell phone. Everything was going to be all right. Ryan explained the situation to Eric, then answered questions, assuring him more than once that Sara was all right.

The conversation made her feel warm and content, drowsy even, the antithesis of terror. Almost anticlimactic.

Ryan hung up the phone. "He wants me to bring you to the station. You up for the drive?"

She nodded, standing up, surprised when she stumbled. "I'm just a little sleepy. Shock, I guess."

Ryan frowned, slipping an arm around her. "Maybe I should take you to the hospital first, make sure you're all right."

"No." She shook her head, feeling as if everything was moving in slow motion. "I'd rather go to Eric. I need to see him." She tried to smile, but the effort was just too much. "You understand, don't you?"

"Of course I do." His smile was warm, but his eyes were sad, and she wondered why, but unfortunately her brain wasn't quite up to figuring it out.

"Ryan?" she slurred, the kitchen blurring into a wash of colors. "I think maybe I'd better go to the hospital after all. Something's definitely wrong with me." She leaned against him, grateful for the support.

"Just hold on to me, Sara," he crooned, helping her walk to the door. "I've got you now."

Eric was out of the car almost before it skidded to a stop. He ran up the walk, remembering the first time he'd come this way, not sure of his reception, hoping for so much more. This time he knew what she thought. Knew that she loved him. Only this time she might be gone forever.

The glass in the door had been shattered, the frame still intact. "Sara?" he called, still running forward, almost tripping over the prone figure at the door. Forcing himself to stop, to treat the area like a crime scene, he knelt by the body.

Male. Not Sara, his brain screamed.

Automatically he felt for a pulse. It was faint, but it was there. Carefully, he rolled the body over, turning it faceup.

Nate Stone.

"He alive?" Tony flanked him, staring down at the man who'd led them on such a wild dance.

"Yeah." Eric stood up, eyes reassessing the scene. "He's got a pretty deep gash on the back of his head. That's probably what brought him down."

"Looks like he was trying to get inside." Tony nodded toward the glass.

"But something stopped him. If Sara or Jenkins stopped Nate, then where the hell are they?" Eric frowned, still trying to piece it together. "This doesn't feel right."

"You check inside," Tony said, reaching for his cell phone. "I'll call it in."

Eric was already moving forward, gun drawn. The door was locked, which caused relief and alarm all at the same time. Reaching through the broken glass, he flipped the lock, swinging the door open, then stepped into the hallway.

Everything was dark, the only disruption the glass scattered on the floor. "Sara?" As before, the name echoed through the empty hall, unanswered. Edging up the stairs he worked his way to the bedroom, swinging around the doorjamb, his eyes searching every nook and cranny.

Clothes were draped over a chair, and a towel had been thrown across the bed. He reached out to touch it, the dampness indicating she'd been here recently. Holstering his gun, he walked into the bathroom, breathing deeply, her perfume still lingering in the air. The counter was littered with cosmetics, a brush teetering on the edge. She'd obviously been in a hurry.

To get back to him.

The thought echoed through his brain, taunting him, and his gaze locked on a small jewelry box. Open, the blue velvet lining highlighted the gold of Sara's wedding ring. He wasn't certain why she'd taken it off, but he was certain that the act was momentous. She wore the ring like a shield, using it to hold the world at bay.

Spurred on by anger and fear, he tore through the rest of the house, searching every corner, finally, standing alone in the empty kitchen.

"If she was here, she's gone now."

Eric spun around to look at his partner, Tony's face mirroring his own anguish. "Did Nate say anything?"

Tony shook his head. "He's still out. But the paramedics are here, and they don't seem to think he's in any danger. Just a nasty bang on the head."

"Any sign of Jenkins?"

"He's dead. I found him in the bushes. His neck's broken."

"Nate?"

"It would make sense, except that you haven't found Sara. Are you sure you looked everywhere?" Tony's voice was gentle, but Eric rounded on him anyway.

"Positive. There's no blood in the house. And no body. She's not here."

"So what the hell happened?"

Eric clenched a fist, trying to focus; he wouldn't help Sara if he had a meltdown. "I don't know. The front door was locked. Nate was obviously trying to get in when someone hit him."

"Well, it wasn't Jenkins. From the looks of it, I'd say he's been dead a while."

"So that leaves Sara. But if she did it, then where the hell is she? None of this makes any fucking sense."

"There's no sign of anyone outside." A uniformed officer came in through the back door. "But there are footprints. Heading toward the alley."

"Get the techs out there. Maybe they can tell something from the tread. And have someone check this kitchen." Eric barked the orders, but to the man's credit, he simply nodded and turned to make it so.

"Let's get the hell out of here," Tony said. "Nate's on his way to the hospital. And the sooner we question him, the sooner we can begin to piece together what happened here."

Eric nodded, still fighting against his fear. He had to hold on. Had to keep focus. It was the only way they were going to find Sara.

Sara opened her eyes slowly, trying to remember where she was. The room didn't look familiar at all. She started to sit up, but just turning on to her side sent her head reeling, the world tilting on its axis, her stomach roiling. Lying back, she breathed deeply, closing her eyes, concentrating on stilling the chaos inside.

The last time she'd felt like this she'd been in college, head hanging over the toilet, fighting the effects of one too many glasses of Blue Nun. Only this time she hadn't been drinking.

Memory came back with a vengeance.

Nate.

She blew out a breath, forcing herself to open her eyes. To focus. She needed to talk to Eric. To tell him what had happened. She sat up, fighting for equilibrium, her beleaguered brain finally taking in her surroundings.

She wasn't at the hospital. She wasn't anywhere she recognized at all. The room was a kaleidoscope of color: apple green curtains over what appeared to be a boarded-up window, an orange hang-ten throw rug on the floor, and a bedspread that could have passed as the original model for flower power. The bedside table was piled with battered books, the top one called *Wildfire at Midnight,* the one below it *The Tropic of Capricorn.*

Everything was battered, dingy almost. An old snapshot from the sixties, right down to the rows of beads hanging in the doorway. She inched her way to the edge of the bed, and with a concentrated effort, tried to stand.

Teetering, she reached out to the night table for balance, then slowly took a step forward. One step followed another, and although she felt light-headed, she held away moving to stand by the window. It was indeed covered with boards, the night visible through the cracks, dark and inscrutable.

She frowned, her mind trying to play out the events that had led her here. She'd been with Ryan. He'd talked to Eric, and then they'd been heading for the hospital. Ryan had said that Jenkins was handling Nate. Was it possible that Nate had somehow managed to turn the tables? Could he have overtaken Ryan as well?

She struggled to remember, but everything was fuzzy. She remembered Ryan being there. Remembered all that had led up to his appearance but try as she might, she couldn't remember leaving. Didn't remember anything really except drinking coffee and needing Eric.

Coffee.

Her stomach churned, threatening revolt, but she fought the urge, turning back to face the room again, her eyes drawn to the back wall. Filled with shadows, it appeared to be lined with record albums, some of them filed, some hanging on the wall like artwork. Intuitively, she recognized the artist, her blood turning to ice, but her mind refusing to accept what her eyes were telling her without confirmation.

Still fighting nausea, she walked to the wall, pulling out one album and then another, her heartbeat ratcheting up with each discovery. *Songs for Swinging Lovers, Come Dance With Me, Songs for Young Lovers, Strangers in the Night.*

Frank Sinatra.

They were all Frank Sinatra. She shuddered violently, the enormity of the thought sending her stomach into spasms again. This time her stomach won, and she scrambled for a wastebasket, making it with only seconds to spare.

Gasping for breath, she perched on the edge of the bed again, jumping at the sound of the door opening, Ryan's smiling face nailing the truth down once and for all.

"You're awake." He sounded as if he'd spirited her away for a romantic weekend, his expression concerned, caring. "I'm sorry I had to spike the coffee, but I was fairly sure you wouldn't come any other way."

She fought the urge to throw up again. "Where are we?"

"Someplace safe." He walked over to the bed, reaching out to touch her, but she shied away, pushing herself back against the headboard. "Ah, Sara. Don't turn away. There's nowhere to go. Besides," he stroked her cheek, his eyes almost sorrowful, "we don't have much time."

The words were terrifying, robbing her of strength, reality warping, twisting into something evil. She thought of the other women, sharing their horror, their last minutes on earth, then closed her eyes, pulling an image of Eric front and center.

Eric. Her future. A lifeline amidst all the madness. She couldn't die here, not like this. Not when for the first time in two years, she had a reason to live. No. She wasn't going down without a fight.

Shifting so that her back blocked the nightstand, she edged closer to Ryan. "What do you mean?" she asked, forcing a smile. "We have all the time in the world now that we're finally together."

He frowned, obviously confused by her about-face. "But you're in love with Eric."

Sara fought the urge to retch, and shook her head, her hand closing on a book. Not the best of weapons, but it would have to do. "I had no idea you were interested. Why didn't you tell me?"

"I did." He studied her, weighing her words, suspicion mixing with hope. "And you told me that if it weren't for Charlie and Tom, you'd have fallen for me. Don't you remember?"

"Of course I remember," she lied, leaning closer, feigning interest, her insides collapsing in on themselves as the reality of his words drove home.

"Well, I did it. I got rid of them. But you still didn't come to me."

With energy born of raw hatred, she swung the book, the spine connecting with his head with a satisfying *thwunk*. Then she hit him again, the second blow catching him full in the face, the force driving him off the far side of the bed, his head cracking against wallboard.

In an instant she was running for the door, yanking it open, beads swaying with the motion. She slammed it behind her, searching for a lock, a dead bolt. She sure as heck wasn't going back for the key, so she dragged a chest of some sort in front of the door. The door opened inward so the chest wouldn't stop him for long, but he'd have to move it, and that bought precious time.

The hallway was short, two doors; one a bathroom, the other a closet. Ignoring both, she ran through the opening at the end of the hallway, skidding to a stop, taking precious seconds to orient herself.

A living room. She was standing in a living room. Sparsely furnished. A table, a couch, and in the corner what passed for a kitchen. Another door opened off the adjacent wall. But it was too small for a hallway, and was definitely not the front door.

A noise from behind her set her heart racing. Ryan was up and moving. She pivoted, eyes searching, dismissing the boarded window and a cubby that looked like a pantry or closet, finally settling on an alcove on the same wall as the door, almost hidden by shadows.

A crash, followed by a curse, echoed down the hallway. Ryan had hit the chest. Sara ran for the alcove, praying that it held the front door and that the door was unlocked.

One out of two didn't count.

The door was there, but the double-key lock mocked her, the sound of Ryan's footsteps in the hall signaling that her time had run out.

"Where the hell is Sara?" Eric's voice was contained, but that didn't stop his anger from contaminating every word.

Nate Stone shrank back against the pillows of his hospital bed, shooting a pleading look at Tony, who was leaning against a wall by the door, arms crossed, his expression inscrutable.

"Don't look at him. Look at me," Eric demanded.

"But I've already told you. I don't know where Sara is." The man was just this side of terrified, and despite the evidence, Eric found himself wondering if Nate was actually capable of the atrocities he'd been accused of.

"Then tell us what you do know." Tony straightened, coming to sit beside the bed, his voice gentle, playing good cop to Eric's bad cop, which was probably just as well because Eric's stance was not an act.

Nate swallowed, then drew in a shaking breath. "I went to Sara's to take her the contact sheets from the shoot she did with Allison Moore's family. I thought we could discuss the article. But when I got there, I found Jenkins."

"You just happened to be poking around the shrubbery?" Eric asked, not even trying to contain his sarcasm.

"The wind caught the sheets and they blew out of my hands. Some of them went into the hedge. That's how I found him." His eyes met Eric's, obviously begging him to believe.

"Seems a bit of a stretch, Nate," Eric growled. "Why didn't you call for help?"

"My cell phone was in the car, and all I could think of was getting to Sara." Nate licked his lips, his gaze darting from Eric to Tony and back again. "I tried to open the door, but it was locked, so I started pounding and screaming for her. I was afraid something had happened, that whoever had killed the officer had hurt her. But then I saw her. In a flash of lightning. Only she was backing away from me, as if I were something to be afraid of. So I threw a rock at the door. I wanted to break the glass and get in. To warn her." He shot another look at Eric, then faced Tony again, his anxiety apparent. "The next thing I remember is coming to here."

"So, according to your story, Sara was alive the last time you saw her."

"Yes." Nate nodded. "She was definitely alive."

Anger mixed with hope, leaving Eric torn between relieved and frantic. "Then where the hell is she?" He banged his hand down on the tray table, the plastic top rattling in the sudden silence.

Nate winced. "I told you. I don't know."

Eric threw his hands up in frustration. "This isn't getting us anywhere."

"Look, I'm not the Sinatra killer," Nate pleaded. "I swear it."

"Then maybe you can explain why your fingerprint was found on the boom box left at Molly's." Eric waited, watching, everything hanging on their ability to get Nate to confess, to tell them what he'd done with Sara.

"I turned it off."

Eric frowned; Nate's answer surprising in its simplicity. And something Claire said moved front and center. Molly had been tied, and she wouldn't have had the strength to get the ropes off. At least not by herself. "You called it in. You helped Molly."

Nate nodded, his eyes filled with tears. "I came by to see if she wanted to go to lunch. I wanted to talk to her about something. She was really good at listening. But when I got there, the door was open, and I could hear music playing. I knocked, but she didn't answer, so I went inside and found her there." He covered his face with his hands, the memory overwhelming him. "I untied her and pulled her off the chair. Then I called for help."

"Why didn't you stay with her?"

"I didn't want anyone to know I'd been there." Nate looked up, his face crumpling in on itself. "I even tried to wipe everything clean."

"But Molly's blood was on the phone." Tony's frown was intense, and Nate winced.

"I put it there. It was easy enough. There was blood everywhere." Nate stared down at his hands. "I wanted to cover my tracks. I thought if you knew, considering my past, you'd think it was me. Like before."

Not only had the man not come forward, he'd tampered with the scene. Eric fought to contain his anger. "You're talking about the Wichita Falls murders."

Nate nodded. "It wasn't me, but the detectives there wouldn't listen. They just took a look at my past and assumed I was the one."

"They had to have more reason than that, Nate."

"There was a witness who said she saw a man loitering in the area of the first murder. She picked me out of a lineup. But she recanted later, said she really hadn't been able to see that well."

"So they dropped the charges." Tony shrugged, his tone purposefully flippant.

"That didn't matter; the damage was already done. You can't imagine what it was like. Everyone in town thought it was me. I couldn't walk down the street without people whispering. I can still see their faces. It was like I was a monster or something. Only I hadn't done anything. Don't you see, I couldn't go through that again. I just couldn't."

"So you didn't tell anyone you were with Molly."

"But I called. That has to count for something, right?" The tears fell, his misery a tangible thing. "I didn't hurt

Molly. And I didn't hurt Sara. They're my friends. Don't you see? I couldn't hurt my friends. That's why I broke Sara's door. I was trying to help her. And I want to help you. But I can't tell you what I don't know."

Eric ran a hand through his hair, disappointment threatening to unravel his hard-won control. Nate was sticking to his story and they weren't any closer to finding Sara. Which left them absolutely nowhere. Sara was out there somewhere, and he didn't have a fucking clue.

A policeman entered the room holding an envelope, but before he could say anything, Eric's phone rang. Leaving the officer to Tony, he turned his back, plugging an ear so that he could hear. "D'Angelo."

"It's Brady. Claire got a hit on the print from your car. I'm faxing the report over to the hospital, along with the file. It's a prior from New Orleans. Guy by the name of Roy Graham. The record dates back almost eighteen years, so the picture is questionable. And to top it off the guy's apparently been clean ever since. There's not a whisper of him in Louisiana or Texas. But I thought you'd still want to see it. Stone give anything up?"

"No. He swears he's innocent." Eric looked over at Nate, frustration peaking again.

"And still no word from Sara?"

He shook his head, the silence answering for him, then clicked the phone off, and turned to face Tony. "Brady's sending something over."

"Way ahead of you." Tony slit the envelope, pulling out the contents. "Hanson brought it." He tipped his head toward where the officer was still standing, then looked down at the paper in his hand. "Son of a bitch." He held out the sheet, his expression grim.

Eric took the page, eyes narrowing as he studied the picture there. Roy Graham couldn't have been more than fifteen, but his features were clear—the line of the nose, the set of the eyes, even the fall of his hair exactly the same as Ryan Greene's.

Chapter 29

"Sara." Ryan's voice was harsh, his breathing heavy. Which meant she'd hurt him. Small comfort, but she'd take what she could get. Moving faster than she'd have thought herself capable, she dashed through the second doorway, quietly shutting the door behind her.

This room was smaller. Probably meant to be a bedroom, it was obviously being used as a storeroom. Grabbing boxes at random, she piled them in front of the door, knowing they wouldn't hold him back for long, but hoping to buy enough time to escape.

The light switch was behind the boxes, but there was a floor lamp off to her left. She ran over to it, turning the switch, praying that it worked, relief rushing through her when it did.

The light was weak, casting long shadows across the room, making it hard to make anything out except her immediate surroundings. Still, it was better than before. Determined to see more, she took a step forward, staring into the dark, waiting for her eyes to adjust, immediately regretting the action.

There was someone in the room with her. Someone sitting. Watching.

She pressed backward against the boxes that blocked the door, her mind scrambling to figure out how Ryan could possibly have gotten in. Then she heard him behind her, felt him slamming against the door.

Someone else was in front of her.

Despite her fear, she inched forward again, straining into the shadows trying to see. As if on cue, the lamp flickered, then brightened. A scream rose and died, terror drying her mouth, cold sweat prickling along her arms and hairline.

Directly across from her, sitting in a chair, was a store mannequin—a woman dressed in moth-eaten clothes whose faded colors still reflected the electric patterns of the sixties. Her features had been carefully altered, twisted into something sadistic. Terrifying. Human body parts replaced plastic, fingers curling inward, eyes staring at nothing, hair lank and bloodstained, a decaying, swollen tongue protruding between molded lips.

Sara tried to step backward, to escape the monster, but stumbled instead, falling forward, her hand brushing against the cold, lifeless fingers. She jerked back, swallowing bile, heart hammering as she scrambled to her feet, desperate for escape. The window here was boarded shut, too, but she didn't let that stop her, pulling at the boards, trying to wrench them free, working until her hands were bloody.

All the while knowing that *thing* was behind her, staring at her through Molly's eyes.

The boxes tumbled to the ground with a crash, and Ryan was in the room. The window boards still refused to yield. Sara yanked harder, splinters driving into her fingers and palms, tears of sheer terror streaming down her face.

"Sara," he said, his voice deceptively gentle.

She turned to face him, bending her knees slightly, determined not to go without a fight.

"You've hurt yourself." His concerned gaze raked across her, settling on her bleeding hands.

She launched herself at him, hitting him with the full weight of her body, her intention to knock him to the floor. But this time he was ready, taking the hit, and then twisting around to grab her, arms viselike around her chest. "That was a mistake, Sara." There was anger in his tone, coupled with regret.

She fought against him, but it was useless, his superior strength subduing her with ease. "After all I've done for you," he whispered, his breath hot against her ear, "the least you can do is stay with me. Besides," he said, turning her toward the mannequin, "you haven't met my mother."

"He's not here." Eric slammed his hand down on the credenza in Ryan Greene's foyer, the resulting pain helping him to focus.

"We didn't think he would be." Tony's voice was overly solicitous. A concerted effort to keep him calm. "It's too obvious. That's why we've got people searching the tax records for a second residence. You said he mentioned lake property."

"Yeah. At the party. But he could be anywhere, and time is ticking away." Eric clenched a fist, still fighting his surging emotions. Alternately angry, then terrified, he couldn't stop thinking about Sara, imagining the worst.

"So we'll find it. And we'll find Sara." Tony reached over to lay an awkward hand on Eric's shoulder. "And, in the meantime, we search the house."

"Right." Eric sucked in a breath, pulling all his years of training into play. He could do this. He had to. "Maybe it'll help to go over what we do know." He started up the stairs, Tony following. "Roy Graham was born in New Orleans. Dad out of the picture, mom on drugs. According to the records they faxed, Mom was arrested several times for solicitation, but never served time. When the kid was around twelve, Mom disappeared and he was put in foster care." They stopped on the landing, Eric turning to face Tony. "Except it didn't stick. He ran away, played loose with the rules, and wound up being arrested."

"But by then," Tony opened a cupboard and slid out a box, randomly pulling out the contents, "Mom was back in the picture because she bailed him out. So the happy family is reunited and, as far as public records go, sinks into oblivion. We've got nothing more on either of them. No tax records, no driver's licenses, nada. It's as if they simply ceased to exist."

"Until now."

Tony nodded. "Claire's running Roy's fingerprints through the computer for confirmation that the two men are one and the same and Brady's searching for additional background on Ryan. But my gut says Roy Graham is Ryan Greene."

"So we've got a guy with a lousy past who reinvents himself. None of which gets us any closer to finding Sara." Eric hit a box with a swipe of his hand, spilling the contents on the floor; another detective, working down the hall, looked up at the disturbance.

"That's sure as shit not going to help." Tony's eyebrows drew together in warning. "Look, if this is too hard—"

"I'm fine." Eric cut him off with a wave of a hand, bending to pick up the fallen paper. "It's just that you know as well as I do that after the first twenty-four hours a missing person is most likely gone for good." He couldn't bring himself to say her name, the act threatening the precarious hold he had on his emotions. "Every second counts."

"We've got every able hand working the case, and they're working as fast as they can."

"Detectives, I found something I think maybe you should look at." A tech stood in the bedroom doorway, holding out a narrow black book. "It was hidden in the closet ceiling."

Eric grabbed the book, flipping pages. The pictures were old. Yellowed at the edges. Most of them pictures of Ryan as a child. The usual poses—Christmas, birthdays. Eric turned another page, Tony looking over his shoulder. The photo here was larger and more faded, as if this page had been looked at more than the others, exposed to the elements.

A mother and a child sat on the steps of a ramshackle apartment building, the ironwork on the stoop bearing the unmistakable mark of New Orleans. The boy gazed up at his

mother with intense adoration; the mother smiled provocatively at the camera, seemingly unaware of the child.

Ryan and his mother.

A mother who looked exactly like Sara.

"You're out of your mind." Sara struggled against Ryan's
hold, averting her eyes from the abomination in front of her.

"Not in the way you think." He twisted her arms behind
her, and she tried to jerk free, but he was faster, his arms
tightening around her.

"You just said that *thing* was your mother."

"I didn't say that at all." He sounded so rational, so normal. As if everyone had dismembered body parts in their
spare room. "I said you haven't met my mother. This is obviously only a likeness." He reached out with one hand to
caress the mannequin. "The clothes were actually hers, but
the rest is just a re-creation." He smoothed his hand over the
bloodied hair. "I like to think of it as a work in progress, a
reminder that ultimately I have the power."

"That," Sara jerked her head toward the mannequin, "is
not a sign of power. It's the work of a monster."

Ryan spun her around, his eyes shooting fire, his fingers
digging into her shoulders. "I am not a monster. In fact, I
have amazing control. If I didn't, believe me, you'd already
be dead."

She forced her gaze to meet his, an attempt to hold her
own, to let him know that she wouldn't go easily, but fear
was a seductive thing, and it clawed at her from the inside
and out, threatening any attempt at dignity. "Why are you
doing this, Ryan? I thought we were friends."

" 'Friend' is a relative term, Sara." He smiled slowly, the
gesture far more chilling than his anger. "And I'm afraid
your definition is very much different from mine. As for doing this, I'm not the one who's at fault. That responsibility
lies completely with you. I gave you every opportunity to
prove yourself worthy, but you failed me. And in doing so
confirmed that you're no better than her." His expression

darkened as he turned toward the mannequin, his grip loosening ever so slightly.

Sara seized the opportunity and jerked away from his grasp, spinning to the right, colliding with the mannequin. Fighting her revulsion, she grabbed an arm, ripping it off the body, swinging it like a bat.

Plastic connected with Ryan's skull, and without waiting to see the results, she sprinted through the door, veering left down the hall toward the bathroom. Ryan cursed somewhere behind her and she froze for an instant, heart beating wildly in her chest.

"Sara, there's nowhere to run."

His rage was palpable, and the tenor of it was enough to set her moving again. She dashed into the bathroom, slamming the door behind her, and wedged a stool under the door handle.

She flipped on the light and turned her back to the door, her breath coming in ragged gasps. The room was narrow, barely more than a closet, with a sink, a toilet, and a tub, the latter at the end of the room, swathed in an ebony shower curtain.

Crossing the floor in two strides, she ripped back black plastic, exposing a small window above the tub. Like the others it was boarded shut, but this time there was only a single board. Hope surged through her as she stepped into the tub and up onto the far edge, her attention focused on the board.

Ignoring the pain in her hands, she pushed her bloody fingers under the edge, prying upward. The board creaked, and gave an inch or so. Pushing her hand farther beneath the board she pulled again, this time feeling it pull free.

It clattered to the floor of the tub, the sound of wood on enamel no doubt giving her away. But Sara didn't care. With shaking hands, she opened the lock and shoved up the window, freedom just inches away. Behind her, the door rattled but held. She pushed herself over the sill, squirming in an effort to squeeze through the tiny opening.

Halfway through, a loop on the waistband of her jeans caught in the sash, stopping forward motion. She reached

back, struggling to free herself, feeling the precious minutes
ticking away. With a violent crash the bathroom door splintered open, the metal stool scraping across the tile floor.

Terrified, she twisted, trying to rip the denim. But it refused to yield. Hands closed on her calves, and Ryan yanked
her backward, her elbows and hands slamming forcefully
against the window frame.

She kicked wildly, trying to loosen his grip, but in seconds he'd pulled her back, his body pinning her against the
wall, his face a mask of pain and rage. "You bitch." He hit
her with the back of his hand, the force slamming her head
against the wall. "I'll teach you to run away from me."

Grabbing her hair, he yanked her toward him, and hit her
again, this time with his fist, white heat exploding through
her head. She tried to raise her hands, to protect herself, but
he was too fast, his fist descending again and again, his face
contorted with rage.

She opened her mouth to scream, praying that somebody,
somewhere would hear, but there was no sound, pain robbing her of voice, her vision blurring, fading, darkness
beckoning, cool and safe.

With something akin to relief, she let the velvety black-
ness carry her away, certain that this must be death, her only
regret that she couldn't tell Eric good-bye.

"I don't know what I'm supposed to do." Eric ground
his teeth, staring blindly out the car window. They had finished at Ryan's with no further leads and, lacking clear direction, were heading back to the station, each passing hour
lessening the odds of finding Sara alive. "She could be
anywhere."

"The lake house is still our best bet," Tony said, not taking his attention from the road. "And if it's out there, we'll
find it. Brady has the whole department working on it."

"And in the meantime?" Eric knew the answer, but
couldn't bring himself to put it into words.

Tony shrugged. "We wait."

"While that bastard does God knows what to her?" His stomach twisted as his imagination went into overdrive. Frustration warred with anger, both emotions laced with equal amounts of fear and dread.

"Don't go there, Eric," Tony warned, as usual seeing more than Eric wanted him to. "It's only going to make it worse. You have to keep your head clear. It's the only way you can help her."

Eric slammed a fist into the dashboard. "Except that I can't help her if I can't find her." As if on cue, Tony's cell phone rang, and Eric reached for it, pulling it off the dash and powering it on. "D'Angelo."

"Eric. Glad I caught you." Brady's voice was husky, a sure sign he was excited. Eric's heart rate ratcheted up a notch, and he held his breath, waiting. "I've got some news."

"So spill it." He hadn't meant to snap, but every second was important, and his patience was stretched thin.

"We searched the tax records and couldn't find any lake property deeded to Ryan Greene." Eric tightened his hand on the phone, disappointment like acid in his gut. "So we tried the alias," Brady continued, "and we got a hit. The house is on the lake, about a quarter mile up a track near the end of Lime Creek Road."

"Lime Creek Road," Eric repeated, his mind obediently doing the math. "That's about twenty minutes from here if we push it. We're on our way."

The lieutenant sighed. "All right. But I don't want you guys going in without backup."

"Then they'd better get moving," Eric said, terminating the call.

"I take it Brady wants us to wait for the cavalry." It was a statement not a question.

"There's no way I'm going to wait, Tony. I've got to find her." Eric looked over to meet his partner's gaze, emotions raw and exposed. "It may already be too late." His heart twisted inside him, pain cresting so white-hot he wasn't certain he could endure it.

"So we'll go." Tony said, his expression set with grim determination. "And we'll find her. You've just got to hold on to that thought."

Eric clenched a fist, thinking of all the times he'd said those exact words to someone. And of all the times they hadn't meant a goddamned thing.

Chapter 30

Sara hurt, the throbbing pain threatening to split her skull in two. She tried to change positions, to roll over, but something impeded the action, cutting sharply into her wrists and ankles, this new pain pushing her firmly into consciousness.

She opened her eyes. Or at least one of them. The other refused to function, the attempt shooting needles through her eyelid and cheek. Waiting a moment for the sensation to subside, she tried again, relieved when both eyes opened, albeit the left one swollen at half-mast.

She had trouble at first remembering where she was, but the sight of the Day-Glo wallpaper sent a shard of terror piercing through her.

Ryan.

She twisted her head, trying to find him, realizing that she was tied in place, hands above her head, feet anchored securely to the footboard. Cold air wafted across bare skin, bringing the horrified discovery that her shirt was open, her breasts bare. She stifled a sob, and pulled angrily at her bindings, collapsing back against the bed when the pain became unbearable.

"You're awake." He materialized from the shadows on the far side of the bed, the mattress squeaking as he sat next to her. "I was worried that perhaps you wouldn't." Chameleonlike, his rage seemed to have vanished, the face hovering above her reflecting only concern.

She gagged, pain and fear combining to make her stomach churn. "You hurt me." Her voice came out a whisper, the simple movement of her lips and throat sending fresh waves of agony rocking through her.

"I'm sorry about that, Sara. But you brought it on yourself. There's no escape, and the sooner you accept that fact, the happier we'll both be." He reached over to smooth back her hair, but she twisted her head to avoid his touch.

Anger flashed in his eyes, and he grabbed her face, forcing her to look at him. "All this time I thought you were different. But you're not. You're just like her." He released her in disgust, his smile brittle.

"Your mother?" she gasped, her own anger dispelling some of her fear. "Is that what this is all about?"

"My mother was a whore," he spat out the words, and she forced herself to meet his gaze, her heart clenching at the hatred she saw reflected there. Then, almost as if he were metamorphosing, his features froze into a mask of disinterest, his anger seemingly vanishing on a whim.

Walking over to the stereo, he pulled out an album. "This was her room, you know. At least as much of it as I could re-create. These were hers, too." He waved the record cover at the wall. "She was always listening to Frank Sinatra. Dreaming about him, collecting his albums, savoring them as if they were alive."

He yanked the record from the cover, putting it on the turntable, the first melancholy notes of "I Will Wait for You" filling the air. "Sometimes I think she loved Sinatra more than anything else in the world." He turned to face her, eyes still glittering with hate.

"Then why did you immortalize her?" The statement was macabre at best, but in a sick, warped kind of way it held truth.

"Because I loved her," he said, as if those four words explained everything.

Hate and love were part of the same circle after all, only in Ryan's world the emotions had obviously taken on a life of their own, morphing into something insidious.

Sara watched him warily, trying to find something of the Ryan she knew, some way she could reach him. Reason with him. Even as she had the thought she knew it was futile. The man she'd known was a caricature, a mask to hide the monster within.

He came to sit beside her again, his hand idly tracing the curves of her stomach. "Mother was beautiful, Sara, just like you. The kind of woman every man wants to sink himself into." His fingers dug into the her belly, twisting her skin.

"But she chose me. I was the only one who could make her happy. I knew just how to touch her, to please her." His hand slipped lower, and Sara squirmed to move away, the ropes making it impossible. "She taught me what it was to be a man."

"You had sex with your mother?" The words were out before she could stop them. And Ryan's eyes turned angry again.

"It wasn't sex. It was love." His grip tightened, his fingers hurting her. "She loved me."

"That isn't love, Ryan," Sara whispered, the idea of a mother debasing love into something so twisted making her forget for a moment who she was talking to. "That's perversion."

The blow caught her by surprise. Her ears rang with the force of it, the pain in her head intensifying. "You don't know anything about her. About us. We were a team, she and I. Until *he* came along." He stood up, agitated now, his hands clenching and unclenching.

Sara shrank back, afraid that he was going to hit her again, but instead he began to pace, his eyes filled with an anger that reached out from the past.

"He was nobody. A hustler with a voice. But all she saw

was Sinatra. And just like that he was between her legs. Telling her a kid was nothing but a liability. The bastard." He spat the curse out, his eyes narrowing to slits. "She left me for him. Just like that, she was gone." He sank down on the bed, rocking back and forth, following the beat of the music, more a little boy than a man.

"I waited for her. I knew she'd be back. She'd never desert me. Not for someone like that." He frowned, determination setting his chin, memories driving his expression. "And it paid off. The son of a bitch ran out on her, and she came crawling home. Wanting me again."

He stood up, walked over to the bureau and opened a box, pulling out a knife. It glittered in his hand, and he caressed it with a finger, turning back to smile at her. "Only me."

Sara tugged against the ropes that bound her, oblivious to the pain as she struggled to free herself. He was insane. She could see it in his eyes. And he thought she was his mother. Her left hand twisted against the rope, almost slipping free.

Ryan moved with unexpected speed, the knife now held firmly against her throat. She froze, not doubting for a moment that he'd use it. "I warned you about struggling." The tip of the knife bit into her neck as he traced a line across it, and then bent to taste the trail of blood. "I'd hate to have to end this before it's even started."

She saw regret flash through his eyes, and felt the knife shift. Self-preservation kicked in. She didn't want to die. Not here. Not like this. "Weren't you angry with your mother? For leaving you, I mean?" The words came out on a rush of air, tumbling over each other. She fought to keep her breathing even, to keep herself calm, willing him to move the knife, to turn his anger back where it belonged.

He lifted the blade, considering the question. "I loved her more. And I wanted her. A son belongs with his mother." He looked to her for agreement, and Sara forced herself to nod.

"We were happy after that. I was older, more capable of fulfilling her needs. Everything was perfect." He ran the knife back and forth over his leg, as if in his mind he were sharpening it. "Then *he* came back. Bringing apologies and Sinatra. And she betrayed me again." His hand stilled, and he lifted the blade, staring into it as if it were a mirror.

"So I killed him. I thought it would please her. Prove my love. But she called me a fool, said I was only a boy." Ryan gripped the knife, anger cresting again in his eyes. "After all I'd done for her, she rejected me. *Me.*"

He slammed the knife into the dresser, the sound spitting through the room, a counterpoint to Sinatra's crooning. Pivoting, he picked up an album, sliding out the ebony disk. "You know what I did, Sara?" His smile was twisted, his eyes wild. "I broke the record." With a snap the album splintered, pieces flying across the room. He held up a jagged piece. "I used this to rape her, to prove once and for all that I was a man. Her man." He pulled the knife from the dresser, dropping the record shard.

"And then you know what I did?" His voice was almost singsong now, as if he'd recited the story many times to himself, his tone almost gleeful. "I slit her throat and watched her die."

"Your mother?" Sara's words came unbidden, as if they had a life of their own, her horror mixing with mind-numbing fear.

Ryan nodded. "So I cut them into pieces and left them for the bayou fish to eat." He tilted his head, watching her, his gaze assessing, his mood shifting like lightning. "I thought I'd put it all behind me, Sara. Made a new life for myself. A respectable life. But then you came along."

He moved toward her, eyes wild, the knife still clutched in his hand, and Sara screamed, the sound harsh in the sudden stillness of the room.

"There's the house." Tony pointed at the shadowy building under the canopy of trees and it was all Eric could do to keep from jumping from the moving car, the burning question whether the man was in residence.

And, more important, whether Sara was with him.

"Stop here. No sense in advertising our arrival." Faint light shone through what appeared to be blinds on the windows. Eric's heart pounded, every nerve ending on high alert.

Tony killed the engine, letting the car glide to a halt. Eric wrenched the door open, intent on heading for the house.

"Wait." Tony was out of the car, too, opening the trunk. "Kevlar."

Eric frowned with impatience, but returned to his partner, taking the vest and slipping it on. Tony followed suit, and then motioned Eric to follow him. Using the trees for cover, they moved toward the house, passing a car, the same make and model as Ryan's. Tony stopped long enough to feel the hood mouthing the word "warm."

Nodding his understanding, Eric drew his gun and moved cautiously toward the house, alternating with Tony as he moved forward, taking turns watching each other's backs.

The building was more a shack than anything else. Square and ugly, it squatted on a rocky outcrop, surrounded on three sides by live oaks and on the fourth by the dark, murky water of the lake. Its walls were weather-beaten, the roof sagging inward as if it were too tired to remain upright.

Not exactly high-stakes real estate.

Most of the house was dark, light spilling only from the south side, adjacent to the lake. Signaling Tony to cover him, Eric ran forward, keeping low, up onto the ramshackle porch. In comparison to the rest of the house, the door was new. And locked. The dead bolt holding secure as he turned the knob.

With enough time and the proper tools, he could probably jimmy the lock, but he had neither, so he moved back into the shadows, this time following Tony as they worked their way around to the lighted side of the house.

There were two windows here, both boarded shut, the first glowing dimly, the second brighter, its light cascading onto the lawn, escaping through cracks between the boards. Fighting the urge to try to crash through them, Eric inched forward until he was under the first window.

Popping up, he tried to peer through the boards with no success. Either the light was too dim, or the boards too close together. And to complicate things even more, the window had been boarded shut from the inside, adding a layer of glass to the mix.

Smothering a curse, Eric bent again and edged toward the other window, Tony right behind him. This time Eric could hear movement inside, along with the wisp of a melody. His blood froze as he recognized the recording.

Frank Sinatra.

Holding his breath, he rose until his eyes were level with the windowsill, shifting until he could see through the crack.

At first there was only color, green, orange, and pink, but then, as his eyes adjusted to the light, he could make out Ryan pacing back and forth in front of what looked like a bookcase, a knife big enough to gut a bear in his hand.

Fighting to stay calm, he pivoted slightly, enough to see rope anchoring something to the end of the bed. Beyond that an open doorway led out into what appeared to be a hallway. Squinting, he rose slightly, using a different crack for a peephole. White Keds came into view. And ankles. Beautiful slim ankles that he'd recognize even in the dark.

Ryan had Sara.

Ducking back down, he returned to Tony, whispering his discovery. Together they retreated to a safe distance, Eric fighting the urge to batter the door down with his bare fists. "I've got to get in there."

"We ought to wait for backup," Tony insisted. "They can't be too far behind us."

"Between the distance and coordinating with the county for jurisdiction, I bet they're still a half hour out, minimum. Ryan will kill her before then."

"You don't know that." Tony folded his arms, digging in for a fight.

"I don't *not* know it either, and I'm not taking chances with Sara's life."

Tony opened his mouth in rebuttal, but Eric cut him off

with an angry wave of his hand. "I think I can get in through the other window. The sash is rotten. It won't take much effort to break the lock and open it."

"There're still the boards to deal with."

"Nothing a tire iron won't take care of."

"And the noise?" Tony uncrossed his arms, a signal that he was weakening.

"Between the music and Ryan's voice, I doubt he'll hear anything. Besides, you'll be standing watch, so you can signal me if something tips him off." Eric blew out a breath, willing his friend to understand. "I can't just sit here, Tony. If we can get in there, Sara's got a chance. If not—" He spread his hands, the gesture underscoring his thoughts.

"All right. We'll do it your way." Tony was already moving back toward the car, returning minutes later, tire iron in hand. "You ready?"

Eric took the tire iron, temporarily holstering his weapon. "Let's do it."

Years of teamwork stood in their stead, Tony moving soundlessly to watch through the window, Eric using the tire iron to pry the lock off the rotten window. It fell with a muffled thud, and Eric waited for Tony's thumbs-up before lifting the window to attack the boards nailed inside.

They were surprisingly easy to pull off. Still, it seemed a painfully slow process, first loosening the board and then pulling it carefully through to the outside.

Once or twice, at Tony's command, he stopped, waiting with pounding heart for Tony's okay. But finally the space was big enough for him to crawl through.

This was it. Now or never. Sara's life was in his hands.

He'd spent his whole life trying to protect the world from scum, but it had never been personal. No matter the outcome, he'd been okay. Nightmares maybe, but nothing that was in any way personal.

This mattered—at a soul-deep, can't-live-with-it-if-you're-wrong kind of level.

He shot a look at Tony, wanting support, knowing he

probably wouldn't get it. But he was wrong. His partner—his friend—was there by the window, offering a leg up.

"She's the only thing that counts." Tony's whisper was like a clarion call. Sounding truth, giving him strength.

"All right. Then I'm there." He boosted himself through the window, not worrying about the broken boards, the only thing that mattered finding Sara—keeping her alive.

Chapter 31

The knife plunged downward, and terror ripped through her. But no additional pain followed, the knife embedded in the pillow by her head, the sound of steel against feathers ratcheting through her as if it had been the real thing.

"Why didn't you kill me?" The words were ripped out of her, born in horror and fear, cold sweat sending shudders rippling through her, relief tempered by the certain knowledge that he was toying with her.

"I can't." Ryan's words were equally tormented, and Sara twisted her head to look at him. He pulled the knife free, staring down at it as if is he'd never held one before.

"Why?" she whispered, some part of her still needing to understand, needing to justify his tortured dementia.

He looked up at her with eyes she recognized. The man she'd considered a friend. "Ryan?" The tears came, the aftereffect of fear and relief. There was nothing noble about terror. It leveled the field. An enemy no one could beat.

"In the beginning, I only watched you, Sara. In the city, at work, sometimes even at home. I made a copy of your keys so I could come and go as I pleased. Day or night. I saw everything—your intimate best. But it wasn't enough." He paused, his hand tightening on the knife. "I wanted to feel you, Sara. To show you how much I cared." He slid the blade under her breasts, his eyes devouring her, his free hand tracing the crest of her nipple. "You're so like her," he said, his voice broken. "I thought she'd come back to me."

"But I'm not your mother, Ryan. I'm not." She begged him, trying to reach that part of him that had been her friend, wondering if there'd been signs, something she'd ignored or missed, something that would have hinted at the devil within, warned her off, kept her safe. "Please, let me go."

He shook his head. "It's gone too far. I thought I could keep you separate. Keep you safe. Until you were ready." His eyes were full of regret. "But I can't. You're no better than she was—always choosing someone else."

"How could I have chosen you, Ryan? I was married. For God's sake, I had Charlie. He was a little boy," she whispered, the words catching in her throat, her chest constricting in agony. She yanked at the ropes that bound her, wanting to hurt him, to punish the man who had killed her son. "He was my baby."

"He was in the way." Ryan turned to face her, his face devoid of emotion.

Hot tears rolled down her cheeks, her body shaking, the pain of her loss so intense it vanquished her fear. "I loved him."

"No, you loved the idea of him. The idea of family, Sara. That's what was important to you."

She shuddered, guilt racking through her. There was truth embedded in insanity. She had wanted a family. Wanted it with every part of her being. But that didn't change the fact that she'd loved them. "They were my life, Ryan."

"No. They weren't. You told me so, remember? All I did was clear the way for you."

The horror of his words settled inside her, wrapping around her like an insidious cancer. Tom and Charlie were dead because of something she'd said to a madman. She jerked her left arm forward, the ropes cutting deep, the pain only serving to drive her onward. She pulled harder, the muscles in her shoulder burning like fire.

"Stop it," he barked, the knife back at her throat. "I'll decide when it's time for you to die." He'd found her breast again, the feel of his skin against hers making her gag, his touch repulsive. "We've come this far. There's no sense in rushing things."

"I'd rather be dead than with you." She bit out the words, hating him with every fiber of her being.

"You'll get your wish soon enough." He twisted her nipple, the pain feeding her fear. She gritted her teeth, trying to stay focused, to find a way to fight. As if reading her mind, he smiled, the gesture devoid of humor. "It all would have been so different if you'd come to me, Sara."

"You mean my family would still be alive." The thought ate at her, even though she recognized the fallacy of the logic. She was falling into his insanity, letting it cloud her thinking.

"And all the others." Ryan released her, reaching over to pull the tattered remains of her shirt across her breasts, the torn material not quite reaching.

A new realization worked its way front and center, this one no less horrifying than the other. "You killed them because of *me*?"

"I had no choice." He aimlessly drew circles on the bed with the point of the knife, his eyes never leaving hers. "I'd waited so patiently and instead you threw yourself at Tom's fraternity brother."

"Phil?" Incredulity mixed with an overwhelming sense of dread. "What does he have to do with any of this?"

"You threw yourself at him." His hand tightened convulsively on the knife.

"I went to dinner with him. He was Tom's friend. There was nothing between us." She was trying to reason with a madman, insanity breeding insanity.

"Liar," he shrieked, hitting her with the hilt of the knife, leaving blood hot against her cheek. "I saw you looking at him. Laughing with him. You even brought him home with you."

"To talk." She stressed the words, turning away from him, tears of pain and anger salty against her tongue.

"Not to talk." He grabbed her chin, forcing her to look at him. "To fuck. You wanted to fuck him. Admit it, Sara."

She glared up at him, willing herself courage. This wasn't Ryan. This was the bastard that had hurt Molly. The man who'd killed innocent women. In her name.

"I could have killed you then." He lowered his head, his breath fetid against her lips, his fevered gaze boring into hers. "But I didn't." His grip tightened, the skin of her face stretching until she thought it would pop. "I didn't."

"You killed them instead." She twisted to try to break free, but he moved with her, his fingers viselike on her chin, the knife now resting against her throat.

"I told you I didn't have a choice. I love you, Sara." Coming from him the words were an abomination. "And they were so like you. The mouth, the hands, the eyes."

"Oh, my God," she shuddered, choking on her bile, thinking of Molly. "The mannequin isn't your mother, is it? The mannequin is me."

"You're so like her, Sara. Too much so." He spit the last out in anger, his face changing yet again. "I wanted us to have a happy ending."

"Surely you knew that was impossible?"

"Nothing is impossible." He said the words, but his tone was bitter, as if he didn't really believe them. "You were my second chance. I couldn't let anything happen to you." He shook his head, releasing her chin, the knife dipping lower, circling her breast. "But someone had to pay."

"That's why you called me." She was beginning to follow his twisted logic, and the thought terrified her. "You wanted to prove to yourself that I was still alive. That it had all been a fantasy."

"I knew you'd understand." His smile was empty. A caricature. His face a reflection of the demons that drove him. "It was easy enough in the beginning. Hookers are stupid people." He dismissed them with a toss of his head, disgust coloring his expression.

"You set Lydia up. Told her it was me who wanted to meet her." Sara felt tears prick her eyes, surprised she had any left to shed.

He shrugged. "It worked."

"And Allison?" She wasn't certain she wanted to know, but as long as he was talking, she was alive, and despite the pain, she wanted every precious minute.

"Her hair was just the same color as yours." He reached out to twirl a strand around his finger.

Sara fought the urge to gag, and tried to twist away, but he jerked her back, using her hair to pin her in place. "She begged me for her life, Sara. I wonder if you'll beg me, too."

Sara shuddered, her imagination filling in the blanks, then closed her eyes, forcing herself to let go of the images, to focus on the present, as horrific as it might be. "You knew about Nate, didn't you? About his past. You were going to let him take the fall."

"The idiot told me everything." His eyes were shrewd suddenly, lucidity mixing with madness. "I took it as a gift and it worked like a charm. The poor bastard never saw it coming."

"And Molly?" Her friend's name came out of its own volition, Sara's mind blanching at the thought of the horror Molly had endured. "How did she fit into your plan?"

"The bitch mocked me. She convinced you to throw my flowers away. I needed for her to understand the degree of her transgression."

"So you took her eyes?" Sara fought not to show her revulsion, the image of the mannequin filling her mind.

"An eye for an eye." He paused for a moment, tilting his head to one side, smiling as if the idea had only just occurred to him. "It was fair, don't you think?"

He was watching her now, waiting for her agreement. He

sounded so certain Sara was suddenly unsure of her own convictions, right and wrong converging, nothing really clear.

"You're insane," she whispered, wishing she could just disappear, knowing with certainty that any semblance of the man she had known was gone forever.

"On the contrary," he laughed, the sound frightening in its simplicity, "I've never been more clearheaded. Everything I've done has been for you, Sara. For you and me."

"There is no you and me." She spit the words out, enunciating each one as if he were deaf.

"Of course there is." He backhanded her, the impact sending shards of pain shrieking through her head. "You just refuse to accept the fact. Instead, you cling to thoughts of men like D'Angelo."

He'd meant the name as a curse, but to Sara it was salvation. Something wonderful to cling to in the midst of this nightmare. Ryan turned the knife so that the point dug into her belly, the resulting pain almost welcome, a focal point to keep her mind from giving in to the horror.

"You tried to kill him, didn't you, like Tom and Charlie?" She forced herself to concentrate on the fact that Ryan had failed, that no matter what happened to her, Eric was safe.

"I needed him gone." He tightened his hand on the knife, hatred shining in his eyes. "He was distracting you." The knife dug deeper as he stroked her face, his eyes raking over her, glazed with passion. "Surely you realize I couldn't let you leave me. Not again."

"But I was never yours." She raised her eyes to meet his gaze, ignoring the pain, determined to defy him to the last.

"You have always been mine." He bent to kiss her, moving the knife back to her throat. "And I've been waiting a very long time."

She wasn't sure suddenly who he was talking to, who it was he wanted so desperately. Her or his mother. Some twisted amalgamation of them both, she imagined. In his mind, they were the same. And in taking her, he was trying to reinvent his past, trying to make the unthinkable acceptable.

But it wasn't possible. No matter how hard he tried.

She twisted her head, trying to avoid Ryan's touch, turning her mind instead to thoughts of Eric and her love for him. Facing death, the only real regret she had was that they hadn't had more time.

She closed her eyes, some part of her giving up, letting go. But even as she did so, another part of her, the part that had only just begun to live again, rebelled, muscles tensing with the anger ripping through her.

She was not going to give up. Not now. Not ever.

Opening her eyes, her gaze locked with Ryan's. "I love Eric, Ryan. And no matter what you do to me, nothing will ever change that fact. I will *never* be yours."

"Then you'll belong to no one." Ryan raised the knife, his voice flat and emotionless, at odds with the tears in his eyes.

And Sara knew with certainty that this time he wouldn't miss.

Eric's heart leapt into his throat, his finger tightening on the trigger of his gun. Ryan held the knife with the precision of a surgeon, his anger apparent even with the distance between them. Sara's face was battered and blue, her left eye swollen almost shut, clotted blood distorting her eyebrow and cheek.

Eric wanted to shoot the bastard, to end this thing once and for all, but there was no way to get a clean shot. Not with Sara in the way. Tony, flattened against the wall directly behind him, shook his head, concurring with Eric's thoughts.

He'd never felt so helpless in all his life. If they rushed Ryan, he would surely kill her. Even if Eric could get off a shot, it would most likely be too late. Sara would be dead.

Which meant he had to think of another option.

Emotions held at bay, he focused on the scene, assessing the possibilities. What he needed was a way to get Ryan away from Sara. A distraction.

As if his thoughts were reaching out to her, she twisted away from Ryan, her face turning toward the door. With an intake of breath, he shifted so that he was visible, withdrawing as soon as he saw recognition in her eyes.

"The music's stopped, Ryan." Sara's voice came out a harsh whisper, as though talking were painful, but even so she managed to make the words provocative. "We can't do this without Sinatra."

Ryan eyed her doubtfully, his forehead creased with a frown.

"He's part of it all, isn't he? A final touch to the perfect ending?"

Ryan ran his hand across Sara's breasts, and Eric's entire body tensed, Tony's hand on his arm the only thing stopping him from rushing the bastard.

"You know how good the music makes us feel," Sara crooned. "Please, Ryan."

Eric's rage crested, the white-hot pain leaving him feeling impotent. She was dancing with the devil, and it was up to him to see that she didn't have to pay the price.

As if hearing his thoughts, she turned to him, her expression determined, full of trust, and he knew that everything he'd ever needed, ever wanted, was right there in her eyes. He loved her more than life, and he sure as hell wasn't going to let Ryan Greene take her away from him. He tightened his hand on his gun as Ryan straightened, his expression still skeptical.

"Come on, you bastard," Eric whispered. "Just a few feet more."

"Please, Ryan?" Sara cajoled, arching her back provocatively. "If this is all we have, I want it to be perfect."

Doubt faded, and Ryan's smile was slow and lascivious, his hungry gaze devouring Sara's flesh. With a last lustful look at Sara, Ryan moved around the end of the bed, reaching out to turn on the music. Eric waited one beat, and then another, and then with a nod at Tony, burst into the room, taking aim. "Drop the knife, Ryan. It's over."

Ryan spun around, his face contorting with rage. "D'Angelo," he hissed, then pivoted, throwing the knife, the blade glistening as it arced through the air toward Sara.

Eric screamed a warning, and dove for her, his only thought to reach her before the knife did.

A gunshot rang out as he made contact with the bed, Sara's body beneath his, the knife bouncing against his vest, clattering harmlessly to the floor. Rolling once more, he was upright again, his gun trained in Ryan's direction, but Tony was already there, bending over the body, Ryan's blood spattered across the record albums.

Eric holstered his gun and ran back to Sara, jerking free the knots that bound her hands and feet, pulling her into his arms, the knowledge that her heart was beating against his hand the sweetest sensation in the world.

"I've got you," he whispered, and he felt her burrowing tighter against him. He reached down to tip up her face, his eyes searching hers, needing to reassure himself that everything would indeed be all right.

"Always," she answered, her mouth curving upward with the hint of a smile.

He pulled her close again, her head against his heart, as Sinatra's voice echoed through the room. There would still be barriers to overcome, wounds to heal. But they were alive, and they were together. And for the moment that was more than enough.

♫ ♪ ♫ ♪ ♫

"Looking for the light of a new love,
To brighten up the night I have you, Love,
And we can face the music together
Dancing in the dark . . ."

Epilogue

The air smelled of roses, sweet and fragrant, bursting with new life. New beginnings. Sara couldn't remember ever being this happy. She smiled up at Eric as they danced, the music matching her mood.

"Have I told you how beautiful you look, Mrs. D'Angelo?"

Sara smiled up at her husband, lifting her hand to caress his face. "Have I told you how much I love you, Detective D'Angelo?"

"Not for at least an hour." He laughed, pushing her out into a spin, then pulling her close, her breath catching in her throat at the passion in his eyes.

"We're not being fair to our guests, you know."

"I say let them fend for themselves." He massaged the small of her back, sending shivers of desire racing through her. "Today is for us, after all."

"You'd never know it to look at them." Sara tipped her head in the direction of the crowd of wedding guests. Their friends eating cake, drinking champagne, and generally having a marvelous time.

Molly was holding court in her wheelchair, her sunglasses tinted the exact color of her bridesmaid's dress. Nate hovered nearby, her ever faithful attendant, their friendship forged in the fires of hell, his devotion, surprisingly, just what Molly seemed to need as she worked to reclaim her life.

Jack was over by the bar, chatting up a pretty girl who

worked in the APD forensic lab. He hadn't wanted to come, but Sara had insisted. He was part of her life. Part of her family. And nothing would change that. Whatever lay between them, they'd find a way to work it out.

Tony and Bess danced by them, Bess's bridesmaid's dress tight across her rapidly expanding belly. Tony winked as he whirled by, his smile for both of them. *Together*. Mr. and Mrs. Eric D'Angelo. Sara smiled, her heart full.

Ryan had tried to take everything. To destroy all that she loved. But in the end, despite the horror of what he'd done, she'd survived. And built a new family, a new life—with Eric. Her life bittersweet in so many ways, she still felt triumphant. Good had managed to conquer the day. And now it was time to move on—to walk into her future unfettered by the past.

"Penny for your thoughts?" Eric's breath was warm against her ear.

"I was just thinking how lucky we are."

His arms tightened around her, his lips against her neck. "Funny, I was just thinking how lucky I was going to get."

"*Eric*." She pushed back in his arms, pretending outrage.

"What?" he grinned. "I'm not allowed to fantasize about my wife?"

"Only if you share the fantasy with me." She laughed, the tulle of her dress swirling around their legs, the fire in his eyes reflected in her own.

Eric bent to kiss her, his mouth possessing hers, the heat between them nearing combustion. Their bodies melded together as they danced, two hearts beating as one, the music surrounding them both like an old friend.

Look for these exciting novels
of suspense by

Dee Davis

MIDNIGHT RAIN

"Taut suspense, wicked humor, powerful romance—
Midnight Rain has it all."
—Christina Skye

For undercover FBI agent Katie Cavanaugh this was supposed to
be a routine job—go in, get the evidence, catch a killer. But from
the moment she lays eyes on John Brighton the intense charge in
the air between them tells her that the stakes will be higher this
time around. Posing as his physical therapist allows Katie firsthand access to him but she can't let the intimacy of living together cloud her judgment. She will need her instinct sharp if she is
going to find him guilty . . . or prove his innocence.

Left for dead along a deserted highway, John awakes to find
himself the lead suspect in a murder investigation. The only
bright point in his life is Katie. Warm and beautiful, she is the
one person he thinks he can trust. But as a net of suspicion
closes in, John and Katie must work to unravel the maze of
secrets and lies that threaten to keep them apart forever. . . .

Published by Ivy Books
Available wherever books are sold

DARK OF THE NIGHT

"Intrigue, deception, and murder make *Dark of the Night* a great way to spend your entertainment hours. Author Dee Davis is making quite a name for herself in the romantic suspense field."
——*Romantic Times*

When she was only eight years old, Riley O'Brien survived the tragic deaths of her mother and sister. As a result, she vowed never to desert her father, a brilliant young congressman whose star was on the rise. Twenty-one years later, Riley stands by her father's side as he makes a bid for the presidency. Growing up in the political spotlight, she has become an expert at hiding her feelings. But her defenses are about to be shattered.

Investigative reporter Jake Mahoney resents wasting his time covering an ice princess at a presidential campaign rally. But when a car bomb throws him—literally—on top of the candidate's daughter, Jake quickly realizes that Riley O'Brien is pure fire. Their attraction is instant, and possibly fatal—as dangerous secrets from the past explode into the present, destroying one life after another in a nightmare of blind ambition. . . .

Published by Ivy Books
Available wherever books are sold

JUST BREATHE

"A wonderful, not-to-be-missed, stay-up-late read."
—*Philadelphia Inquirer*

Former CIA agent Matthew Broussard came to Vienna to catch a killer. But when his only lead is shot dead, he is left without answers and with an injured witness in his arms. The enticing young woman may be his last chance to resolve the tragedy that still haunts his past. He cannot let her out of his sight, even if it means getting close to someone again.

For aspiring travel writer Chloe Nichols, escorting a tour group of wealthy ladies through Europe was supposed to be anything but thrilling. Then she is rescued from an assassin's bullet by a stranger on the train—a perfectly handsome stranger who saves her life with a kiss and asks her to pose as his fiancée. Chloe believes Matthew is trying to protect her, until the seductive charade becomes part of a lethal international conspiracy in which no one is what they seem—including her captivating hero. . . .

Published by Ivy Books
Available wherever books are sold

*Subscribe to the Pillow Talk
e-newsletter—and receive all these
fabulous online features directly in
your e-mail inbox:*

- Exclusive essays and other features by major romance
  writers like Linda Howard, Kristin Hannah,
  Julie Garwood, and Suzanne Brockmann

  - Exciting behind-the-scenes news from
    our romance editors

- Special offers, including contests to win signed romance
  books and other prizes

- Author tour information, and monthly announcements
  about the newest books on sale

  - A Pillow Talk readers forum, featuring feedback
    from romance fans. . .like you!

Two easy ways to subscribe:
Go to www.ballantinebooks.com/PillowTalk
or send a blank e-mail to
join-PillowTalk@list.randomhouse.com

Pillow Talk—
the romance e-newsletter brought to you by
Ballantine Books